"I just have to

"There is that," Fel...
unfazed by the insult. "What sort of monster do you suppose I am, Princess?"

Briar couldn't tell if he was asking the question with sincerity. She wasn't sure she cared. But as she looked at him a picture began to form in her mind. His eyes were gold, glinting with heat and the possibility of a kind of cruelty she didn't want to test. There was something sharp about him, whip-smart and deadly.

"A dragon. Clearly," she said, not entirely sure why she had provided him with the answer.

"I suppose that makes you the damsel in distress," he said.

"I'd like to think it makes me the knight."

"Sorry, darling," he said. "I kissed you awake not eight hours ago. That makes you the damsel."

"If we're going on fairy tales then that should make you Prince Charming, not the dragon."

He chuckled. "Sadly this is real life, not a fairy tale. And very often the Prince can be both."

*Three innocents encounter forbidden temptation
in this enticing new fairy-tale trilogy
by* New York Times *bestselling author Maisey Yates...*

Once Upon a Seduction...

Belle, Briar and Charlotte have lived sheltered lives,
far from temptation—but three billionaires are
determined to claim them!

Belle has traded herself for her father's freedom—
but the dark-hearted Prince keeping her prisoner
threatens to unleash an unknown sensuality...

Meanwhile Briar awakens to find herself abducted
by Prince Felipe—who blackmails her
into becoming his royal bride...

And Charlotte is reunited with the billionaire who
once climbed a tower to steal her innocence—and
Rafe is about to discover the secret consequences!

Find out if these young women can tame their
powerful men—*and* have their happily-ever-after!

The Prince's Captive Virgin
June 2017

The Prince's Stolen Virgin
August 2017

The Italian's Pregnant Prisoner
October 2017

THE PRINCE'S STOLEN VIRGIN

BY
MAISEY YATES

MILLS & BOON

All rights reserved including the right of reproduction in whole
or in part in any form. This edition is published by arrangement with
Harlequin Books S.A.

This is a work of fiction. Names, characters, places, locations and
incidents are purely fictional and bear no relationship to any real
life individuals, living or dead, or to any actual places, business
establishments, locations, events or incidents. Any resemblance is
entirely coincidental.

This book is sold subject to the condition that it shall not, by way of
trade or otherwise, be lent, resold, hired out or otherwise circulated
without the prior consent of the publisher in any form of binding or
cover other than that in which it is published and without a similar
condition including this condition being imposed on the subsequent
purchaser.

® and TM are trademarks owned and used by the trademark owner
and/or its licensee. Trademarks marked with ® are registered with the
United Kingdom Patent Office and/or the Office for Harmonisation in
the Internal Market and in other countries.

First Published in Great Britain 2017
By Mills & Boon, an imprint of HarperCollins*Publishers*
1 London Bridge Street, London, SE1 9GF

© 2017 Maisey Yates

ISBN: 978-0-263-92531-9

Our policy is to use papers that are natural, renewable and recyclable
products and made from wood grown in sustainable forests. The logging
and manufacturing processes conform to the legal environmental
regulations of the country of origin.

Printed and bound in Spain
by CPI, Barcelona

Maisey Yates is a *New York Times* bestselling author of more than fifty romance novels. She has a coffee habit she has no interest in kicking, and a slight Pinterest addiction. She lives with her husband and children in the Pacific Northwest. When Maisey isn't writing she can be found singing in the grocery store, shopping for shoes online and probably *not* doing dishes. Check out her website: maiseyyates.com.

Books by Maisey Yates

Visit the Author Profile page
at millsandboon.co.uk for more titles.

For my mom and dad, who read to me always
and made me fall in love with books—
most especially fairy tales—from the beginning.

My favorite stories always ended with
"they lived happily ever after." And they still do.

CHAPTER ONE

Once upon a time...

BRIAR HARCOURT MOVED quickly down the street, wrapping her long wool coat more tightly around her as the autumn breeze blew down Madison Avenue and seemed to whip straight on through to her bones.

It was an unseasonably cold fall, not that she minded. She loved the city this time of year. But there was always a strange sense of loss and nostalgia that mixed with the crisp air, and it was difficult for her to figure out what it was.

It would hover there, on the edges of her consciousness, for just a moment. Then it would slip away, like a leaf on the wind.

It was something to do with her life before she'd come to New York; she knew that. But she'd only been three when she'd been adopted by her parents, and she didn't remember her life before them. Not really. It was all impressions. Smells. Feelings. And a strange ache that settled low in her stomach.

Strange, because she loved her parents. And she loved her city. There shouldn't be an ache. You couldn't miss something you didn't even remember.

And yet, sometimes, she did.

Briar paused for a moment, a strange prickling sensation crawling up the back of her neck. It wasn't the cold. She was wearing a scarf. And anyway, it felt different. Different than anything she had ever experienced before.

She paused then turned around. The crowd behind her parted for a moment and she saw a man standing there. She knew, immediately, that he was the reason for the prickling sensation. He was looking at her. And when he saw that she was looking back, a slow smile spread over his face.

And it was like the sun had come out from behind the clouds.

He was beautiful. She could see that from here. Dark hair pushed back from his forehead, making him look carelessly windswept. There was dark stubble on his jaw, and something in his expression, in his eyes, that suggested he was privy to a host of secrets she could never hope to uncover.

He was… Well, he was a man. Nothing like the boys that she had been exposed to either at school or at various functions put on by her parents. Christmas parties at their town house, summer gatherings in the Hamptons.

He wouldn't stumble around, bragging about conquests or his beer pong score. No, never. Of course, she also wouldn't be allowed to talk to him.

To say that Dr. Robert Harcourt and his wife, Nell, were old-fashioned was an understatement. But then, she was their only child, and she had come to them late in life. Not only were they part of a different generation than many of her friends' parents, they had always made it very clear that she was precious to them. An unexpected gift they had never hoped to receive.

That always made her smile. It made the ache go away.

It didn't feel like a chore to do the best she could for them. To do her best to be a testament to all they'd put into raising her. She had always done her very best to make sure they were happy they'd made that decision. She'd tried—so very hard—to be the best she could be. To be perfect.

She had done her deportment lessons and her etiquette. Had done the debutante balls—even though it hadn't appealed to her at all. She had gone to school close to home, had spent every weekend back with her parents so they wouldn't worry. She'd never even considered rebelling. How could you rebel against people who had chosen you?

Except, right now, she felt a little bit like disregarding their concern. Like moving toward that man, who was still looking at her with those wicked eyes.

She blinked, and just as suddenly as he had appeared he was gone. Melted back into the crowd of black and gray coats. She felt an unaccountable sense of loss. A feeling that she had just missed something important. Something extraordinary.

You wouldn't know if it could have been extraordinary. You've never even kissed a man.

No. A side effect of that overprotectiveness. But then, she had no desire to kiss Tommy Beer Pong or his league of idiot friends.

Tall, sophisticated-looking men on bustling streets were another matter. Apparently.

She blinked then turned back around, heading back in the direction she had originally been going. Not that she was in a hurry. She was on break from school, and spending the days wandering her parents' town house wasn't terribly appealing. So she had decided she was going to go to the Met today, because she never got tired of wandering those halls.

But suddenly, the Met, and all the art inside, seemed lackluster. At least, in view of the man she had just seen.

Ridiculous.

She shook her head and pressed on.

"Are you running away from me?"

She stopped, her heart slamming against her breastbone. Then she whirled around and nearly ran into the object of her thwarted feelings. "No," she said, the word coming out on a breath.

"You seemed to be walking quickly, and with great purpose."

Oh, his *voice*. He had an accent. Spanish, or something. Sexy and like the sort of thing her brain would weave out of thin air late at night when she was trying to sleep, concocting herself the perfect mystery dream date that she would likely never find.

He was even better-looking up close. Stunning, even. He smiled, revealing perfect teeth. And then, he relaxed his mouth. There was something even more compelling about that. About being able to examine the shape of his lips.

"I wasn't," she said. "I just…" Somebody bumped into her as they walked by quickly. "Well, I didn't want to be in the way," she said, gesturing after the person, as if to prove her point.

"Because you had stopped," he pressed. "To look at me?"

"You were looking at *me*."

"Surely you must be used to that."

Hardly. At least, not in the way that he meant. Nobody likes to be different, and she was different in a great many ways. She was tall, first of all. Which was one refreshing thing about him. He was at least five inches taller than her height of five eleven, which was a rare and difficult thing to come across.

But yes, that was her. Tall. Skinny. All limbs. Plus, her hair was never going to fall in the effortless, silken waves most of her friends possessed. It took serious salon treatments to get it straight and she often questioned if it was worth it. Though, her mother insisted it was.

She was the opposite of the typical blonde beauty queen in her sorority or at any of the private schools she had attended growing up.

She stood out. And when you were a teenager, it was the last thing you wanted.

Though, now that she was in her early twenties, she was beginning to come to terms with herself. Her first instinct still wasn't to assume someone was staring because they liked what they saw. No, she always assumed they were staring because she was out of place.

"Not especially," she said, because it was honest.

"I don't believe that," he said. "You're far too beautiful to walk around not having men snap their necks trying to get a look."

Her face grew warm, her heart beginning to beat faster, harder. "I'm not really… I'm not supposed to talk to strangers."

That earned her a chuckle. "Then perhaps we should make sure to become something other than strangers."

She hesitated. "Briar. My name is Briar."

A strange expression crosssed his face, though it was fleeting. "A nice name. Different."

"I suppose it is." She knew it was. Yet another thing that made her feel like she stood out.

"José," he said, extending his hand.

She simply stared at it for a moment, as if she wasn't quite sure what he intended her to do. But of course she did know. He wanted to shake her hand. That wasn't weird. It was what people did when they met. She sucked in a sharp breath and allowed her fingers to meet his.

It was like she'd been hit by lightning. The electricity was so acute, so startling, that she immediately dropped his hand, taking a step back. She had never felt anything like that before in her life. And she didn't know if she wanted to feel it again.

"I have to go."

"No, you don't," he said, insistent.

"Yes. I do. I was on my way to… I was just going to… to a hair appointment." A lie easily thought of because she'd just been pondering her hair. But she could hardly tell him she was going to the museum. He might offer to walk with her. Though she supposed he could offer to take her to a salon, too.

"Is that so?"

"Yes. I have to go." She turned away, walking away from him quickly.

"Wait! I don't even know how to get in touch with you. At least give me your phone number."

"I can't." For a whole variety of reasons, but mostly because of the tingling sensation that still lingered on her hand.

She turned again, taking too-long strides away from him.

"Wait!"

She didn't. She kept on walking. And the last thing she saw was a bright yellow taxi barreling down on her.

* * *

Warmth flooded her. The strangest sensation assaulted her. Like she was being filled with oxygen, her extremities beginning to tingle. She felt disembodied, like she was floating in a dark space.

Except then it wasn't so dark. There was light. Marble walls. White. With ornate golden details. It was so clear. A place she'd never seen before, and yet…she must have.

Slowly, ever so slowly, she felt like she was being brought back to herself.

First, she could wiggle her fingertips. And then, she became aware of other things. Of the source of the warmth.

Lips against hers. She was being kissed.

Her eyes fluttered open, and in that instant she recognized the dark head bent over hers.

The man from the street.

The street. She had been crossing the street.

Was she in the street still? She couldn't remember leaving it. But she felt… Tied down.

She opened her eyes wider, looking around. There was a bright, fluorescent light directly above her, monitors all to her side. And she was tethered to something.

She curled her fingers into a fist and felt a sharp, stinging sensation.

She looked down at her arm and saw an IV.

And then, all her focus went straight back to the fact that she was still being kissed. In a hospital bed, presumably.

She put her hand up, her fingers brushing against his cheek, and then he pulled away.

"*Querida*, you're awake." He looked so relieved. Not

like a stranger at all. But then, he was kissing her, which was also unlike a stranger.

"Yes. How long was I...? How long was I asleep?" She posed the question to the nurse that she noticed standing just behind him. It was weird that he had kissed her. And she was going to get to that in a moment. But first she was trying to get a handle on how disoriented she felt.

"You were unconscious. Only for an hour or so."

"Oh." She pushed down on the mattress, trying to sit up.

"Now be careful," he said. "You might have a concussion."

"What happened?"

"You crossed the street right in front of a taxi. I was unable to stop you."

She vaguely remembered him calling after her, and her continuing to walk on. Feeling slightly frantic as she did. Logically, she knew that her parents were overprotective. She knew that they had been hypervigilant in instilling the concept of stranger danger to her, but she had taken it on board, even knowing that it was a little bit over the top.

They had told her that she had to be particularly careful because Robert was a high-profile physician who often worked with politicians and helped write legislation pertaining to the healthcare system, and that made him something of a target. She had to be extra vigilant because of that, and because of the fact that they were wealthy.

It had made her see the bogeyman in any overly friendly stranger on the street as a child, but she supposed it had kept her safe. Until she had met *him* and run out in front of a car.

Her parents. She wondered if anyone had called them. They wouldn't be expecting her home until evening.

"Excuse me..." But the nurse had rushed out of the room, presumably to get a doctor? She didn't know why the woman hadn't stopped to check her vitals.

"My father is a doctor," she said, looking back up at José. That was his name. That was what he had said his name was.

"That is good to know," he said, a slight edge in his voice that she hadn't heard earlier.

"If he hasn't been called already, somebody should get in touch with him. He's going to want input on my treatment."

"I'm sorry," José said, straightening.

Suddenly, his face looked different to her. Sharper, harder. Her heart thundered dully, a strange lick of fear moving through her body.

"You're sorry about what?"

"It isn't going to be possible for your father to have input on your treatment. Because you're going to be moved."

"I am?"

"Yes. It seems to me that you are stable, and that has been confirmed by my nurse."

"Your nurse?"

He sighed heavily, lifting his hand and checking his watch. Then he adjusted the cuff on his jacket, the mannerism curt and officious. "Yes. My nurse," he said, sounding exasperated as though he was explaining something to a small child. "You do not have to worry. You will be treated by my doctor once we arrive in Santa Milagro."

"Where is that? I don't understand."

"You don't know where Santa Milagro is? I do question the American school system in that case. It is truly a shame that you had to be brought up here, Talia."

Something niggled at her, something strange and steep. As deep as those wistful feelings she often felt when the air began to cool. "My name isn't Talia."

"Right. Briar." His smile took on a sardonic twist. "My mistake."

"The fact that I don't know where Santa Milagro is is not the biggest issue we have. The biggest issue is that I'm not going to see your doctor. You're just a crazy man that I met on the street. For all I know you stole that coat—it is a really nice coat—and you're actually an insane vagrant."

"A vagrant? No. Insane? Well. That matter is fully up for debate. I won't lie."

"José—"

"My name isn't José. I'm Prince Felipe Carrión de la Viña Cortez. And you, my dear Briar, are mine by rights. I have spent a great many years looking for you, and now I have finally found you. And you're coming with me."

CHAPTER TWO

PRINCE FELIPE CARRIÓN DE LA VIÑA CORTEZ had yet to lose sleep over any of his actions. As long as he steered clear of covert murders to further his political status, he was better than his father.

A low bar, certainly. But Felipe liked a low bar. They were so much easier to step over.

And while this might be the lowest he'd stooped, it was also going very well. Surely if he wasn't supposed to have Princess Talia she wouldn't have delivered herself quite so beautifully to him.

Well, the part where she was hit by a taxi was perhaps not ideal, but it had certainly made the second half of his scheme easier. Because she was now confined to a hospital bed, being wheeled through an empty corridor—something he was pleased he'd arranged, because she was yelling for help, and it was much nicer to not have to deal with anyone trying to come to her aid—and he was going to have her undergo a quick check by a privately hired physician before having her loaded onto the plane.

He was covering all his bases, and truly, being quite generous.

Though he supposed the kiss hadn't been wholly necessary. But remembering the way she had jolted when she'd seen him on the street, he had wondered. Wondered if there was enough electricity between them to shock her awake.

It had worked, apparently.

Other men might feel some guilt over kissing an unconscious woman. Not this man.

Not with this woman.

She was owed to him. Owed to Santa Milagro. She should be thankful that he was the one who had found her. Had it been his father…

Well. Yet more reasons Felipe would be losing no sleep over this. Life with him would be a kindness by comparison.

Though it was clear to him that his princess did not see it now.

"Are you insane?" She was still shouting, and he was becoming bored with it.

"As previously mentioned, it is entirely possible that I'm crazy. However, hurling it around like an epithet is hardly going to help."

She looked up at him, her dark eyes blazing, the confusion from earlier cleared from them. Even now—in a hospital gown—she was beautiful. Though her rich skin tone would be better served in golds, colors like gems. Not the sallow, white and blue cloth her slight curves were currently covered by.

No, he would see her dressed like a queen, which she soon would be. His queen. Once his father died and Felipe assumed the throne.

He had a feeling his father would be distinctly unhappy to know that Felipe had managed to track down the quarry his father had spent so many years searching for. Good thing the old bastard was bound to his bed.

Though, even if he was not, Felipe had the support of the people, and at this point, the support of the military. He supposed considering treason in the form of dispatching his own father was probably not the best course of action.

Though, if the old man was healthier, the likelihood of him considering it would be much higher.

There would be no need to do that. No. Instead, he would bring Talia back to the palace, and he would parade her before his father like a cat might deliver a bird to its master. Except the old king was not Felipe's master. Not anymore.

He passed the nurse a large stack of US dollars after she helped load the princess into the back of the van he had hired. He would not be paying anyone with anything traceable. No. He wanted all of this to go off without a ripple in the media.

Until he decided to make the tidal wave.

This would be one of his grandest illusions, and he was a master of them. Sleight of hand and other trickery so that he would be consistently underestimated on the world stage. Because it suited him. It suited him endlessly.

Well, that wasn't true. The end was coming.

Talia was a means to it.

"To the airport," he said to his driver as the van was secured.

"The airport?" She was sounding quite shrill now.

"Well, we aren't swimming to Santa Milagro. Not in your condition, anyway."

"I am not going with you."

"You are. Though I appreciate your spirit. It's admirable. Particularly given that you're currently in a hospital bed. I will have you undergo a preliminary examination before we get on the plane."

The physician he'd hired moved from his seat over to where Talia was. He proceeded to examine her, taking her blood pressure, looking at her eyes. "You may want to order a CT scan once you get back to your country," the older man said. If he was feeling any compunction about being involved in this kidnapping, he was hiding it well.

But, considering the amount of money that Felipe was throwing at him, he should hide it well.

"Thank you. I will make sure she has follow-up appointments. I do not want her broken, after all."

She did not look relieved by that news, though in his opinion she should.

"If you have any integrity at all," she said, reaching out and grabbing the doctor by the arm, "then you'll tell somebody where I am. Who I'm with."

The older man looked away from her, clearly uncomfortable, and withdrew his arm.

"Talia," Felipe said, "he has been paid too well to offer you any help."

"You keep calling me Talia. And I'm not Talia. I don't know who Talia is."

Well, that was certainly an interesting development. "Whether or not you know who Talia is—and that I question—you are her."

"I think maybe you're the one who hit your head," she said.

"Again, sadly for you, I did not. While I may not be of sound mind, I certainly know my own mind. This... Well, this has been planned for a very long time. You think it accidental that I encountered you on a busy street in New York City? Of course not. The most random of encounters are always carefully orchestrated."

"By some sort of higher power?" she asked, her tone wry.

"Yes. Me."

"I have no idea who you are. I have never heard of you, I have never heard of your country, so I can only imagine that it is the size of a grain of rice on a world map. While we're talking size, I can only assume that plays a factor in a great many things, since you seem to be compensating."

He chuckled. "If I were not so secure I might be offended by that, *querida*. Anyway, while I am a believer in the idea that size matters in some arenas, when it comes to world events, often the size of the country is not the biggest issue. It is the motion of the… Well, of the cash flow. The natural resources. And that, my country has in abundance. However, we are going through a few structural changes. You are part of those changes."

"How can I be part of those changes? I'm a doctor's daughter. I'm a university student. I don't have a place on the world stage."

"And that is where you're wrong. But we're not going to finish having this discussion here."

He had paid the good doctor for his silence, that much was true, but he did not trust anything when a larger payday had the potential to come into play. And when news of Briar Harcourt going missing hit the media, there was a chance that the man would go forward with his story.

That meant that the details revealed in the van needed to be limited. Soon, however, they arrived at the airport, and the vehicle pulled up directly to Felipe's private plane.

"Don't we have to go through customs? I don't have… Well, I don't have a passport."

"Darling. You're traveling with me now. I am your passport. Does she need the IV any longer?" He posed that question to the doctor.

"She shouldn't," came the grave reply.

"Then remove it," Felipe commanded.

The doctor did so, carefully and judiciously, putting a Band-Aid over where the needle had been.

"She is not hooked up to anything else?"

"No," the doctor replied.

"Excellent." Felipe reached down, wrapping his arms around Talia and hoisting her up out of the bed. "Good help is all very well and good, but in the end it's always better to do things yourself."

She clung to him for a moment, clearly afraid of falling out of his arms and getting another head injury, and continued to hold on to him while he got out of the van and began to stride across the tarmac toward the plane.

And then she began to struggle.

"Please do not make this difficult," he said, tightening his hold on her, not finding this difficult at all, though he would rather not end up with a bruise if it could be helped. If he was going to be marred, he preferred for it to happen in the bedroom. At least then, there would be a reward for his suffering.

Hell, sometimes the suffering was just part of the reward.

"The point is to make this difficult!"

"I have never had a woman resist getting on my private plane quite so much."

"But you've had them resist. That says nothing good about you."

He sighed heavily, taking them both up the steps and into the aircraft. His flight crew immediately mobilized, closing the door and beginning the process of readying for takeoff. As they had been instructed prior to his and the princess's boarding.

"You say that as though it should bother me," he said, setting her down in one of the plush leather chairs on the plane before sitting down in the chair across from her. "Don't bother to try and get up and unlock the door. It can only be unlocked from the cockpit now. I made arrangements for some high-security additions to be added to the plane before coming to get you."

"That seems stupid," she said. "What if we need to get out and the pilots can't let us out?"

He chuckled, reluctantly enjoying the fact that she seemed so comfortable running her mouth even though she had absolutely no power in the situation. "Well, I can actually control it from my phone, as well. But don't get any ideas about trying to do it yourself. It requires fingerprint and retina recognition."

"Fine. But if the plane catches fire and we need to get out and somehow your fingerprints have melted off and you can't open your eyes and we die a painful death because of your security measures…"

"Well," he said. "In such a case I will feel terribly guilty. And, I imagine continue the burning in hell."

"That's a given."

"Are you concerned for the state of my eternal soul?"

"Not at all. I'm concerned for the state of my present body." She looked around, and he could tell the exact moment she realized she had nothing. That she was wearing a hospital gown, that she had no identification, no money and no phone.

"I do not intend to harm you," he said, reaching down and straightening his cuffs. "In fact, that runs counter to my objective."

"Your objective is to…improve my health?"

"Does it need improving? Because if it does, I most certainly will."

"No," she laid her head back, grimacing suddenly. "Okay. Well, right now it needs slight improvement because I feel like I was hit by a taxi." She sat upright, slamming her hands down on either side of her, her palms striking the leather hard, the sound echoing in the cabin. "Oh, yes! Because I was hit by a taxi!"

"Regrettable. While I orchestrated a great many things, that was not one of them. I would never take such a risk with you."

"Maybe now is a good time for you to explain yourself. Since we've established I'm not going anywhere. And I assume that Santa Milagro is not a quick and easy flight. I suppose we have the time."

"In a moment." The engines fired up on the plane, and they began to move slowly. "I like a little atmosphere. And I don't want to be interrupted by takeoff."

The aircraft began to move faster and he reached across to the table beside him, opening the top and pressing a button. An interior motor raised a shelf inside, delivering a bottle of scotch, along with a tumbler.

As the plane began to ascend he opened the bottle and poured himself a generous measure of the amber liquid. He did not spill a drop. That would be a mistake. And he did not make mistakes.

Unless he made them on purpose.

"And now?" she pressed.

"Do you want to change first?" He took a sip of his drink. "Not that the hospital gown isn't lovely."

Her face contorted with rage. "I don't care what I'm wearing. And I really don't care what you think of it."

"That will change. I guarantee it."

"You don't know very much about women, do you?"

He set his glass down on the table. "I know a great deal about women. Arguably more than you do."

"You don't know anything about this woman. I don't know what kind of simpering idiots you normally capture and drag onto your plane, but I'm not impressed by your wells, by your title, by your power. My father did not raise a simpering, weak-willed idiot. And my mother did not raise a fool."

"No, indeed. However, they were raising a princess."

"I'm not a princess."

"You are. The Princess of Verloren. Long-lost. Naturally."

"That is… That is ridiculous."

"It is the subject of a great many stories, a great many films… Wouldn't you think that something like that, a story so often told, might have its roots in reality?"

"Except this isn't *The Princess Diaries* and you are not Julie Andrews."

He chuckled. "No, indeed." He took another sip of his scotch. Funny, alcohol didn't even burn anymore. Sometimes he missed it. Sometimes he simply assumed it was a metaphor for his conscience and found amusement in it. "A cursory internet search would corroborate what I'm telling you. King Behrendt and Queen Amaani lost their only daughter years ago. Presumed dead. The entire nation mourned her passing. However, in Santa

Milagro it was often suspected the princess had been sent into hiding."

"Why would I be sent into hiding?"

"Because of an agreement. An agreement that your father made with mine. You see, sometime after the death of his first wife, the king fell on hard times. His own personal mourning affected the country and led the nation to near financial ruin. And so he borrowed heavily from my father. He also promised that he would repay my father in any manner he deemed acceptable. He more than promised. It is in writing." Felipe lifted a shoulder then continued, "Of course, at the time King Behrendt felt like he had nothing to lose. His wife was dead. His heir and spare nearly grown. Then he met a model. Very famous. Originally from Somalia. Their romance stunned all of Europe for a great many reasons, the age gap between them being one of them."

"I know this story," she said, her voice hushed. "I mean, I have heard of them."

"Naturally. As they are one of the most photographed royal couples in the world. What began as a rather shocking coupling has become one of the world's favorites."

"You're trying to tell me that they are my parents."

"I'm not *trying* to tell you that. I *am* telling you that. Because when it came time to collect on the king's debt… My father demanded you."

"He did?"

"Oh, yes. Verloren, and indeed the world, was captivated by your birth. And when you finally arrived, a great party was given. Many gifts were brought from rulers all over the world. And my father—not in attendance because he was any great friend of yours, but because your father was obligated—came, but it was not with a gift. It was a promise. That when you were of age he would come for you. And that you would be his wife."

Her skin dulled, her lips turning a dusky blue. "Are you… Are you taking me to your father? Is that what this is?"

He shook his head. "No. I am not delivering you to my father. For that, you should be thankful. You will not be his wife."

"No," she said firmly. "I will not be."

He looked up at her then, his eyes meeting hers. She looked fiery, determined. Anger glittered in those ebony depths, and perversely he ached to explore that rage. Sadly, it would have to wait.

"You will not be my father's wife," he repeated, pausing for just a moment. "You will be mine."

CHAPTER THREE

SHE LOST CONSCIOUSNESS after that. And really, she was somewhat grateful for that. Less so when she woke up feeling disoriented, cocooned in a bed of soft blankets in completely unfamiliar surroundings.

At least when she woke up this time it wasn't because he had kissed her.

Though, he was standing on the far side of the room, his arms crossed over his broad chest, his expression one of dark concern. Perhaps that was an odd characteristic to assign to concern, but she had a feeling the concern wasn't born out of any kind of goodness of his heart, rather over the potential thwarting of his schemes.

His schemes to make her his wife. She remembered that with a sudden jolt.

She sat up quickly, and her head began to throb.

"Be careful, Princess," came a slow, calming voice. "You do not have a concussion, but you have certainly been through quite a lot in the past twenty-four hours."

She became aware that a woman was standing to the left of her bed. A woman who had that kind of matter-of-fact bedside demeanor she typically assigned to physicians.

"Are you a doctor?" she asked.

"Yes. When you lost consciousness on the flight, Prince Felipe called and demanded that I make myself available to him as soon as the plane landed. I told him it was likely stress and a bit of dehydration that caused the event." She sent him a look that carried not a small amount of steel.

"I have indeed been placed under stress," Briar said. "Since he kidnapped me."

The woman looked like she was about to have an apoplexy. "Kidnapped. Lovely."

"Did you have a criticism, Dr. Estrada?" Felipe asked, his tone soft but infinitely deadly.

"Never, Your Majesty."

"I thought not."

"Perhaps you ought to criticize him," Briar said.

"Not if she would like to retain her license to practice medicine here in Santa Milagro. Also, not as long as she would like to stay out of the dungeon."

"He would not throw me in the dungeon," Dr. Estrada said, her tone hard. "However, I do believe he might strip me of my license."

"Do not think me so different from my father," he said, his tone taking on a warning quality. "I will have to assume control of the country soon, and I will do whatever I must to make sure that transition goes as smoothly as possible. I would like to give you all that I have promised," he said, directing those words to the doctor, "but I cannot if you don't help me in this. I am not evil like my father, but I am entirely focused on my goals. I will let nothing stand in my way." He rolled his shoulders backward, grabbed the edge of his shirtsleeve and pulled it down hard. "I am hardly a villain, but I am...morally flexible. You would both do well to remember that."

"You can't exactly issue threats to me," Briar said, "as I've already been kidnapped."

"Things can definitely get worse," Felipe said, a sharp grin crossing his lips. "I'm quite creative."

A shiver ran down her back and she thought wildly about what she could do. There was no hope of running, obviously. She wasn't feeling her best, even if she didn't have a concussion. She was also stranded in a foreign country with no ID, no money, nothing but a hospital gown.

"Help me," she said to Dr. Estrada, because she had no idea what else she could do.

"I'm afraid I can't," the woman said. "Except when it comes to your medical well-being. You can take a couple of these pain pills if you need them." She set the bottle on the nightstand.

"I might take the whole thing," Briar responded.

"I will not tolerate petulant displays of insincere overdoses." Felipe walked across the room, curling his fingers around the pill bottle and picking it up. "If you need something I am more than happy to dispense it. Or rather, I will entrust a servant to do so."

He was appalling. It was difficult to form an honest opinion on his personality, given that he had kidnapped her and all. That was the dominant thing she was focused on at the moment. But even without the kidnap, he was kind of terrible.

"That will be all, Dr. Estrada," he said, effectively dismissing what might have been Briar's only possible ally. "She would not have helped you," Felipe said, as if reading her mind. "She can't. You see, my father has had this country under a pall for generations. People like Dr. Estrada want to make a difference once the old king is dead—and he is closer and closer to being dead with each passing moment we spend talking. I would prefer that he live for our marriage announcement, however. Still, if he does not, I won't lose any sleep over it. The sooner he dies, the better. The sooner he dies, the sooner I assume the throne. And change can begin coming to the country."

"There's nothing you can do until some old, incapacitated king dies?"

He waved a hand. "Of course there is. If there was nothing that could be done, Dr. Estrada wouldn't have been here at all. In fact, she's somebody that I've been meeting with for the past couple of years, getting a healthcare system in place, ready to launch the moment I assume power. I have pieces in a great many strategic places on this chessboard, Princess. And you were the last one. My queen."

"I don't understand."

"Of course you don't. But you will. Ultimately, this will benefit your country. Your parents."

"My parents live in New York," she said, gritting her teeth. "I don't care about anybody else."

He made a tsking sound. "That's quite heartless. Especially considering the king and queen assumed great personal cost to send you to safety."

"I might feel something more if I knew them," she said, ignoring the slight twinge of guilt in her chest. "As it is, I'm concerned that the mother and father I know are going to be frantic, looking for me."

"Likely they will be. But soon, very soon, I will be ready to announce to the world that we are engaged."

"And what's to keep me from flinging myself in front of the camera and letting everybody know that I'm not

your fiancée, I'm a kidnap victim? And you are dangerously delusional."

"Oh," he said, "you've got me there. Something I
didn't think of. I've only been planning exactly how my
ascendance to the throne would go for the past two decades. But here, you have completely stumped me with
only a few moments of thinking." He laughed, the sound
derisive. "Your country, your father's country, owes mine
an astronomical amount. I could destroy them. Bankrupt
them. The entire populace would spend the remainder
of their days in abject poverty. A once great nation top-
pled completely. I, and I alone, have been the only thing
standing in the gap between my father and his revenge
on Verloren. My own had to go neglected so that I could
protect yours. I spent every favor on that. Used every
ounce of diplomacy to convince him that it was not the
time to move on Verloren. I placated him with ideas that
I had gotten leads on your whereabouts." He shook his
head. "I did a great deal to clinch this. If you think you're
going to thwart me with a temper tantrum then you are
truly delusional."

"Well, I was hit by a taxi."

He laughed again. "True. I should have given the
driver a tip. He made this all that much easier. Anyway,
you will be well taken care of here."

"I just have to marry a monster."

"There is that," he said, looking completely unfazed
by the insult. "What sort of monster do you suppose I
am, Princess?"

She couldn't tell if he was asking the question with
sincerity. She wasn't sure she cared. But as she looked
at him, a picture began to form in her mind. His eyes
were gold, glinting with heat and the possibility of a kind

of cruelty she didn't want to test. There was something sharp about him, whip-smart and deadly.

"A dragon. Clearly," she said, not entirely sure why she had provided him with the answer.

"I suppose that makes you the damsel in distress," he said.

"I'd like to think it makes me the knight."

"Sorry, darling," he said. "I kissed you awake not eight hours ago. That makes you the damsel."

"If we're going off fairy tales then that should make you Prince Charming, not the dragon."

He chuckled. "Sadly, this is real life, not a fairy tale. And very often the prince can be both."

"Then I suppose a princess can also be a knight. In which case, I would be careful, because when you go to kiss me again I might stab you clean through."

He lifted one dark brow. "Then the same goes for you. Because the next time I go to kiss you, I might decide to swallow you whole instead."

There was something darkly sexual about those words, and she resented the responses created in her body. No matter that he was… Well, insane almost by his own admission, he was still absurdly beautiful.

And that, she supposed, was ultimately what he meant about the dragon and the prince being one and the same. On the outside, he was every inch Prince Charming. From his perfectly tailored jacket and dark pants, to his classically handsome face and picture of exquisite masculinity that was his body.

But underneath, he breathed fire.

"I am announcing our engagement tomorrow. And you will not go against me."

"How do you know?"

"Because I'm going to allow you to call your parents tonight. At least, the people you know as your parents."

"They'll send someone for me. They'll contact that… They'll contact the president if they have to."

"They won't," he said, his voice holding an air of finality. "And you know why? Because they do know the whole story of how you came to be theirs. They know exactly who you are, and they know why they cannot interfere in this. They were charged with keeping you safe from me, and they failed. Now, there is nothing that can be done. Once you have passed into the possession of the dragon… Well. It is too late. Tell them everything that I told you. And they will confirm what I've said. You don't have a choice. Not if you want to keep your homeland from crumbling. Not if you ever hope to see things actually fixed. This is bigger than you. When you speak to them, you'll know that's the truth."

Then he turned, leaving her alone with nothing but a sense of quiet dread.

"I will be having an engagement party in the next week or so," Felipe said, staring fixedly out the window at the view of the mountains.

"That seems sudden," his friend Adam said on the other end of the phone.

Adam was recently married to his wife, Belle, after years of isolating himself on his island country, lost in grief after the death of his first wife, and hiding the terrible scars he had received from the accident that had made him a widower. But now things had changed. Since he had met Belle, he had come back into the public eye, and he seemed to have no issue with public appearances.

All the better as far as Felipe was concerned, because he wanted to have as much public support as possible.

"It isn't," Felipe said. "Believe me."

"Why do I get the feeling this is the sort of thing I don't want to know the details about?" his other friend Rafe said, his tone hard.

"You likely don't," Felipe said. "But I would happily give them to you. You know I have no shame."

He didn't. Though he was hardly going to engage in unbridled honesty and a heart-to-heart with his friends about the current situation. That wasn't how he worked. It wasn't the function he fulfilled in the group.

He'd cultivated the Prince Charming exterior long ago. Out of necessity. For survival. Image had been everything to his father, and the older man had always threatened Felipe and his mother with dire consequences if Felipe were to reveal the state of their lives in the palace.

The consequences of behaving otherwise were dire, and he had discovered that the hard way.

So he had learned, very early on, not to betray himself. Ever. He kept everything close to his chest, while appearing to give the whole world away.

"I would like details," Adam said, "before I know what sort of circus I'm bringing my pregnant wife to."

"Congratulations," Felipe said. "Please make the announcement before you come to my party. I don't want the impending arrival of your heir to overshadow my engagement."

"I suppose that's about all the sincerity I can expect out of you," Adam said, his tone dry.

"Probably. But you see, I have found a long-lost—presumed dead—princess. And, I'm making her my wife. This is good for me for more than one reason. All political things, I won't bore you with them. Suffice it to say, this party is going to be quite the affair."

"I see. And how exactly did you find this princess?"

"Well, there's an app. I just opened it up and trapped her inside a little ball."

Adam snorted. "I wish that were true, Felipe. But I have a feeling that a lot more skullduggery was involved."

"There was skullduggery. I cannot deny the existence of skullduggery. Ultimately, I consider that a good thing since skullduggery is a sadly underused word."

"I do not need details," Rafe said. "But is my support of you going to damage the value of the stock in my company? That, I do need to know."

"And I need to know if she is the princess of any country possessing nuclear weapons. Because again, my support cannot endanger my people," Adam added.

"If the actual details of how I came in to possession of the princess were released, it might in fact cause you both trouble. But they won't. First of all, her parents owe an astronomical amount of money to my country. As much as they might want to contest the marriage, they won't be able to. And, once she is more familiar with the situation, she will feel the same way."

"So, you're forcing her into marriage?" Adam asked.

"Do I detect a hint of judgment in your voice?" Felipe returned. "Because if I remember correctly you came into possession of your wife when you took her prisoner."

"That was different."

"How?"

"Because *I* did it," Adam said. "Plus, I wouldn't do it now."

"Because love has changed you and softened you. I understand. Sadly, I'm not looking for love." The very idea almost made him laugh. "No chance of softening. But I do believe that in the end this is going to be the best thing for Santa Milagro. If it isn't the best thing for one woman, when all of my people could be benefited, I have to say I'm going to side with my people."

"So," Rafe said, slowly. "You are asking us to attend your engagement party, where you will announce your intention to marry a woman that you kidnapped, who doesn't want to marry you, but who will have to pretend as though she does so that you don't bring terrible consequences down on her mother and father, and her entire country."

"Yes," Felipe said.

"That sounds about right," Rafe responded.

"My wife will be…unhappy," Adam said.

"Then don't tell her. Or, tell her that's how all the girls meet their husbands these days. Stockholm syndrome."

Adam growled. "I'm not going to keep it from her."

"Fine. But I do expect that she fall in line," Felipe said, having not considered that his friend's potential loose cannon of a spouse might be an issue. Who knew what Belle might say to the press?

"Belle does not *fall in line*," Adam said. "It isn't in her nature. However, I will explain the sensitive political situation. I know she would not wish to cause harm. And while I don't trust that you won't cause any harm, Felipe, I do trust you're trying to prevent greater harm."

"Of course. Because I'm an altruist like that. Details will be forthcoming, but of course I had to call and give you the good news myself."

"Because you're such a good friend," Rafe said, the words rife with insincerity.

No, the truth was, they were friends. True friends, the

kind that Felipe had never expected to have. The kind that, he imagined, had prevented him from becoming something entirely soulless.

They had some idea about his upbringing. About the way that he was. But mostly, he showed them the face he showed the world. Prince Charming, as he had just discussed with Talia.

The dragon, he kept to himself.

Usually.

CHAPTER FOUR

BRIAR WAS ABOUT to give in to despair when there was a knock on the door. She knew immediately that it wasn't Prince Felipe, as she had a feeling he didn't knock. Ever.

She was proven correct when a servant came through the door after she told her to come in.

"This phone is programmed so that you may call your parents," the woman said. "I will give you some privacy."

She turned and swept out of the room, leaving Briar there with the phone. The first thing she tried to do was call 911, which was stupid, because she knew that it wasn't an emergency number in Santa Milagro. The phone wasn't connected to the internet, so she couldn't search any other numbers, but she had a feeling that even if she could it was programmed to only connect to one other number.

She should dial them immediately. After all, except for when she was at school, this was the longest she'd gone without contact with them. And even when she'd been at university it had been…different. She'd been in an approved location, doing exactly what they'd asked her to do.

Right now she was…well, somehow rootless, even as she learned the truth of where she'd come from. On her own, in a way she never had been before, even while she was being held captive.

For one moment, she thought about not calling. It was a strange, breathless moment, followed by her stomach plummeting all the way to her toes, even as she couldn't believe she had—for one moment—considered something so selfish.

They were probably sick with worry. And it was her fault, after all. She was the one who had approached Felipe. She was the one who had opened herself up to this. She had failed them. After trying so hard for so much of her life to make sure she could be the daughter they deserved to have, now they were going through this.

With shaking fingers, she dialed her parents. And she waited.

It was her father who answered, his tone breathless in rush. "Yes?"

"It's me," she said.

"Briar! Thank God. Where are you? Are you okay? We've been searching. We called the police. We've called every hospital."

"I know," she said. "I mean, I knew you would have. But this is the first chance I've had to call. I wasn't…I've been kidnapped," she said. As much as she didn't want to cause her parents any alarm, kidnapped was what she was; there was no sugarcoating it.

Her father swore violently, and a moment later she heard the other line pick up. "Briar?" It was her mother.

"I'm okay. I mean, I'm unharmed. But I'm in…"

"Santa Milagro," her father said, his tone flat.

The world felt like it tilted to the side. "You know? How do you know?" He had told her they would. But she realized that up until that moment she truly hadn't believed him.

"Perhaps it was a mistake," her father said slowly, "to keep so much from you. But we saw no other way for you to have a normal, happy life. It wasn't our intention to keep your identity from you, not really. But we didn't know what kind of life you would have if you knew that you were a princess that couldn't live in a palace. If you knew that you had parents who had given birth to you across the world, who didn't want to give you up but had felt forced into it."

"It was selfish maybe," her mother said, her tone muted. "But your mother and father did agree. They agreed that it would be best if you knew only us. They agreed it would be best if you didn't feel split in your identity. But we all knew it couldn't go on forever. We simply hoped this wouldn't be the reason."

Briar felt dizzy. "Am I Talia? Princess Talia. That's what he keeps calling me. Is that true?"

"It is true." Her father said it with the tone of finality.

"How? How can everybody just keep something like this from me? This is my life! And yeah, you were always overprotective and everything, but I didn't realize it was because I was in danger of actually being kidnapped by some crazy prince from half a world away." She took a deep breath. "I didn't realize it was because I was…a princess."

It felt absurd to even think, let alone say.

"It lasted longer than we thought it would," her mother said, her voice soft. "And I can't say that I've been unhappy about it. You're all we have, Briar. And to us, that's who you are. Our daughter. We wanted so badly to protect you." She heard the other woman's voice get thick with tears. "We failed at that."

Briar felt…awash in guilt. A strange kind. They were distressed because of her. Because they had been embroiled in this and probably hadn't a clue what the best way to handle it was. Of course there wasn't exactly a parenting book called *So You Have to Keep an Endangered Princess Safe While Raising Her as Your Own.* It might hurt, to find all this out now, but she certainly couldn't blame them.

"He says I have to marry him," she said, her voice hushed.

"The king?"

"Prince Felipe," she said.

The sound of relief on the other end of the phone was audible. "At least he's not… His father is a devil," her father said. "That was why your birth parents, the king and queen, sent you away from your country. Because they knew a life with him would destroy you."

"I don't want to marry Felipe, either, though," she said. "I don't want to be a princess. I just want to go back home."

There was a pause. A silence that seemed to stretch all the way through her.

"I'm afraid that's impossible. Now that he has you… It would be catastrophic to your birth parents…if any of this were to get out. The money that was borrowed by Verloren. Because any business done with King Domenico would be considered a blight on your mother and father. They would never recover from it. And the consequences to the country would be severe if Santa Milagro decided that the terms of the deal had been violated. The national treasury would be drained. People would have nothing. No food, no housing. No healthcare."

As he spoke those words, she felt weight settling on her shoulders. A new one added with each thing he listed would be denied to the citizens of her home country—a home country she couldn't even find on a map—if she chose not to comply.

"So I have to… I have to marry him?"

"Unless you can convince them there is some other alternative," her father said. "I'm not sure what else can be done. You are beyond our reach. This is something we never wanted for you."

Fury filled her anew. "But you knew it could happen. You knew all along, and I didn't."

"We never wanted you to be afraid of your own shadow," her mother said.

"Well, I don't want to be afraid of my own shadow. But I should have been warned to be afraid of charming Spanish men who tried to talk me up on the street." She hung up, and as soon as she did the door swung open. And there was Felipe.

Immediately, she was filled with regret.

He crossed the room, taking the phone from her hand. Why had she hung up? Who knew how long it would be before she was able to speak to her parents again.

"I assume everything that I said would be confirmed was?" he asked.

"I assume you were listening in, based on your perfect timing."

He smiled. "You know me so well already. We're going to be the perfect married couple."

"I don't understand. Marry somebody else. Why does it have to be me?"

He reached out then, grabbing hold of her hand and tugging her up out of bed. She was still wearing nothing more than the hospital gown, and she felt a breeze at her backside. She gasped, realizing that there was nothing but a thin pair of white cotton panties separating her from being bare back there.

His golden eyes were blazing then, blazing with that kind of fire and intensity she had sensed was inside him. And more than that. Fire, and brimstone. She had the sudden sense that there was hell contained inside this man. And whether it was just the shock wearing off, or a sudden connection with the reality she found herself in, for the first time she was afraid of him. Really afraid.

She found herself being dragged over to a window. Heavy drapes obscured the view, and he flung them back, roughly maneuvering her so that she was facing the vista before them. A large, sprawling city, nothing overly modern. Villas with red clay roofs, churches with tall steeples and iron bells hanging in the towers. And beyond that, the mountains.

"Do you see this?" he asked. "This is my country. For decades it has been ruled by a madman. A madman more concerned by power—by shoring up all of the money, all of the means through which he could blackmail—than caring for the people that live down there. And in that time I have spent decades doing what I can do in order to change things once I assume the throne. Working toward having the military on my side. Toward earning as much money as I could personally to make a difference the minute I had control. I have been making contacts and arrangements behind the scenes so that the moment my father's body is put into the dirt a new dawn will rise on this country. I never wanted to take it by civil war.

No, not when the cost would be so dear in terms of life. At least, I didn't want to take it in an open civil war. But that is exactly what I have been fighting for years. Playing the part of debauched playboy while I maneuvered in the background. You are part of that plan. And I will be damned if I allow you to do anything to mess it up. There is no amount of compassion that could move me at this point, Princess. Nothing that will stir me to change my path. I will be the King of Santa Milagro. And you... You can be the queen. You can help fix all the evil that has befallen my people, and you can improve the lives of yours, as well. Or you can go back to life as a bored sorority girl in the city. I'm sure that's an existence, as well. And all of these people... Well, they can slide into the sea."

She had to smooth her fingers over her eyebrows to make sure they hadn't been singed off during that fiery tirade. "Am I really so important to your plans?"

"Everybody knew that you were supposed to marry my father. And the things he would have done to you... But if you marry me, and you do so willingly...it will mend the fences between Santa Milagro and Verloren. It will do much to fix the image of my country—and me— in the media. I need everything in my power. Absolutely everything. All the pieces that I have set out to collect. I will let nothing fall by the wayside. Including you."

"And if I don't?"

"I didn't think I could possibly make that more clear. If you don't there will be destruction. For everyone. Everyone you love. Everyone you will love."

She blinked. "Are you going to have people killed?"

"No. I'll only make them wish they were dead."

"And how will that help your *improve your image* attempt?" she asked with a boldness she didn't feel.

"I'm not so stupid that I would go about it in the public view. But your New York parents...they are vulnerable. And suitably low visibility. Nonetheless, I can ruin them financially. He works with American politicians. And believe me, if I offer the right incentives, I can decimate his patient base, his reputation. Because far better to have an alliance with a prince than continue to support a specific physician."

Ice settled in her stomach. She believed him. Believed he would do that. Harm her parents. And if she allowed that...what sort of daughter would she be? They had protected her all her life. The least she could do was protect them in kind.

He smiled, and something in that smile made it impossible for her to doubt him. And then his expression shifted, and he returned to being that charming-looking man she had seen on the street in New York. "Now, you can't possibly meet my people in that hospital gown. Rest for tonight. Tomorrow... Tomorrow we shall set about fashioning you into a queen."

Felipe walked into his father's room. It was dark, the curtains drawn, none of the lights on.

"Good evening, Father," he said, sweeping toward the bed.

"Your jacket is crooked," his father said by way of greeting.

Felipe lifted his arm, tugging his sleeves down, hating the reflex. "It is not," he returned. "And you're very nearly blind, so even if it was, there would be no way for you to tell."

It was a strange thing, seeing this man in this state. He had always been fearful to Felipe when he'd been a child. And now, here he was, drained, shrunken. And still, something twisted with something sour whenever he looked at him.

This man, who had abused and tortured him and his mother for years. A slap across her face when Felipe was "in disarray."

He could remember well his mother being hit so hard it left an instant bruise beneath her eye. And then her makeup artist had been charged with making it invisible before they went to present themselves in the ballroom as the perfect royal family.

A facade of perfection. Something his father excelled at. He had convinced his country of the perfection of his family and the perfection of his rule. The citizens of Santa Milagro slowly and effectively stripped of their freedom. Of art, education and hope.

All things Felipe would see restored. Though he would never be able to fix what had become of his mother, at least he could restore Santa Milagro itself.

There had always been the temptation to try and claim the country by force, but that would only entail more loss of life.

There was enough blood shed already. Blood that felt as if it stained his hands.

"Is that any way to talk to your dying father?"

"Probably not. But since when have I cared? I only wanted you to know something."

"What is that?"

"I found her. The princess."

His father stirred. "My princess?"

A smile curved Felipe's lips. "No. She's mine now. I'm

going to make her my wife. There is nothing you can do about it. Not from your deathbed."

"You're a bastard," his father said, his voice thin, reedy and as full of venom as it had ever been. But he had no power now.

"Don't I wish that were true," Felipe said, twisting his voice into the cruelest version of itself he could manage. Projecting the sort of cruelty that he had learned from the man lying before him. "If only I were a bastard, rather than your flesh and blood. You have no idea how much I would pay to make that so."

"The feeling," his father said, the words broken by a ragged cough, "is mutual." He wiped a shaking hand over his brow. "I never was able to break you."

"Not for lack of trying," Felipe said. "But I do hope that I will go down in history as one of your greatest failures. The only truly sad thing is that you will not be here to see it."

He turned to leave his father's room. Then paused. "However, if you're still alive by the time the wedding rolls around I will be sure to send you an invitation. I'll understand that you won't be feeling up to attending."

He continued out of his father's room then, striding down the hall and on to the opposite wing of the palace where his rooms were. It was only then that he acknowledged the slight tremor in his own hand.

He flung open the doors to his chamber, crossing the length of the space, and took a large bottle of whiskey from the bar that was installed at the back wall. He looked at the glass that he kept positioned there—always, for easy access—and decided it was not needed. He took the cap off the bottle and lifted it to his lips, tilting it back and trying to focus on the burn as the alcohol slid down his throat.

It took so much more for him to feel it now. So much more for him to feel anything.

He slammed the bottle back down onto the bar. And he waited. Waited for something to make that feeling of being tainted go away. It was because he had gone into his father's room. Or maybe it was because of the princess who resided down the hall against her will.

Or maybe it was just because his father's blood ran through his veins.

Felipe roared, turning toward the wall and striking it with his forearm, his fist closed. He repeated the motion. Over and over and over again as pain shot up to his shoulder, and all the way down to his tightly closed fingers.

Then he lowered his arm, shaking it out. He took a deep breath, the silence in the room settling over him. He looked down, and he noticed a trail of blood leaking out from beneath his now crooked shirtsleeves.

He frowned. Then reached down and grabbed hold of the fabric, straightening his cuffs. And took another drink.

When Briar awoke the next morning she was greeted by three stylists. A man dressed in a shocking green coat, wielding a pair of golden scissors. A woman in a skin-tight fuchsia dress, and another wearing a pale blue top and a navy-colored skirt.

"The prince has ordered that we help prepare you for your public debut," the woman in pink said, her features seeming to grow sharper as she examined Briar.

"I don't normally wear hospital gowns," she said, her

voice stiff. "But I kind of left home without a chance to gather any of my clothes."

The woman waved a hand, the shocking neon fingernails a blur against her brown skin. "None of them would have been acceptable anyway. I'm confident in that fact."

After that, she found herself being plucked from bed and herded into the bathroom where she was instructed to get into the shower, where she would find acceptable soaps. She bristled at the idea that somehow what she had used before wasn't acceptable, but gladly walked into the massive tiled facility and stood beneath the hot spray for longer than was strictly necessary.

Then she began to scrub her skin with the toiletries provided and had to concede the fact that it was essentially like cleansing herself with silk. Perhaps, she also had to concede that as nice as the items in her childhood home were, they weren't palace material.

Then she got defensive again when she was seated in front of a vanity and that man with the golden scissors began to paw at her hair.

"Don't cut too much off," she all but snarled.

"I'm sorry," he said, "where did you go to school for hair?"

"I didn't. But it's grown out of my head for the past twenty-two years, so I have to say I'm pretty well educated on that situation."

He appraised her reflection in the mirror, squinting his eyes. "No. Not more than I am. You should not have straight hair."

"Well, clearly I disagree with you," she said, feeling defensive.

"Your bone structure agrees with me."

There was no argument after that. And she had to

admit that when he was finished she appreciated the curls in her hair in a way she didn't normally. He had managed to find a nice middle ground between the tightly wound natural curl and the board-straight style she normally aimed for. The fact that she didn't hate it was a little bit annoying.

She had a similar interaction with the stylist who was intent on choosing silhouettes that Briar normally avoided. She was averse to things that clung too tightly to her curves, but the woman in bright pink seemed to think that Briar needed to show off a bit more.

The makeup artist didn't believe in subtlety, either, and by the end of it Briar barely recognized the woman in the mirror. Or rather, she almost did. Because the tall, slim creature with her eye-catching curls and slim figure wrapped tightly in a blaze-orange dress, bright pink blush on her cheeks and gold on her lips, looked more like Queen Amaani than she did herself.

It was becoming more and more difficult to deny the reality of the situation.

Although, resemblance didn't confirm genetics, but her parents had told her it was true. And even if they hadn't…it would be very difficult to push it aside now.

"Beautiful," the man in green said.

She felt complimented, but at the same time didn't really want the compliment as she was being made beautiful for a man she didn't really want to feel beautiful for.

She said nothing, but her beauty team didn't seem to care. Instead, they packed up their things and left as quickly and efficiently as they had arrived.

Briar wobbled on the high heels she was wearing then sat quickly on the edge of the bed. She put her hand to her chest and looked at the mirror that hung across the room, looked at the wide-eyed, undeniably beautiful woman staring back at her.

She was a princess. Really and truly. And she was supposed to marry a prince who was quite possibly the maddest bastard on the planet.

The door to her room opened again and a man she hadn't seen before appeared. "His Majesty would appreciate it if you would join him for breakfast. Provided you are dressed suitably."

"Does that mean he didn't want me to show up in a hospital gown?"

The servant didn't react, his expression carefully blank. "He did not specify."

"Well, I imagine I'm suitable." She stood, following him out of her bedroom. She had been tempted, if only for a moment, to deem herself unsuitable and stay in her bedroom. But she had been in there for two days and eventually she was going to have to face her adversary. Face the man who claimed he was going to marry her whether she wanted him to or not.

And she was going to have to try to get out of it.

She walked silently with the servant, the only sound in the corridor the clicking of her high heels on the flagstone. The man opened the door to what she presumed was the dining room and stood to the side. "This way."

He didn't enter with her. Instead, she heard the doors close firmly behind her and found herself standing alone in a cavernous room with Prince Felipe. He was seated at the opposite end of the table from her, a newspaper to his left, a cup of coffee to his right.

"Good morning," he said.

Then, from behind the paper, he produced a velvet

ring box. He set it firmly in front of him then said nothing more about it. "Have a seat," he said.

"As you wish," she returned, taking her seat in the farthest possible place from him, nearest the door.

"That is not what I meant," he said.

"But it is what you said."

He chuckled and folded the paper then retrieved the ring box and picked up his cup. He stood then, and she was reminded of how tall he was. How imposing. He walked across the room and sat down next to her. If he was fazed at all, he didn't show it.

"You seem to have woken up in a good mood, Briar."

"That's the first time you've called me that," she said. "Apart from when you were pretending to be José."

"I suppose it doesn't benefit me to be at odds with you," he said, tilting his head to the side, a dent appearing between his brows. As though he was truly considering this for the first time. "If you are more comfortable being called Briar in conversation, then I will call you that. However, in public I will refer to you by your given name."

"A given name I don't remember being given."

"Do any of us really remember being given our names? I know I certainly don't." He placed his index finger firmly against the top of the ring box and slid it toward her. "See if this is to your satisfaction."

"It won't be," she said, not making any move toward the box.

"I doubt that. The diamond is practically large enough to eradicate world hunger."

"Then eradicate world hunger. Don't put it on my finger."

"I will make a donation to charity that matches the value. Put it on your finger."

"No," she responded. "I have been given no real compelling reason why I have to actually marry you. It's only because you're choosing to consider me payment for a debt, which I think we can both agree is a bit archaic. You say that your father is a monster, so I don't understand why you want to be monstrous, as well."

"Because I will be a better monster," he said. "Anyway, I have explained my terms, and they will not change."

"Well I don't—"

"Do you want to meet your parents? King Behrendt and Queen Amaani?"

A strange, yawning void opened up inside her chest. One that she hadn't realized was there until that moment. And she flashed back to earlier when she had seen her reflection in the mirror and realized how much she favored the queen. Realized that there was most certainly truth in the stories she had been told about her lineage.

She loved the mother and father she knew, and nothing could ever replace them. But she had other parents. Parents who hadn't actually wanted to give her up. Parents who had done it for her protection.

A king and queen who had lived halfway across the world from her for almost her entire life. A king and queen that she could meet.

That longing was an ache, so acute, so intense, that it stole her breath.

But she refused to respond to him. Apparently, she didn't need to, because only a moment later it became clear that her longing must have been written across her features.

"Excellent," he said. "If you ever want to meet your

parents, if you want to see the palace again… We can always attend the annual ball they throw every year in October. I hear you loved it when you were a little girl. There is always spiced cider, which I'm told was your favorite."

It hit her in the chest with the force of a brick. That feeling. That nostalgia. That hook she felt in her gut whenever the air began to chill and the leaves started to fall.

It was what she remembered. Oh, she didn't remember it in pictures. Didn't remember it as an actual event. But it lived somewhere inside her. Resided in her bones. It transcended specific moments and images and existed in the realm of feeling. Deep and powerful. It was a root; she couldn't deny it. It always had been. A part of her that connected her to the earth, that ran beneath the surface of all that she was. That had formed her into who she was now.

She wanted to see it. She wanted to connect that with something real. With something more than a feeling.

"You remember," he said, the amusement in his voice almost enraging. "And you do want it. More than anything. You have very expressive eyes, *querida*. All the better for me."

All the better for him to manipulate her, he meant. And he was doing it. Doing it with all the skill of a master. She suddenly felt like a puppet whose strings had been cut. Like someone who had been restrained all her life, who was left standing there with an endless array of choice.

Her parents weren't here. She didn't like Felipe, and he needed her. Which meant she was under no pressure at all to behave a certain way. As long as she was here, she was doing his bidding and he couldn't—and wouldn't—

lash out at her so long as she didn't bring her behavior into the public eye.

She didn't have to behave. She didn't have to do anything for anyone.

She didn't have to be perfect.

"Of course I want to meet my parents," she said, not bothering to soften her tone. "Who wouldn't want to understand where they came from?"

"It will be impossible for you to meet your family, of course, should you fail them in the way that you are suggesting you might."

"They sent me across the world, pretended I was dead, in order to avoid this fate for me."

"No, they wished for you to avoid my father. However, a marriage of convenience is not uncommon between royals. And I am not my father. Believe me. It matters. That is not just an incidental. Had the marriage been set between you and I from the moment you were born...they would have happily handed you over. What I can offer them, what I can offer your country, and what yours can offer mine, is no small thing. Conversely, what I can do if you disappoint me on this score is no small thing. Do you honestly think that your mother and father would be content to allow you to marry a doctor on the Upper East Side?"

"They sent me to be raised by one. I'm not entirely certain why one wouldn't be good enough for me to marry."

"But you were never intended to live there forever. You were always meant to come back and assume your place. Tell me... What did you expect to do with your life?"

"I was an art major."

He made a dismissive sound. "So you're poised to become an incredibly useful member of society. I'm terribly sad to have interrupted that trajectory."

Anger fired through her veins, and since she wasn't worried about making friends with him, she let it show. "Art is important."

"Of course. It's the thing that people worry about after all of their necessities are met."

"It's one of the things that makes the world beautiful. It gives people hope. It's part of moving from surviving to living."

A smile curved his lips. "I seem to have found a bit of passion in you. That is encouraging. I would put you in charge of the art program. For all the schools in my country. You will have the opportunity to change the face of education in this country. My father has kept things quite austere, it may not surprise you to learn. When I say he has been something of an evil dictator I am not exaggerating. That is not the kind of job offer you're going to get in Manhattan. What else are you going to do with that degree? You going to marry someone successful and plan all his parties for him? I grant you that often princesses can be quite decorative, but my queen will not be. I will use you in whatever capacity you see fit, whatever way you can find to improve my country."

He spoke with…well, sincerity, which was the most surprising thing. That he seemed to so easily hand this to her. The chance to reconnect with her parents, with her heritage, and the chance to make a difference. All by using the subject that she was most passionate about.

"And you should see the art collection we have in the palace. Just sitting in the basement waiting to be curated. Our museums need to be opened. We have been in the dark ages. It is time that we come into the light. And if—as you say—art is a part of living and not surviving, then help my people live."

It was strange, because she could actually see that he cared about this. About his country. That of all the things in the entire world, this might be the only thing that mattered to him. She might be at a disadvantage here, but so was he. Because he cared about this. And he needed her. Needed her to cooperate. Needed her to help insulate his image.

"And if I get up in front of the entire world when you try to announce our engagement and tell them that you kidnapped me?" She had to ask.

"If I go down, Princess, we are going down in flames together. I promise you that. I'm not a man to make idle threats. I have been lying in wait for years, waiting for the moment when I might liberate my kingdom, when I might save my people. Believe me when I tell you I will not be stopped now. I would not say that I am a man consumed with serving the greater good. I don't really care about whether it's good or not. I care about serving my goal. My goal is to make this country great. My goal is to liberate the people in it. Whatever I have to do."

He slid the ring closer to her again. "Now. Put it on."

She hesitated for a moment before reaching out and curling her fingers around the box. Then she opened it slowly. Her breath caught in her throat. It truly was beautiful. A stunning diamond set into an ornate platinum setting. Definitely designed to tempt a woman on the fence about accepting a marriage proposal.

If it was a show of love it would be personal.

It hit her then, with the speed and impact of a freight

train, what it would mean to marry him. It would mean never having a real boyfriend. It would mean never falling in love. And it would mean...

She looked up at him, her heart slamming against her breastbone. Images flashed through her mind. Him touching her. Kissing her. She had never kissed a man before, unless you counted that time he had kissed her when she was unconscious. And she didn't really. Except, it was difficult not to. Because it had most certainly been the first time another person's lips had touched hers. And thinking of it now made them burn.

"Did you have questions?" he asked.

"I don't have another choice. Do I?"

"We always have choices. It's just that the results of those choices are going to be better or worse. You have one choice that doesn't ruin a great many lives. That isn't having no choices."

"One requires me to be completely selfish, though." And if she decided to walk away from him, she supposed that she could go back to life as she had always known it. She would simply ruin an entire nation that she hadn't known much about until this week. Would never meet her parents. But she could go back to how things were. Could pretend that none of this had happened.

"And if I were you, that is perhaps the choice I would make."

His dark eyes glittered, and she had a feeling that his comment had been calculated. Because the moment he had said that, she had known that her decision was made. She wasn't him. She wasn't, and she never would be. Her parents had always instilled in her the fact that having money as they did didn't make her better, didn't make them better. That she had been given a great many advantages and was responsible for making the best of those advantages.

She had been intent on doing that. As soon as she had finished school she had planned on getting involved in inner-city art programs, in establishing funds and foundations. She was being given the opportunity to do that here. And more.

The influence she would have as a queen was inestimable.

She wrapped her hand around the ring box. "Okay. I'll do it."

He didn't smile. Didn't gloat. No, he reacted in a completely different way to what she had imagined he might do. His handsome face set an expression of grim determination. "Good. And it is done. The announcement will be made tomorrow. And we are going to have a ball celebrating our engagement. I have already sent out invitations."

"Ahead of my acceptance?"

"I never doubted you."

The words hit her strangely, bounced around inside her chest, ricocheting off her heart. They made her angry, but they made her feel something else, too. Something she couldn't quite put a finger on. Something she didn't want to put a finger—or anything else—on.

"Perhaps you should. Someday I might surprise you."

He shook his head. "Good people are rarely surprising, Briar. It's bad people you have to watch out for." He stood then. "You should order yourself a coffee." He turned to walk out of the room.

"Are you a bad person?"

His expression turned grave, deadly serious, which

was strange. "I am… Whatever I am, I am beyond help. If I were you, I wouldn't try."

Then he left, leaving her alone with her fear, her doubt and a diamond.

CHAPTER FIVE

IT WAS THE headline the next morning. That Prince Felipe Carrión de la Viña Cortez was engaged to the long-lost Princess of Verloren. He assumed it was not the best way for the king and queen to discover that he had found their daughter, but he was going to send them an invitation to the engagement party so they could hardly be too upset.

Though he didn't think they would come. No, they would assume that it was some kind of trap, of course. It would take time. It would take time for anybody to trust that he wasn't as conniving as his father.

Starting with the kidnapping of a princess was perhaps not the best opening move, all things considered. But that was one thing that he and Briar were going to have to discuss.

He flung the doors to her bedchamber open, unfazed by the gasp and eruption of movement that resulted. He saw nothing but a flash of curl and a blur of brown skin as she dashed behind a changing screen.

"I'm not dressed!"

"And I'm your fiancé," he said. "Which is exactly what I came to speak to you about. You cannot behave this way in my presence. I cannot have the world thinking that I forced you into this."

She poked her head out from the side of the divider. "But you did."

"Sure. But we're not going to advertise that, are we? It undermines my aim for building bridges between nations."

"Well, God forbid you could build an actual bridge," she said, disappearing behind the divider again. He heard the rustle of clothes.

"Don't dress on my account."

She made an exasperated sound then appeared a moment later wearing a black pencil skirt and a bright green crop top. She was stunning. She had been from the beginning, but the new wardrobe, the makeover, provided to her by his staff, had truly brought out the uncommonness of her beauty. It had elevated her from mere beauty to someone who would turn heads everywhere she went.

Exactly what he wanted in a queen.

He enjoyed her ability to stand up to him, as well. Had she no spine at all he would have kept her, certainly, but it would have been a much greater trial. It would have made him think too much of his mother.

And he knew where that ended.

"I'm not going to stand in front of you in my underwear."

"You will eventually."

She paled slightly. "Well. We'll cross that bridge when we come to it."

"The bridge you just accused me of not building?"

"It's a different bridge, obviously."

"Just clarifying. I wish to give you a tour of the castle."

She looked startled by that. "Why?"

"Because you live here. And you will live here for the foreseeable future. Don't you want a tour of your home?"

"I guess it's practical. But I don't know why you're giving it to me."

"I am going to be your husband. And we are going to be required to make a great many public appearances together. You will have to learn to act as though my presence doesn't disgust you."

"I was never a very good liar," she said, looking at him with those fathomless dark eyes, her expression almost comically serene.

"Well, get better at it." He extended his arm. "Shall we?"

She accepted the offered arm slowly, curving her fingers around him as though she thought he was a poisonous serpent. Something about that light, tentative touch sent a shock of heat through his body.

That electricity that had been there from the moment he had seen her pulsed through him with renewed strength. She had been quite pitiful after her accident, and that—along with the logistics of convincing her to marry him—had pushed some of that attraction onto the back burner. But he was reminded now. With ferocity. He was also reminded that it had been a very long time since he'd had a woman in his bed. He had been too focused on getting all the pieces in play to see to the typical pleasures he filled his time with.

"You've seen the dining room already," he said, indicating the room to their left. "My chambers are that way. My father is kept in another wing entirely, and you have no reason to ever set foot in that part of the palace." The old man might be incapacitated, but he still didn't want Briar anywhere near his father.

The shock of protectiveness that slammed into his chest surprised him. Briar—as far as he was concerned—

was a means to an end. He did not have particularly strong feelings about her. But he did have particularly strong feelings about his father and the sort of influence he wielded over women. He didn't want that old man to put one drop of poison into Briar's ear. Not when he knew full well that it was the sort of poison that could be fatal.

"I don't think I want to, all things considered." She hesitated for a moment. "He's really dying?"

"Any day now, truly. His body has been failing him for quite some time. There is no hope left. Nothing to be done. Just waiting for him to choke on his spite and bile."

"You don't sound…sad at all."

"I'm not. I thought I had made that perfectly clear. I hate my father. I'm not simply ambivalent toward him. I loathe him. My legacy shall be upending his."

She said nothing to that, though she shifted to the side of him, the soft swell of her breast brushing up against his biceps. A simple touch, one that would have barely registered had it been any other woman. At any other moment. But he was going to marry this woman.

For the first time, that part of the plan truly settled in his mind. She would be the mother of his children. And he would need her to be…happy. That had not been part of the plan when he had first conceived it. He had not considered her happiness—her feelings of any sort— when he had decided that he needed to bring her here and make her his. Why would he? Considering that would run counter to his objective. He didn't like anything getting in the way of his objective.

And considering it now had nothing to do with the goodness of his heart. If he possessed a heart he very much doubted it had any goodness in it. But she would give birth to his children, and she would need to be there for them. He knew too well the alternative.

Suddenly, the promise of art programs was much more than simple bribery. "I meant what I said," he said. "About the art collection. About the programs. You will be in charge of those. You can appoint an entire team to help you with teaching, with organization. I will give you a very generous budget. The country has fallen on difficult financial times under my father's rule, but I have made billions on my own. And I have kept it all out of the country, tightly under my control so my father couldn't get his hands on any of it. But that will change once he's gone."

She stopped walking, looking at him, her expression full of confusion. "Why are you giving me this? It's for your country, right? It isn't for me."

"My aim is not for you to be miserable."

"Why do you care?"

"Because I know what it's like to exist beneath the rule of a totalitarian regime. My father was a dictator to the country, but he was even worse to those who lived under his roof. It will not be so, not in my house. I will not subject my wife or my children to such things."

Her mouth dropped open. "Children."

"Of course we will have children. The single most important act for a ruler is to produce an heir, is it not?"

"I...I suppose. I hadn't really thought about it."

"Of course you haven't. You were raised as a commoner. But it is a requirement. I have to carry on my line."

She frowned. "But I... But we..."

"Do you not want children?"

She frowned. "I...I do. I... Things are different now,

because I'm going to meet my parents. My biological parents. But I always wanted someone in my life that I shared a genetic bond with. Which is silly. It doesn't matter. Blood doesn't matter. All that matters is that somebody loves you. And my parents—the ones that raised me—they love me. But still."

"You don't have to explain yourself to me," he said. "I'm a man entirely driven by the need for vengeance. I'm hardly going to call your motives into question."

"Yes, I want children. But I didn't anticipate having them… Now. Or with…" She was blushing. Her cheeks turning a dusky rose.

"With me?" He finished for her.

"Well. Yes. You're a stranger."

"I won't be. By that point." They wandered down the long hall, and all the way to a pair of blue, gilded double doors that were firmly closed. "This is where we will hold the ball where we celebrate our upcoming nuptials." He flung them open then reached out for her this time. "Come with me, Princess."

She took his hand reluctantly, but eventually curved her delicate fingers around his. He smiled. He knew full well how to put people at ease, but he hadn't done the best job with her since that first day. Since that first moment.

He would do well to charm her. She would certainly be happier. And he knew how to charm women. He had been told a great many times that he was very good at it. And, if the notches on his bedpost were any indicator, it was the truth. It would not cost him to turn on that part of himself for this woman.

Now that he had her, now the she had agreed…

"Do you know how to dance?"

She laughed. "Of course I do. I had an entire…coming out."

"A debutante?"

"Yes."

"You really are excellent. And your parents did a wonderful job raising you. Because they knew that this would ultimately be where you'd land."

She frowned. "Well. If what you say is true, then they hoped I would end up back in my country and not in yours at all."

"Perhaps." He shifted their positions, keeping hold of her hand, then he wrapped his arm around her waist and pulled her up against him. "Would you care to practice?"

Her dark eyes widened, her full lips falling open. "I don't need to practice."

"The world will be watching when we take our first dance as a couple. It is not enough to simply know how to dance. You have to know how to move with me." And with that, with no music playing and no sound in the room but their feet moving over the glossy marble, he swept her into the first step of a waltz.

She followed beautifully, her movements graceful, but her expression spoke far too readily of her feelings.

He leaned in slightly. "You must work at looking as though my touch doesn't disgust you."

As he spoke the words, he realized that he must work at making sure his touch didn't disgust her. Yes, the relationship had started with force, but there was no reason it could not be mutually satisfying. Oh, there would never be any love, nothing like that. He didn't believe in the emotion. Even if he did, he wasn't capable of feeling it. But they could have a reasonable amount of companionship.

They could certainly have more than violence and death. Than aching loss. Yes, they could have more than that.

He moved his hand slowly down the curve of her waist, settling it more firmly on her hip. She looked up at him, her dark gaze meeting his, the confusion there evident. He knew why she was confused. She didn't find his touch repellent at all. And she couldn't figure out why.

"Don't feel bad," he said, keeping his voice soft. "I'm very experienced at this. I promise you I could take you from shouting at me in anger to screaming my name in pleasure in only a few moments."

Color suffused her cheeks and she tried to pull away from him. He held her firmly. Didn't let her leave. Kept on dancing. "You're ashamed of that. Of the fact that you enjoy me touching you." He was fascinated by that. That somebody would waste one moment being ashamed of something that brought them pleasure. He'd had very little of it in his childhood, and he could admit that he had possibly gone overboard with it once he had gotten out from beneath his father's roof. Once he had discovered women. Once he had discovered that, as profoundly terrible as his father could make him feel, a woman's hands on his skin, a soft touch, could make him feel that much better.

But whether or not it had been too much, he didn't regret it. No. He never let himself regret feeling good.

"I don't understand," she said, her voice flat, not bothering to deny the accusation.

"There's very little to understand with chemistry, *querida*. And there is very little point in fighting ours. We are to be married, after all." Her flush deepened and she looked away from him. "Did you imagine that you would be a martyr in my bed? I promise you, you could start out as serene and filled with sacrifices as Joan of Arc, but in the end, when I made you burn, it would not be in the way you're thinking."

"You're so arrogant," she said, her voice vibrating with some strong emotion he couldn't place. "Assuming that I'm not comfortable with this because I feel shame. It didn't occur to you that maybe—just maybe—I'm not feeling exactly what you think?"

"Sorry," he said, knowing he didn't sound apologetic in the least. "But you're a little too late in your denial. And even if your words haven't already betrayed you, your body betrays you, Princess. Your eyes..." He lifted his hand, tracing a line just beneath her left eye. "They've gotten darker looking at me, your pupils expanding. This speaks of arousal, did you know?"

She swallowed visibly. "My eyes are dark. I sincerely doubt you noticed anything of the kind."

"All right. Then let's move on. There is color in your cheeks. You're blushing."

"Perhaps I'm angry. Maybe that's why."

"I suspect you're angry, as well. More at yourself than at me." He moved his thumb down the curve of her cheek, to her lower lip, sliding it slowly over that soft, lush skin. "You're trembling here. And your breathing... It has grown very shallow. Quick."

"And that," she said, her voice unsteady now, "could be fear."

"Yes. But you don't strike me as the kind of woman who scares easily."

"I don't suppose being hit by a taxi and kidnapped, then taken half a world away, scaring me, would qualify as *scaring easily.*"

He laughed. "No. I don't suppose it would. Still…"
He moved his thumb even slower across her lower lip. "I
don't think you're afraid of me. I think you're afraid of
what you might do." He moved in slowly and she sucked
in a sharp breath, drawing backward. "Yes. You're afraid
of what you might want. That's the scary thing, isn't it?
Knowing that I'm not Prince Charming. Knowing that
I am the monster. And wanting me anyway. That does
make you unique. Most women only know the surface.
Most of them have not had the pleasure of being kidnapped by me. They want the facade. You know what's
underneath and you want me still. I wonder…"

A strange sense of disquiet filled his chest and he did
his best to ignore it. He couldn't afford to be growing a
conscience now. Couldn't afford to be concerned with her
or her feelings. He needed to seduce her. She was supposed to be his wife, after all. He was hardly going to
live in a sexless marriage. Then again, he wasn't entirely
sure he was going to remain faithful during the course
of their marriage. That would depend. On a great many
factors. Namely what would keep the peace in the palace. It was entirely possible that she would not want all
of his attentions focused on her.

But as he had realized only a few minutes ago, her
happiness was going to have to come into consideration.
Something new, and strange. Needing to care about the
emotions of another person. If only to keep her from…
Well. He had no desire to repeat the sins of his father.
That was as far as he would go with that line of thinking today.

"What do you wonder?" she asked. It was strange that
she seemed to be asking the question genuinely. That
she did not seem to be teasing or testing him. He had

a very limited amount of experience with people who were genuine in any fashion. But Briar seemed genuine. She was sharp, and she possessed a rather whip-smart wit. But even so, there was something…well, something untested about her. Young. Innocent. In his circle, in his world, there were very few innocent people. Everyone was guilty of something.

He supposed eventually he would find out what she was guilty of. Because there was no way she was everything she seemed on the surface. Nobody was.

Still. The way she asked the question…

"I wonder if it would be the same for anyone," he said, his voice hard. "Perhaps you're not unique. Perhaps any woman, faced with the possibility of marrying a prince who was set to become a king, given the chance to be a queen, would overlook the fact that I'm a bit…beastly."

"I'm not looking anything over," she pointed out. "You're holding quite a few things hostage—including me—in order to get me to agree to the marriage."

He found himself oddly relieved by that, and he didn't know why. "That is true."

He was still touching her lower lip, and the color in her cheeks was only growing more intense. "You can stop that now," she said.

"I'm not sure that I want to."

"Well, I want you to."

He dropped his hand down to his side. And he was gratified when she let out a long, slow breath that he was certain spoke of disappointment. She wished that he would push harder. She did. Whether she admitted it or not, she did.

"It must be nice," he said, releasing his hold on her

and stepping back from her. "Releasing all responsibility in a situation."

"What are you talking about?"

"I'm a kidnapper. A kidnapper, a blackmailer… Well, it's not a long list, but it is a fairly damning one. You, on the other hand… What are you? Victimized, I suppose. You have no other option but to marry me. And certainly, it benefits you in a great many ways, but you're able to claim that you're not actually swayed by the title, by the money…when in fact, you might be."

"Stop it," she said. "You're twisting the situation. It's bad enough without you adding gaslight."

He drew back, feeling as though she had slapped him. He *was* manipulating the situation, and he found that it was something of an impulse on his end. Which ran counter to the fact that he had just realized he needed to do something to make her happy. But he didn't know how to…have a real conversation. He didn't know how to do anything other than poke and prod, and attempt to make himself come out with the advantage.

He didn't know how to connect.

She seemed to. She had asked a question. And it had been genuine. Part of his answer had been, as well.

"Very well," he said, moving away from her. "We can finish for the day."

"What else am I supposed to do with my time?"

"Anything you like. Except for returning to New York. But I have informed my staff of the position that you will be filling after our marriage, and it's possible that you can begin organizing the art collection right away."

She looked shocked. "I can?"

He waved a hand. "Yes. Why would I prevent you

from doing that? It was one of the things I used to bribe you with."

She blinked. "I suppose so."

"I don't want you to be miserable. Sure, the foundation for the marriage might be kidnapping and blackmail, but I don't see why you can't enjoy yourself."

"You know I think that might be the most honest thing you said since we met."

"What?"

"That you don't understand why I can't enjoy myself even though I've been blackmailed and kidnapped."

"The situation is what it is. Make of it what you will. I suppose I will see you again for our engagement party."

She looked relieved. Relieved that she wouldn't be seeing him for a while. Well, that was going to have to pass. But there was time.

He turned and walked away from his fiancée, the woman who was wearing his ring, who didn't even want to be in the same room with him. And he ignored the tightening in his gut and below his belt as he did. She was beautiful, but she wasn't special.

No woman was. No one person was. He wasn't sentimental; he didn't believe in that sort of thing.

But as he walked down the corridor toward his office he had to make a concerted effort to banish the image in his mind of that wide-eyed, genuine look that had been written on her face when she had asked him what he wondered. With nothing but curiosity. Nothing but honesty.

And as he sat down at his desk he did his best to banish the grim thought that her honesty wouldn't last long. Not with him. That kind of openness, the little bit of innocence that she possessed, would be snuffed out by the darkness inside him.

It was as inevitable as her becoming his queen. And as necessary, as well.

There was nothing that could be done. And he would waste no time feeling guilty about it.

Guilt was for men who could afford to have consciences. He was not one of those men.

CHAPTER SIX

THE ENGAGEMENT PARTY came more quickly than Briar was prepared for. The moment when Felipe was going to present her for the entire world to see as his fiancée. Yes, the world at large knew, but this was different. This was the first time she was actually going to make an appearance. The first time she was going to have to contend with it.

She had been presented with two couture gowns to try on for the event. And her stylists were currently in a heated debate as to whether or not she should choose the pink or the blue.

Both were cut dramatically, designed to show off her figure, and billowed around her feet. Ultimately, she went with the blue. Because when she twirled, it moved effortlessly with her body. That, and it had a little bit more give around the hips. She had a feeling that she was going to need it. She was naturally thin, much to the chagrin of most of her friends at university, but even she felt a little bit constrained by a gown after a long evening of standing around eating. And the delicacies here at the palace really were amazing.

She supposed if one had to get kidnapped, getting kidnapped by a prince really was the way to go. Good food, good lodgings. And really amazing clothes.

As she was zipped into the beautiful blue gown, she looked down at the ring sparkling on her left hand. Right. There was that. The fact that her particular kidnapping had come with a fiancé. But also with a royal title. Of course, she supposed she had that title on her own.

Her stomach lurched a little bit when she remembered that her parents—her birth parents—had been invited to tonight's event. Would they come? Would this be the first night she saw them since she was a little girl? And what would she do? She had a feeling that she would crumble. Break down completely, which she hadn't done once since she had been kidnapped from her home in New York. That was strange, she realized then. That she hadn't cried yet.

She supposed part of it came down to the fact that she was afraid if she shed even one tear she would shed endless tears, and then they might never stop.

She sucked in a deep, shuddering breath and looked at her reflection. At the woman staring back at her who was less a stranger now than she had been a week ago. With the expertly applied makeup and the beautifully styled curls.

Panic fluttered in her breast, and she had to look away.

This wasn't the time to have a meltdown. She was going to have to save it for later. She would pencil it into her brand-new schedule. A gift from Prince Felipe. At least, she had been told. True to his word, she hadn't seen him between that moment in the ballroom and today.

There was a very large part of herself that was grateful for that. What had happened was…confusing. The fact that he had made her feel things. The kinds of things she had felt that first moment when she had seen him standing there on the street.

And she kept turning over what he had said to her. About what it meant that she liked him even knowing he was a monster. Well, like maybe wasn't the word for it. That she was attracted to him.

That she *wanted* him.

She turned away from her reflection, pressing her hand against her stomach.

"You will be fine, Princess," the stylist said, reading her nerves incorrectly. That was fine. She didn't care if he thought she was nervous about going to the ball. Well, she was. But it had to do with her parents. And it had to do with him. The man that she should be disgusted by. The man that she should hate.

The man that made her feel things no other man ever had.

She was herded down the hall, to an antechamber that was seemingly outside a private entrance to the ballroom. She knew that guests had already arrived. She also knew that she was going to be presented, along with the prince, in a formal way.

She understood all of that. She hadn't grown up as traditional royalty, but growing up as she had, with her father occupying a very prominent position in high places, she had been American royalty in some regards.

Ceremony was part of that upbringing. She supposed that was helpful. Of all the things that she did have to worry about at least she didn't have to learn this entirely new language of formality.

She didn't know what she expected. Didn't know who she had expected to guide her into the ballroom. But she hadn't expected Felipe. Or maybe she had, and there was simply no way for her to prepare herself for the sight of him.

He was… Well, it simply wasn't fair how good he looked in a suit. He really should look monstrous. Because she knew that he was one. That he was selfish. That he was willing to do anything to meet his ends, no matter who he heard. It didn't matter. It didn't diminish the intensity of his masculine beauty.

The perfection of those broad shoulders, the exquisitely sculpted face that was a work of art all on its own.

"You look beautiful," he said as though he had pulled the word she was thinking right out of her head. Except, she had been thinking that he was beautiful. And she would rather die than confess that. Still, she had a feeling that he knew. It seemed evident in the glint in those dark eyes, in the slight quirk of his full mouth.

He certainly wasn't a man who possessed humility. Why was that appealing? Why was anything about him appealing?

You're going to marry him. You're going to marry him and sleep with him.

Her entire body went hot. She shouldn't be thinking about this. Not now.

Really, she was going to have to put off thinking about it for as long as possible. And then when she did, she was going to have to wait until she was alone. Until he wasn't standing right in front of her acting like a visual reference for what was going to happen. So that she wasn't tempted to imagine what he might look like without those layers of fabric over that masculine physique.

She should be appalled by him. If there was any justice, if there was any logic involved in hormones, she should be appalled.

She had always thought herself above this kind of

ridiculousness. Apparently, she had just been waiting for the right kind of wrong man to get hot and bothered over.

"Are my parents in there?" That was the one thing she had to know.

"You're welcome," he said, his tone dry. And it took her a moment to remember that he had just called her beautiful. Well, she wasn't going to thank him for that. Mostly because she wanted to keep her interactions with him anything but cordial. For now. She supposed, since she had agreed to marry the man, she had to relax that eventually.

Maybe around the time that she let herself think about being intimate with him.

Maybe.

"Are they in there or not?"

"They are," he said. "And they have requested a private audience with you, which I will grant them after we've been formally introduced."

Suddenly, she felt dizzy, but rather than reaching out to steady herself against the wall, she found herself pitching forward. She stretched her hand out, her fingertips coming into contact with his chest. Then she swayed. And he caught her around the waist, pulling her up against his body. "Are you okay?"

She looked up at him, or rather, at his Adam's apple, at the sharp line of his jaw, and then the wicked curve of his lips. She could feel his heart raging beneath her palm. And she wondered if his heart always beat so hard, if it always beat so fast. "No," she said, her tone hushed. "How can I be okay? I always knew that I was adopted. I always knew that I had birth parents out there somewhere. But I never expected to meet them. I certainly didn't expect them to be a king and queen. And I didn't expect them to have given me up reluctantly. To have given me up to protect me."

She found herself blinking back tears and wondering if her mascara was waterproof.

And he looked… Well, for the first time since she had met him Felipe looked afraid. As if her tears terrified him.

"I'm sure it will be fine," he said, his tone stiff suddenly.

"How can it be fine?"

"I only had one set of parents, and they were never particularly useful to me. Neither were they particularly loving. You seem to have two sets of parents who were quite fond of you. How can it not be fine?"

There was something strange about the way he said that, but then, there was something strange about the way he talked about emotion in general. The way he talked about connections with people, or the lack of them. She had noticed that the day they danced in the ballroom. It made her sad. Almost.

"I don't know how to face this. I don't know how to handle any of this. A week ago I was just Briar Harcourt. And now I'm…I guess I'm a long-lost princess."

"You were found," he said. "You are not lost anymore."

She didn't say, as she took hold of his arm and allowed him to lead her toward the double doors of the ballroom, that she felt more lost now than she ever had. No, she kept that observation to herself. And then the doors opened, and they walked out to the top of the stairway, where they were announced as Prince Felipe and Princess Talia. It was strange, and it felt somewhat detached, since the name still didn't feel like her own. But as they descended the stairs the sense of fantasy faded. And she felt the moment as sharp and real as anything had ever been.

Strange, because this was something out of a movie. Strange, that it was the first moment that felt truly real in the past week. Or maybe it was just the events catching up to her. The undeniable reality of the whole thing. The fact that if it was a dream she would have woken up by now, and she could no longer pretend that she might.

Then she saw them. Well, she saw Queen Amaani. A near mirror image of herself. A beautiful, dark-skinned woman standing there holding her husband, King Behrendt's, arm. She had a heavy golden crown on her dark hair, signifying her ranking.

The king himself had piercing blue eyes, a strong nose and neatly kept gray hair and beard. Clearly much older than his wife, he was still a handsome man, his presence announcing his status more clearly than a crown ever could.

Briar found herself clutching Felipe's arm as though without him she would collapse completely. It was a perverse thing, that she found herself leaning on his strength in this moment. She should push him away. She should push him away and run to her parents. But she was afraid that if she let go of him she would crumble to the floor.

The people in the ballroom blurred into indistinct shapes, the men a wave of black, the women a watercolor rainbow. All she could see was her mother and father. And Felipe. She could still see him. She could feel his warmth. Could feel his strength.

She swallowed hard as she approached the king and queen.

"Let us step out onto the balcony," Felipe said, leading the way, holding on to her as he led her through the crowd and out toward a large balcony that overlooked the gardens.

Nobody followed them, and then she realized that there were guards preventing anyone from leaving the ballroom and interrupting the reunion.

Suddenly, Briar found herself enveloped in her parents' arms. And that was when she lost hold of everything. Of her emotions. Of her control. And she let the tears fall.

There was nothing to say. Because it transcended words. She supposed that there would be time to ask about what had happened in the years since they had seen each other. Though she gathered quickly that they knew things like what she had majored in, and that they had been sent photographs all through her growing up. She was the one with the real deficit. The one who knew nothing of her past, the one who knew nothing of her family. Of her country, of the palace that she had once called home, of her half brothers and their wives and children.

But there would be time for all of that later. Because for now, there was nothing but this. But this deep, happy, devastatingly sad reunion that she had been waiting for all her life without even realizing it.

She looked up and saw Felipe studying them as though he was looking at something he simply couldn't understand. She shouldn't be looking at him now. Except, he had been instrumental in this reunion. But without his father she wouldn't have been given up in the first place. But then, she wouldn't have known the parents that she loved so dearly, the mother and father who had raised her. Everything was mixed up in her head and she didn't know how she felt anymore. Didn't know if she was happy, didn't know if she was sad. Didn't know if she was angry at that devastatingly handsome man standing apart from them, or if she felt sorry for him.

If she wanted to run from him, or if she wanted to draw closer to him.

"Sadly," he said finally, "we cannot stand out here all night."

King Behrendt looked up at Felipe, his expression stern. "Haven't you and your people robbed us of enough time already?"

"It is unfortunate," Felipe returned. "However, in the future you will have endless time to spend together. I do not intend to keep her from you. In fact, I intend to ensure that we have brilliant relations between our two countries. This is a reunion. Not simply for our families, but for the goodwill between Verloren and Santa Milagro. I understand that you might not appreciate the tactics. But Briar has agreed to marry me. I'm sorry, Princess Talia has agreed to marry me."

Queen Amaani looked stricken by the use of her other name. But she stepped forward. "Which name do you prefer?" she asked Briar, her voice soft.

"I don't know that I prefer either one," she said. "I'm just getting used to everything."

"We've always known what they called you," she said. "If that's what you want to be called, if you want to be Briar, you can be."

"I'll be Talia," she said, not sure if she meant it or not. But she didn't want to cause these people any more pain. Not after all they had been through.

"We can find another way," her father said, his expression hard as he looked at Felipe.

Briar shook her head, because she knew they couldn't. It was just that her father was too proud to acknowledge anything else. "You don't have to. I've been away for a long time. I haven't had the chance to be part of this. To be part of royal life. To serve my country in any way. This is how I can do it." She realized, as she spoke the words, that she meant them.

Her parents gave her one last lingering hug before they headed back into the ballroom, with promises to have her travel to Verloren as soon as possible, and promises to visit the palace in Santa Milagro often.

"I think," said Felipe, walking up slowly behind her, pressing his hand against her lower back, "that I will call you Briar."

It sent a strange, electric jolt through her. To have him touch her. To have him say that. She didn't know why that affected her. The thought that he would call her Briar.

"You don't have to," she said.

"I'm going to."

She stopped walking and turned to face him. He kept his hand planted firmly on her lower back. "And if I don't want you to?"

"I still will."

She frowned. "Why?"

He examined her closely, something in his dark eyes sharper, clearer than usual. It was then that she realized that lazy, indolent manner he sometimes threw over himself like a cloak was exactly that. Just something he put on.

She wondered about the real man. The one who wasn't a monster or Prince Charming. The man beneath all of that. Then, just as quickly as she wondered about that, she wondered if he even existed anymore. Or if he had been buried underneath a rock wall that he had carefully constructed around any and all authenticity.

"Because I should think you would like it if your entire past wasn't erased."

"It might be less painful." To just pretend that her childhood in New York, her family, her friends, didn't exist anymore. To pretend that Briar didn't exist anymore. That thought made her feel hollow.

"Life is painful," he said. "Loss is painful."

"You're acknowledging that I'm experiencing loss at your hand?"

"Circumstances are what they are. It doesn't have to be a loss. Unless… Did you have a lover back home?"

She shook her head. "If I did I never would have talked to you on the street in the first place." Maybe she should have lied. Maybe that would have been better. To make him think that she had another man in her life. But he would find out soon enough that it wasn't true. If he hadn't figured it out already. If this question wasn't just another piece of bait.

Because he seemed to know what she was feeling before she did. Seemed to understand what was happening in her body even when it mystified her.

"Because you felt it, too," he said, his voice like a touch, skimming over her entire body. Touching her in places no one ever had before.

She wanted to deny it. Wanted to pretend she had no idea what he was talking about. And she really didn't want to question what he meant when he said that she had felt it, too. As if he had felt something. Something other than the thrill of a hunter spotting his quarry.

She didn't want to get drawn into this. Didn't want to get drawn into looking at him and searching for humanity. It was much better if she only looked at the facade. If she only looked at the monster. Much better if she never tried to search behind that rock wall.

And yet she felt the pull, the tug toward him. The undeniable need to understand him. Maybe that wasn't so bad. Maybe it wasn't so dangerous. To try and understand the man she would supposedly spend the rest of her life with.

"What did you feel?" she asked. "When you saw me."

"You were beautiful. I responded to that. I'm a man, after all."

"There are a lot of beautiful women."

"Yes. But there are very few women who represent payment for an outstanding debt owed to my country." Something shifted in his expression. He was so difficult to read. His moods seeming to shift like sand without giving any warning. "Did you know my father had renounced marriage at the point when he announced he would claim you? He did not intend to take you as a wife. He intended to make you a mistress. On your sixteenth birthday."

Horror pierced through her. "He did?" She blinked rapidly. "But what about your...? What about your mother?"

"At that point she was dead. And anyway he never cared about her. He had mistresses all through their marriage. He paraded them about the palace whenever he saw fit. Women who were younger, women who weren't made weary by a lifetime of abuses and indignities. And he made sure that my mother knew they were infinitely more desirable than she would ever be. He made sure to let her know that she was a failure. For a great many reasons, though I was one of them. She never could keep me in line. Never could keep me in my place. My father demanded that one small thing from her, and she couldn't do that, either. And so he made her life hell. In part because he enjoyed doing it. In part because of me."

"He…he showed you that sort of thing was normal," she said, wondering how he'd ever had a hope of developing a conscience.

"Yes. But I knew they weren't. I knew that intending to take a woman some forty years younger than him—not a woman, a girl!—and make her his plaything was wrong. I never intended to use women that way. I never intended to use you that way. But I did recognize that you would be useful. That your symbolism could be changed."

"How very strange. Because I have never felt like a symbol. I've only ever felt like a girl."

"I'm well aware that you're neither of those things. You are not a symbol." He moved nearer to her, brushing the backs of his knuckles over her face. "You're far too warm. You're too alive. But also… You're not a girl. You're a woman."

For the first time, she felt like one. With his finger slowly drifting over her skin, those dark eyes pinning her into place, she didn't feel like a tall, awkward girl who was hopelessly different than everyone around her. Didn't feel like a simple curiosity. Didn't feel like a child in sophisticated clothes playing at something she was not.

No, in this moment, rooted to the spot, she felt every inch a woman. And she wanted to find out why that was. Wanted to respond to everything that was male in him and explore what it all meant. But it was all tangled up. Jumbled together with the reality of the situation. And then weighted down completely by the diamond on her finger, as if it were a millstone.

Perhaps she was simply succumbing to the insanity of the situation. Perhaps she had lost her mind completely.

Did it matter? That was the real question.

He let his fingertips drift down to the edge of her jaw then traced the line to the center of her chin. He tilted her face upward, his mouth a breath away from hers. She felt like she was being lifted off the ground. Her lungs, her body, filled completely. Expanding until she felt like she might burst with whatever feeling was taking her over. It was strange, and it was foreign. She wasn't entirely sure she liked it. Wasn't entirely sure she didn't.

"Your Majesty," a voice came from behind them.

Felipe dropped his hand and took a step back. "What is it?" he asked without ever taking his eyes off her.

"Prince Felipe. It's your father."

At that, Felipe turned and faced the man who had joined them on the terrace. "What is it?"

"The king is dead."

Something went horribly blank, flat in Felipe's eyes. She could feel ice radiating from his skin. He said nothing for a moment. And then, he tilted his face upward, his expression one of schooled arrogance, overlaid with a breathless lack of remorse.

Then he finally spoke, a strange smile curving his lips. "Long live the king."

CHAPTER SEVEN

"I SUPPOSE WE will be making more than one announcement tonight," Felipe said, his tone hard.

Then he straightened the cuffs on his jacket and walked back into the ballroom. Leaving Briar standing there by herself feeling utterly helpless. His reaction was frightening, and she didn't know what to do with it. Didn't know why she cared. Didn't know why it hit her quite so squarely in the chest and made it so hard for her to breathe.

Then she saw people begin pouring out of the ballroom. Heading back up the stairs, leaving the party much sooner than she was sure they had been planning. She lifted the front of her gown and hurried inside. She could hear Felipe shouting, but didn't understand what he was saying as he was speaking in Spanish.

Then he switched to English. "The party is over," he said. "My father is dead. I will be assuming the throne now. But we will not dance anymore tonight. Go home. Everybody get out."

And his word was obeyed for, after all, he was the king.

The only people who hesitated were her parents. She looked between Felipe and her mother and father, then she went to the king and queen. "You should go," she said, reaching out and placing her hand over her mother's.

"Are you certain you'll be all right?" the other woman asked.

She looked back at Felipe, who was standing there perfectly smooth and unruffled. She knew it was a lie. She just did. Whether or not it made any sense, she knew. This was another of his games. Another of his facades.

"Yes," she said. "I'll be fine. Leave me with him."

That left her in the ballroom, empty all except for herself and Felipe. And she realized that it had not been the moment she had accepted his proposal, not the moment he had placed the ring on her finger, that she had truly chosen this, chosen him. It was now.

She wasn't sure she would ever be able to explain why. Only that he needed her. He needed someone. She didn't know who else it would be.

The tables were still laden with food, and there was music being piped in over the speakers. But no one else was there. Not a single guest, not a single servant. With the chandelier glittering above and all the lights lit, casting the golden room in a fierce glow, it all seemed rather eerie. Particularly with the deep emotion radiating from the man who stood before her.

Apparently, she was with him. She had a feeling that she had been from the moment she'd first set eyes on him. Her world had shifted then. Regardless of what had happened since, in that moment…she had connected with him.

"Are you all right?"

He looked at her, the expression on his face indicating that he was surprised to find her still there. "Of course I am. Why wouldn't I be?" He straightened his sleeves, then his hands moved to the knot on his tie, and he straightened that, too, even though it hadn't been askew at all.

"Your father is dead."

"Yes. And I am now the king. And everything that I have wanted to do for the past two decades can now come to fruition. I'm more than all right."

He didn't look it. He didn't sound it.

"Felipe," she said, taking a step toward him.

He turned abruptly, gripping the edge of one of the tables that was laden with food, and he turned it over. She gasped and took a step back as glass shattered on the marble floor, champagne running through the tiles like a river.

"I feel better," he said. "Yes. I feel better."

"That was a waste of food."

"I'll make a donation. Around the time I make a donation that matches the cost of your ring. Do you find that acceptable?"

"I wasn't… I was just…"

"My father had not one quality to redeem him, Briar," Felipe said. "Not one. He victimized every person who walked through his life. And this—" he swept his hand to the side, indicating the mess he had just made "—would have appalled him. He could not abide disorder. Could not abide disorder while he created chaos inside everyone who lived underneath his roof. I always found that the greatest irony. He claimed he wanted everything to run smoothly while he ruined my mother from the inside out. Tell me, does that make any sense?"

She shook her head. "No."

"No. It doesn't. I will not make you miserable. I promise you." He began to pace, his movements agitated. He gripped the edge of his sleeve with his thumb and fore-finger and straightened it again. Then he repeated the action again. "Because it makes no sense. I'm not a soft man. I don't believe in love. I don't believe in romance. But I can certainly accomplish the amazing feat of not being a cruel bastard."

She stood where she was for a moment, not moving away from him, but not moving forward, either. She wasn't sure if another explosion of violence was going to come. She wouldn't be surprised if it did. He was all barely leashed energy and a strange kind of manic emotion that she had never seen before.

It turned out, she didn't have to move toward him at all. Because a moment later he was closing the distance between them. His dark eyes blazing into hers. And then, those eyes were all she saw. All she saw as he wrapped his arm around her waist and drew her hard up against his body.

She couldn't breathe. She didn't even have a moment to react. Because then, his mouth was crashing down on hers, his lips taking hers, consuming her. She had never been kissed before, so she didn't know what she had expected. But it hadn't been this. No, she never could have anticipated this, not in her wildest fantasies.

Because in her imagination a kiss had always been a sweet thing, romantic thing. In her fantasies, a kiss was meant to be shared with someone you loved, or at the very least someone you cared about. She couldn't claim that she cared about Felipe at all.

But that didn't seem to matter. Because while there wasn't…caring, there was something else. Something hot and reckless that burned through her like wildfire. And whatever he had been before, whatever she thought about him, was consumed by it, leaving behind nothing but ash. Making it impossible for her to remember how she had gotten here, and who she was. If she was Princess Talia, or Briar Harcourt. If she was a prisoner, a forced bride, or if she was kissing this man simply because he was the only man she had ever wanted.

For a moment she simply stood there, stood and marveled at the kiss. As his tongue slid over the seam of her lips, requesting entry. She didn't know what to do. Didn't know what she wanted. Her heart was thundering so hard she was certain that he could hear it. Certain that he could feel it butting up against his own chest as close as he was holding her.

Her arms were pinned to her sides, her hands curled into fists.

But then, his hold on her changed. He shifted, spreading his fingers, holding on to her in a way that was firm, sure and comforting in the oddest way. Then with his other hand he cupped the back of her head, tilting his head and granting himself access to her mouth, tasting her deeply.

After that she was lost. Completely and utterly. In the sensations that were pouring through her body like a liquid flame, in his heat, his presence, the strength of his body. And in the need that she hadn't realized her body was capable of feeling.

She had always thought she was somewhat dispassionate. After all, she had never even been tempted by the boys she had gone to university with. But that was the problem. The problem, which she had realized that first moment she had laid eyes on Felipe. They were boys. They were nothing but boys, and he was a man. A man who called to everything woman inside her. The man who made her realize that she was a woman.

The man who made her realize what a wonderful thing that was.

Her breasts ached, and he tightened his hold on her, crushing her up against that hard, muscular wall of his chest. She wanted him to touch her. Wanted his hands on her, not just this kind of passive contact that teased her with what she wanted without actually giving it.

As if he read her mind, he shifted, and instead of putting his hands on her he simply let her feel what she did to him. Let her feel the evidence of his own arousal, pressed up against her belly like an iron rod.

She had never been close enough to a man to experience anything like this. And she... She loved it. She was glorying in it. In the effect that she had on him. She didn't feel awkward. She didn't feel different. She felt *singular*. She felt *beautiful*. That she had the power to affect this man—this glorious, intoxicating man—in the way that she was... How could she feel anything but wholly, purely *desired*?

Except that he was the man who had kidnapped her. The man who had forced her into this engagement. Those thoughts swirled around in her mind along with the fog of arousal. She knew that she should grasp on to those little bits of sanity. But she didn't want to. She didn't want sanity. Not now. She just wanted this. This kind of reckless madness that she was certain would be her undoing.

But she was undone already, wasn't she? She had been cautioned all her life, told to be careful, and it was all because she was running from this man. But here she was, she was in his palace, she was in his arms, and he was consuming her. It was too late. She had been taken by the dragon, and she might as well give in to this, as well. There was nothing else that could be done. And in this moment, it seemed the most logical thing of all to give him this, too.

He growled, reversing their positions and pressing her back up against the wall. Against the windows that overlooked the garden outside. She knew that—despite the fact it seemed they were in isolation—there were still hundreds of people milling around the palace. She didn't care. She didn't care about anything. Nothing but this.

He moved his hands, dragging them down so that he was gripping her hips, his blunt fingertips digging into her skin. But she liked it. Loved that feeling of him anchoring her to the earth, because she still felt like she was in danger of floating away.

Then his hands moved upward, and he gripped the neckline on her dress, tearing the delicate fabric, exposing her breasts to his hungry gaze. She gasped, wrenching her mouth away from his, the breath dragged from her lungs in long, unsteady pulls.

"Felipe," she said, gasping his name, but he didn't seem to listen. Didn't seem to hear. He was like a man possessed—his dark eyes wild, desperation pouring from him in waves. This was the real man. It was, and she knew it. Shaken, unhinged, broken. Needing something that she wasn't certain she knew how to give. Something she wasn't sure she wanted to give.

She had only known him a week. And in that time she had pledged her life to him. But she had not fully known what it might mean to pledge her body to him, as well. She still didn't. But then he lowered his dark head, sucking one tightened bud deep into his mouth, groaning harshly as he did.

She lifted her hands, not sure if she was moving to hold him to her or push him away. Instead, she ended up threading her fingers through his dark hair, resting them there as he continued to lavish attention on her breasts. And she wondered, just for a moment, what sort of woman she was. She flashed back to those words he had spoken to her. Knowing that he was a monster, she still wanted him.

And seeing him like this now, she wanted him even more. She liked this man better than the playboy she had met the first day. Liked him more than the twisted, cynical prince who always seemed intent on scoring points off her. She liked him sharp, liked him dangerous, with rough edges that could easily cut her all the way down to the bone.

Or perhaps *like* wasn't the word. Perhaps it was something deeper than that. Something that cut through the loneliness of that careful childhood she'd led. That strange sense of isolation, of feeling wrong, feeling different, that had always followed her wherever she went.

No, *like* was not the correct word. She wasn't sure that she *liked* any of this. But it was driving her, creating a need inside her as quickly as it satisfied it.

She had spent her entire life fully in control. Of her actions, of her desires, of everything around her. Being so entirely without it was terrifying. Liberating. She should tell him to stop. She should want him to stop. She wasn't going to. She didn't want to.

She had a feeling she knew where this was going. She might be inexperienced, but she wasn't innocent of the way things went between men and women. Though she wasn't sure she had any way of knowing how she would withstand it. What the consequences might be for her. It was like helplessly clinging to a speeding train, unsure of whether she should ride it out or jump off. Unsure of which might do more damage.

"I have to," he said, his voice sounding frayed, tortured, as he tilted his head to the side, sliding his tongue down the column of her neck, all the way down to her collarbone and down farther still, tracing the outline of one tightened nipple. "I have to," he repeated again, tearing her bodice completely so that the whole front of her gown was gaping wide.

She clung to his shoulders, the glass against her back warm now from her body being pressed against it for the past few minutes. She looked beyond him, at the empty ballroom, still all lit up as though it was expecting a crowd. But it was just the two of them now. Just the two of them and the broken glass on the floor and whatever ghosts Felipe was contending with.

He took hold of the flimsy skirt of her gown, curling his fingers around it and tugging it upward, past her hips. Then he pressed one hand between her thighs, bold fingers moving beneath the waistband of her panties, and then on through her slick folds. She was wet for him. There was no hiding it. Not from him, not from herself.

What does that say about you, I wonder?

Those words rolled to her head again, and she pushed them away. It didn't matter what it said about her. She didn't care. She had always cared. Had always tried to be the perfect daughter. To do exactly what her parents had told her to do. To earn her position in their household. No, they had never acted as though she had to do that, but it didn't matter. She had put that weight there. Had done her best to follow their rules, had done her very best to succeed, to be a monument to all that they had poured into her.

This stood in antithesis to that.

This served her. The immediate. The moment. The physical, yawning need inside her. And whatever the consequences might be after, she couldn't bring herself to think of them now. Couldn't bring herself to care.

He pressed one finger inside her then drew it back out again, rubbing it over the sensitized bundle of nerves at the apex of her thighs. She gasped, letting her head fall back, and he took advantage of that vulnerable position, pressing a hot, openmouthed kiss to the tender skin on her neck.

And all the while he created wicked magic between her legs with his fingers. Made her feel things that she had never imagined possible. Things that she had certainly never managed to make herself feel, no matter how hard she'd tried on long, lonely nights in her bedroom. This was different. This was different because it was him. Because she had no control over what he might do next. Over how hard or soft he might touch her, how quickly he might stroke her, or when he would pull away again.

Then he growled, removing his hand and gripping her hips again, pressing her more firmly against the window. He took hold of one wrist and raised it up over her head, before going to collect the other, pinning that one down, as well, holding her fast with one hand.

He tried to hold her skirt in place with his free hand, but quickly became frustrated and wrenched the skirt to the side, rendering it nothing more than an expensive strip of silk. Her panties suffered the same fate. And she realized she was standing there wearing nothing but the facsimile of a dress in front of this man who might as well be a stranger.

But could he really be considered a stranger now? Now that he had touched her in the most intimate place on her body? Not when she had let him. Surely, they were more than strangers now.

He kissed her then, deep and hard, and she could feel him shifting against her, but it didn't click exactly what was happening until she felt something hot, blunt and hard pressing up against the entrance of her body. Her stomach went into a freefall, nerves assaulting her. Of course she had known where this was going.

She felt a shock of nerves, but then he was kissing her so long and deep, and her head felt dizzy with desire and pleasure. And nerves didn't matter anymore. Only how much she wanted him.

He flexed his hips upward, breaching the barrier there, a sharp, tearing sensation assaulting her, making her feel as though she couldn't breathe. He was too much. Too big. She was too full and it didn't feel good. She wiggled her hips, trying to get away from him, but she was trapped completely between the hard, uncompromising window, and the hard uncompromising man. And he was too far gone to realize that she was in distress.

He only gripped her harder, retreating from her body before he thrust back inside her again. Only this time, it didn't hurt quite so bad. This time, a part of her welcomed the feeling of fullness. He retreated again then returned to her. And with each thrust pleasure began to edge out pain. Desire consuming fear.

And then she gave herself up to it, to him. Opened herself to him, rolled her hips in rhythm with his movements. There was nothing gentle about it. Just like her first kiss—which had happened an astonishingly short time ago—this was void of the kind of sweetness and gauzy romance she had always imagined the act would contain.

But she didn't mourn it. Because she had never wanted anyone else. She wanted him. So how could it be anything other than perfect?

It was a messy kind of perfect. A broken kind of perfect. But as the pleasure built, deep and intense inside her, she realized she didn't care. He rolled his hips up against hers, and bliss broke over her like a wave on the rocks.

She just shook and rode it out. As she shuddered out her pleasure, turning her face into the curve of his neck, doing her best to hold back the tears that began to push against her eyes, pressure building to almost unbearable levels.

He tightened his hold on her, his thumb and fingers digging so hard into her wrists she was certain it would leave a bruise. And then, he let out a harsh, feral growl as he found his own release. He released his hold on her, burying his fingers into her massive curly hair and claiming her mouth in a kiss that mimicked the act they had just finished.

This was no sweet, silent afterglow. It was a conflagration that still raged on in spite of their release.

And when it was done, he took a step away from her, regarding her with wild, dark eyes. "You will spend the night in my bed tonight," he said, the words a command and not a request.

And then, he turned away from her, striding away from her, not offering her so much as a comforting touch.

In spite of the heat that was still coursing through her body, she shivered.

CHAPTER EIGHT

SHE HAD BEEN a virgin. And he had taken her against a wall—no, a window—with absolutely no finesse.

Then he had left her standing there in a tattered dress, the bright streaks of blue a shocking contrast to that smooth, brown skin. Her small, high breasts and that dark thatch of curls at the apex of her thighs exposed, her hair a dark halo around her face.

Had left her standing there with the command that she join him in his bed tonight, when the fact of the matter was no one should come anywhere near him tonight. And he shouldn't inflict himself on anyone.

What had been in his mind? Sending everyone away as he had? He had come into the ballroom, waiting for the surge of triumph to flood his veins. Waiting for a sense of completion. Waiting for his lips to form the words to an eloquent speech.

About dark ages rolling forward into the light. But instead he had cleared the room.

Instead, he had done what he seemed compelled to do from some dark place inside him that had purchase on his soul, that he seemed to have no control over, and that was to sabotage the moment. To break. To destroy.

And he still felt no relief. No sense of completion.

Nothing but an end. A dark, blank end that offered him nothing but more emptiness. Like a chasm had opened inside him, one that had always been there, but one he now had to admit might always be.

His father was dead. That was supposed to be the key.

But now he couldn't yell at the old man. Couldn't scream at him and demand answers. Could never shout at him about the fact it was his fault Felipe's mother was dead. How it was all his fault.

Felipe swallowed hard, trying to get a handle on himself, on his control. This control he had long prized so much. He should not have Briar come to his room. He should deal with his demons alone.

But he would have her again. Because there was no other choice. Because the hollow feeling inside him was threatening to consume him, and the only moment of peace he'd had since his father's aide had come and announced the old man's death had been when he was buried in Briar's tight, welcoming heat.

It occurred to him as he flung open the doors to his chamber that she might not come. That she might go back to her room. Might hide from him.

She should. There was no question about that.

But if she did he would go after her.

There was also no question about that.

With shaking hands, he poured himself a glass of whiskey then stared down at the amber liquid. He was dangerous enough as it was. Unsteady, unstable. Disorderly. There was no greater sin in his father's eyes and there never had been.

The thought made a smile curve his lips. He might have wasted some opportunities tonight, but he had rebelled in a rather spectacular fashion. His father had prized all that surface order. Never mind if beneath the surface everything was jagged and destroyed.

Destroying the ballroom appealed to that part of him that wanted to wound the old man still. That hoped his ghost had watched the whole thing.

He looked down at the glass. As on edge as he was he wasn't entirely certain he should add alcohol to the equation. For Briar's sake and for no other reason. And so, he tilted the glass to the side before cocking his arm back and flinging it against the wall.

"I imagine that's a bit too disorderly for you as well, Father," he said.

There was every chance the old man could hear him. That he was now haunting the halls like the malevolent spirit he had always been. It would be fitting. This palace was full of ghosts; Felipe had never thought differently, no matter that his father had tried to tell him otherwise.

He was failing again. Which seemed to be what he did. Failing at not being a horror to the woman he was intent on taking as his wife. But then, he wasn't sure he was capable of being anything other than this. Anything other than the creature his father had set out to create.

He gripped the edge of the bar, lowering his head. He had to be different. He had to. If for no other reason than for Santa Milagro. His people had lived in darkness long enough.

Of course, he had no idea how he was supposed to remedy that when he feared he had no light inside him.

Then the door to his bedchamber opened and he lifted his head, turning it to look behind him. It was Briar. She was no longer wearing the shredded ball gown that he had left her in downstairs. She had changed into a long, flowing robe in a luminous pink that contrasted beautifully with her smooth, dark skin. She had washed her makeup off, leaving her looking young and freshly scrubbed. He had to wonder if she had been so eager to wash his touch from her body.

But she was here. And he felt almost certain she had brought some light in with her. Perhaps that was the key. Perhaps she was the key to more than he had originally imagined.

He ignored the slight twisting feeling in his chest that questioned this reasoning. That forced images of his mother to swim before his mind's eye.

"You came," he said.

"Yes," she said, scanning the room slowly, her eyes falling to the broken glass and spilled alcohol on the floor. "Clearly you can't be trusted around food at the moment."

"I can't be trusted around you, either," he said, his tone hard. "And yet, here you are."

She clasped her hands in front of her, wringing her fingers. "You asked me to come."

"I confess, I thought I might have to go retrieve you from the depths of your room. I thought I might have frightened you."

She lifted one elegant shoulder. "I'm not frightened of you."

He narrowed his eyes. "Truthfully?"

She released her hold on her hands, one fluttering slightly as she made a dismissive gesture. "Well. I suppose I am afraid of you. But not enough to hide from you."

"Is that because you've accepted your fate or because you find yourself fascinated by me?" The answer was important.

She frowned, a small dent growing between her eyebrows. "I think it took you stealing me away from the city for me to think I could do anything other than accept my fate, actually. And when I say that, it isn't because my life was terrible. I don't mean it in that way. It's just that it seemed predetermined. Like the path had been set since the beginning of my life. And then you showed me that I had no idea. None at all. I didn't know where I had started, and I had no idea what was out there, what was hunting me—so to speak. I would say that never in my life have I been at a point where I was more likely to accept the way things are than I am right now. And yet, here I am."

Something shifted inside him, a rumble of satisfaction beginning in his chest, growing. "Perhaps because I was your first man?"

Color tinged her cheeks. "You could tell?"

"Yes."

"And you did it anyway?" She tilted her head to the side, a strange expression on her face.

"It wasn't forefront in my mind. It was afterward. If I had stopped and thought about it while it was happening, I would have realized. As it was, I didn't put everything together until it was too late."

She looked somewhat appeased by that. "Okay."

"Does it matter to you?"

"I don't know if it matters. Well, yes, it does. I wouldn't like to think that it meant nothing to you. I have never wanted a man before. I wasn't a virgin because I was waiting for anything. I mean, nothing moral. I wasn't waiting for you, or some other mythological husband. I was just waiting for somebody that I wanted. I was waiting for the moment I didn't want to say no. And that happened downstairs with you. I don't know why.

I just know that it was different. That it changed something in me. So yes, if it meant nothing to you I would find that painful."

He felt a smile touch the corner of his lips. He walked toward her, closing the distance between them. Then he reached out, pressing his thumb against the center of her lower lip. "You want to be special to me, *querida*?"

She trembled beneath his touch, her dark eyes questioning. Searching. She wouldn't find anything. Not in him. Nothing but more darkness. That endless, blank pit that existed in his chest. Selfishly, he wanted her answer to be yes. And yet, he knew that he should want nothing from her. And he should rejoice if she wanted nothing from him.

Still, he waited. And he hoped. A strange, costly thing for a man like himself. To reach for a flame, wondering if it was going to warm him, or if the action would simply snuff it out.

"That's not so shocking, is it?" she asked, her voice hushed. "We... We were intimate with each other. Of course I want it to matter."

"Intimate?" He could honestly say he had never considered sex intimate. It was a release. It was bodies, only bodies. And long ago he had determined to detach himself from his body when he needed it to be so. To be able to make it so he felt no pain while undergoing excruciating torture.

To feel nothing but pleasure when he was in the arms of a woman—no matter what he might feel inside.

A body was simply that. Fallible, temporary. Losing himself in someone else's had never felt like anything more than pleasure.

And yet she called it intimacy. She had never wanted

another man. Had never allowed another man to touch her. He was not sure if he knew how to make someone special to him, but it seemed that he might be special to her.

He was equally at a loss as to what he was supposed to do with that.

But it satisfied him. Satisfied something inside him he had not known existed until that very moment. It was the deepest kind of satisfaction, satiating him in a way his orgasm hadn't even managed to.

"Yes," she said, her voice soft. She lifted her hand, pressed it flat against his chest. "What we did was intimate. Something that you don't share with just anyone." She frowned. "Or do you?"

"I have," he said, with no shame at all. "Desire exists to be satisfied."

"I don't think that's true. I think what makes desire matter is that it can't be satisfied in any time. What makes it so deep is that it's reserved only for certain people. For certain moments."

He wrapped his fingers around her wrist, held her hand more firmly against his chest. "As the woman who just confessed to having never felt it before? You say that, but what if it were another man to fire these feelings inside you? If it were to happen again, would you simply accept his advances as you did mine?" The thought was like acid, eating through his mind and sliding on down to his chest where it began to burn around the edges of the blackness there.

She shook her head. "No."

"So that makes me important?" He tightened his hold on her. "That means I'm important to you."

He never had been. Not to anyone. Not to his cruel,

sadistic father or his broken, fragile mother. He wanted it. More desperately than he had ever wanted anything, and he didn't care what that meant. Because he only understood want in a very singular way. Wanting was having as far as he was concerned. So he would have this. And he would feel no compunction about it.

"I said I would marry you," she said, looking away from him. "But you never answered if I was important to you."

"I said I would marry you," he said, parroting her words back to her. "Do you see any other women around here wearing my ring?"

She shook her head.

"There's your answer," he said. And then, the phone in his pocket vibrated. He said a curse then took it out, looking at the screen.

It was Rafe. The bastard really did have lousy timing. Why had he decided to have friends?

"We didn't get a chance to speak tonight," his friend said. "You threw everyone out of the palace."

"I'm surprised you left without being forced," he said to his friend, all the while keeping his eyes on Briar.

"Oh, Adam and I were forced," Rafe returned. "Though Adam was forced by his bride, who felt that your wishes should be respected. Because she simply doesn't know you well enough to know when you should be ignored."

"And what's your excuse?"

"I didn't suppose, given the disadvantage of my lack of sight, that I should engage your royal guards in a fight."

Felipe laughed. "Please. We both know you still had the advantage in the fight, Rafe."

"True enough."

"I assume that Adam was involved in this goodwill mission. You checking on my mental well-being." He took that moment to look at Briar more fully, to allow his gaze to travel over her beautiful curves. To truly relish just how flimsy that nightgown she was wearing was. He needed this phone call to be short.

"Your father has passed away. It isn't a small thing."

"It's better that he's dead. It was a cruelty of fate that he drew breath for as long as he did. There are a very great number of people who die far too young and don't deserve it."

"They say the good die young," Rafe pointed out.

"Then you and I are both safe."

"We are that," Rafe said, his tone hardening slightly. "We are that. I should be dead already. And likely would be if I were worthy of life."

Rafe's cynicism was one of the many reasons Felipe counted him a friend, when in general he found friendship to be pointless.

"Right now I'm grateful to be alive. I outlived that old bastard—" his gaze returned to Briar "—and I have a promising evening before me."

"You're with your fiancée, I assume," Rafe said.

"Yes. So you'll understand that I have to cut this call short."

"A word of caution," Rafe said. "This woman you have… I did a bit of research. And Adam described her to me. She is too soft for you, my friend. Far too young."

"Very much," Felipe returned, his eyes never leaving Briar, who was blushing beneath his frank appraisal. "She's too innocent for me, as well."

Her gaze sharpened, her mouth dropping open as she

realized she was the topic of discussion. She, and her virginity.

"That's even worse," Rafe said. "You have to be careful with women like that."

Felipe laughed. "Please. I spent my entire childhood at the mercy of a sadistic old man. I'm not in any danger."

"That makes it even clearer to me that you might be. Men like you and me… We can't be broken by the hard things. It's the soft things. Believe me. I know of what I speak."

Rafe had never given the details of how he lost his eyesight. All he and Adam knew was that there had been an accident. But Felipe had long suspected a woman had been involved in some capacity. This… This confirmed it. Except, Felipe had a difficult time imagining his friend falling prey to a woman, no matter how soft or beautiful she was.

"I'll keep that in mind." He hung up then. He wouldn't be keeping it in mind. Not tonight. Tonight he wanted only one thing. And as he advanced on his beautiful fiancée, he could think only that she had much more to be afraid of than he did.

"You were talking about me," she accused.

"Yes."

"Who was it?"

"A friend."

"You have friends?" Her eyes widened. If it wasn't objectively such a surprising thing that he had friends, even to him, he might have been offended. Instead, he found himself amused.

"I do. Two of them. And to answer your question, yes, they have myriad issues. Definitely not normal."

"I suppose I'm not normal, either."

He wrapped his arm around her waist, drew her up against his chest. "I don't need you to be normal. I need you to be mine."

She looked at him, marveled at him as though he were some kind of curiosity. Something she had never seen before, and was trying to figure out. Then she lifted her hand, drawing her fingertips lightly across his cheek.

He growled, taking hold of her wrist again and holding her steady as he brought his lips down to hers. As he claimed a kiss that he needed more than his next breath.

And then, Rafe didn't matter at all. Neither did the ghosts of his past. The ghost of his father that was likely rattling chains and wandering restlessly down the halls even now.

Nothing mattered but this. But her. But her beauty, her delicacy. The fact that he should stay away from her, because she would be so easily bruised, crushed like a delicate rose.

Perversely, he wanted it. Wanted to see the effect that he had on her. Wanted to ruin her. To make her his. Like he had wanted to ruin everything in this whole damn palace from the moment he had found out his father was dead. Disorder. That was what he wanted. Utter chaos. And he would be the king of it.

That drove him on. Spurred him to deepen the kiss. To crush his mouth against hers, to swallow the sounds she made, whether they were of pleasure or protestation, he wasn't entirely sure. But he was consumed by this. Consumed by his need for her.

He knew nothing else, and that was a blessed relief. He opened his eyes, looked at his own hands, holding on to her face, at his sleeves. Those damn sleeves. He released his hold on her, wrenching his jacket off, then working at the buttons of his shirt before he cast it to the ground, as well.

He hadn't been naked the last time they had been together. Hadn't felt those soft, sweet hands pressed up against his skin. Well, he needed it now. Needed it more than he needed his next breath. And as much as he wanted her to be marked by him, he wanted the same in return.

"Touch me," he demanded, his voice rough, a stranger's voice. He had learned to conduct himself with the manner of a gentleman. Had learned how to be suave, how to be smooth. How to cover up the monster inside by pretending to be a man of impeccable manners.

That was gone now. Cast to the ground with his clothes. Shattered like the glass he had broken against the wall. She already knew. She knew he wasn't that. That he never could be. Because he had shown her the truth. And she was still here. Said that she still wanted him. That she wanted to mean something to him.

Foolish girl. Inexperienced *girl*. She was everything that Rafe had said. Too soft. Too innocent. Too young.

But he was his father's son.

He pushed that thought to the side. He didn't want to examine it, not now. Couldn't. There was no possibility of thought, not now.

His father was dead anyway. And all the duplicity he had lived under, the extreme control, the calculated air of not caring at all…it was dead with him.

He didn't need it anymore.

He was king now. And he would do as he wished.

Inexperienced fingers brushed against his throat, moved down his chest. "Like you mean it," he growled, his lips against hers as he issued the rough command.

Her touch grew firmer, a bit more confident, and she dragged her fingertips down his washboard-flat stomach, to the waistband of his pants. "Yes," he said, the word rough and encouraging. "Like that."

She fumbled with his belt, and he clung to her as she pushed his pants down his thighs, taking his underwear with it. Leaving him completely naked standing in front of her. He watched her expression closely, tried to read her thoughts. It seemed as though she didn't know where to look, her dark eyes darting every which way as she examined his body.

"Have you never seen a naked man before?" Oh, he liked that. Liked this far too much. That he was corrupting her. That he was altering her in ways that were irreparable.

She shook her head. "I mean, in pictures."

"You've never undressed anyone. Never touched them. Never watched a man get hard because of you."

"No," she said. "Until you I had never been kissed."

Without being conscious of making the decision to do so, he found himself closing the distance between them. Growling as he took her into his arms and kissed her with all the uncivilized ferocity inside him.

She whimpered, her hands trapped between them, her palms resting on his chest. He was hard, throbbing and insistent against her body, and he knew that she could feel it. That she could feel just how affected he was by her. Just how much he wanted her. There was nothing civilized about this. But perhaps, just maybe, it was intimate. Because this was beyond him in a way that sexual desire had never been before.

This seemed to be tangled up in emotions in a way

that the need for release never had been. And it had been so from the moment he had taken her downstairs. When he had turned that table over, ripping the mask of the civilized prince off and letting the monster free. He had done that. In front of her. For her. Almost because of her. It was as though she reduced his control in ways that he could scarcely understand. Ways he certainly had not given permission for.

But strangely, she didn't seem to fear him. Didn't seem to fear that at all.

None of it made sense. That she would be the one to see that side of him, and yet not be afraid. That he would be the one to make her desire for the first time, when he was little more than a villain to her. The man who had ripped her from her life and dragged her into this. Into his domain.

But he didn't need sense. Not now.

"Now," he said, the words pulled from him, "you have been kissed."

She nodded, her kiss-swollen mouth soft, completely irresistible. And he leaned in to devour her again. It made no sense. That she was so receptive to this. To him. She should be disgusted by him. By the beast he had transformed into from the moment he had brought her back here to the palace. Or rather, from the moment he had revealed to her his intentions to take her back to his country.

But then he supposed that he should be disgusted by those things, as well. He wasn't.

He needed her. Needed her to rule his country in the best way. And more than that, now he wanted her. Wanted her in his life, in his bed. Wanted to be inside her. He would not deny himself.

And so, he could feel no guilt.

"Shall I teach you something?"

She looked up at him, her dark eyes luminous. Then she licked her full lips. "Yes. Teach me."

CHAPTER NINE

HIS HEART THUNDERED HARD, the blood firing through his veins hot and fast. He drew himself away from her. "Get down on your knees for me."

"The floor is hard," she said, her expression blank.

"That is true," he said, sweeping her up into his arms and crossing into his bedchamber. "We shall make it a bit more comfortable for you." He set her down in front of his bed, on the plush rug there. "Will this be a little more gentle on your royal knees?"

She blinked. "I…"

He cupped her chin, gazed into her eyes. "Kneel for me."

She complied, and he had to close his eyes, grit his teeth tight, to keep from coming then and there. She hadn't even touched him, but that simple act of compliance did more for him, did more to him, than a thousand illicit acts before had ever done.

"Take off that gown," he said, indicating the belt that held her robe closed. "I need to see you."

With shaking fingers, she undid the knot, let the silken fabric slide down her shoulders. And there she was, naked before him on her knees, her black hair tumbled over her shoulders, her sleek curves so enticing it took all his control to keep himself from lifting her back up into his arms and tumbling her onto the bed. To keep himself from burying himself inside her body again, and forgetting these little power games.

It occurred to him then, that if she was a virgin it was entirely possible she wasn't on any sort of birth control. He had taken her earlier without a condom, and he had no intention of using one this time, either. The idea of her pregnant, growing round with his child, only sent another shock of satisfaction through him. Then she would truly be bound to him. Forever.

She would not be able to leave. At least, not easily.

Ah, yes, your father's son.

He pushed the thought away again as he tangled his fingers in her hair and drew her toward his body. "Take me in your mouth," he said.

She looked up at him, uncertainty on her face. Perhaps she would reject him now. And perhaps, that was what he had been pushing her toward the entire time. Maybe that was what he wanted. To find her breaking point. To find the point at which she would become disgusted with him. For it had to exist. The fact that she had wanted him up until this point made no sense to him.

But, she did not pull away. Instead, she adjusted her position, lifting her hand and curling her fingers tentatively around his length. Then she leaned forward, her slick tongue darting out over the head of his arousal before she slowly took him inside her mouth.

And then, whatever he had imagined might happen, whatever guidance he thought he might give, was lost completely. There was nothing. His mind was blank and his body was on fire. She had absolutely no skill, was clearly not a woman who had ever touched a man before, and yet, it was the most erotic experience of his life.

Because it was just for him. As she had said. It was an intimacy. It was special. And that mattered. It mattered to a man who had never had such a thing before. A man who had never even known to hope for such a thing. She wanted him. She wanted him when she had wanted no other man before him.

She gave to him, generously. Gave him far more than he deserved. Those inexpert hands moving in rhythm with her lips and tongue as she lavished pleasure on him. Like a woman would do for her beloved, not for her kidnapper.

Not for a man who had commanded she get down on her knees and give him pleasure as though it was his due.

And then, he was no longer able to control himself. He tightened his fingers in her hair, pulled her head back. "Not like this," he said.

She rocked back on her heels, wobbling, and he caught her by the wrist, drawing her up against his body and claiming her mouth in a searing kiss.

He tumbled her backward onto the bed, groaning loudly as every inch of her naked body pressed against every inch of his. She was impossibly soft. Refined. Delicate. Lovely beyond measure.

Not for him.

And he felt… He felt like a criminal, getting away with the perfect crime. Which was—he discovered in that moment—an intensely satisfying feeling. To be in possession of something far too lovely, far too fine, for a man such as himself.

Perhaps other men might feel guilt.

He was not other men.

He was a monster. And she knew it. She wanted him still.

He groaned, lowering his head, taking one tightened nipple between his lips and sucking hard. She arched beneath him, a raw sound on her lips.

"Why do you want me?" he asked, the question surprising even himself, the words broken, torn from a part deep inside himself he had not known existed.

She looked at him, her dark eyes glazed, her expression full of confusion. "What?"

"You're too good. You're too soft. Why do you want me? It doesn't make any sense. You should be disgusted by me. Don't you understand that? I'm not a good man. You are a good girl. A very good girl. Soft and fragile. Protected. Protected from monsters like me. And yet, here you are, flinging yourself at me. It makes no sense."

"You asked for me," she said simply. "That's hardly me flinging myself at you."

He growled, taking her other nipple into his mouth and sucking on her until she gasped, until she arched against him again. And then, he released her. "There you are. Flinging yourself at me. And I need to know why."

"Did it ever occur to you that it's because you're everything I don't have? You're hard, where I'm soft. Dangerous. And I've been so protected, just like you said. And you are... Well, you're a bit bad, aren't you?"

She lifted her hand, touched the side of his face, and he turned, grazing her fingertip with his teeth. "Just a bit."

"Maybe I've been just a little bit too good, then. Maybe people need both, and I don't have any of my own. So, I need some of yours."

He rolled his hips against hers, felt slick, receptive

flesh beneath his unyielding hardness. "You need my darkness," he said.

She gasped, grabbing hold of his shoulders. "Yes."

He needed her light. Dammit, but he needed it. He wouldn't say it, not now. Couldn't say it. Because he was too consumed by the need to be inside her.

He pressed the head of his arousal against her entrance, slid inside inch by excruciating inch, torturing them both with that slow penetration. Belatedly, he was concerned that she might be sore. But he banished those concerns quickly enough. They paled in comparison to his need. His need to have her. To consume her in the way she was consuming him.

To have her light.

Darkness had been his constant companion, but right now he felt like he was standing on the edge of an abyss that was something beyond darkness. And only she was keeping him from falling completely.

He lost himself in her, burying his head against her neck as he chased that white-hot flame of release that he could only find in her. She grabbed hold of him, her fingernails digging into his skin, sounds of pleasure escaping her lips as she met his every thrust with one of her own.

Then she grabbed hold of his arms, a raw scream on her lips as she found her own release, her fingernails scraping a long trail down his forearms, all the way to the backs of his hands.

Marks from their encounter he wouldn't be able to hide. Disorder. Beautiful chaos. Found within his princess.

No. His queen.

And as she convulsed around him, he gave in to his

own release, flinging himself into the darkness. Because he knew that her light would be there when he reached the bottom.

The next few days passed in a flurry of activity. Briar scarcely saw Felipe in the light of day. But at night... Yes, she saw him at night. It didn't matter if she retreated to her own room, in that case, he would come and find her. He would find her, and he would make love to her for hours. Tapping into parts of herself she hadn't known existed.

But in the morning he was always gone. She had a suspicion that he never fell asleep with her. But rather, waited for her to drift off before succumbing himself.

It was times like this she felt her isolation keenly. The separation from her mother. If she was back in New York she could talk to Nell about this. Well, in some vague terms. She wouldn't go talking about everything they'd done in detail.

Her cheeks heated.

She wasn't quite sure how she had found herself in this situation. Bonding—physically at least—with the one man she should be most distant from.

When she tried to think of her life before Felipe, before coming here, it all seemed hazy. She supposed that wasn't a good sign. That for some reason these past weeks in Santa Milagro seemed bolder, more colorful, than the life before she had arrived here ever had.

She wondered if it was a trick, too. Some magical spell that Felipe had over her, even though she didn't believe in magic. Or rather, she hadn't before discovering she was a princess, and being spirited away to a foreign country by a prince that was far too handsome and far too wicked for anyone's good.

The very strange thing, though, was the fact that even though she had stepped into this life that was entirely unknown to her, had stepped into a role she had never imagined she might fulfill, she felt more herself than she ever had.

And it wasn't just because she had been happily creating art programs, working out grants and funding for various schools and cataloging the artwork long forgotten in the years since King Domenico had shuttered the museums.

Art had always made her feel alive, it was true, but it was more than that. Perhaps it was because Felipe seemed to require nothing from her other than that she stand by his side, and that she make herself available to him when he had need of her body.

Otherwise, he didn't want a particular sort of behavior from her. At least, not that he'd said. There was no pressure to present herself as something perfect or demure, not when she was in his presence. He liked to push her, and he seemed to enjoy when she provided him with a spirited response.

He certainly seemed to enjoy that in the bedroom. Thinking of it even now made her cheeks heat. She pressed the back of her hand against the side of her face, cool skin pressing against hot, making her shiver.

She was currently digging through a room in the back of the palace that seemed to have been abandoned. There were a great many artifacts that she wanted cataloged for the museums, and she was doing her best to sort through what she might have different appraisers come and have a look at, and what probably didn't have any value beyond the sentimental.

She had been doing a lot of historical research on her adopted country, trying to give context to all the various pieces she was discovering. It seemed that the poor nation had only experienced pockets of peace and prosperity, while mostly enduring long stretches of time with kings who were tyrants.

But the people had created beautiful things, even during their oppression. Almost most especially during their oppression.

In the palace she had mostly found personal collections. Portraits of past rulers and their relatives, pieces of the crown jewels, which had been stowed in a very secure vault. She would prefer they be on display than sitting in the back growing tarnished. Felipe seemed to have no opinion on the matter, so she was proceeding.

But in the rooms she had discovered only yesterday, it was different. The jewelry was not cataloged. It was not organized at all. And yet, it seemed to be of amazing quality. Millions of dollars in gems hidden in drawers. Beautiful paintings—still life and portraiture—hidden behind canvas. Hand-carved furniture beneath tarps.

She let out a long, slow breath and dragged one large tarp off a piece that sat against the back wall. Her eyes widened as she looked over the beautiful chest of drawers. Different pieces of wood were inlaid to create a representation of the mountainous skyline visible from the windows here in the tower.

Thin strips of gold separated the different pieces of wood, and she had a feeling it was real precious metal. She brushed her fingertips over the mountain peaks, over the sun, positioned in the upper left-hand corner of the bureau.

There was so much hidden beauty here. She couldn't help but think it might be a metaphor for the man she was going to marry. She paused for a moment, Felipe's handsome face swimming before her mind's eye.

He was such a puzzle. Charming and smooth one moment, then rough and out of control the next. He seemed to crave order, his appearance never anything but perfectly polished. And yet, the night his father had died he had laid everything in his wake to ruin, including her.

She felt her cheeks grow even hotter.

What a ruin it had been.

She took a fortifying breath and turned away from the chest of drawers, making her way across the room to a shapeless mass covered by canvas that she assumed was more framed paintings of various sizes. She dragged the canvas down and was rewarded with exactly that.

Landscapes in gilt-edged frames, a painting of fruit on a table. She enjoyed looking at this sort of thing. Because it proved that people had always been people. Compelled to capture the things around them. Compelled to take some kind of snapshot of their dinner for the world to see.

She carefully moved the first couple of paintings to the side and paused when she saw a portrait of a woman she had never seen before.

She was beautiful. Her black hair was swept up into an elegant bun, a golden crown on her head. Her crimson lips were curved into a half smile, one that seemed to contain wicked secrets. It reminded her of… Well, it reminded her of Felipe.

"What are you doing?"

She jumped, turning at the sound of Felipe's voice.

"Just exploring the rooms. I'm handling the art, as we discussed. Getting everything ready for the museums."

"That isn't art," he said, his voice taking on a strange tone.

She frowned. "It is a painting."

"It's my mother," he said, swift and hard.

She looked between him and the painting, speechless for a moment. "I…I can see it, actually."

He laughed. "Can you? I had thought that she and I bore no resemblance at all."

"You do," she said softly, not sure if it was the right thing to say. She couldn't read his mood. But then, she so rarely could. Trying to grasp Felipe's motivations or feelings was a lot like grabbing hold of a handful of sand. You could wrap your fingers around it for a moment, but then it all slid away into nothing.

"I would prefer if her things stayed here," he said.

"I didn't realize these were your mother's things."

He nodded once. "Yes. I think they have been in here untouched since the day she died."

"How old were you when she died?"

"Seven," he said, his tone detached now.

He crossed the room, making his way over to the window. It had bars over it, she had noticed earlier. She had thought very little of it then, because often windows that were so high up had a precaution of some kind in place so that no accidents happened. But for some reason, when he made his way there, when he pressed his fingers against the pane of glass, she wondered about them.

"She died here," he said, the words conversational.

"Was she… Was she ill?"

"In a manner of speaking. She was not well, that's certain."

She didn't say anything. If there was one thing she had learned about Felipe—and she had actually learned several—it was that if he wanted to say something he would eventually. And if he didn't, there was no amount of pushing that would get him to speak. There were other ways of dealing with him that were much more effective.

She took a moment to think about those ways, curling her fingers into fists as she imagined running her palms over his face. It would be rough now, because it was late in the day and dark stubble covered his jaw. She liked that. Liked when he was a bit unshaven. A bit feral.

She liked herself that way, too. Which was surprising, she had to admit.

He pressed his palms flat against the window, and she noticed his gaze dropped to his shirtsleeves. But she didn't speak then, either. She was collecting bits of information about him. Had been from the moment she had first laid eyes on him. He fascinated her. He called to something deep inside her that she couldn't explain, not really. Except that… He seemed to need her. And in every other situation in her life, she had needed those around her.

It wasn't a bad thing. It was just that she'd had to make sure she behaved, make sure she was good so that she could somehow make her presence worthwhile.

He had needed her so badly he had kidnapped her. And perhaps there was some kind of twisted logic trying to make that a good thing, but then again, maybe there was no logic at all.

Maybe it was all just a feeling, and that was okay, too.

"My cuffs weren't straight," he said.

She looked down at them now, saw deep scratches

extending from them now, lending him a look that was much less than civilized. Marks she'd left on him.

Marring his perfection. Making a mockery of hers.

She felt her face heat.

"What?" She found herself taking a step toward him.

"That was the start of it. I was never quite so orderly as my father would have me be. And he took it out on my mother. He demanded perfection that could never be achieved, particularly when he himself was creating chaos beneath the surface." Felipe tapped the glass then turned to face her. "I did not have a nanny. My father demanded that my mother care for me. Otherwise, what was her use?"

"How did you… How did you know about all of this? It doesn't seem right that a little boy should have heard all this going on between his parents."

He flashed that wicked smile, but there was no joy behind it. "That was never a concern. In fact, my father demanded I bear witness to all manner of indecency he subjected my mother to. If I misbehaved and she had to be slapped across the face, he wanted me to see it. And vice versa. He much preferred punishing her for my sins and me for hers. You see, it's so much more painful to watch your mother be struck because you spoke at a moment when you should not have than it is to be hit yourself." He looked back at the window. "She was always quite delicate. Like a bird. She escaped him. She flew away."

"She left him?" Briar asked, searching for clarity.

"She jumped out the window." He wrapped his knuckle against the glass. "That's why there are bars. I suppose my father didn't want to lose another family member in the same way. It would begin to reflect poorly on him."

He said the words so dispassionately, and Briar found

herself unable to breathe through the grief that exploded in her chest like a bomb. For his mother. For him. It seemed unfathomable that a small boy should lose his mother that way.

It seemed equally unfathomable that the woman in that portrait, the woman who had most certainly started out with as much spark in life as Felipe himself had, could have been reduced, tormented, until she felt that was her only escape.

"Felipe… I'm so sorry. I don't understand how he got away with that. With tormenting you both. What did the public think?"

"That it was an unfortunate accident. And of course, my father controlled the press. And no one would ever question what he had decreed."

"So no one knew. No one has ever known."

"No," he said, his tone hard. "We had to perform. For the nation, for the world, pretend that everything was okay when we were…when we were dying."

"What does that have to do with your cuffs?" she asked, her eyes falling to his sleeves. It was one of his many obsessive-looking mannerisms. He straightened his jacket and dress shirt constantly. She had seen him do it frequently from that first meeting.

"There was a state dinner. And my father chose to make that the issue of the day. My jacket sleeve was rolled up, or it was ill fitting, something." A crease appeared between his brows, and there was a measure of confusion in his dark gaze. She had a feeling that he remembered all of it. But that he preferred not to. That he preferred not to show himself and get all of the details right, because the details were so horrifying. "She tried to protect me. She brought me up here. And then my father followed us. And he poured all of his rage out on to her. He struck her. Again, and again. And then she… She went to the window. Then she was gone." He frowned. "I thought about following her. But I thought…I thought it could not be safe. And yet if my mother had just jumped out the window how could it be dangerous?"

His expression went blank. "All of that was answered for me later."

Her throat worked, but she could force no words to her lips.

Felipe regarded her closely. "Have I shocked you?"

She pressed her hand to her breast. "Of course you have. It's a terrible story. It should be shocking. You saw her… You saw your mother…"

"Yes," he said, that same detached tone she had heard from him many times prevalent now. "You can see now why I hate him so much. My father. There was nothing good about him, Briar. Nothing at all."

She nodded silently, swallowing hard.

She looked around the room, surprised that he was standing there. That he was standing so near that window. Had she endured something like that she doubted she would ever have been able to set foot in that room again.

"You're wondering how I'm in here," he said. "It's okay. I understand that it must seem strange to you. That it would seem strange to a great many people. People with a heart. But I cut mine out a long time ago, Briar. Because so long as you care it is dangerous. So long as you care you can be broken. My father tried to break me. He made me come in here. Told me that he would not allow for me to become softer, weak, would not allow me to build a shrine to a dead woman. So I learned." He looked around the space. "There is no real power in this room, anyway.

The real power was in plotting my father's downfall. The real power is in the fact that I now have control of this nation, and that I will right the wrongs that have been perpetuated against the people here. That I will write the history books and I will make sure my father's name is nothing but dirt. These are just four walls and a window. And anyway, the memories are with me wherever I go. I don't have to be here."

For the first time she truly believed he had a monster inside him. One made of memories; one comprised of the past horror he had lived through. And it most certainly drove his actions now. But it wasn't him. It wasn't. All she could do was picture a small boy who had been abandoned. Who had seen something no one should ever see.

Who had thought—naively—that he could perhaps fly out that same window to be with her, because in spite of all the indignity, in spite of all the abuse he had suffered, there was still trust inside him.

Trust that, she had no doubt, had been broken that day.

"You have a heart, Felipe," she said, the words strangled.

He frowned. "I don't. And why would I want one?"

She couldn't answer that. Except, she wanted him to understand that he wasn't broken. That his father didn't have the power to keep him in that blank, emotionless state he had been forced to assume to protect himself. The old man was dead, and he had no power. Not now. She wanted him to know that. Wanted him to understand.

Why? For you? Because you wish it were true?

She took a step back, those thoughts halting her words. Maybe. Maybe it was about her. And about what she wanted him to need from her. She swallowed hard, trying to catch her breath.

She shook her head. "I don't know."

She knew why she wanted him to have one. She wished that she didn't. She wished that she could ignore those thoughts. That she could deny the feelings rushing through her like a wave.

They shouldn't be possible. She should hate him. It shouldn't matter how terrible his childhood was; it shouldn't matter that he was broken, that there was no way he could possibly know how he was supposed to treat another person. He had kidnapped her. Was forcing her into marriage, or as good as forcing her, and she needed to remember that.

The trouble was that she did remember it. All too clearly.

And still…

Still, he made her body tremble. Still, he made her heart ache.

"I know what I need to do. For my country. I don't need a heart to accomplish those things." He closed the distance between them, brushing his knuckles over her cheekbone. "And have I not been kind to you?"

"You kidnapped me."

He waved his hand. "Have I not given you pleasure, *querida*? I believe that I have."

Pleasure isn't love. But she didn't say that. "Yes."

"I don't need a heart for such things. I only need this." He took hold of her hand and pressed it against the front of his slacks, over his hardening arousal.

She couldn't even be angry with him. That was the problem with Felipe.

"You're a very bad man," she said, no censure in her voice. "Do you know that?"

"Yes," he responded flippantly.

Then he kissed her as if to prove that didn't matter, either. And he proved it quite effectively.

Warmth flooded her body, flooded her heart. And there was simply no denying the truth. She loved him. She loved him and it mattered whether or not he had a heart because she needed him to have one so he could love her, too.

Later she might try and figure out if all of this was crazy. Might try and figure out why she felt this way. Right now she just clung to him. And felt a kind of certainty she had never experienced before. She didn't feel different. She didn't feel wrong. Like a misshapen piece shoved into the only available space.

But she wanted—so very much—to be all he needed, and she hoped that she could be. That she could be enough. That she could be...

This was her place. Here with him. Felipe was king, and in order to rule he would need a heart. Whether he believed it or not.

So she was determined to give it back to him.

CHAPTER TEN

FELIPE HADN'T INTENDED to confess all of that to Briar earlier. There was something about her. Something that got beneath his skin, got beneath his defenses. Well, he imagined it was the same thing that got beneath his pants. And frequently. Nothing to be too concerned about.

Neither were the headlines currently calling into question whether or not he was a sociopath. Considering he had broken with tradition and declined to give his father a funeral.

He didn't know why he would make a show of burying a dictator, and he had said as much to the media. Implications had been made—more than implications—that he was no different than the old man. That his lack of compassion—whether or not his father had deserved it—was indicative of a flaw in him, as well.

He could not be certain that wasn't the case. Nobody could be.

He strode out of the media room, tearing at the lapel mic he had been wearing. He was done giving interviews for the time being.

Another error, and he was damned if he could figure out what the hell was driving him. He'd spent years married to a facade, and he couldn't seem to find it now. He was damaging that which he sought to build with his inability to simply play the part he ought to.

Though he didn't know why he was surprised.

He destroyed. It was what he did. No matter whether he wanted to or not.

He was surprised to see Briar walking toward him, dressed as though she was prepared for an evening out. She was wearing a green silk dress that conformed to her curves, with a hemline that fell well above the knee, showing off those endless legs he was so fond of. Of course, he preferred it when they were wrapped around him.

He had half a mind to grab her and drag her to his room now. Whatever plans she had. She was his, after all. His queen. To do with as he pleased. If he wanted her, then she would have to cancel her plans and see to him. He paused, frowning. He wondered if that was the sort of thing his father thought about his mother. About anyone in his life. They were his. His to use as he pleased.

"I was looking for you," she said, her bright smile at odds with the thoughts currently chasing around his head.

"Were you?"

"Yes. I thought we might go out for dinner."

"If you haven't seen the headlines today I have created something of a scandal. Perhaps it would be best if we stayed in."

She looked stubborn. Mutinous. She was quite difficult to argue within that state, he had learned. "I have seen the headlines. People are calling your character into question, and it isn't fair. Of course you shouldn't have thrown a large public funeral for your father. It would have been a farce. I understand that. And that's the entire point of the two of us going out. You want me because you needed my help in softening your image. Well, let me do that."

"I'm not sure I understand."

"We will ostentatiously make an appearance together going for dinner. The entire nation will see that whatever the press says I'm on your side. Whatever anyone says, I stand with you."

Her words rang with the kind of conviction he didn't deserve.

"I'm not certain it will accomplish anything."

Her dark brows lowered. "I am," she said, her tone every inch that of a queen.

"You've grown very comfortable with your new role."

She tossed her head back, her curls bouncing with the movement. "Would you prefer that I remain uncomfortable with it? I think it would be much more effective for both of us if I were comfortable. And I think it would be best for you if you complied with my plan."

"Answer me this, my queen. Are you kidnapping me?"

A smile curved her lips. "Yes."

"Then I suppose I have no option but to comply."

The press was waiting outside the gates to the palace, and when the limousine he and Briar were riding in exited the gates they were nearly mobbed. Briar held on tightly to his arm, glaring out the window. "I would have us present a united front," she said, her tone stiff. "Because I believe that what you did was right. You did it for you, and for your mother. And whether or not anyone else ever understands the full circumstances... I do."

Those simple words caused a strange shift in his chest, and he didn't pause to examine them. Her soft fingertips were drifting down past his arm, over his thigh.

"Careful," he said, his tone full of warning. "The flash photography may make it so they can get shots through the window."

He didn't know how effective the tinted glass would be against those high-powered bulbs.

"I don't care," she said. "Like I said. Let them see that I stand with you. That you're mine.

"I'm going to have the car drop us off a little way from our destination." She tapped on the glass, and the driver lowered the divider. "Leave us just near the university," she commanded.

He quite liked seeing her like this. So at ease with her position. So perfectly at ease in his life. It made him feel much less like questioning himself. Much less like he might be the villain, as he was worried he might have been a few moments earlier.

"There are no restaurants over by the university," he said, reaching out and brushing some of her hair from her face. "Unless you intend to have us eat fast food."

"I'm not opposed to a French fry, Felipe. But that isn't what I have in mind for us tonight. I have a plan. But we need to make sure we're seen a little bit more before we get down to it."

He wrapped his arm around her, burying his face in her hair, his lips touching the shell of her ear. "I'm more than happy to get down to it. We don't even need to have dinner."

"Later," she said, her dark eyes burning with promise. "I promise later."

For some reason, those words caught hold of something in his chest. Sparked a memory. A feeling. One of loss. The kind of loss he hadn't truly allowed himself to feel since he was seven years old.

He caught hold of her chin, held her face steady. "Is that a promise? A real promise? One you won't break."

"Have I ever denied you my body?"

She had not. And still, he couldn't quite credit why that was. "No."

"Then trust me."

He couldn't remember the last time someone had asked him to trust them. Moreover, he couldn't remember the last time he had actually trusted someone. He wanted to. He found that he very much wanted to.

"I will hold that in reserve," he said finally.

The car pulled up to the university, and he and Briar got out, Briar taking hold of his hand as though it was the most natural thing on earth. He couldn't remember the last time anyone had asked him to trust them, and he couldn't remember the last time he had held a woman's hand, either. Had he ever? He had lovers from time to time, fairly frequently, in truth. But their interaction was confined to the bedroom. That meant there was no reason for them to ever walk around with their fingers laced together.

This touch was not... Well, it wasn't sexual. And in his life that meant it was pointless. Except it didn't feel pointless. It felt very much like something essential. Felt very much like air. He couldn't explain it even if he wanted to. He found he didn't. He found he just wanted to enjoy the feeling of her soft skin against his.

It only took him a moment to realize she was taking him to the museum.

"Are you subjecting me to a gala?" He looked at her sideways. "Because I must warn you I am not in the temperament required for a gala."

She narrowed her eyes. "What temperament is required for a gala?"

"Something much more docile than I'm capable of."

She made a dismissive sound. "You don't need to be docile." She tugged on his hand, drawing him toward the entrance. "Of course, this is our own private gala. And our own private dinner."

"I thought the point of coming out was to be seen?"

She pushed open the museum door. "It is. Well, it was. But we were seen as much as I intend for us to be tonight."

She looked at him, her expression slightly mischievous. It made his heart beat faster, made his groin tighten. She grabbed hold of the door and pulled it shut, and impish grin tugging at the corners of her mouth.

"If I didn't know any better I would say you had lured me here to seduce me," he said. He disliked his own tone. It was far too dry, far too insincere, when there was absolutely nothing insincere about Briar. Or this act. He closed some of the distance between them, pressing his hand to her cheek. "That was not a complaint, mind you."

She lifted her own hand, covered his with it. "I didn't take it as one."

"You set dinner out for us?" he asked, doing his best to keep himself from poking at her. From twisting the conversation into something overly light and familiar.

"Well, people who work for you set dinner out for us. I don't know how to cook." She cleared her throat. "But I didn't bring you here to try and impress you with the food."

She turned the lights on, and the entire antechamber lit up, the antique chandelier that hung in the entry blazing into glory. Everything was clean. A statue placed just at the foot of the staircase well lit, showcasing the marble, and the incredible skill of the artist.

"It's nearly ready," she said, nearly bursting with excitement. "I wanted you to see this. I wanted you to see what you have made it possible for your people to have." She turned a circle, her arms spread wide. "All of this history. All of this beauty. It's part of the fabric of this country and it's been hidden from them for so long. But now it won't be. Now everyone can come and see this. Everyone can experience this."

He was humbled. Not so much by the art, not even by the work she had put in here. But by her exuberance for it. The happiness that she felt. Why should she be happy? Why should she be happy here with him? And excited for this task he had assigned to her as something she should be grateful for when he had uprooted her from her home? He didn't understand it. He didn't understand her.

And he didn't understand the kind of unfettered joy she seemed to radiate.

Moreover, he didn't understand the passion that she had for art. For something that seemed to exist for no other reason other than to be beautiful. For no other reason than to be looked at. It was a frivolous beauty, and he had never found much beauty in life at all. But she seemed to relish it. Seemed to worship it almost.

He wondered what it must be like to care like that. To feel like that. To live for something beyond the grim march to a goal.

"Come this way," she said. "They've set a table for us in my favorite wing."

"What is your favorite wing?" he asked, finding that he was unable to wait for the answer to that question to be revealed naturally.

She paused. "Impressionists." She smiled, her expression pretty, clearly pleased with the fact that he had asked.

"Why?" he persisted as he followed her down a long corridor, and into a large, open showroom with paintings mounted on each wall. A table was set in the middle with plates covered by trays. There were no candles, and he found that didn't surprise him.

She wouldn't expose her beloved art to anything that might burn it.

She was clearly puzzled by his question. "I don't know. I mean, I do know. But it's hard to put into words. It speaks to my soul in a way that…resonates beyond language."

Those words put him in the mind of something that resonated in him. It brought to mind images of his hands on her skin. The contrast of his fingers gliding over her dark beauty, an erotic kick to the gut that shocked him every time. The feel of her…of being over her, in her… there was nothing on earth like it.

He'd had sex more times than he could count, with more women than he cared to count. This reached beyond that. He imagined she would not enjoy him comparing their physical relationship to the art she loved so much. But he had no other frame of reference.

"It's not as detailed as some styles," she continued. "It's not perfect. There's something almost…messy about it when you look up close. Chaotic. And yet, when you stand back and you look at the whole picture it creates something beautiful."

"Why does that appeal to you so? You seem like nothing more than perfection to me, Princess."

She tilted her head to the side, her expression full of speculation. "I suppose it's because I like to think that…

if someday I should ever become…something other than what I have tried to be, then somebody would look at me and try to see the beauty. That somebody would step back and see who I am as a whole. And find me lovely."

"You could never be anything less than beautiful," he said, his voice rough. "It would be impossible."

"You're talking about physical appearance. And it isn't that I don't appreciate that," she said, looking down. "It's just that… That isn't all there is. And it isn't really my primary concern. But I always felt that…my parents—the parents I was raised with, not the king and queen—were older when they took me in. And they loved me. They have always behaved as though I was their own. But they never had any children before me. I was the first. And I could tell that though I brought them joy I brought them an equal measure of anxiety. And I did my very best to transcend that. To make up for it. To be worth the sacrifice. Because before I came into their lives they had so much less responsibility. So much less worry. I always felt like I had to do something to offset that. To be the girl that was worth that sacrifice."

"That is quite the feat. For a young girl to attempt to be perfect. To try and justify your existence. A child should never have to do that." His existence had always had purpose, for he was his father's heir. And then in end, his purpose—no matter that it had been a secret one— had been to right the wrongs his father had committed against his people.

But she had wondered. Had wondered what she should do to make herself worthwhile, when she should have known all along she had a kingdom depending on her. When she should have known she had parents in the US and in Verloren who cared for her.

She had not. It had all been hidden from her.

He despised his role in that. The role his family had played in that. His father. But then, that was nothing new. His father ruining lives. Him ruining lives.

"I can't remember any different," she said, her tone soft. "It has always been that way for me. For as long as I can remember."

"Except, you *can* imagine different. If not, you wouldn't like these paintings quite so much."

"Perhaps not."

She stopped talking then, directing him toward the table that was set for two, any staff who might have placed the settings now conspicuously absent.

"If I didn't know any better I would think you were trying to seduce me," he said.

She smiled, her earlier sadness vanishing. "I am," she said, her tone light, cheerful, as she picked up a glass of wine and lifted it to her lips.

"You should know that you don't need to go to so much effort. In fact, you don't need to go to any effort at all. Showing up is about all it takes."

Her expression changed, and suddenly, she looked slightly wistful. "Is that true of me? Or is it true of all women that you…that you do this with?"

"I have never done this with another woman. Oh, of course I have had lovers, Briar. But I have never…I have never *associated* with a woman outside the bedroom."

"Never?"

He shrugged. "You have never had a relationship, either. Why is it so alarming that I haven't?"

"Well, I had never had a sexual relationship with anyone, either. It seems like one should…lead to the other. So yes, *alarming* is the word I would use. That you've been physically intimate with someone and never…"

"You use the word *intimate* to describe sex often, but to me seeking physical release with someone was nothing." He could see by her expression that those words had hurt her. "In the past," he said, softening his tone, not quite sure why he felt the impulse to do so, only knowing that he did not like that he had been responsible for putting that desolate expression on her beautiful face.

"So I'm different?" She sounded so hopeful, and he wondered why on earth she would waste her hope on him.

"It is so important to you to be different." Suddenly the words that she had spoken when they had walked in and spoken of the Impressionists clicked together with these. And he understood. More than that, he cared. Whatever that meant.

"It is not so unusual that a woman would want to be special to her lover." She slid her wineglass back and forth, her focus on the dark liquid.

"Yes, but that is the thing." He pressed his hand over hers, stopping the nervous movement. "You are more than my lover. You are to be my wife. You have more power, more position, in my life than any woman ever has."

She smiled, clearly pleased by that. And he was happy that he had made her smile. He couldn't recall ever taking such pleasure in someone else's happiness before. Except… Dimly, in the recesses of his mind he could remember trying to make his mother happy when his father had just been being an ogre. Could remember trying to make her smile in spite of the abuses they had both suffered.

As if the antics of a little boy could heal the actions of a madman.

They hadn't. Clearly. If they could have, his mother would still be here. She wouldn't have leaped out a window rather than continue to suffer at the hands of his father. Rather than continue to try to deal with a little boy who would always make that situation untenable. Order. His father had wanted order and he hadn't been able to give her that much. Hadn't realized that if he'd simply...

He tugged on his cuffs.

No, he had never been enough. Not when it counted.

Much like then, that smile on Briar's face probably didn't extend as far down as it needed to go. Much like then, he imagined he would be found wanting. But Briar would be queen. And she would have her art. She would have this place. And they had their passion. He would be faithful to her. He remembered then that he had never told her so.

"I will not repeat the sins of my father," he said.

"Which sins?"

"I will be faithful to you."

She blinked. "I didn't realize that was ever up for debate," she said.

"I had not promised you fidelity."

She frowned. "I thought that was a given with marriage. Unless you're an awful person. Like your father."

"I kidnapped you," he said simply. "At what point did you begin thinking I was a decent man?"

"You've never hurt me. I understand why you did what you did," she said, looking down at where his hand was still pressed over the top of hers. "I understand why you need my help. And I'm honestly happy to give it."

Suddenly, he didn't like that. Didn't like that she was offering him help. That she was putting herself forward as another mark of her perfection. He didn't want that.

Perversely, he wanted her to be with him because she wanted to be.

There was no logic in that. To want that from the woman he had forced to accept his proposal.

Offer her freedom. See what she does.

No. He could not do that. She couldn't have her freedom. She could not be given that opportunity. Because he needed her. He did. Whatever he wanted, he would have to be content with what they had.

There was no reason he should not be. He had everything he wanted.

He would not be everything she wanted, that was inescapable. For this was not the life she had chosen for herself. And why did he care about that at all? Only a few weeks ago he would not have. He had not. He had kidnapped her from a hospital for God's sake.

And now, sitting here in this quiet museum with her, his hand pressed over the top of her knuckles, he burned. Ached. Wanted more than he should. Wanted things that conflicted with his goals.

"If you're offering martyrdom to me—the kind of martyrdom that you gave your parents—then I will state for the record that I don't want it."

"You want me to help with your cause. To comply with your wishes. You never cared why I was giving it before. You threatened me, in fact, if I didn't give it. How can it not be martyrdom?"

"You're offering me your help, saying that you understand, looking at me with those angelic eyes of yours… Pity. You look at me like I'm a dog you *pity*. I may have taken that from my queen, but not from my lover."

"I'm trying to help. I'm trying to do what's expected of me. I'm trying to find my place here. This is for me as much as it is for you. I never knew where I fit. All my life I didn't know. I felt wrong. I knew I had come from somewhere else. I knew that. There were people all around me who can trace their lineage back to the May-flower and I couldn't trace mine back to my parents. I couldn't remember the first four years of my life. Well, apparently, I was born to be royalty. So here I am. And I'm trying my very best. To make this mine. To make a place for myself. And you're accusing me of playing at empty perfection."

He didn't know why he was pressing this. Didn't know why he cared at all. Mostly, he didn't know why there was a howling, wrenching pain in his chest when he thought of her simply lying back and doing her duty for him.

He wanted to mess her up. Mess them both up.

"I have pushed you every step of the way," he said. "And you... You seem completely and utterly compelled to prove your worth. Why should I think it's anything different?"

She stood, pushing her chair back, her dark gaze level with his. "What do you need? You need some sort of sym-bol that I'm here on my own? That I'm making choices? That this isn't about me simply complying quietly?"

She reached behind her back, and he heard the soft sound of a zipper. Then she stepped out of her dress. The shimmering fabric fell to her hips, and she pushed it down all the way to the floor.

"When have I ever complied quietly when it comes to you, Felipe?" She unhooked her bra, pushed it down her arms and then sent her panties along the same path, until she was standing naked before him wearing noth-ing more than a pair of high heels that made her impos-sibly long legs seem all that much longer. "I screamed and shouted at you as you kidnapped me from the hospital. I refused you until…"

"Perhaps only until you found that there was enough here to make compliance worth it." He was pushing. Pushing hard. And he wanted to see how hard she would push back.

She moved to him, and he stayed seated in his chair, allowed her to curl her fingers around the back of it, to lean over him, her breasts hovering temptingly close to his lips. "Do you think I'm weak? Do you think I'm frightened of you?"

"I think you should be." He lifted his hand and touched her chin. "I ruin people." Then he tilted his face up and scraped his teeth along the underside of her chin. "If you think that by playing perfect you can somehow outrun that fate, then I have news for you."

"Perhaps you should ruin me. Perhaps…we all need to be a little bit ruined. Like one of my paintings."

It so closely echoed his earlier thoughts that it blanked his mind for a moment. But she seemed to be able to read him. That she seemed to…understand him. And that she had not run in the other direction.

He placed his hands on her shoulder blades then slid his fingertips down the elegant line of her spine, to the perfect curve of her ass. He was already so hard he hurt, his arousal pressing against the front of his slacks.

He reached up then, forking his fingers in her hair, curling his fingers around the massive curls and tugging her head back as he pulled her more firmly onto his lap, rolling his hips upward, well aware that he was rubbing his hardness against that place she was already wet and needy for him. She was undoing him, he couldn't deny it. But he would see her undone, as well.

If he was going to break, she would break along with him. They would break together.

He leaned forward, pressing a kiss to the pounding pulse at the base of her neck, then tracing a trail up to her jaw with the tip of his tongue, along upward to her lips, where he claimed her fiercely, with no delicacy at all.

She gasped, her fingers working clumsily on the front of his shirt, tearing at his tie, at the buttons there. And then she gave up, hands moving to his belt buckle, tugging at the fabric until she freed his erection. She curled her delicate fingers around him, her hand small and dark, soft, over that rock-hard arousal, the contrast an aphrodisiac that nearly sent him over the edge.

"Show me," he said, planting his hands on her hips, holding her steady over him. "Show me how much you want me."

Keeping her hand on him, she tilted her hips forward and guided him toward her slick entrance, placing him there, slowly lowering herself onto him. His breath hissed through his teeth and he let his head fall back, let himself get lost in all that tight, glorious heat.

It was tempting to close his eyes, to shut everything out except for that sensation. But he forced himself to keep them open, so that he could look at her. So that he could watch the glorious bounce of her breasts as she rocked herself up and down over him.

He looked beyond her shoulders, at all the art that was mounted on the walls. She rivaled all of it. Made these masterworks as finger paintings in his eyes. He slipped his hands up to her narrow waist, holding her hard as she moved.

Then he leaned forward, capturing one of her nipples with his mouth, sucking it in deep. She let out a low, hoarse sound and her pleasure exploded all around him. She didn't close her eyes; instead, she looked deep into his, her expression one of fierce intensity and concentration.

This was just for him. She had never even kissed another man before him. She had certainly never come for another man. And here he was, buried deep inside her, wringing out every last bit of her pleasure, taking it on as his own. He didn't deserve it. Didn't deserve her. And yet, he couldn't stop. Couldn't fathom not taking this. Not taking her.

She tossed her head back at the last moment, planting her hands on his shoulders as she ground her hips against his, extracting each and every possible wave of pleasure from him, her climax a fierce and wild thing he didn't deserve in the least.

When she righted herself, when she looked at him again, he was the one who had to look away. He was undone by that emotion in her eyes. A vulnerability that ran beneath the strength he had just seen. The kind of vulnerability a man like him could exploit. A softness he could so easily destroy.

The sort of thing he would do well to be gentle with. And yet he found himself tightening his hold on her. Driving himself up inside her as he chased his own release. As he allowed that white-hot wave to wash over him, to steal every thought, every doubt, from his mind. At the moment he was inside Briar. And she was all around him. Her soft skin, her delicate scent, everything that she was filling him, consuming him.

A soft smile curved her lips, an expression of wonder on her face. She cupped his head in her hands, sliding her thumbs along the line of his jaw as she gazed down at him. No one had ever looked at him like this before. As if he were a thing they had never before seen. As if he were something magic.

He should explain to her that he was not magic. He was not unique. And he would only destroy her.

Instead, he found himself reaching up, wrapping his hands around her wrists, pulling her more firmly against him, forcing her to wrap her arms around his neck. His lips pressed against hers, and when he spoke it was nearly a growl. "We will be married next week. Then you will truly be mine."

Her lashes fluttered, a slight hint of shock visible in those dark eyes. But then she smiled. "I'm glad."

She shouldn't be. And he had a feeling in time she wouldn't be. But self-sacrifice was for another man, a better man. And if he was a man capable of those things, perhaps he would be worthy of her.

And so it was an impossible situation. For *her*.

As for him, he would have what he wanted.

The dragon inside him was content. And the man... Well, the man wanted her already, all over again. As though she had opened up a need inside him that he'd never before known existed. One he was afraid would never entirely be satisfied again.

Good thing they would have a lifetime for him to try and exhaust it.

Then she did something he could not have anticipated. She leaned forward, kissing him softly, sweetly. And then she spoke.

"I love you."

CHAPTER ELEVEN

SHE HADN'T INTENDED to say that out loud. But now that she had she couldn't regret it. Wouldn't regret it. How could she? She had fallen in love, for the first time in her life. With this wild, untamable man who had suffered unimaginable loss. Who had endured unimaginable pain. And she just wanted to give to him. She wanted him to feel everything that she did. This bright, intense emotion in her chest that made it difficult for her to breathe, that made her want to cry and laugh and shout all at the same time.

She felt brave, and she felt frightened. She felt more than she had ever felt in her life. And she felt everything. How could she not share it?

"I wasn't looking for that," he said, his voice flat. Hands planted on her hips, he removed her from his lap, and she felt the loss of him keenly, leaving her body and her heart feeling cold. She wrapped her arms around herself, raised goose bumps covering her arms.

"That's all right. I offered it anyway."

"Why? Because it makes you feel better about accepting my proposal? Make no mistake, Princess. It is not a proposal, but a demand. You do not have to offer anything in return. Unless it's simply to salve your own conscience." He narrowed his dark eyes. "Is that the issue? You're disturbed by the fact that you enjoy the body of a man you don't love? So you had to manufacture emotions in order to justify your orgasm?"

Heat seared her cheeks, wiping out the cold sensation that had rocked her only moments earlier. "I don't feel the need to justify any orgasm I've had with you," she said, not quite sure where her boldness was coming from. "I wanted you, and I was never ashamed of that, regardless of the emotions involved. I had never wanted a man before, and I can't think of a better reason to be with someone and wanting them the way that I wanted you. That isn't why I love you."

A cold, cruel smile quirked the side of his mouth. "Go on, then. Enumerate the reasons you find me emotionally irresistible. I can provide you with several reasons why you find me physically irresistible, as I'm not a modest man, neither am I unaware of the charms that I present to women. So if any of it has to do with my body I shall have to sadly inform you that your reasoning is neither original nor rooted in finer feelings. That is lust, my darling, and nothing more."

She recognized this. This kind of bitter banter that played at being light but was designed to cut and wound, was designed to keep the target at a distance. He had done it from the beginning, and only recently had he made an effort to connect with her in ways that went deeper than this. But he was retreating.

He was also misjudging her. Sadly for him, she did know him. More than just his body, and she saw this for exactly what it was.

She wanted to fix it. Wanted to find a way to be what he needed. To be…

She wanted so much to keep him. To have his heart and not just his body. To be the wife he didn't know he wanted.

She wanted to be perfect for him.

"You are strong," she said. "Determined. You believe in doing what's right, even if you have to do the wrong things to accomplish it. Your moral code might not be the same as what the rest of the world would call good, but you have one. And it is strong."

He laughed. "Yes. So very strong. In that I do everything within my power to establish myself as a better ruler than my father, to ensure that my place in the history books is superior to his. To create a country richer in resources and wealth, to forge better alliances with neighboring nations. If you imagine me to be altruistic, I will have to disappoint you on that score. I'm simply much less base than my father was, much smarter about how I might wield my power."

"It suits you to say that, and I can guess at why that might be. But that isn't the beginning and end of it. I know it, whether you do or not."

"You suppose that you know my motivations better than I do?"

"Yes. Because I think you're hiding from your motivations. I think you hide from a great many things, and I can't blame you. You were forced into hiding as a child because of the way that your father treated you."

He laughed, hard and flat. "Oh, no, Princess, do not make the mistake of imagining that I am some little boy trapped inside a man's body, still cowering in fear. That little boy was obliterated long ago. I did learn how to survive, and it was by hardening myself. I might not have thrown myself out the window that day, but my mother took a piece of me with her, and I gladly surrendered it. Love. I am not capable of it, not anymore. And I don't want to be. So whatever you say, whatever you feel you must force yourself to feel for me… Understand that I cannot return it. I will gladly take your body, Briar, for I am not a good man, and I'm not a soft man. All that I can give you in return is pleasure."

Once again, she found herself standing before him naked while he was clothed. Vulnerable while he seemed impenetrable. But she knew that wasn't the case. Knew that it was all an illusion. She was naked because she was strong. It takes a great amount of strength to stand before somebody without any covering, not on her body, not on her soul.

He, on the other hand, was desperately concealing all that he was. Was trying so hard to protect himself with that barrier that he had placed between them. And she could understand it in a great many ways. Sometimes she wondered if she had held herself apart from friends, from men, if she had set about to working so hard on this idea of perfection and earning her place because she was afraid of loss. Because even though she couldn't remember her life before going to live with her parents in New York, that feeling, that emptiness, lived inside her. A memory that didn't reside in her brain, but in her heart.

"I don't believe that," she said, her tone muted. "I don't believe that it's all you have inside you. Maybe it's all you feel you can give right now, but I don't think it's all we'll have forever. And I can wait. I can wait until you love me."

"I won't," he said, the words clipped, hard. "I cannot."

Her throat tightened, tears stinging her eyes. "Then I suppose I'll have to love you enough for both of us."

"You're still going to marry me?"

She nodded. "Of course I am. We didn't start here because of love. Why should it end because of a lack of it?"

It was easy to say, but she felt…devastated. A part of her destroyed that she would have said didn't exist. Because how could she hope for Felipe to love her? How had they gotten here? It still mystified her in some ways.

That she had gone from being terrified of him, from hating him, to needing him more than she needed her next breath. But he was… He was the most extraordinary man. So strong. And most definitely not loved enough.

Right then she felt a surge of anger—not at his father, but at his mother. For leaving him. How dared she? Why couldn't she have stayed for him? Shouldn't love have been enough to make her stay and protect that little boy? Or try to find a way to escape, but with him?

She would stay. No matter what he said he could give. Because she did believe that in the end he would find more for her. That they would have more. No one had stayed for him; no one had ever truly demonstrated their love for him. Well, she would be the first one. Even if it hurt.

She would be what he needed, because it was what she needed.

"Very pragmatic," he said, his tone as opaque as his expression.

"It's not, actually," she said. "It's just… Perhaps a bit blindly hopeful. But I feel like one of us needs to be, Felipe. You want your country to have beauty. You want it to be filled with the kind of light it's been missing… Well, I think one of us needs to believe in it in order for that to be accomplished, don't you?"

He reached out, gripping the back of her neck, drawing her to him, kissing her fiercely. "You're welcome to hope for that, Briar. You're welcome to believe in it. But don't be surprised when all you're met with is darkness."

She had difficulty talking to Felipe over the next few days. But at night he remained as passionate as ever. He announced the wedding to the media that very next day, and Briar's head was spinning with how quickly an elaborate event could come together when you had unlimited wealth and power.

She had a wedding dress fitted to her in record time, the design altered so that it was unique only to her. A menu had been planned, elaborate cakes conceptualized. Somehow, a massive guest list had been amassed, with RSVPs coming in fast. If anyone had something else to do, they had certainly rearranged their schedules quickly enough.

The wedding of Prince Felipe Carrión de la Viña Cortez to the long-lost Princess Talia was definitely a worldwide curiosity. The kind of event that everyone wanted to be included in.

For her part, Briar felt numb. Her parents—both sets—had been invited to the wedding and she felt strange and had trepidations about seeing both of them. Mostly because she had a feeling they would all try to talk her into calling it off. Even though everyone involved knew that was something that couldn't be afforded. Plus, at this point, she didn't want it called off.

Regardless of what he had said to her the other day, she still loved him. In fact, watching him put this wedding together, watching him contend with matters of the state, with his new position, only made her love him more.

The morning of the wedding dawned bright and clear,

the preparations being made about the palace awe-inspiring as far as Briar was concerned. But she didn't have a chance to observe the decorating process to the degree that she wanted to, because she was accosted by her stylists early in the day and subjected to a beauty regimen that left her feeling like she had run a marathon.

She was scraped, scrubbed, plucked and waxed, left so that she was glowing to an almost supernatural degree. Her hair was tamed into an elaborate up-do, some kind of powder that left her glowing brushed over her face, her lips done in a deep cherry color, her fingernails painted to match.

Large gold earrings with matching gems weighed down her ears, and a crown was placed on top of her head, heavy and unfamiliar.

The gown had a fitted bodice, the skirt voluminous, great folds of white, heavy satin fashioned into pleats, falling all the way to the ground, and trailing behind her in a dramatic train.

She had to admit, she certainly looked like a princess bride. She only hoped that she would be the bride of Felipe's dreams. She clasped her hands in front of her, twisting her fingers. Maybe she was foolish; he certainly thought that she was. To hope that this could ever be more than a bloodless transaction, necessary for him to gain the sort of reputation in the world that he coveted.

But she had to believe it. Someone had to believe in them. Believe in him. She did. And she would do it until… Until he left her no other choice.

She was supposed to marry him, after all. For better or worse. Until death did them part.

Nerves twisted low in her belly and she pressed her

palm up against herself, taking a long, slow breath out, hoping that she would find some sense of calm. Of peace.

Then the door to her bedchamber opened, and her eyes clashed with Felipe's. There was no calm to be had there. Just a sort of dark excitement that hit her all at once like a freight train. There was nothing that could prepare her for the impact, not even after weeks of being his lover.

She wondered if he would ever become common-place, this man who had the face of a fallen angel and the body of a Greek god, and a soul that had every dark thing imaginable crammed into it, until that gorgeous, mortal frame—for however perfectly he was formed, he was mortal—seemed as though it might crack from the force of it.

How could a man such as that ever be common? How could he ever fail to make her feel things? Everything.

How could she ever give up on him? It was inconceivable. Unfathomable.

"You're not supposed to see me before the wedding," she said.

He laughed, flinging himself down onto an armchair. "Because the beginning of our relationship was so auspicious and traditional you're going to concern yourself with superstition now?"

She lifted a bare shoulder. "I suppose at this point we are somewhat bulletproof."

His expression turned dark. "Nothing is. Are you prepared for this?"

"I don't know. Can anyone really prepare for something they've never done before? Lifelong commitment and all of that."

"And if you marry me," he said, his tone uncompromising, "it will be a lifelong commitment."

She couldn't quite place the thread running under-neath those words, hard and angry-sounding though they were. There was something else. But with Felipe there was always something else. There had been from the first moment she had met him. He covered it all up with that world-weary cynicism of his, with that brittle banter de-signed to make the recipient die of a thousand small cuts.

But there was more. He was just so very desperate to hide it. She wanted to uncover it. But that probably would be bad luck before their wedding. If she did that, he could well and truly crack. Spilling all the dark things out into the room. She wasn't afraid of that. She knew the day would come eventually.

She just thought that maybe…just maybe…it wouldn't happen right before they took their vows. Anyway, while she wasn't afraid of it, she had a feeling that he might be.

"I know that, Felipe. If you recall, I love you, so it isn't really going to be a great burden for me to bind myself to you for the rest of my life. Actually, when you love someone you consider that something of a goal."

He flinched when she spoke those words, as though she had struck him. "So you say," he responded.

"Did you want me to throw myself on the ground and scream about how I shan't marry you, because you're a brute and I cannot possibly fathom a future with you? It would be both embarrassing and disingenuous. Plus, I would mess up my hair."

"It would make more sense than this," he said, stand-ing, waving his arm at her standing there in her wed-ding gown. "You are far too serene. Far too accepting of your fate."

"You say fate, I say destiny."

"They end in the same place, Princess," he said, his

tone brittle. "Either way, I expected a bit more in the way of hysterics on this day of days."

"Why? Haven't I demonstrated to you over the past weeks that I'm here with you? You threw everyone out of that ballroom, Felipe. You told everyone to leave, and yet I remained. You told me about your mother, we stood together. I showed you my artwork. I gave you my body. I have continued to do so every night in the days since, and I will do it every night after. You're the only one who seems to be perturbed by the impending wedding. The one that you literally crossed the world and committed a crime to make happen."

He scowled, his dark mood rolling off him in waves. "I am not. What surprises me is your lack of emotion." He prowled across the room, stopping in front of her. "You should feel something. You should do something."

"I professed my love. It's really not my fault you don't acknowledge that as an emotion, Felipe. But there are other emotions beyond rage. Beyond grief. Beyond hatred. They are no less valid."

"Yes, you seem overjoyed."

She blinked, the corners of her lips tugging down. "I'm not sure that I am overjoyed," she said honestly. "I'm slightly afraid. Of how it will be between us. Of what might happen along the way. Of the ways in which you might hurt me. But I love you. And I've made my decision. I'm not going to pretend. I'm not going to paste a smile onto my face when my feelings are more complicated than that."

That seemed to light a match on the gasoline of his anger. "So you admit you are not thrilled to marry me. All your posturing about love and forever was simply that. Why don't you fight against it? Why don't you do something other than stand there grimly prepared to do your duty? Lying to both of us about how you feel so you can try to justify what's about to occur? Why do you have to be so damned perfect all the time?" He wrapped his arm around her waist, pulling her hard against his chest.

"I'm not," she said, her voice strangled. "I'm not. And I don't know what I have to do to show you that that isn't what this is. Stripping naked in a museum wasn't enough? Telling you about how hard I worked all that time to earn love… That wasn't enough?"

"No," he said, his voice rough, "it's not enough. You're here because you want access to your family. Because now you're afraid to leave, because you're afraid of the state you believe the nation in. You're a martyr," he said, spitting those words, "and what you do is for your own conscience. So that you can feel important. So you can feel special. And if you have to call it love in order to make yourself feel better then you will. But that's not going to insulate you against a lifetime with me, Princess."

He said those words as though they were intended to push her away, and yet he tightened his hold on her as they escaped his lips. And she was not such a fool.

She reached up, grabbing hold of his tie. "I don't need insulation. Don't you dare accuse me of being weak. Don't you dare accuse me of lying to myself, or to you, about my feelings. I spent my life trying to simply get through and make no waves. Trying to be worthy of the sacrifice my birth parents had made for me, and of the upending of the lives of my parents who raised me. You're right. I did spend my life trying to be perfect. Trying to do the right thing. The best thing. Trying to do my best to make sure nobody regretted taking me on. But that's not what I'm doing with you. I'm not afraid of you. I'm not afraid to fight against you. I'm not afraid to push you. Do not mistake me, King Felipe. When I say I am prepared to stand as your queen it is not so that I can be an accessory to you. Not so I can stand demurely at your side. I intend to make a difference. I intend to make a difference not just in this country but in your life. If I have to push you then I will do so. If I have to fight you, I will do that, too. You will never become your father, Felipe, because I will not allow it. Because I see more in you, and I see bettering you. You might not know it's there, but I do. *I do.*"

He wrapped his fingers around her wrist, pulled her arm back, prying her fingers off his tie. "Do you think my mother thought she would be crushed beneath the boot heel of my father? I highly doubt that was her goal. And yet… And *yet.*"

"I'm not your mother," she said, brushing her fingertips over his lips, satisfied when he jerked beneath the touch. "And you're not your father."

"Such confidence in me," he said, parting his lips, scraping his teeth over her fingers, leaving a slight stinging sensation behind. "For what? And why?"

"Love, Felipe. The very thing you keep dismissing as a lie. As an incidental. It's not. It's everything. It's what will keep you grounded. It's what keeps me here with you. I want to be here with you. I want to be what you need. I want to be perfect for you."

Her words echoed between them, and they made her stomach sink.

It was all so circular.

She had been consumed with being perfect for her mother and father, and then she'd come here and found a freedom in her lack of caring. But now she did care. Now she loved him. And she was back to trying to be whatever she had to be.

She could see the moment he heard it, too. The moment he realized what it meant.

"Was it love that saw my mother jumping from a window, Briar?" he asked, his voice rough. "Because that's the only love I've ever known," he said, his voice rough, harsh. "It's soft and weak. It can be used against you. Used to destroy you."

"You think you'll destroy me, Felipe? And you're angry at me for believing differently? Is that what's happening here?" Nerves ate at her as her own words began to fray. Would he destroy her? He had the power to do so now. Now that she cared.

"Why should you believe in me at all?" he asked, his tone harsh. "There is nothing good in that. Nothing good that could possibly result from it."

"What do you want? You want to drag me kicking and screaming down the aisle so that you can be thought of as a villain by your people? That isn't true, because you care about your reputation. So I can only imagine it's yourself you're playing the villain for. But I can't for the life of me figure out why."

"You're trying to figure me out as if I am a puzzle, *querida*. But you assume there are pieces for you to assemble. I am broken beyond repair. I told you already, my mother took her last leap with my heart, and there is no fixing that. But more important, I don't want it fixed."

"Stop trying to be so damned messed up all the time," she said, shooting his words back at him. "Don't commit yourself to this. You accuse me of being a martyr, but what are you, Felipe? You're determined to atone for your father's sins, but must you punish yourself for them, as well?"

"Someone has to," he said. "The old man is dead, and for all that I hope he's burning in hell, the only assurance I have that things will ever be right is what I fix in this life."

"But you can't have anything good while you work at that?"

"I can't…" He closed his mouth, a muscle working in his jaw. "I cannot afford distraction."

She knew that wasn't what he'd been about to say. That there was something else. But she also knew he wasn't going to let his guard down enough to actually speak with any honesty. There was something about this—whether it was the wedding, the sight of her, or the declaration of love—that unnerved him. That…that scared him. And no matter how deep he might deny it, she could see it.

If she could just make him see. She needed him to see. She had to make him understand that she could be what he needed. That she could fix this. That…

It hit her again, what was happening now.

She had convinced herself that if she behaved in a certain way she could earn his love. Could make him see that she wasn't a burden. That she was everything he needed. That in the end, he would be happier for having her in his life, if she would only just…find the perfect way to be.

She couldn't step back into that. She couldn't do that to herself. Mostly, she could not be the woman he needed her to be if she did. He was so afraid of breaking her. And if she didn't learn how to stand on her own, he might, and it wouldn't even be his fault. She couldn't force him to change. No amount of smiling prettily and inviting him into her bed could do that. He was going to have to love her.

She was going to have to demand that. Not sit around and wait for it.

She was going to have to make waves. There was no other option. She was going to have to take a risk that in the end she wouldn't be worth it. It was the one thing she had always feared most. That ultimately, she would be far too much of an inconvenience for her parents if she stepped out of line. That everyone would find her to be too much trouble to care about. Unless she acted just so. Unless she contributed just enough.

She had stopped. She had to stop or it would go on forever. And it could not.

She took a deep breath and looked up at him, trembling from the inside out. "I love you, Felipe," she said, the words steady.

"So you have said."

"Do you love me?"

"I already gave you my answer."

"I know. But I have to ask again. Because I have to be absolutely certain."

"I cannot," he said, his voice rough. "It is not in me."

She nodded slowly. "I understand. And I need you to understand this. I can't marry you. Not without your love."

"Oh, so suddenly now you require love. Before you said this was never about love, and it wouldn't change."

"Well... I changed."

"What do you want from me? You want me to lie to you, say the words and they will somehow have the magic power to force you to walk down the aisle?"

Her throat started to close up, her hands shaking, misery threatening to overwhelm her. She wanted—with almost everything she had, everything she was—to throw herself on the ground in front of him and tell him she didn't mean it. That she would marry him no matter what. That she would stay with him forever and just hope that everything worked out okay.

And she would grow dimmer and dimmer. And he would consume her. In the end, it would sign both of their death warrants. For their happiness, at least.

"No," she said, forcing the word through her tightened throat. "I would know. If you turned around and said it to me now I would know that you didn't mean it."

"And so you have forced me into an impossible situation."

"You forced us into an impossible situation, Felipe. Because you are not the monster that you seem to think you are, not the monster that you wish you were. You kidnapped me, you dragged me here. And if you had been truly awful it would have been easy for me to resist you. But the fact is you aren't. You're simply broken. And whatever you say, you're more that little boy who lost his mother all those years ago than you are a dragon. But I can't fix it for you. I've tried. And I will break myself in the process. You're right. I can't martyr myself to this cause. You asked me to reconsider. That's what you came here for. To push me away. To make it so that I would leave." She blinked hard, tears threatening to fall. But she wouldn't let them. "Congratulations. You've won."

"There is an entire room full of guests waiting for us to say our vows, Princess. You would disappoint them?"

"I would disappoint them now rather than devastate myself later. It has to be done. I have to go. And if, when I am gone you are able to look inside yourself and find that heart you seem to think doesn't exist... Then you can come and find me."

"And if you leave," he said, his lip curling up into a sneer, "you know that I will make things very difficult for your mother and father."

She nodded slowly; this time a tear did track down her cheek. "I know."

"And you will have failed everyone," he said, the words hard, cruel. "You will have failed me, you will have failed Santa Milagro, you will have failed your adoptive parents, the king and queen, and Verloren herself. Is that what you want?"

She shook her head. "No. It isn't what I want. It's the last thing I want. But sadly, I could never be Princess Talia. I could never be the person I was born to be. I've only ever been able to be Briar Harcourt. She doesn't want any of those things. But she does want to be loved. And at the end of the day, I think she deserves it." She shook her head, battling with the ridiculousness of speaking about herself in the third person. But it was so hard to say what she knew she needed to say. "I deserve to be loved. I deserve it. I don't need to earn it. I shouldn't have to. Someday, Felipe, I'm going to find a man who wants me. One who didn't track me down to the ends of the earth simply because I presented a political advantage to him. But a man who would track me down to the end of the world if I could offer him nothing but a kiss. If I came with no title. If I was only me. I have...I have never been able to say that I thought I deserved such a thing. That I've possessed enough value to be worthy of it. But now I do."

She looked down at the ring, sparkling on her finger. A ring that represented a promise that would now not be fulfilled. She slipped it off, held it out to him. "I suppose I'm the monster now," she said softly, dropping the gem into his open palm. "But I'm a monster that you created. You made me more myself than I have ever been. But I fear that if I stay here it won't last. It will only fade away as I try everything in my power to please you, to make you love me the way that I love you. We both deserve more than that. Because it will only be a self-fulfilling prophecy, don't you see? I will begin to feel I don't deserve love, as I cannot earn it. And you will become the monster you were always afraid you were while you break me slowly into tiny pieces. I won't do that to you. I won't do it to me."

She stood, and she waited. Because whatever she had said if he was to fling himself at her feet, if he was to grab her and pull her into his arms and confess his undying love, she would surely stay. Even if it was a lie. It would take nothing. A half a beat of his heart, a flutter of his eyelash, an upward curve to his lip. Just a sign. A small one, and she would crumble completely, all her good intentions reduced to ash.

"Get out," he said, his voice hard.

"What?"

"You heard me. Get out of my sight. Get out of my palace." He cocked his arm back, threw her ring across the room with a ferocity that shocked her. It was a gem of near inestimable value and he had cast it aside as though it was garbage.

Still, she didn't obey him. She simply stood, shocked, unable to move.

"Get out!" He shouted now then turned to the side and grabbed hold of her vanity, tipping it over onto its face, the glass shattering from the mirror, small bottles of perfume smashing on the tile and sending heavy, drugging scents into the air.

She jumped backward, pressing her palm against her chest, her heart fluttering in her breasts. But still she felt rooted to the spot.

He advanced on her, radiating fury, his eyes a black flame. "Do you think I'm joking? Do you think I am anything less than the product of my father's genetics and upbringing? Do you think I am anything less than a monster? Get out of my sight. Pray that I never see you again, Princess, because if I do I cannot promise you I will not make you my prisoner again. But this time, it will be far less pleasurable for you, I can assure you."

"Felipe…"

He reached out, gripping her chin, the hold hard and nearly painful. "I do not love you. I do not possess the capacity. But oh, how I can hate. You do not want to test the limits of that."

He turned and walked away from her then, and perversely she missed his touch. Even though it had hurt. Because this was worse. This total separation from him. This finality. It was for the best, and she knew it. By doing this she had revealed his true colors. Had uncovered the truth as it was in his heart. If he could not love her to keep her with him, then he never would.

"You had best not be here when I return," he said finally before he walked out the double doors to her room, closing them behind him with a finality that reverberated through her entire frame.

She looked around the room, panic clawing at her. She didn't know what to do, didn't know where to go.

She took a breath and tried to keep calm. She had just done what needed to be done. But she felt terrible. She didn't feel better at all, and she had a feeling it would be a long time before she did. She waited a few moments. Waited until she was certain Felipe wouldn't be standing out there in the hall.

And then she flung the doors open, picked up the front of her dress and ran through the empty corridor. She ran until her lungs burned. Until she reached the front of the palace, going straight out the doors and across the courtyard. There were steps that led up to an exit point that she knew would be less watched, and she tried to scramble up them, taking them two at a time. And then she slipped and fell, her knees hitting the edge of the stones, her dress trailing behind her. She just lay there for a moment, feeling like this was a perfectly fitting moment for how she felt inside.

But then she pushed up, getting back to her feet. Because there was nothing else to be done. She had made the decision. And there was no going back. She had decided that she was worthy of love. No matter what she submitted herself to, or refused to submit herself to. She should be more than payment for her father's debt.

She should be more than Felipe's humanizing face that was presented to the people. More than a perfect daughter.

She was Briar. No matter who she had been born as. That was who she had become. And she needed to keep on becoming that. Because it was ongoing. Because she wasn't finished. And if she stayed here and allowed her desire to please him to become all that she was...

She couldn't. No matter how badly it hurt to leave. She would only hurt them both if she stayed.

CHAPTER TWELVE

FELIPE HAD CERTAINLY created headlines on his wedding day, but they were not the headlines he had hoped they might be. No, rather than photographs of the happy couple, the news media was filled with photographs of him storming into the chapel and demanding everybody leave. A repeat of the night his father had passed away, and proof that he was no more stable than the previous ruler, at least, so said a great many of the papers.

His lungs were burning as he walked up the stairs to the tower. He didn't know why he was going to the tower. One of the things his father had done early on—shortly after his mother had killed herself—was drag Felipe back up to the tower. He had demanded that he stand there. Demanded that he look out the window and see that there was no longer anything there.

"There is nothing," his father had said. "No ghosts. No bodies. She is gone. And she isn't coming back. This place holds no power. Emotion has no place here. And it certainly shouldn't sway you as a ruler."

Felipe laughed cynically as he remembered that. Of course his father would say that emotion had no power. But he didn't mean anger. He didn't mean rage.

It struck him then, with clarity—a disturbing clarity—that he held a similar worldview. That love didn't count. That happiness was something that could easily be destroyed. Those were the emotions he had banished from himself. All while retaining the kind of toxicity his father had carried around with him.

He walked across the room, making his way over to the window. He wrapped his fingers around the bars. Briar had left him, and it was for the best that she had done so by going out the front door and not flinging herself from a tower.

He also despised that she had taken his words and thrown them back at him. That she had done exactly what he had been trying to get her to do. He had wanted her to leave, in the end. But he had thought that…

Perversely, he had hoped that in the end that love, that he felt was such a folly, that he considered a weakness, would prove to be the thing that was strong enough to hold her to him. It was wrong, particularly when his aim had been to get her to call the wedding off, and yet, part of him had hoped.

He had goaded her. He had pushed her. And in the end she had made the right decision; he knew it because he didn't possess the kind of softness in him that she deserved. He knew only how to break things. How to break people.

Pushing his hand through the bars, he rested his palm on the window. "I am sorry, Mama. I truly am." And then he pounded his fist against the glass, watching it crack, splinters embedding in his skin. He relished that pain. As he had done earlier. As he had done for a great many years. Punishing himself because his father was no longer able to do it.

And, oh, how he loved to break things. Because the old man wanted order. And Felipe wanted to defy that.

And then you straighten your shirtsleeves like a naughty boy.

He pounded his forehead with his bleeding fist then lowered his hand slowly, his heart threatening to rage right out of his chest.

For the first time he wondered if he was not like his father. He wondered if he was merely controlled by him. If he had allowed the old man to gain access to him. No. He was going to make his country better. He was going to atone.

And yet you let him steal your ability to love, with all that fear he gave you. You let him cost you Briar.

He gritted his teeth. No, letting Briar go had been a kindness. Because as she had said to him it would only damage them both in the end if the two of them were to be together.

He thought of her, of everything she had told him about the way she had grown up. So afraid that she would be found unworthy. So desperate to prove her value.

All she had to do for him was simply breathe.

The thought of her… Well, it created a pain in his chest that was so severe it blotted out the pain in his hand.

What was it? All of this pain. He wasn't supposed to be able to feel anything. He had made sure. He had promised himself.

He curled his fingers around the window bars again.

He had promised her.

He hadn't been brave enough to follow her. And so he had done what he thought was best. He had sent the most vital part of himself with her. Had consigned it to the grave. Because he had failed her. In the end, it had been his fault.

He clutched his chest, unable to breathe. His heart. His *heart*. Of course, he knew that his heart was there physically. It was the metaphorical heart he had long since surrendered. But if so then why did it hurt so badly now? Why did it feel as though he was going to suffer cardiac arrest because he didn't have Briar with him? Why did standing here in this room, the room where he had witnessed his mother's death, feel like he was submerged under water and he couldn't breathe? Like his chest was going to explode. If you didn't have a heart…then why the hell was it breaking?

Why was he standing here imagining days filled with darkness? Days without her soft hands touching his skin. Without her looking at him as though he was a person of value. Without her telling him that he mattered? Why was he imagining those things and not the loss of all his political alliances? Because that was all she should mean. It was all she should have ever meant. He should be mounting an attack. Plotting revenge against her for taking herself away from him and ruining his plans. He did not allow such things. He never had.

But the problem was, she was already perfect for him. She didn't even have to try. And without her…without her he was nothing.

He reached into his pocket and pulled out his phone, and without thinking, he dialed Adam's number. Felipe was not the kind of man who depended on the kindness of friends or strangers. Indeed, he had done his very best to never need anyone's kindness. Mostly because he had grown up with none, and had never assumed it would be there when he needed it.

But he needed something now. And he didn't know where else to turn.

"Adam," he said.

"I'm surprised it took you this long to call. Considering your wedding was just dramatically called off."

"Yes. Well. I didn't think I needed anything to deal with that. She's gone. What's done is done. There's nothing I can do to fight that. Nor do I want to. At least, I didn't think so."

"I see. It turns out you're not so happy to have lost your fiancée?"

Felipe felt like he'd been stabbed in the chest. "No. And I'm not thinking about the political ramifications. All I can think of is her. She is… She is impractical for me in every way. She's young. She was innocent." His body warmed just thinking of how far she had come in the past weeks. "She is soft and giving. She is everything I'm not. I shouldn't miss her. I shouldn't want her. And yet…"

"I could have told you that it is a grave mistake to take beautiful young women captive," Adam said, his tone dry. "I have a bit of experience with that."

"You were also the most humorless, angry man I had ever met before Belle came into your life. How did you change? I need to know. I need to know if it's possible."

Adam hesitated for a moment. "I was content to go through my life feeling nothing," he said finally. "The loss of my first wife was more than I could bear. At least, I thought so. I thought I had been damaged beyond the capacity for feeling. I wanted to be. But Belle came softly, and because of that I did not know I needed to arm myself against her. I was so certain that as her captor I held the upper hand. Ultimately, she was the one who captured me. Her love changed me. And the fact that I had to become something different to be worthy of it. It does not just happen as you sit idly by, Felipe. You must choose it. You must choose love instead of darkness. Because that's the only way that it can win in the end. But once you do… Light wins every time. It swallows the darkness whole."

"Perhaps your brand of darkness, Adam. I fear mine might have the power to absorb the sun."

"If that is how you choose to see it, if that is the power you choose to give it, then I believe it. Light and dark exist in the world, Felipe. Good and evil. Love and hate. We must all choose, I suppose, which of those things we give the most power. Which of those things get to carry the most weight. In the end, I chose love. Because anything else was to submit to the unthinkable. A life without Belle. If you can imagine life without Briar, then I suppose you don't need to change at all. But if this present darkness that you're in feels too suffocating, too consuming… Turn on the light, my friend."

"Talia." Queen Amaani walked into the room. It could be no one else. After a week in Verloren she could recognize the other woman by the sound of her footsteps. There was something about the way she glided over the tile, even in heels. She was like an ethereal being.

And Briar looked like her. She was her daughter; there was no denying it.

She was also the daughter of Dr. Robert and Nell Harcourt from New York, who had raised her and loved her and done their best to protect her from a threat they'd had no power against.

Living at the palace in Santa Milagro, then coming

here, truly underscored that fact. How much power the players in this game possessed, that Dr. Harcourt and his wife did not. It was strange, though. That realization didn't make her feel more indebted.

It made her feel…

Well, she felt as if it was the proof of love she'd always been looking for.

It had always been there. She'd just put so many of her own fears up in front of it.

She turned to face the queen, her heart pounding hard. "Briar," she said. "Call me Briar, please?"

The other woman's beautiful face looked shocked, but only for a moment. Then she smoothed it into rather serene calm. "If that's what you prefer, of course."

Briar smiled, knowing the smile looked as sad as she felt inside. "It's more…I've been thinking a lot. About who I am. And what I want. I'm so happy that I've been able get to know you and…and I'm sorry—" her throat tightened up "—I'm sorry that we couldn't have known each other better. I'm sorry that it…is this way. But I was blessed to have a wonderful upbringing with the people you chose to care for me. And…I became the woman they raised me to be. I wanted to be Talia for you. I wanted to please you. But I need to be Briar."

Felipe had always seen her as Briar. Always. Even when she'd told her mother and father to call her Talia, he had known.

He had known long before she had.

Funny how that wretched man could be so insightful about her behavior, and have such a huge blank when it came to his own.

Then the queen did something unexpected. She knelt down in front of Briar, her hands on Briar's lap, her face full of sadness. "I know. And it is… The reason we chose the Harcourts was because we had known them for years. Because we trusted them. Because we knew that they would help you grow into the woman you were meant to be. I'm sorry we failed you. I'm sorry you suffered at the hands of that madman…"

"He's not a madman," she said, surprised by her own vehemence. "He's…lost. And he's hurt. But he's…" Tears filled her eyes. "I love him. And I would be with him still except…it couldn't be like it was. With him convinced he had forced my hand. With me trying to earn his love. It has to be different. If he comes for me again, it has to be because he wants me. Not because he wants a wife he thinks will make him look good. And I need to go with him because I love him. Not because he kidnapped me from a hospital."

The queen's eyebrows shot up. "From a hospital?"

Briar sighed. "It's a long story."

The queen rose to her feet and sat in the chair next to Briar. Then she snapped her elegant fingers. A servant appeared. "Tea," she said. Then she turned her focus back to Briar. "I have time for long stories. The two of us have much catching up to do, Briar."

CHAPTER THIRTEEN

FELIPE HAD NEVER imagined coming to Verloren. Especially not without armed guards. Or an entire battalion. Not considering the relations between the two countries. It was one of the many reasons he had wanted Briar in the first place. She was a convenient human shield. One that forced the nations to be friendly.

But he was coming now as an enemy, with no defenses. With nothing. Nothing except a whole lot of darkness inside him that he wanted so desperately to shine a light on.

Briar's light.

Whether he deserved it or not, that was what he was here for.

He didn't expect a hero's welcome, but he didn't expect to be put in chains the moment he showed up at the palace, either. And yet he was. He also allowed it, because the last thing he could afford was the kind of scandal that would erupt if he committed an act of violence in a foreign palace.

And he also couldn't afford to do anything that Briar might disapprove of.

Especially not with her father, the king, looking on as he was led into the palace throne room.

"King Felipe," he said. "It is a surprise to see you. You will forgive the precautions. But last time you were around a member of my family without chains, you took her against her will."

He did not bother to correct the king by saying that last time he had been around the man's daughter he'd been the one to tell her not to return. And that before that she'd been in his arms—in his bed—willingly.

Felipe didn't want to die. Not today.

Perhaps after he met with Briar, perhaps if she rejected him. But not before he had the chance to try.

"I welcomed you to my palace without chains," Felipe pointed out.

"I was also invited. What is your business here?"

"I'm here to see the princess."

"You're here to claim a debt that isn't yours to claim, and was never meant to extend to my daughter," the older man said, standing. "I refuse. Even if it means war. I should have done that years ago."

"I am not here to claim her, as a payment or otherwise. I am here to speak to her. I'm here to tell her…"

"Here to tell me what?"

He looked toward the doors that led in deeper to the palace and saw Briar standing there. It was strange to see her dressed so casually. Wearing just dark jeans and a gray T-shirt, her hair loose and curly, her face void of makeup.

Strange, and yet she was even more beautiful to him now than she had been in the most beautiful of ball gowns. Because this wasn't a memory. This was now. She was here standing before him, and he had made a decision.

That made her the most beautiful she'd ever been to

him. It made this the most beautiful moment, in a world that had—to this point—been mostly darkness and pain for him.

"I am in chains," he said, lifting his wrists to show her.

"Oh, well…good. Now you'll have an idea of what it's like to be held against your will." She crossed her arms, cocking her hip to the side, her expression serene.

"Is there a chance, as I am in chains, I might speak to you alone? I can't do anything in this state, after all."

Her father's expression turned sharp. "Absolutely not."

Briar held up her hand. "Yes. I need to speak with him. I need to hear what he has to say."

The old king paused then looked at his guards. "Let us go. Briar, if you have need of us, you know what to do."

She nodded. "Thank you."

Once the king and his henchmen had exited the room, Felipe turned his focus back to Briar. "He called you Briar."

"Yes. I'm not Talia. I…explained that to them yesterday. I need to be…me. And that's Briar. Briar Harcourt. It doesn't mean I can't visit here. And I would like to get to know them. But…I'm me."

He knew what it meant. She didn't have to explain. Because he knew her. He could honestly say he had never known anyone else quite as well. And certainly no one had known him.

"Briar." He just wanted to say her name. Wanted to watch her respond to him. To his words. To his voice. Wanted to confirm that she wasn't neutral to him. No. No, she was not. It took three steps for him to close the space between them and when he did, he looped his arms around her, trapping her in the chain, pulling her up against him.

"I'm not here to steal you," he said, leaning in, pressing his lips to hers. "But I am here for you."

"You said…" Her voice wobbled.

"That I would not claim you. Not for revenge. Not for payment. But I want you." He drew her even closer, wrapping the chain around his wrists to make it so she couldn't pull away. "I *need* you."

"Why do I feel like you're trying to take me captive again?" she whispered, her dark eyes glittering.

"Impossible," he said. "I'm the one in chains. I suspect I have been for a very long time. But it took the desire to be free for me to truly recognize my limitations. When I wished so much I could hold you, but knew I could not because it would only harm us both. Because…because if I am in chains then holding you means having you in them, as well, and you were right. It would have only destroyed us both. That has long been my fear. That I destroy, rather than build. That I am my father's son, and I can only break things, even the things I love."

"And you're holding me in chains now," she pointed out.

"Yes, but this is literal, because I want you against me. Touching me. The other was metaphorical."

"I see," she said, the side of her mouth quirking upward. "But none of it matters if you haven't found the key."

"To my chains? Oh, I have. The metaphorical chains. Not these. Your father will have to release me from these."

She lifted her hands, taking hold of his face. "Unless you're going to tell me how you found the key, you can shut up."

He took that opportunity to wrap the chains yet another time around his wrist, hauling her closer as he dipped his head and claimed her mouth with his. When they parted, they were both breathing hard.

"You," he ground out. "You're the key, Briar. To all of this. To me."

"I am?"

"Yes," he said. "You. Not as a princess, but as a woman. You made me see...you made me see for the first time in years. You shone a light on my darkness. And even more than allowing me to see, you saw me. You saw me and you wouldn't allow me to hide."

"You saw me," she said, the words husky. "You made me stronger. You made me fight."

"It was in you all along," he said. "That fight. You just had to come up against a dragon to find it."

She smiled. "I like that."

"And I love you." The words scraped his throat raw. He couldn't remember if he'd ever spoken them before. He didn't think he had. "All my childhood I'd been too bound up in fear and abuse to...to feel much of anything. I dismissed it. I dismissed it as something that didn't matter because I didn't truly understand. I didn't know what it meant to love someone, or to have them love you. I didn't understand the power of it. I thought...I thought that perhaps my mother's death was something I could have fixed. If I had done more. If I had been better."

"No," she said, pressing her fingertips to his lips. "No. You were a little boy, Felipe. Of course you couldn't have stopped it."

"It felt like it was me," he said, his voice strained. "That I was the one who broke her."

"No, Felipe. It was him."

"I know. I know now. There was only ever one person who could have stopped the hell we lived in, and that was my father. And that small thing. That thing he taught me meant nothing...love. It would have healed so much, Briar. If he would have had it for me, for my mother. For anyone but himself. Love is not a negligible thing. I have come to believe that it is the only thing."

"I love you, Felipe." She smiled at him. And it was like the sun had risen after the darkest night, shining a light in the hidden corners of his soul.

He kissed her again, and he felt something lift away from him. A weight, a darkness that had rested upon him for longer than he could remember. He had tried to banish it with anger, with hate. With vengeance. But nothing had taken it from him. Until this. Until her love.

Love was stronger.

That was how the princess slew the dragon. Not with a sword. Not with a magic spell.

But with love.

And they lived happily ever after...

* * * * *

If you enjoyed
THE PRINCE'S STOLEN VIRGIN
by Maisey Yates
make sure you read the first part of her trilogy
ONCE UPON A SEDUCTION…
THE PRINCE'S CAPTIVE VIRGIN
Available now!

And keep an eye out for the final installment,
Rafe and Charlotte's story
Coming October 2017!

In the meantime why not explore another
trilogy by Maisey Yates?
HEIRS BEFORE VOWS
THE SPANIARD'S PREGNANT BRIDE
THE PRINCE'S PREGNANT MISTRESS
THE ITALIAN'S PREGNANT VIRGIN
Available now!

Santiago's voice was low, controlled, but Belle felt his cold fury. He was all gorgeous on the outside, she thought. Too bad his soul was even harder than his body.

"You made your choice," she whispered. "You abandoned us. This baby is mine now. Mine alone."

He lifted a dark eyebrow. "That's not how paternity works."

"It is if I say it is."

"Then why tell me you're pregnant at all?"

"Because three days ago I was foolish enough to hope you could change. Now I know it would be better for my baby to have no father at all than a man like you." She lifted her chin. "Now, get off my land."

Growing dangerously still, Santiago stared at her, jaw tight.

"Let me tell you what's going to happen, Belle." As he looked at her his voice was low and deep, almost a purr. "You're going to marry me."

Was he crazy or was she?

"Marry you?" Belle gasped. "Are you out of your mind? I hate you!"

"I'll admit I made a mistake, trusting you. I should have known better. I should have known your innocence was a lie. I shall pay for that…" He moved closer, with a gleam in his dark eyes. "But so will you."

Secret Heirs of Billionaires

There are some things money can't buy…

Living life at lightning pace, these magnates are no strangers to stakes at their highest. It seems they've got it all… That is until they find out that there's an unplanned item to add to their list of accomplishments!

Achieved:

1. Successful business empire

2. Beautiful women in their bed

3. *An heir to bear their name?*

Though every billionaire needs to leave his legacy in safe hands, discovering a secret heir shakes up his carefully orchestrated plan in more ways than one!

Uncover their secrets in:

Look out for more stories in the
Secret Heirs of Billionaires series, coming soon!

CARRYING THE
SPANIARD'S CHILD

BY
JENNIE LUCAS

All rights reserved including the right of reproduction in whole
or in part in any form. This edition is published by arrangement with
Harlequin Books S.A.

This is a work of fiction. Names, characters, places, locations and
incidents are purely fictional and bear no relationship to any real
life individuals, living or dead, or to any actual places, business
establishments, locations, events or incidents. Any resemblance is
entirely coincidental.

This book is sold subject to the condition that it shall not, by way of
trade or otherwise, be lent, resold, hired out or otherwise circulated
without the prior consent of the publisher in any form of binding or
cover other than that in which it is published and without a similar
condition including this condition being imposed on the subsequent
purchaser.

® and TM are trademarks owned and used by the trademark owner
and/or its licensee. Trademarks marked with ® are registered with the
United Kingdom Patent Office and/or the Office for Harmonisation in
the Internal Market and in other countries.

First Published in Great Britain 2017
By Mills & Boon, an imprint of HarperCollins*Publishers*
1 London Bridge Street, London, SE1 9GF

© 2017 Jennie Lucas

ISBN: 978-0-263-92531-9

Our policy is to use papers that are natural, renewable and recyclable
products and made from wood grown in sustainable forests. The logging
and manufacturing processes conform to the legal environmental
regulations of the country of origin.

Printed and bound in Spain
by CPI, Barcelona

USA TODAY bestselling author **Jennie Lucas**'s parents owned a bookstore and she grew up surrounded by books, dreaming about faraway lands. A fourth-generation Westerner, she went east at sixteen to boarding school on scholarship, wandered the world, got married, then finally worked her way through college before happily returning to her hometown. A 2010 RITA® Award finalist and 2005 Golden Heart® Award winner, she lives in Idaho with her husband and children.

Visit the Author Profile page
at millsandboon.co.uk for more titles.

To my husband, my own fairy-tale hero.

CHAPTER ONE

BELLE LANGTRY HAD hated Santiago Velazquez from the moment she'd laid eyes on him.

Well, not the *exact* moment, of course. She was only human. When they'd first met at their friends' wedding last September—Belle had been the maid of honor, Santiago the best man—she'd been dazzled by his dark gorgeousness, his height, his broad shoulders and muscular body. She'd looked up at his dark soulful eyes and thought, *Wow. Dreams really do come true.*

Then Santiago had turned to the groom and suggested out loud that Darius could still "make a run for it" and abandon his bride at the altar. And he'd said it right in front of Letty!

The bride and groom had awkwardly laughed it off, but from that moment, Belle had hated Santiago with a passion. Every word he said was more cynical and infuriating than the last. Within ten minutes, the two of them were arguing; by the end of the wedding, Belle wished he would do the world a favor and die. Being the forthright woman she was, she couldn't resist telling him so. He'd responded with sarcasm. And that had been their relationship for the last four months.

So of course, Belle thought bitterly, he would be the one to find her now, pacing the dark, snowy garden behind Letty and Darius's coastal estate. Crying.

Shivering in her thin black dress, she'd been looking

toward the wild Atlantic Ocean in the darkness. The rhythmic roar of the waves matched the thrumming of her heart.

All day, Belle had held her friend's adorable newborn as Letty wept through her father's funeral. By the end of the evening reception, the pain in Belle's heart as she held the sweetly sleeping baby had overwhelmed her. Gently giving the baby back to Letty, she'd mumbled an excuse and fled into the dark snow-covered garden.

Outside, an icy wind blew, freezing the tears against Belle's chapped skin as she stared out into the darkness, heartsick with grief.

She would never have a child of her own.

Never, the ocean sighed back to her. *Never, never.*

"Belle?" a rough voice called. "Are you out here?"

Santiago! She sucked in her breath. The last man she'd ever want to see her like this!

She could only imagine the arrogant sneer on the Spaniard's face if he found her crying over her inability to have a child. Ducking behind a frost-covered tree, she held her breath, praying he wouldn't see her.

"Belle, stop trying to hide," he said, sounding amused. "Your dress is black, and you're standing in the snow."

Gritting her teeth, she stepped out from behind the tree and lied, "I wasn't hiding."

"What are you doing out here, then?"

"I just needed some fresh air," she said desperately, wishing he'd leave her alone.

A beam of light from a second-floor window of the manor house illuminated the hard lines of Santiago's powerful body in the black suit and well-cut cashmere coat. As their eyes met, electricity coursed through her.

Santiago Velazquez was too handsome, she thought with an unwilling shiver. Too sexy. Too powerful. Too rich.

He was also a selfish, cynical playboy, whose only loyalty was to his own vast fortune. He probably had vaults big enough to swim in, she thought, and pictured him doing a backstroke through hundred-dollar bills. In the meantime he mocked the idea of kindness and respect. She'd heard he treated his one-night stands like unpaid employees. Belle's expression hardened. Folding her arms, she waited as he strode through the snow toward her.

He stopped a few feet away. "You don't have a coat."

"I'm not cold."

"I can hear your teeth chattering. Are you trying to freeze to death?"

"Why do you care?"

"Me? I don't," he said mildly. "If you want to freeze to death, it's fine with me. But it does seem selfish to force Letty to plan yet another funeral. So tedious, funerals. And weddings. And christenings. All of it."

"Any human interaction that involves emotion must be tedious to you," Belle said.

He was nearly a foot taller than her own petite height. His shoulders were broad and he wore arrogance like a cloak that shadowed him in the snow. She'd heard women call him Ángel, and she could well understand the nickname. He had a face like an angel—a dark angel, she thought irritably, if heaven needed a bouncer to keep lesser people out and boss everyone around. Santiago might be rich and handsome but he was also the most cynical, callous, despicable man on earth. He was everything she hated most.

"Wait." His black eyes narrowed as he stared down at her in the faint crystalline moonlight frosting the clouds. "Are you crying, Belle?"

She blinked hard and fast to hide the evidence. "No."

"You are." His cruel, sensual lips curved mockingly. "I know you have a pathetically soft heart, but this is pushing the limits even for you. You barely knew Letty's father, and yet here I find you mourning him after the funeral, alone in the snow like a tragic Victorian madwoman."

Normally that would have gotten a rise out of her. But not today. Belle's heart was too sad. And she knew if she showed the slightest emotion he'd only mock her more. Wishing desperately that Santiago hadn't been the one to find her, she said, "What do you want?"

"Darius and Letty have gone to bed. Letty wanted to come out and look for you but the baby needed her. I'm supposed to show you to your guest room and turn on the house alarm once you're brought in safe and sound."

His husky, Spanish-accented voice seemed to be laughing at her. She hated how, even disliking him as much as she did, he made her body shiver with awareness.

"I changed my mind about staying here tonight." The last thing she wanted was to spend the night tossing and turning in a guest room, with no company but her own agonizing thoughts. "I just want to go home."

"To Brooklyn?" Santiago looked at her incredulously. "It's too late. Everyone wanting to get back to the city left hours ago. The ice storm just closed the expressway. It might not reopen for hours."

"Why are you even still here? Don't you have a helicopter and a couple of planes? It can't be because you actually care about Letty and Darius."

"The guest rooms here are nice and I'm tired. Two days ago I was in Sydney. Before that, Tokyo." He yawned. "Tomorrow I leave for London."

"Poor you," said Belle, who had always dreamed of traveling but never managed to save the money, even for an economy ticket.

His sensual lips curved upward. "I appreciate your sympathy. So if you don't mind wrapping up your self-indulgent little *Wuthering Heights* routine I'd like to show you to your room so I can go to mine."

"If you want to go, go." She turned away so he couldn't see her exhausted, tearstained expression. "Tell Letty I'd already left. I'll get a train back to the city."

"Are you serious?" He looked down at her skeptically. "How will you reach the station? I doubt trains are even running—"

"Then I'll walk!" Her voice was suddenly shrill. "I'm not sleeping here!"

Santiago paused.

"Belle," he said, in a voice more gentle than she'd ever heard from him before. "What's wrong?"

Reaching out, he put his hand on her shoulder, then lifted it to her cheek. It was the first time he had ever touched her, and even in the dark and cold the touch of his hand spun through her like a fire. Her lips parted.

"If something was wrong, why would I tell you?"

His smile increased. "Because you hate me."

"And?"

"So whatever it is, you can tell me. Because you don't give a damn what I think."

"True," she said wryly. It was tempting. She pressed her lips together. "But you might tell the world."

"Do I ever share secrets?"

"No," she was forced to admit. "But you do say mean and insulting things. You are heartless and rude and…"

"Only to people's faces. Never behind their backs." His voice was low. "Tell me, Belle."

Clouds covered the moon, and they were briefly flooded in darkness. She suddenly was desperate to share her grief with someone, anyone. And it was true she couldn't have a lower opinion of him. He probably couldn't think less of her, either.

That thought was oddly comforting. She didn't have to pretend with Santiago. She didn't have to be positive and hopeful at all times, the cheerleader who tried to please everyone, no matter what. Belle had learned at a young age never to let any negative feelings show. If you were honest about your feelings, it only made people dislike you. It only made people leave, even and especially the ones you loved.

So Santiago was the only one she *could* tell. The only one she could be truly herself with. Because, heck, if he permanently left her life, she'd throw a party.

She took a deep breath. "It's the baby."

"Little Howie?"

"Yes."

"I had a hard time with him, too. Babies." He rolled his eyes. "All those diapers, all that crying. But what can you do? Some people still seem to want them."

"I do." The moon broke through the clouds, and Belle looked up at him with tears shimmering in the moonlight. "I want a baby."

He stared down at her, then snorted. "Of course you do. Romantic idiot like you. You want love, flowers, the whole package." He shrugged. "So why cry over it? If you are foolish enough to want a family, go get one. Settle down, buy a house, get married. No one is stopping you."

"I…I can't get pregnant," she whispered. "Ever. It's impossible."

"How do you know?"

"Because…" Belle looked down at the tracks in the snow. The moonlight caused strange shadows, mingling her footsteps and his. "I just know. It's medically impossible."

She braced herself for his inevitable questions. Medically impossible how? What happened? When and why?

But he surprised her.

Reaching out, he just pulled her into his arms, beneath his black cashmere coat. She felt the sudden comfort of his warmth, his strength, as he caressed her long dark hair. "Everything will be all right."

She looked up at him, her heart in her throat. She was aware of the heat of his body against hers.

"You must think I'm a horrible person," she said, pulling away. "A horrible friend for envying Letty, when she just lost her father. I spent all day holding her sweet baby and envying her. I'm the worst friend in the world."

"Stop." Cupping her face, he looked down at her fiercely. "You know I think you're a fool…existing in a pink cloud of candy-coated dreams. Someday you will lose those rose-colored glasses and learn the truth about the heartless world…"

She whispered brokenly. "I—"

He put his finger on her lips. "But even I can see you're a good friend."

His finger felt warm against her tingling lips. She had the sudden shocking desire to kiss it, to wrap her lips around his finger and suck it gently. She'd never had such a shocking thought before—she, an inexperienced virgin! But as little as she liked him, something about the wickedly sexy Spaniard attracted —and scared—her.

Trembling, she twisted her head away. She remembered all those women he'd famously seduced, those women she'd scorned as fools for being willing notches on his bedpost. And for the first time, she sympathized with them, as she herself fully felt the potent force of his charm.

"You're lucky, actually." Santiago gave her a crooked half grin. "Babies? Marriage? Who would want to be stuck with such a thankless responsibility as a family?" He shook his head. "No good would have come of it. It's a prison sentence. Now you can have something better."

She stared at him. "Better than a family?"

He nodded.

"Freedom," he said quietly.

"But I don't want freedom." Her voice was small. "I want to be loved."

"We all want things we can't have," he said roughly.

"How would you know? You've never wanted anything, not without taking it."

"You're wrong. There has been something I've wanted. For four months. Someone. But I can't have her."

Four months. Suddenly, Belle's heart was beating wildly in her chest. He couldn't mean…couldn't possibly mean…

Could Santiago Velazquez, the famous New York billionaire, a man who had supermodels for the asking, really want *Belle*—a plump, ordinary waitress from small-town Texas?

Their eyes held in the moonlight. Sparks ran through her body, from her earlobes to her hair to her breasts to the soles of her feet.

"I want her. I can't have her," he said in a low voice. "Not even if she were standing in front of me now."

"Why not?" she breathed.

"Ah." His lips twisted. "She wants love. I see it in her face. I hear it in her voice. She craves love like the air she breathes. If I took her, if I made her mine, she would turn all her romantic longings on me. And be destroyed by it." He looked down at her, his eyes dark and deep. "Because as much as I want her body, I do not want her heart."

Behind the soft silver halo on his black hair, she could dimly see the shadow of the manor house, and hear the ocean waves pounding on the unseen shore.

Then Belle's eyes suddenly narrowed.

He was playing with her, she realized. *Toying* with her. Like a sharp-clawed cat with a mouse. "Stop it."

"What?"

She lifted her chin. "Are you bored, Santiago? Do you want some company in your bed and I'm the only one around?" She glared at him. "Other women might fall for your world-weary playboy act. But I don't believe a word of it. If you really wanted me, you wouldn't let anything stand in the way, not my feelings and certainly not the risk of hurting me. You would seduce me without conscience. That's what a playboy does. So obviously, you don't want me. You're just bored."

"You're wrong, Belle." Roughly, he pulled her against his body, beneath his expensive black cashmere coat. She felt his warmth as his dark eyes searched hers hungrily. "I've wanted you since Darius and Letty's wedding. Since the first time you told me to go to hell." His sensual lips curved as he cupped her cheek and looked down at her intently. "But whatever you think of me, I'm not in the business of purposefully making naïve young women love me."

Her whole body was tingling with energy, with fear, with a feeling that could only be desire. She fought it desperately.

"You think I'd immediately fall in love with you?"

"Yes."

She gave an incredulous snort. "You have no problems with your ego, do you?"

His dark gaze seared her. "Tell me I'm wrong."

"You're wrong." She gave a careless shrug. "I do want love, it's true. If I met a man I could respect and admire, I might easily fall in love. But that's not you, Santiago." She looked at him evenly. "No matter how rich or sexy you might be. So if you want me, too bad. I don't want you."

His expression changed. His eyes glittered in the moonlight.

"You don't?" Reaching out, he ran his thumb lightly against her trembling bottom lip and whispered, "Are you sure?"

"Yes," she breathed, unable to pull away, or to look from his dark gaze.

He ran his hand down her arm, looking down at her as

if she were the most beautiful, desirable creature on earth. "And if I took you to my bed, you wouldn't fall in love?"

"Not even remotely. I think you're a total bastard."

But even as she spoke, Belle couldn't stop herself from shivering. She knew he felt it. The corners of his lips twisted upward in grim masculine satisfaction.

Softly, he ran his hand down through her hair. Her body's shivering intensified. As she breathed in his scent of sandalwood and firelight, she felt the strength and power of his body against hers, beneath his long black coat.

"Then there's no reason to hold back. Forget love." He gently lifted her chin. "Forget regret, forget pain, forget everything fate has denied you. For one night, take pleasure in what you can have, right here and now."

"You mean, take pleasure in you?"

She'd tried to say the words sarcastically, but the way her heart was hammering in her chest, her tone came out wrong. Instead of sarcastic, she sounded breathless. Yearning.

"For one night, let me give you joy. Without strings. Without consequences. Stop thinking so much about the future," he said in a low voice, his hand cupping her cheek. "For one night, you can know what it feels like to be truly, recklessly alive."

His black eyes seared hers, and the cold January night sizzled like west Texas in July as an arc of electricity passed between them.

Give herself to him for one night, without consequences? Without strings?

Belle stared up at him, shocked.

She'd never slept with anyone. She'd never even gotten close. She was, in fact, a twenty-eight-year-old virgin, an old maid who'd spent her whole life taking care of others, while failing to achieve a single dream for herself.

No. Her answer was no. Of course it was.

Wasn't it?

He didn't give her a chance to answer. Lowering his head, he kissed her cheek, his lips lingering against her skin, moving slowly. Sensuously. She held her breath, and as he drew back, she stared at him with big eyes, her whole body clamoring and clanging like an orchestra.

"All right," she heard herself say, then gasped at her own recklessness. She opened her mouth to take it back. Then stopped.

For one night, you can know what it feels like to be truly, recklessly alive.

When was the last time she'd felt that way?

Had she ever?

Or had she always been a good girl, trying so hard to please others, to follow the rules, to plan out her life?

What had being good ever done for her—except leave her heartsick and alone?

Santiago's dark eyes gleamed as he saw her hesitate. He didn't wait. Wrapping his large hands on her jawline and then sliding them to tangle in her hair, he slowly drew his mouth to hers. She felt the warmth of his breath, sweet like Scotch, against the tender flesh of her skin.

His sensual mouth lowered on hers, hot and demanding, pushing her lips apart. She felt the delicious sweep of his tongue, and the cold winter air between them heated to a thousand degrees.

She'd never been kissed like this before. Never. The tepid caresses she'd endured seven years ago were nothing compared to this ruthlessly demanding embrace, this— dark fire.

She was lost in his arms, in the hot demand of his mouth, of his hands everywhere. Desire swept through her, a tidal wave of need that drowned all thought and reason. She forgot to think, forgot her own name.

She'd never known it could be like this...

She responded uncertainly at first, then soon gripped his shoulders, clutching him to her.

All her hatred for Santiago, all her earlier misery, transformed to heat as he kissed her in the dark winter night on the edge of the sea, invisible waves crashing noisily against the shore.

She didn't know how long they clung to each other in the cold night, seconds or hours, but when he finally drew away, she knew she'd never be the same. Their breath mingled in the dappled moonlight.

They stared at each other for a split second as scattered snowflakes started to fall.

Wordlessly, he took her hand and pulled her toward the house. She heard the crunch of frozen snow beneath her scuffed black flats, felt the warmth of his hand over hers.

They entered the nineteenth-century mansion, with its dark oak paneling and antique furniture. Inside, it was dark and quiet; it seemed everyone, including the household staff, had gone to bed. Santiago closed the tall, heavy door behind them and punched a code into the security system.

They rushed up the back stairs, hardly able to stop kissing long enough to stumble to the second floor.

Belle shivered. She couldn't be doing this. Impulsively offering her virginity to a man she didn't even like, let alone love?

But as he pulled her into a guest bedroom at the far end of the hall, she couldn't even catch her breath. His long black coat fell to the floor, and he pulled her into his arms. Cupping her face in his hands, he ran his thumbs along her swollen lower lip.

"You're so beautiful," he whispered, running his hands through her long brown hair tangled with ice and snowflakes. "Beautiful, and *mine*..."

Lowering his mouth to hers, he kissed her hungrily. Heat flooded through Belle, making her breasts heavy, swirling low and deep in her core. His hands stroked her deliciously, mesmerizing her with sensation, and by the time she realized he was unzipping her black dress, it was already falling to the floor.

An hour ago, she'd hated him; now she was half-naked in his bedroom.

Setting her back onto his bed, he pulled off his suit jacket, vest and tie. He never took his eyes off her as he unbuttoned his black shirt. His bare chest was chiseled and muscular, curving in the light and shadow. Falling beside her on the bed, he pulled her against him with a growl, kissing her with a hot embrace. He nibbled down her throat, and she tilted her head against the pillow, closing her eyes. He cupped each breast over her white cotton bra and reached beneath the fabric to stroke and thrum the aching nipples beneath.

Unhooking her bra, he tossed it to the floor and lowered his head to suckle one breast, then the other. The sensation was so sharp and wild and new that she gasped, gripping his shoulders tightly.

Moving up, he covered her gasping lips with his own, plundering her mouth before he slowly kissed down her body to her flat, naked belly. His tongue flicked her belly button. Then he kept going down further still.

His hands gripped her hips. He nuzzled between her legs, and she felt the warmth of his breath between her thighs. He held her firmly, gently pressing her legs apart, kissing each of her thighs before he pulled her panties off. Pushing her thighs apart, he teased her with his warm breath, then, with agonizing slowness, he lowered his mouth and tasted her.

The pleasure was so unexpected and explosive that her fingernails dug into his shoulders as his tongue slid against her, hot and wet.

Holding her hips, he worked her with his tongue until

she gripped the blanket beneath her, holding her breath until she started to see stars. He licked her softly one moment, then the next plunged his tongue inside her. She heard a voice cry out, and realized the voice was hers.

He swirled his tongue against her, increasing his rhythm and pressure until her back started arching from the bed. He pushed a single thick finger inside her, then two, stretching her wide. She gasped as the pleasure built almost too high to bear. Higher—higher—then—

Soaring to the sky, she exploded into a million pieces, falling to the earth in gently chiming shards. It was like nothing she'd ever experienced. It was pure joy.

Lifting up from her, he ripped off the last of his clothes. Positioning himself between her legs, he gripped her naked hips. As she was still gasping with pleasure, he pushed his huge, thick shaft inside her.

He'd dreamed of this.

For four months, Santiago had dreamed of seducing the sinfully beautiful woman who'd made it such a point to scorn him. He'd dreamed of having her deliciously full curves in his arms, her body naked beneath his. He'd dreamed of kissing her full pink lips and seeing her lovely face darken with ecstasy. He'd dreamed of taking her, filling her, satiating himself with her.

But now, as he finally pushed inside her, he felt a barrier he had not expected. He froze. He'd never once dreamed of this.

"You're a virgin?" he breathed in shock.

Slowly, she opened her eyes. "Not anymore."

He set his jaw. "Did I hurt you?"

"No," she said in a small voice.

Something in her expression made him tremble. Something in her voice spoke directly to his soul. He felt a strange emotion in his heart: tenderness. He bit out, "You're lying."

"Yes." Her soft, slender arms reached up around his shoulders and pulled him down, down, down against her, tempting him to his own ecstasy and ruin. "But don't stop," she whispered. "Please, Santiago…"

Hearing his name on her lips, he sucked in his breath. How could even a romantic, idealistic woman like Belle Langtry be an untouched innocent, in this modern world? *A virgin.* Santiago was the only man who'd ever touched her, this infuriating, exhilarating, magnificent woman.

His soul felt the danger of getting close to any woman so innocent and bright. It made him want to flee.

But his body, held still deep inside her, felt the opposite as he looked down at her beautiful face, glowing with wanton desire. He shuddered. Ravaging hunger built inside him, thrilling his nerves, coursing down his limbs and centering at his hard core barreled deep inside her.

He lowered his head to hers. His kiss was gentle at first, then deepened, turning to pure light. His hands roamed slowly down her naked body, cupping and caressing her breasts.

She had the most perfect body, curvy and ripe. Any man would die to have a fiery goddess like this in his bed. And that this goddess was also a *virgin*…

He shuddered a little, and without realizing it, pushed deeper inside her. The soft whisper of a moan escaped her as he lowered his lips to suckle her breasts. Her breath changed to a gasp of ecstasy.

Gripping her hips, he very slowly started to ride her, even as he kissed her lips and caressed her breasts. He sucked her earlobe and slowly licked and nibbled down her neck. He felt her body lift beneath his as new pleasure rose in her, and she began to kiss him back hungrily.

He started to lose the last shreds of his self-control. She

was wet, so wet, and somehow her tight sheath accepted all of him. His thrusts became deeper as he wondered if the size of him would be too much for her. But it wasn't. He felt her tighten around him, gripping her fingernails into his shoulders. But that small pain only added to his building pleasure. When he heard her low gasp rise to a scream of joy he could no longer hold back. His eyes closed in pure ecstasy, his head tossing back as he filled her deeply, until his own roar exploded in the deep dark silence of the bedroom. Flying in a whirlwind, he experienced pure sexual joy such as he'd never known before as he spilled himself into her.

He fell back to the bed against her, eyes closed, cradling her body against his own. For ten seconds, as he held her, he felt a deep peace, a sense of home, sweeter than he'd ever known.

Then his eyes flew open. He was filled with regret so great it tasted like ash in his mouth.

"You were right," Belle sighed, a hopeful smile on her lovely heart-shaped face. "I feel recklessly alive. That was like nothing I ever dreamed. Pure magic." She pressed back against his naked chest, pulling his arms more tightly around her, as she said dreamily, "Deep down, maybe you're not all bad. I might even like you a little."

Santiago looked down at her grimly in the moonlight from the bedroom window. He'd just known ecstasy that he'd never experienced before.

With a virgin.

A *romantic*.

Sleeping with Belle had done strange things to him. His body had never known such deep pleasure. And his soul…

She yawned. "I just hope no one heard us."

"They didn't," he said harshly. "Letty and Darius are in the other wing, and this house is made of stone." Stone like his heart, he reminded himself.

"Good. I'd never live it down if Letty knew, after everything I've said about you."

"What did you say to her?"

"I said you were a selfish bastard without a heart."

His shoulders tightened. "I'm not offended. It's true."

"You're funny." She looked up at him sleepily. "You know, no matter what you think, love and marriage aren't always a prison sentence. Look at Letty and Darius."

"They *look* happy," he said grudgingly, then added, "Looks can be deceiving."

Her forehead furrowed. "Don't you believe in anyone? Anything?"

"I believe in myself."

"You're a terrible cynic."

"I see the world as it is, rather than as I wish it could be." Eternal love? A happy family? At thirty-five, Santiago had seen enough of the world to know those kind of miracles were few and far between. Tragedy was the normal state of the world. "Do you already regret sleeping with me?"

Shaking her head, she smiled up at him, looking kittenish and shy and so damned beautiful that his heart caught in his throat. "You feel so good to me. I'm glad you're here." She yawned, closing her eyes, cuddling against him. "I couldn't bear to be alone tonight. You saved me…"

Pressing against his chest, she fell asleep in seconds.

Santiago yearned to sleep, as well. His body wanted to stay like this, with her, cuddled in this warm bed, taking solace in each other against the cold January night and all the other cold nights to come.

Warning lights were flashing everywhere.

He looked down at her, sweetly sleeping in his arms, so soft and beautiful, so opinionated and dreamy and kind. So optimistic.

You saved me.

Santiago felt bone-weary. Carefully, he disentangled

himself from her. Rising from the bed, he walked naked to his coat crumpled on the floor. Pulling his phone from his pocket, he dialed the number of his pilot.

The man struggled not to sound groggy. It was eleven o'clock on a cold winter's night. "Sir?"

"Come get me," he replied. "I'm at Fairholme."

Without waiting for a reply, Santiago hung up. He looked back at Belle one last time, sleeping in his bed, so beautiful in the moonlight. Like an innocent young woman from another time. He couldn't remember ever being that innocent, not with the upbringing he'd had.

Whatever Belle might say, she would want to love him. She would try, like a moth immolating herself against an unfeeling flame.

Of course she would. He was her first.

His jaw tightened. He never would have seduced her if he'd known. He had a rule. No virgins. No innocent hearts. He never brought anyone to his bed who might actually care.

And he'd just seduced an innocent virgin. The friend of Darius's wife.

He felt a low self-hatred. After Nadia, he'd vowed never to get involved with anyone again. Why risk your capital on an investment that was a guaranteed loss? Might as well flush your money—or your soul—straight down the drain.

He thought again of *Wuthering Heights*. He'd never read the book, but he knew it ended badly. It was romance, wasn't it? That always ended badly. Especially in real life.

Santiago silently dressed, then picked up his overnight bag. But he hesitated at the door, still hearing the wistful echo of her voice.

Don't you believe in anyone? Anything?

He'd lied to her. He'd told her he believed in himself. But the real answer was no.

Belle would wake up alone in bed and find him gone.

No note would be needed. She'd get the message. He really was the heartless bastard he claimed to be.

As if there was ever any doubt, he jeered at himself. Regret and self-loathing filled him as he turned down the hall.

He wished he'd never touched her.

CHAPTER TWO

SHIVERING IN THE warm July twilight, Belle stood on the sidewalk of Santiago's elegant residential street on Manhattan's Upper East Side. She watched well-dressed guests step out of glossy chauffeured cars, climbing up the steps and ringing at his door, to be greeted by his butler.

A butler, she thought bitterly. Who had a butler in this day and age?

Santiago Velazquez—that was who.

But the butler wasn't the problem. Belle watched a crowd of beautiful young socialites, giggling and preening, hurry up the steps of his brownstone in six-inch heels and designer cocktail dresses.

She looked down at her own loose, oversized T-shirt, stretchy knit shorts and flip-flops. She wasn't wearing makeup. Her brown hair was pulled back into a messy ponytail. She'd fit in at his fancy party like a dog driving a car.

She didn't belong here. And she didn't want to see Santiago again—*ever*—after the cold way he'd treated her after they'd slept together in January. Losing her virginity in a one-night stand with the heartless, cynical playboy was a mistake she would regret the rest of her life.

But she couldn't leave New York. Not without telling him she was pregnant.

Pregnant. Every time she thought of it, she caught her breath. It was a miracle. She didn't have any other word to describe it, when seven years ago she'd been told very firmly by a doctor that it could never happen. Pregnant.

A dazed smile traced Belle's lips as she rested her hands gently over the wide curve of her belly now. Somehow, in that disastrous night when Santiago had seduced her, this one amazing, impossible thing had happened. She'd gotten her heart's deepest desire: a baby of her own.

There was just one bad thing about it.

Her smile faded. Of all the men on earth to be her unborn baby's father…

She'd tried to tell him; she'd left multiple messages asking him to call her back. He hadn't. She'd been almost glad. It gave her a good excuse to do what she wanted to do—leave New York without telling him he was going to be a father.

But her friend Letty had convinced her to make one last try. "Secrets always come out," she'd pleaded. "Don't make my mistake."

So, against her better judgment, here Belle was, stopping at his luxury brownstone on her way out of town. The last place she wanted to be.

Just thinking of facing Santiago for the first time since he'd snuck out of her bed in the middle of the night, she wanted to turn and run for her pickup truck parked two blocks away, then head south on the turnpike, stomp on the gas and not look back until she reached Texas.

But she'd already made the decision to try one last time to give him the life-changing news that he was going to be a father. Belle always tried to do the right thing, even if it hurt. She wasn't going to turn coward now. Not over *him*.

Tightening her hands into fists, Belle waited until the last limousine departed, then crossed the street in the fading twilight. Her body shook as she walked up the stone steps and knocked on the big oak door.

The butler took one look at her, then started to close the

door as he said scornfully, "Staff and delivery entrance at the back."

Belle blocked the door with her foot. "Excuse me. I need to see Santiago. Please."

The butler looked astonished at her familiar use of his employer's first name, as if a talking rat had just squeaked a request to see the mayor of New York. "Who are you?"

"Tell him Belle Langtry urgently needs to see him." She raised her chin, struggling to hide her pounding heart. "It's an emergency."

With a scowl, the butler opened the door just enough for her to get through. The soles of Belle's flip-flops slapped against the marble floor of the mansion's elegant foyer. She had one brief glimpse of the beautiful, wealthy society crowd in the ballroom, sipping champagne as waiters passed through with silver trays. Then she sucked in her breath as she saw the party's host, head and shoulders above the crowd. With his height and dark good looks, Santiago Velazquez towered over his guests in every way.

The butler pointed down an opposite hallway haughtily. "Wait in there."

Through the door, Belle found a home office with leather-bound books and a big dark wood desk. Knees weak, she sank into the expensive swivel chair. Her cheeks still burned from seeing Santiago from a distance. Thinking of seeing him face to face, she was terrified.

The night he'd taken her virginity, passion and emotion had been like a whirlwind, flinging her up into the sky, to the stars, scattering pieces of her soul like diamonds across the night. It had been so sensual, so spectacular. More than she'd even dreamed it could be.

Right until the moment he'd abandoned her, and she'd had to go down to breakfast alone. She'd had to hide her hurt and bewilderment, and smile at Letty and Darius and their baby, pretending nothing had happened, that nothing was wrong. That was how cold-hearted Santiago was. He'd only promised one night, true. But he hadn't even been able to stick *that* out.

Leaving Fairholme, she'd returned to her tiny apartment in Brooklyn, which she shared with two rude, parent-funded roommates who'd mocked her dreams, her Texas accent—which was barely noticeable!—and her job as a waitress. Normally she would have let their taunts roll off her like water off a duck's back, but after her night with Santiago, she'd felt restless, irritable and hopeless, as she continued to be rejected at auditions, with a day job that barely paid the bills.

A month later, when she'd discovered she was pregnant, everything had changed. Her baby deserved better than this apartment shared with strangers, an insecure future and unpaid bills. Her baby deserved better than a father who couldn't be bothered to return phone calls. It was a bitter thought.

Belle had come to New York with such high hopes. After nearly a decade spent raising her two younger brothers, she'd finally left her small town at twenty-seven, determined to make her dreams come true.

Instead, she'd made a mess of everything.

She'd dreamed of making her fortune? She now had ten dollars less in her wallet than when she'd left Texas eighteen months ago.

She'd dreamed of seeing her name in lights? She'd been rejected from every talent agency in New York.

But worst of all... Belle swallowed hard... She'd dreamed that she would finally find love, real love, the kind that would last forever. Instead, she'd allowed herself to get knocked up by a man she hated.

Belle had had enough of New York. She was going home. Her two suitcases were already packed in her truck, ready to go. There was only one thing left on her to-do list.

Tell Santiago Velazquez he was going to be a father.

But now, she suddenly wasn't sure she could do it. Even seeing him in the ballroom, from a distance, had knocked her for a loop. Maybe this was a mistake. Maybe she shouldn't stay...

Santiago pushed through the door. When he saw her sitting in his chair, his glare was like a blast of heat, his tall, powerful body barely contained by the well-cut suit. "What the hell are you doing here?"

After all these months, this was how he greeted her? She stiffened in the chair, folding her arms over her belly. "Good to see you, too."

Closing the door behind him, Santiago pierced her with his hard, black eyes and said dangerously, "I asked you a question. What are you doing here, Belle? I think I made it very clear that I never wanted to see you again."

"You did."

Santiago moved closer in the shadows of the study. "Why did you trick my butler into letting you in, telling him there was an emergency?"

"It wasn't a trick. It's true."

"An emergency. Really." His lips twisted scornfully. "Let me guess. After all these months, you're realized you can't live without me, and you're here to declare eternal love."

She flinched at the cold derision in his voice.

"God help any woman who truly loved you." She took a deep breath, then glared back at him. "Don't worry. I hate you plenty. More than ever."

A strange expression flashed across his features, then he gave her a cold smile. "Fantastic. So why did you interrupt my party?"

He was glaring at her with such hatred. How could she possibly tell him she was pregnant with his baby? "I came to tell you...I'm leaving New York..."

"That's your emergency?" He gave an incredulous laugh. "One more thing to celebrate today, on top of closing a business deal."

Her hackles rose. "Let me finish!"

"So do it, then." He folded his arms, looking down at her as if he were king of the mountain and she was just a peasant in the dirt. "And let me get back to my guests."

She took a deep breath.

"I'm pregnant."

Her small voice reverberated in the silence of the study. His black eyes widened in almost comical shock.

"What?"

Slowly, she rose from the chair, dropping her arms to her sides so he could see her baby bump beneath her pregnancy-swollen breasts and oversized T-shirt. For a moment, he didn't speak, and she held her breath, afraid to meet his gaze. Some stupid part of her still hoped against hope that he would surprise her. That he would suddenly change back to that warm, irresistible man she'd seen so briefly that cold January night. That he'd gather her into his arms and kiss her joyfully at the news.

Those hopes were quickly dashed.

"*Pregnant?*"

She risked a look at him. His jaw was hard, his eyes dark with rage.

"Yes," she choked out.

She never expected what he did next.

Pulling her close, he put his large, broad hands over her cotton T-shirt, to feel the unmistakable swell of her pregnant belly.

He dropped his hands as if he'd been burned. "You said it was medically impossible."

"I thought it was…"

"You said you could never get pregnant!"

"It's a…a miracle."

"Miracle!" He snorted, then narrowed his eyes. He slowly looked her over. "And here I thought you didn't have what it took to be on Broadway. No gold digger ever lied to my face so convincingly. I actually thought you were some angelic little innocent. Quite the little actress after all."

That low, husky, Spanish-accented voice cut right through her heart, and she staggered back. "You think I got pregnant on purpose?"

He gave a low laugh. "You really had me going with the way you defended true love. Letting me find you alone, sobbing in the garden over the fact that you could never, ever have a baby. I'm impressed. I had no idea you were such an accomplished liar."

"I didn't lie!"

"Cut the act, and get to the part where you give me a price."

"Price?" she said, bewildered.

"There's only one reason you would deliberately trick me into not using a condom when you fluttered your eyes and lured me into bed—"

Her voice came out an enraged squeak. "I never did that!"

"And that's money. But I'll admit," he said carelessly, looking her over, "you earned it. No woman has ever tricked me so thoroughly. Except—" His expression changed, then he set his jaw. "How much do you want?"

"I don't want money." The room was spinning around her. "I just thought you had the right to know!"

"*Perfecto*," he said coolly. Going to the door, he opened it. "You told me. Now get the hell out."

Belle stared at him in shock, astounded that any man could react to news of his unborn son or daughter so coldly, refusing to even show interest, much less take responsibility! "That's it? That's all you have to say?"

"What did you expect?" he drawled. "That I'd fall to one knee and beg you to marry me? Sorry to disappoint you."

Belle stared up at him, incredulous. She'd waited for twenty-eight years, dreaming of Prince Charming, dreaming of true love—and *this* was the man she'd slept with!

Anger rose like bile in her throat. "Wow. You figured me out. Yes, I'm desperate to marry you, Santiago. Who wouldn't want to be the bride of the nastiest, most coldhearted man on earth? And raise a baby with you?" She gave a harsh laugh. "What an amazing father you would make!"

His expression hardened. "Belle—"

"You call me a liar. A gold digger. When you know I was a virgin the night you seduced me!" She lifted her chin, trembling with emotion. "Was this what you meant when you called me naïve? Did you decide you wanted to be the one to show me the truth about the heartless world?"

"Look—"

"I never should have come here." Tears were burning the backs of her eyes. But she'd let him see her cry once, that dark January night, and he'd lured her into destruction with his sweet kisses and honeyed words. She'd die before she let him ever see her weak again. "Forget about the baby. Forget I even exist." Stopping at the door, she looked back at him one last time. "I wish any man but you could have been the father of my baby," she choked out. "It's a mistake I'll regret the rest of my life."

Turning, she left, rushing past the snooty butler and beautiful, rich guests who looked like they'd never had a single problem in their glamorous lives. She went outside, nearly tripping down the steps into the cooling night air. She ran halfway down the block in her flip-flops before she realized Santiago wasn't following her.

Good. She didn't care. When she reached her old 1978 Chevy pickup, she started up the engine with a roar. Her hands didn't stop shaking until she was past the Lincoln Tunnel.

From the first day they'd met, she'd known Santiago was dark-hearted poison. How could she have been so stupid to let him seduce her?

For one night, let me give you joy. Without strings. Without consequences.

Belle choked out a sob as she gripped the steering wheel, driving south on the Jersey Turnpike. She was thrilled about the baby, but what she would have given to have any other man as the father!

For the last few months, when Santiago hadn't returned her phone messages, she'd told herself that she and the baby would be better off without him. But part of her had secretly hoped for another miracle—that if she told Santiago she was pregnant, he'd want to be a father. A husband. That they could all love each other, and be happy.

So stupid.

She wiped her eyes. Instead Santiago had not only cavalierly abandoned his unborn baby, he'd insulted Belle and thrown her out of his house for daring to tell him she was pregnant!

The truly shocking thing was that she was even surprised. He'd made his feelings clear from the beginning. He thought babies were a thankless responsibility and love was for suckers.

Belle cried until her eyes burned, then at midnight, pulled over to a roadside motel to sleep fitfully till dawn.

The next day, the hypnotic road started to calm her. She started feeling like she'd dodged a bullet. She didn't need a cold, heartless man wrecking her peace of mind and breaking their child's heart. Better that Santiago abandon them now rather than later.

By the third day, as the mile markers passed and she left the green rolling hills of east Texas behind, she started to recognize the familiar landscape of home, and her heart grew lighter. There was something soothing about the wide horizons stretching out forever, with nothing but sagebrush and the merciless summer sun in the unrelenting blue sky.

Feeling a sweet flutter inside her, Belle put a hand to her belly. "So be it," she whispered aloud. This baby would be hers alone. She would spend the rest of her life appreciating this miracle, devoting herself to her child.

It was still morning, but already growing hot. The air conditioning in her pickup didn't work, but both windows were rolled down, so it was all right. Though she was lucky it wasn't raining because one of them wouldn't roll back up.

As she drew in to the edges of her small town, she took a deep breath. *Home.* Though it wasn't the same, without her younger brothers. Ray now lived in Atlanta and twenty-one-year-old Joe in Denver. But at least here, the world made sense.

But as she pulled into the dirt driveway, she abruptly slammed on the brake.

A big black helicopter was parked in the sagebrush prairie, tucked behind her house.

She sucked in her breath. A helicopter? Then she saw the two hulking bodyguards prowling nearby. That could only mean...

With an intake of breath, she looked straight at the old wooden house with the peeling paint. Her heart stopped.

Standing on the wooden porch, with arms grimly folded, was Santiago.

What was he doing here?

Fear pounded through her as she turned off the engine of her truck.

With a deep breath, Belle got out of her old pickup, tossing her long brown ponytail, slamming the door with a rusty squeak.

"What are you doing in Texas?" She lifted her chin to

hide the tremble in her voice. "Let me guess. Did you think up some new ways to insult me?"

He came down the rickety wooden steps toward her, his black eyes glittering. "Three nights ago, you showed up at my house with a very shocking accusation."

"You mean I accused you of getting me pregnant?" Waving her arm, she said furiously, "Such a horrible accusation! No wonder you wanted me to get the hell out!"

Standing on the last step above her, he ground his teeth. "I was calling your bluff. It was a negotiation. I expected you to swiftly return with a demand for a specific sum of money."

Calling her announcement of pregnancy a negotiation! He was just the worst! A lump rose in her throat. Blinking fast, she turned toward his entourage and helicopter in the field. She said evenly, "How did you find my address?"

"Easy."

"You must have been waiting for hours."

"Twenty minutes."

"Twenty! How?" She gasped. "There was no way you could know when I'd get here. Even I didn't know exactly!"

He gave a grim smile. "That was more difficult."

"Were you tracking my truck? Spying on me?"

"Stop changing the subject," he said coldly. He stepped closer on the packed dirt driveway, towering a foot over her. His black eyes traced the length of her body, from her oversized T-shirt to her shorts to her flip-flops, and a flash of heat coursed through her. "You were telling the truth? The baby is mine?"

"Of course the baby's yours!"

"How can I trust a proven liar?"

"When did I lie?" she said indignantly.

"'I can't get pregnant, ever,'" he mimicked. "'It's impossible.'"

"You are such a jerk." Belle shivered, sweating beneath the hot Texas sun.

His voice had been low, controlled, but she felt his cold fury. He was all gorgeous on the outside, she thought, like melted chocolate with his soulful Spanish eyes and black hair and hard-muscled body. Too bad his soul was even harder than his body. He had a soul like flint. Like ice.

Just when she'd been counting her blessings that he was out of their lives, here he was, pushing back in. For what purpose?

"You made your choice," she whispered. "You abandoned us. This baby is mine now. Mine alone."

He lifted a dark eyebrow. "That's not how paternity works."

"It is if I say it is."

"Then why tell me you were pregnant at all?"

"Because three days ago I was foolish enough to hope you could change. Now I know it would be better for my baby to have no father at all than a man like you." She lifted her chin. "Now get off my land."

Growing dangerously still, Santiago stared at her, jaw tight. Without a word, he turned to stare across the stark horizon against the wide blue sky. Against her will, her eyes traced the golden glow of the sun gleaming against his olive-colored skin, the chiseled cheekbones, the dark scruff on his jaw.

"Let me tell you what's going to happen, Belle." When he looked back at her, his voice was low and deep, almost a purr. "Today, you're going to get a paternity test."

"What? Forget it!"

"And if it's proven that the baby's mine," his black eyes glittered, "you're going to marry me."

Was he crazy or was she?

"*Marry* you?" Belle gasped. "Are you out of your mind? I hate you!"

"You should be pleased. Your plan worked. Admit you purposefully got pregnant with my child to trap me into marriage. Have that much respect for me, at least."

"I won't, because it's not true!"

"I'll admit I made a mistake, trusting you. I should have known better. I should have known your innocence was a lie. I shall pay for that." He moved closer with a gleam in his dark eyes. "But so will you."

A shiver went through her.

"I would never marry someone I hate," she whispered.

"You're acting like you have a choice. You don't." He gave a cold smile. "You'll do what I say. And if the baby is mine…then so are you."

CHAPTER THREE

SANTIAGO VELAZQUEZ HAD learned the hard way that there were two types of people in the world: delusional dreamers who hid from the harsh truth of the world, and those clear-eyed few who could face it, and fight for what they wanted.

Belle Langtry was a dreamer. He'd known that the day they'd met, at their friends' wedding last September, when she'd chirped annoyingly about the bridal couple's "eternal love" in face of their obvious misery. Belle's rose-colored glasses were so thick she was blind.

But then, you'd have to be blind to see anything hopeful about love or marriage. Love was a lie, and any marriage based on it would be a disaster from start to finish. It could only end in tears. He should know. His mother had been married five times, to every man in Spain except Santiago's actual father.

But for some reason, when he'd met Belle, so feisty and sure of her own illusions, he hadn't been irritated. He'd been charmed. Petite, curvaceous, dark-haired, with deep sultry eyes and a body clearly made for sin, she'd gotten under his skin from the beginning. And not just because of her beauty.

Belle hated him, and wasn't afraid to show it. With one glaringly big exception, Santiago couldn't remember any woman scorning him so thoroughly. Not since he'd grown into his full height at twenty, and especially not since he'd made his fortune. Women were always hoping to get into his bed, his wallet, or usually both. He hadn't realized just how boring it had all become until that exact moment that Belle Langtry had insulted him to his face.

She was different from the others. She drew him like a flame in the darkness. Her tart tongue, her apparent innocence, her brazen honesty, had made him lower his defenses. Their single night together had been transcendent and joyful and raw. It had almost made him question his cynical view of the world.

Then, three nights ago, he'd discovered how wrong he'd been about her.

Belle Langtry wasn't different. She wasn't innocent. She'd only pretended to wear rose-colored glasses to hide the fact that she was a cold-eyed liar, just like everyone else, plotting for her personal gain. She wasn't like his mother had been, pathetically desperate for love, deceiving herself to the end of her self-destructive life. No. Belle was like Nadia. A mercenary gold digger who would say or do anything, her eyes always on the glittering prize.

At Fairholme, in the snowy garden that cold January night, when Belle had wept in Santiago's arms as if her heart was breaking, she'd been *lying*.

When he'd softly stroked her long dark hair in the moonlight and whispered that everything would be all right, and Belle had looked up, her big dark eyes anguished beneath trembling lashes, she'd been *lying*.

When she'd told him she could never, ever get pregnant, and lowering his head, he'd kissed her beneath the moonlight scattered with snowflakes, as he tried to distract her from her grief, she'd been *lying*.

Santiago had known Belle was an actress. He'd just had no idea how good. He hadn't been fooled in such a way in a long time.

After she'd invaded his cocktail party and dropped the bomb of her pregnancy news, he'd paced and snarled at his guests, wondering what he'd do when Belle finally returned to make her financial demands. If she was truly pregnant with his child, she had leverage. Because as much as Santiago despised the idea of love and marriage, he would never abandon a child the way he himself had once been doubly abandoned.

What would Belle ask for? he'd wondered. Marriage? A trust fund in the baby's name? Or would she eliminate the middleman and simply ask for a billion-dollar check, written out directly to her?

He'd waited that night, nerves thrumming, but she'd never returned to his town house. The next morning, he'd discovered she'd left New York, just as she'd claimed she intended.

Now, after three days, he knew everything about Belle, except for her medical records, which he expected to have later today. His investigator had easily found her home address in Texas. The GPS of her phone had been tracked through means he didn't care to know, and someone had watched for her highly visible blue 1978 Chevy at the gas station two hours to the east, the only gas station for miles in this empty Texas prairie. He'd simply taken the helicopter here from his large ranch in south Texas.

But he could hardly be expected to reveal his strategies to an enemy. Which was what Belle now was.

From the day they'd met, she'd acted like she hated him. But he'd never hated her.

Until now.

Santiago stared down at her beneath the unrelenting furnace of the sun blasting heat from the Texas sky. He felt a prickling of sweat on his forehead. Wearing a vest, tie and long-sleeved shirt along with tailored wool trousers, he found the temperature brutal. And it wasn't even noon.

Santiago set his jaw. He wouldn't allow Belle to control the situation. Or his baby. He didn't know her goal, but the way she was playing the game—like a professional poker player without a heart—the amount she wanted must be astronomical. And why would it ever stop, when she'd have the leverage to control him for the rest of her life? She could try to control custody, or make their child hate him through her lies. She could leave Santiago like a fish gasping on a hook.

Belle had deliberately misled him, saying she couldn't get pregnant. Later, she'd ambushed him with her news and then fled New York, just to show him she meant business. She'd done all this for a reason. To get the upper hand.

But he wouldn't let her use their innocent baby as a pawn. He couldn't be forced or tricked into abandoning a child. Not after what he'd endured himself as a boy. Belle didn't know who she was dealing with. Santiago would scorch the earth to win this war.

His eyes narrowed. She thought she could defeat him? He'd fought his way from an orphanage in Madrid, stowing away at eighteen on a ship to New York City with the equivalent of five hundred dollars in his pocket. Now, he was a billionaire, the majority owner of an international conglomerate that sold everything from running shoes to snack foods on six continents. You didn't do that by being weak, or letting anyone else win.

Belle was in his world now. His world. His rules.

"I'll never marry you," she ground out, her brown eyes shooting sparks. "I'll never belong to you."

"You already do, Belle," he said flatly. "You just don't know it yet." Turning, he made a quick gesture to his helicopter pilot, who started the engine.

She gave an incredulous laugh over the rising noise of the helicopter. "You're crazy!"

Santiago looked down at her. Even now, despising Belle as his enemy, he felt more drawn than ever. She wasn't conventionally beautiful, perhaps, but somehow she was more seductive than any woman he'd ever known. His eyes unwillingly traced the curve of her cheek. The slope of her graceful neck. The fullness of her pregnancy-swollen breasts.

Belle was right, he thought grimly. He was crazy. Because even knowing her for a lying, almost sociopathic gold digger, he wanted her in his bed more than ever.

"I'd be crazy to abandon my child to you," he said evenly. He looked over his shoulder at the wooden house in the barren sagebrush field, with only a few wan, spindly trees overlooking a dry creek bed. "Or to this."

Following his gaze, she looked outraged. "You're judging me because I don't live in a palace?"

"I'm judging what you've done to escape it," he said grimly. He knew all about how she'd been raised here, and only left a year and a half before. He wondered if her dream of Broadway stardom had always been a cover story, and she'd planned to hook a rich man from the beginning. Maybe even her friendship with Letty had been contrived, to better throw Belle in the path of wealthy targets.

The only thing good about this isolated, bare land was the view of the endless blue sky. The sky above the dry grass prairie was starkly dramatic. You could see forever. The freedom. The unending loneliness.

But there were all kinds of loneliness. You could be lonely surrounded by others, as he'd learned as a child.

His own son or daughter would never know that kind of loneliness. He or she would never feel unwanted, or alone. He would see to that.

He turned away. "Let's go."

"Where?"

"Paternity test."

"Forget it—"

He whirled on her with narrowed eyes. "You hate me," he growled. "Fine. I feel the same for you. But does not our child, at least, deserve to know the truth about his parents?"

She glared at him, her eyes glittering with dislike. Then her expression faltered. He'd found the one argument that could sway her.

"Fine," she bit out.

"You'll take the test?"

"For my baby's sake. Not yours."

He exhaled. He hadn't realized he'd been holding his breath, wondering if he'd have to physically force her into the helicopter—a very unpleasant thought, especially with a woman who was likely pregnant with his child. He was relieved she wasn't being so unreasonable.

Then he realized Belle must have decided to change her strategy. She was just shifting her ground, like a boxer. Santiago's lips pressed together in a thin line. He glanced at his bodyguards, hovering nearby. "Get her things."

As his men reached into her pickup, Santiago took her arm, leading her forward. Within seconds, she was sitting comfortably beside him on a leather seat inside the luxury helicopter.

"I'll take the test, but I'm never going to marry you," she said over the sound of the propellers.

He narrowed his eyes coldly. "We both know this is exactly what you wanted to happen. So stop the act. In your heart, I know you are rejoicing."

"I'm not!"

"Your joy will not last long." He drew closer, his face inches from hers. "You will find that being my wife is different than you imagined. You won't own me, Belle. I will own you."

Her brown eyes got big, and he felt a current of electricity course through his body. Against his will, his gaze fell to her lips. So delicious. So sensual and red. Heat surged through his veins.

He'd always despised the idea of marriage, but for the first time, he saw the benefits. As much as he hated her, it had only lifted his desire to a fever. And he knew, by the nervous flicker of her tongue against her lips even now, that Belle felt the same.

Once wed, she would be in his bed, at his command, for as long as he desired. Because one thing, at least, hadn't been a lie between them.

So why wait?

For all these months, since the explosive night he'd taken her virginity, he'd denied himself the pleasure of her. Both for his own sake and, he'd once believed, for hers.

No longer.

Tonight, he thought hungrily. He would have her in his bed tonight.

But first things first.

Putting on a headset, Santiago spoke to the pilot over the rising noise of the blades whipping the sky. "Let's go."

Sitting in the helicopter, Belle looked through the window across the wide plains of Texas. Far below, she saw wild horses running across the prairie, feral and free, a hundred miles away from any human civilization.

She envied them right now.

"Those are mine." Santiago's voice came through her headset. Sitting on the white leather seat beside her, he nodded toward the horses with satisfaction. "We're on the north edge of my property."

So even the wild horses weren't free, she thought glumly. It was the first time they'd spoken in the noisy helicopter since they'd left the world-class medical clinic in Houston.

"You want to own everything, don't you?"

"I do own everything." Santiago's dark eyes gleamed at her. "My ranch is nearly half a million acres."

"Half a—" She sucked in her breath, then said slowly, "Wait. Did you buy the Alford Ranch?"

He raised a sardonic eyebrow. "You've heard of it?"

"Of course I've heard of it," she snapped. "It's famous. There was a scandal a few years ago when it was sold to some foreigner—you?"

He shrugged. "All of this land was once owned by Spaniards, so some people might say that the Alfords were the foreigners. I was merely reacquiring it."

She looked at him skeptically. "Spaniards owned this?"

"Most of South Texas was once claimed by the Spanish Empire, in the time of the conquistadors."

"How do you know that?"

He gave a grim smile. "My father's family is very proud of their history. When I was a boy, and still cared, I read about my ancestors. The family line goes back six hundred years."

"The Velazquez family can be traced six hundred years?" she blurted out. She barely knew the full names of her own great-grandparents.

"Velazquez is my mother's name. My father is a Zoya. The eighth Duque de Sangovia."

His voice was so flat she wasn't sure she'd heard him right. "Your father is a duke? An actual duke?"

He shrugged. "So?"

"What's he like?" she breathed. She'd never met royalty before, or aristocracy. The closest she'd come was knowing a kid called Earl back in middle school.

"I wouldn't know," he said shortly. "We've never met. Look." Changing the subject, Santiago pointed out the window. "There's the house."

Belle looked, and gasped.

The horizon was wide and flat, stretching in every direction, but after miles of dry, sparse sagebrush, the landscape had turned green. Between tree-covered rivers, she saw outbuildings and barns and pens. And at the most beautiful spot, she was astonished to see a blue lake, sparkling in the late afternoon sun. Next to it, atop a small hill surrounded by trees, was a sprawling single-story ranch house that made the place in the old TV show *Dallas* look like a fishing shack.

"It's beautiful," she said in awe. "The land is so green!"

"Five different rivers cross the property."

Past one of the pens she saw a private hangar, with a helipad and airplane runway stretching out to the horizon beyond. "All this is yours?"

"All mine."

His black eyes gleamed down at her, and she heard the echo of his arrogant words earlier. *If the baby is mine, then so are you.* She shivered.

The baby was his. He now had undeniable proof. When they'd gone to the cutting-edge medical clinic in Houston, she'd gotten the impression Santiago must be a very important financial donor, the way the entire staff had waited on him hand and foot. They'd taken the noninvasive blood test, drawing blood from each of them, then the highly trained lab technicians had promised to rush the results.

"But while you wait—" the female OB/GYN had smiled between them "—would you like to have an ultrasound, and find out if you're having a boy or girl?"

Belle had started to refuse. She'd already decided she wanted to be surprised at the birth. But looking at Santiago's face—his dark eyes so bright, almost boyishly eager as he looked at her—she couldn't refuse. If Santiago truly wanted to be what she herself had never had…a loving father…then she was going to do everything she could to encourage the bond between father and child.

"All right," she'd said quietly, and got up on the hospital bed. A few minutes later, as the doctor ran the wand over the sticky goo on her belly, they were staring at the image on the ultrasound screen. A *whoosh-whoosh* sound filled the room.

"What's that?" Santiago asked in alarm, sitting beside her on the bed.

Belle blinked at him in surprise. She suddenly realized that unlike her, he was hearing that sound for the very first time. Smiling, she told him, "It's the baby's heartbeat."

"Heartbeat?" he breathed. The expression on his darkly handsome face, normally hard and cynical, changed so much he looked like a different man.

"It's nice and strong. Your baby looks healthy," the doctor murmured. She pointed at the ultrasound screen. "Here you can see the head, arms…legs…and…" She turned to them with a smile. "Congratulations. You're having a little girl."

"A girl!" Belle gasped.

"A girl?" Reaching out, Santiago suddenly gripped Belle's hand tightly in his own. "When will she be born?"

"Her growth is on track for her due date in late September," the doctor replied.

"September," he murmured, looking dazed. "Just two months from now…"

Belle saw an expression on his face she'd never seen before. Bewilderment. Emotion. Tenderness.

So he wasn't a total bastard after all, she thought. There was one thing that could reach past his layers of cynicism and darkness. Their baby.

Grateful tears had risen unbidden to her eyes, and she'd gripped his hand back tightly. Their daughter would have a father. A father who loved her.

Now, as the helicopter landed at his Texas ranch, Santiago held out his hand to help her out onto the tarmac. He caught her when her knees unexpectedly started to buckle.

"Are you all right?" he asked, his eyes full of concern.

She gave him a weak smile. "It's been a crazy week."

He laughed. "That's one way of describing it."

She'd never seen him laugh like that, with his whole body, almost a guffaw. It made him more human, and somehow even more handsome, more impossibly desirable. In that instant, as she looked up at his dark, merry eyes, her heart twisted in her chest. She turned away, afraid of what he might see in her face.

"So, what happens now?" she said, relieved her voice held steady.

"Now?" he said. "We start planning the wedding."

She stopped abruptly on the tarmac. "I'm not going to marry you. We can share custody."

His eyes narrowed. "The decision has been made."

"By you. Not by me. And if you think you can bully me into marriage, on this ranch or anywhere else, you've got another think coming." She lifted her chin. "My family might not have an aristocratic history that goes back to infinity, but there are a few things we do have."

"Enlighten me."

"Stubbornness. Pure cussedness. And I'm not going to marry a man I don't love, a man who doesn't love me. I would rather scrub your floors with my tongue!"

Amusement flashed across his handsome face. "That can be arranged. Although," he murmured in her ear, "I can think of better uses for your tongue."

An unwilling fire went through Belle's body. Before she could formulate a response, he took her hand, pulling her toward the sprawling single-story ranch house surrounded by green trees.

Inside the main house, it was light and airy, with large windows and hardwood floors. A smiling housekeeper came forward. "Welcome back to the ranch, Mr. Velazquez." She turned her rosy round face in Belle's direction. "Welcome, miss. I hope you had a nice journey."

Nice didn't quite cover it, but luckily Santiago answered

for her. "It's been a long day, Mrs. Carlson. Could you please serve refreshments in the morning room?"

"Of course, Mr. Velazquez."

He led Belle down the hall, into a large room with a glossy wooden floor and a wall of windows. Comfortable furniture faced the view of green trees and a river turned gold beneath dappled sunlight. She breathed, "It's so beautiful."

"Sit down," he said. He seemed suddenly on edge.

Her knees felt weak anyway, so she let herself fall back onto the soft, plush, white cotton sofa. A moment later, the housekeeper appeared with a tray, which she set down on the table.

"Thank you."

"Of course, sir."

After the housekeeper departed, Santiago handed Belle what looked like a cocktail from the tray. At her dubious look, he explained, "Sweet tea."

Oh, her favorite. She practically snatched it from him. Drinking deeply, she sighed in pleasure at the ice-cold, sweetened, nonalcoholic beverage. Wiping her mouth, she sank back happily into the cushions of the sofa. "There are a few things about you that aren't horrible."

"Like sweet tea?"

"You're not totally a monster."

"You're welcome."

Gulping down the rest of the drink, she held the empty glass out hopefully.

His lips quirked as he turned back to the tray. Refilling her glass with the ceramic pitcher, he poured one for himself. "By the way, if you're formulating a plot to run away, you should know the nearest highway is thirty miles."

"I'm not planning to run away."

He straightened. "You're not?"

"Why would I? You're my baby's father. We have to figure it out. For her sake."

He stared at her. His handsome face seemed tense. He held out a plate. "Cookie?"

"Thank you." Chocolate chip, warm from the oven. As she bit into it, the butter and sugar and chocolate were like a burst on her tongue. She sighed with pleasure, then, feeling his gaze on her, looked up, pretending to scowl. "If you're trying to ply me with delicious food and drink to convince me to marry you, it won't work. However," she added hopefully, "you're free to keep trying."

But he just looked at her, his handsome face strained. He started to say something, then abruptly changed his mind. "Excuse me, I have to go."

"Go? Go where?"

"I'll have Mrs. Carlson show you the bedroom. As you said," he gave a smile that didn't reach his eyes, "it's been a crazy week. Rest, if you like. I'll see you for dinner. Eight o'clock."

He left without another word.

Now what was that all about? Although she wasn't going to complain, since at least he'd left the tray. Taking another cookie from the plate, Belle looked out at the leafy green trees moving softly in an unseen breeze, dappled with golden afternoon light. He'd gone to all that trouble to drag her to his ranch, and now, instead of threatening her into marriage or trying to boss her around, he'd just fed her sweet tea and home-baked cookies, then left her to relax?

But then, people had continually surprised her in life, starting with her own family. Belle couldn't remember her father, who'd died when she was a baby. She'd grown up in that house on the edge of the sagebrush prairie with a stepfather, two younger half brothers and her sad-eyed mother, who tried unsuccessfully to shield her children from both her sorrow and her terminal illness. Belle's stepfather, a wiry, laconic welder, never showed much interest in any of the children. He worked long hours then spent his evenings smoking cigarettes, drinking his nightly six-pack and yelling at his wife.

But when Belle was twelve, her mother died, and everything changed. Her stepfather started yelling at her instead, threatening to kick her out of the house, "Because you're none of mine."

So she'd anxiously tried to earn her keep by taking care of the young boys, by cooking and cleaning. By always being cheerful and smiling. By making sure she was never any trouble to anyone.

A week after Belle graduated from high school, her stepfather died suddenly of a brain aneurysm. Ray was thirteen, Joe just eleven. There were no other relatives, no life insurance and almost no savings. Rather than let her little brothers be turned over to foster care, Belle gave up a college scholarship to stay in Bluebell and work as a waitress to support them, raising them until they were grown.

It hadn't been easy. As teenagers, her orphaned brothers had gotten into fights at school, and Ray had briefly gotten into drugs. Those years had been filled with slammed doors, yells of "I hate you!" and her homemade dinners thrown to the floor.

Barely more than a teenager herself, Belle had struggled to get through it. Heartsick, exhausted and alone, she'd dreamed about falling in love with a man who was handsome and kind. A man who would take care of her.

Then, at twenty-one, she had. And it had nearly destroyed her.

"Miss Langtry?" The plump, gray-haired housekeeper appeared in the doorway with her ever-present smile. "If you're done, I can show you to your room."

Glancing at the empty tray, Belle said dryly, "I guess I'm done."

Pushing herself up from the sofa—a simple act that was getting harder by the day as her belly expanded—she followed the housekeeper down the hall of the ranch house. They turned down another hallway, then Mrs. Carlson pushed open a door. "Here's your bedroom, miss."

The room was enormous, with a tall ceiling, a walk-in closet and an en suite bathroom. This, too, had a wall of windows overlooking the river. But that wasn't the bedroom's most notable characteristic.

Belle stared at the enormous bed.

"Is something wrong, Miss Langtry?"

"Um…" Looking around the enormous bedroom, Belle managed, "This is a really nice guest room."

Her worst fears were realized when the older woman replied with a laugh, "Guest room? I know they say everything's bigger in Texas, but honey, that would be crazy. This bedroom suite is bigger than most houses. It's the master bedroom."

Belle gulped. But before she could think of a good reply to explain there was *no way* she was going to be sleeping with the master in this bedroom, the housekeeper continued to the bathroom, proudly showing off the marble tub, sparkling silver fixtures and fresh flowers, with a skylight overhead. Now this, Belle could appreciate.

"You'll find everything you could need or want… Mr. Velazquez said you were weary and dusty after traveling. We have everything you need for a nice, long bath."

She showed Belle all the perfumes, French soaps, creams, shampoos so expensive that she'd only read about them in celebrity magazines. Belle had always thought rich people must be fools for spending fifty dollars on shampoo when the cheap generic brand got your hair just as clean. But as she sniffed the expensive shampoo tentatively, it did smell nice.

"Mr. Velazquez trusts you'll be comfortable while he

conducts some business this afternoon." She opened a door. Belle followed her into a huge closet, with a chandelier and a white sofa.

The housekeeper indicated a red dress hanging alone in the closet. "He requests that you wear this tonight. Dinner will be served on the terrace at eight."

Looking at the dress, Belle breathed, "It's beautiful."

"There are shoes to match, two-inch heels so you won't be uncomfortable or off balance." She smiled in the direction of Belle's belly. "And also new lingerie." She opened one of the drawers. "Silk. Here. Next to your other things."

Lingerie? Belle blushed, suddenly unable to meet the other woman's eyes. Looking around the huge closet, she saw a few scant clothes that had already been unpacked from her suitcase. But other than that and the red dress, the enormous walk-in closet's racks and shelves were empty. "Where are Santiago's clothes?"

"Mr. Velazquez's clothes are in the master closet."

"Isn't this the master closet?"

"Oh, no." Her friendly, chubby face widened in a broad smile. "This closet is designated just for the mistress of the house, that is, if there ever should be one." Leaning forward, she confided, "You're the first woman he's ever brought to the ranch."

"I am?"

"Goodness. Getting late." Mrs. Carlson looked at her watch. "Everything you'll need is here. We arranged toiletries, lotions, lipsticks, everything we could think of that you might want. My grandson is in a school play down at Alford Elementary tonight. The rest of the staff will be gone by eight."

"You all don't live here?"

"Oh, goodness, no. There are staff cottages on the other side of the lake. You and Mr. Velazquez can be completely alone." Was it her imagination, or did the housekeeper wink? "Good night, miss."

Belle stared indignantly after her. Why had she winked? What did she think would happen if she and Santiago were alone?

Nothing, she thought firmly, and locked the bedroom door to prove it. She glanced at the enormous bed. As comfortable as it looked, she would never share it with Santiago. But since he wasn't here right now…

She climbed onto the soft, comfortable bed as days of worry and weariness caught up with her. Her head hit the pillow and she closed her eyes just for a moment.

When she woke, she realized by the fading sunlight that she'd accidentally slept for hours.

Rising from the bed, Belle saw the red dress hanging in the walk-in closet across the bedroom. Going to it, she let her fingertips stroke the soft fabric. She saw the designer tag and gulped. She didn't know fashion, but even she had heard of that famous designer. And the shoes!

But it would be bad manners not to wear it. Especially since it was the most beautiful thing she'd ever seen in real life, much less worn on her body.

Taking the dress and silk lingerie, she went to the enormous en suite bathroom and took a shower. As she stepped naked beneath the hot, steaming water, with six different spigots coming at her from all sides, she sighed in pleasure as the dust and heartbreak of the last three days were swept away. She tried the shampoo. Maybe the fifty dollars was worth it, she thought in a blissful haze. Though even a bargain shampoo would have been great in a shower like this.

Wrapping herself in a towel, she brushed out her long, wet hair. Opening a drawer, she found boxes of brand-new makeup, the high-end kind from department stores with the nice packaging, all lined up for her use, next to a variety of brand-new perfumes and pricey scented lotions.

She tried it all, then put on the silk bra and panties. She almost moaned. So sensual. So soft.

Finally, she pulled on the red knit dress, which fit perfectly over her swollen breasts and baby bump. The soft fabric felt like heaven against her perfumed skin. Even her hands, which for the last year and a half had always been red and chapped from working as a waitress at the diner, felt soft, from all the lotions. She looked in the bathroom mirror.

Her hair now gleamed, tumbling down her shoulders, dark against her creamy caramel skin. Her cheeks were flushed pink from the heat of the shower. Her lips were ruby red to match the dress. Her brown eyes gleamed in the shadows beneath dark kohl and mascara.

Even to her own eyes, she looked…different.

Was it this place? The dress? The extravagant shampoo?

Or was it being around Santiago, being pregnant with his child, being the first woman he'd ever brought to this famous ranch, spread across five counties of south Texas?

"Most of South Texas was once claimed by the Spanish Empire, in the time of the conquistadors…my father is a Zoya. The eighth Duque de Sangovia."

Santiago, the son of a duke? That surprised her. He didn't seem like a man who'd been born with a silver spoon in his mouth. Oh, he was arrogant enough. But he seemed too rough, like a man who'd had to fight so hard for everything that he no longer gave a damn about the judgment of lesser mortals.

"Your father is a duke? An actual duke?… What's he like?"

"I wouldn't know. We've never met."

That was one thing Santiago and Belle had in common, then. All she had of her father was an old picture of him, beaming into the camera as he held her as a swaddled baby, sleeping in his arms.

If Santiago had never even met his father, that explained a lot. But why did they have different last names? If his father was still alive, why had the two men never met?

Then she was distracted by a more urgent question. Biting her lip, Belle looked down at her belly, prominent in the red dress. She looked at the dress, at the luxurious toiletries, the costly, well-made shoes.

Why was Santiago suddenly being so kind to her?

She couldn't trust it, that was for sure. She'd learned that from their night together. He could be warm and tender when he wanted her, then ruthlessly toss her out of his life like garbage.

There could be only one reason. He'd realized he couldn't bully her into marriage, so he was going to try to seduce her into it.

She wouldn't let him.

She *wouldn't*.

Belle was willing to share custody of their baby. But she wouldn't share her life, her heart and certainly not her body. She would never be Santiago Velazquez's plaything again, and definitely not his wife.

Now she just had to convince him of that, so he'd let her go home.

At five minutes past eight, as Belle walked through the enormous, sprawling ranch house, down the darkened hallways, she felt strangely nervous of how he'd react.

Opening the sliding doors, she went outside onto the terrace that stretched out toward the lake. Fairy lights hung from a large pergola, covered with flowers of pink bougainvillea. The lights twinkled against the twilight as soft music came from invisible speakers.

And she saw him.

Santiago stood at the terrace railing, looking out pensively toward dark water painted red by sunset. Then he turned, devastatingly handsome, tall and broad-shouldered in his tuxedo. And he smiled.

"Welcome," he said in his low, husky voice. Their eyes locked, and held.

And Belle suddenly knew the real reason for her fear. Her heart had known it all along, and so had her body. Her brain had refused to accept it. Now she saw the truth. She hadn't been afraid of Santiago's reaction.

She was afraid of her own. Because when she'd given him her body all those months ago, she'd unwillingly given him part of her heart. And now, as he smiled at her, his eyes twinkling beneath the lights, she caught her breath.

"You're beautiful." Coming closer, he held out a champagne glass. His dark eyes caressed her as he whispered, "Brighter than the stars."

As she took the champagne glass, their fingers brushed. She saw the intention in his eyes, and it rocked her to her core.

Santiago intended to conquer her, just as he'd conquered the world. He intended to win her, as he'd won his billion-dollar fortune. He intended to rule her, as he ruled this isolated Texas ranch, big enough to be its own kingdom.

He intended to possess her as his wife. And he would not be denied.

CHAPTER FOUR

HE'D BEEN WRONG about her. All wrong.

When he'd left New York in pursuit of Belle, he'd been certain she was a gold digger, a cunning, cold-hearted actress, who'd ruthlessly lied in order to conceive his child for her own selfish financial gain.

But that afternoon, at the medical center in Houston, he'd learned otherwise.

Standing in the hallway outside the examination room as he waited for Belle, he'd stared at the doctor in disbelief. "Is this a joke?"

She'd smiled. "I never joke about medical matters."

"What do you mean, she was telling the truth?"

"Miss Langtry had good reason to think she could never conceive a child," the doctor had said. "I just received her medical records from the hospital in Bluebell. Seven years ago, she had a procedure to make pregnancy impossible. Bilateral tubal ligation." She hesitated. "I shouldn't be discussing this with you, but…"

But she was, and they both knew why. Santiago spent many millions of dollars each year supporting her clinic, so uninsured patients could get world-class care without worrying about payment. He still remembered his first winter in New York, at eighteen, when he'd been sick for months but hadn't gone to a doctor because he'd feared the cost.

Now, he said incredulously, "Belle deliberately had surgery to make sure she'd never get pregnant? Why?"

"You'd have to ask her."

"But she was only twenty-one—and a virgin! What crackpot doctor would perform such a procedure?"

"Interestingly, that doctor retired a month later. It turned out he'd been suffering from the early stages of dementia."

"So if she had that surgery seven years ago, how can she be pregnant?" Santiago said.

The doctor hesitated. "Miss Langtry is young…"

"So?"

"There is a risk of healing after that type of procedure. It's rare, but it does happen. The body finds a way. It's even more likely when the patient is young."

Santiago glared at her. "She honestly believed she couldn't get pregnant."

"Yes. Either the procedure wasn't done correctly, or her body healed over the last seven years."

It had been like a punch in the gut.

Everything Santiago had believed about Belle was wrong. She wasn't a greedy climber. She was innocent. She'd been telling the truth all along.

After they left the medical center, as their helicopter flew south from Houston, Belle had refused to meet his gaze, but he hadn't been able to look away from her. Her beautiful face, her lush body, pregnant with his child. Remembering their night together, he'd felt aware of her every movement. He'd thought of nothing but how she'd felt in his arms that night. How she'd gasped with ecstasy. How afterward, she'd cuddled against him so sweetly.

"You feel so good to me," she'd whispered. *"I'm glad you're here. I couldn't bear to be alone tonight. You saved me…"*

Santiago had left her that night because he'd known his life would change, with her in it. And he hadn't wanted it to change.

But his life had changed without his consent. In spite of incredible odds, she was pregnant.

Now there was someone else to think about. His child. Having his paternity confirmed, seeing his daughter pictured on the ultrasound screen in Houston, the idea of a baby had felt truly real to him for the first time. A daughter. An innocent child. She hadn't asked to be conceived, but now it was possible, through no fault of her own, she could be born without a name. Without a father's protection or love.

He couldn't let that happen.

He couldn't let his child be split between parents, and have the same childhood he'd endured, ignored and rejected by his biological father, watching his mother so desperate to be loved that she married man after man, each less worthy than the last.

No. His daughter's life would be different.

She would have a stable home. Married parents. Financial security. His daughter would have a happy childhood, filled with love.

When they'd arrived at the ranch that afternoon, Santiago had already made up his mind. He'd taken Belle straight to the morning room, intending to force an engagement ring on her hand, to blackmail or threaten her into it, if he had to. But something stopped him.

The thought of their daughter.

After the way he'd treated Belle from the moment they'd slept together that cold winter's night, she'd had good reason to despise him. He'd abandoned her. Ignored her phone messages. Treated her badly when she'd actually come to his house to tell him about the baby.

Standing in the morning room, he'd known he could force Belle to marry him, if he chose.

He suddenly didn't want to.

He didn't want to be her enemy. For their daughter's

sake, they needed a better foundation for their marriage, for a happy home, than resentment and hatred.

So Santiago had abruptly changed tactics.

Instead of giving Belle his ultimatum in the morning room, he'd given her time to rest, to regroup, to be refreshed. And he'd taken time to plan his own strategy. He'd organized this dinner with the help of his staff. The dress had already been purchased in nearby Alford, by Mrs. Carlson, but he'd still lacked one thing: a show-stopping engagement ring.

Fortunately, he'd thought with grim amusement, he happened to have one, gathering dust these past years in his safe. The diamond ring was tucked in his tuxedo pocket now, glinting, sparkling, obscene.

He'd tried to give this ring to a different woman, long ago; one he'd loved so much he'd built his billion-dollar fortune in the attempt to win her. Santiago still felt acid in his gut at the memory of the day he'd proposed to Nadia with this very ring, as promised so many years before, only to discover she hadn't waited for him. And the man she'd chosen—

Santiago's shoulders went tight. In the past. All in the past. Starting today, he would treat Belle, the mother of his unborn child, with respect and care. Once he did, she would see reason. She would not refuse his marriage proposal.

The sun was falling into the lake, a red ball of fire burning through the low haze of twilight, when Santiago heard Belle come out through the sliding doors onto the terrace. Turning from the railing, he looked at her.

And was dazzled.

He'd never seen such rampant beauty, all lush curves in that red dress, her dark hair tumbling over her shoulders, her lips invitingly red, black eyelashes trembling over big brown eyes.

"You're beautiful," he breathed, holding out a champagne glass. "Brighter than the stars."

She took the glass. From this close, her skin looked delectably soft. He wanted to kiss her. He wanted to pick her up like a caveman and carry her to bed, to rip off the red dress that clung to every curve, and make love to her until he felt her quiver and shake, until he heard her cry out with pleasure.

She looked up at him, her eyes regretful. "I can't drink champagne."

"It's sparkling juice."

"Juice?" Taking the glass, she gave him a nervous smile. "I can't imagine you drinking anything except black coffee and maybe Scotch."

"We're celebrating."

"We are?"

"And if you can't drink champagne, neither will I."

Her forehead furrowed in the twilight, beneath the fairy lights of the pergola.

"I think I know why you're being so nice to me," she said slowly.

"Because I know I was wrong," he said quietly. "And I'm sorry."

She could have no idea, he thought, how long it had been since he'd said those last two words to anyone. Years? Decades?

"Sorry?" She frowned. "About what?"

"You truly thought you couldn't get pregnant."

Her expression changed. "Why do you believe me now?"

"Dr. Hill told me about your medical procedure."

"She shouldn't have." She stiffened. "That's my private business."

"Not anymore. Anything that relates to you or the baby is my business now." Moving closer, his body thrummed with awareness as his gaze fell to her red lips, then further down still. Her thick dark hair fell in waves over her bare clavicle, over her shoulders, almost to her full breasts straining the red knit fabric of her dress. His body suddenly raged to pull her into his arms, tip her back against the table and ravage her right here and now. He took a deep breath to control himself.

"Won't you join me?"

Turning toward a large stone table nearby, he showed her the dishes, interspersed with big vases of flowers.

"What is it?" she said doubtfully.

"Dinner." He lifted a silver lid off the largest platter. Frowning, she peeked over his shoulder. When she saw the food, she burst into a full-bodied, incredulous laugh that he felt down to his toes.

"Blueberries? Licorice whips? I thought you'd try to serve me something nasty, like caviar!"

"I have only your favorites." He lifted another silver lid, and grinned as he heard her gasp.

"Ham and pineapple pizza!" she exclaimed. "Are you kidding me?"

"With the ranch and hot sauce you like, for dipping," he said smugly. "And for dessert…" He opened a third silver lid to reveal strawberry shortcake, thick sweet cakes covered with plump, juicy strawberries and thick dollops of whipped cream. Now, she looked at him almost in awe.

"How did you know?" she breathed.

"Magic."

"No, seriously."

"I called Letty and asked her what you liked best." He lifted an eyebrow. "She didn't sound particularly shocked to hear from me, by the way."

Her cheeks colored. "She's the only one I told about you. I knew she wouldn't tell anyone you were my baby's father.

Not after what she went through with Darius." Tentatively, she touched the crust. "The pizza is still hot!"

"I told you." He waved a hand airily. "Magic."

She looked at him skeptically.

He rolled his eyes. "There's a hot plate beneath the tray. If you make me explain, it takes the magic away. All that's left is cheap tricks." He started to add, *just like romance*, but stopped himself, since he didn't think it would help his cause. Pulling out a chair, he gave her a sensual smile. "Have a seat."

As they ate together, enjoying fruit, pizza, sparkling water and finally dessert, the sun gradually disappeared beneath the horizon, turning the sky a soft pink against the black lake.

He enjoyed watching her eat. He took pleasure in her appetite. As she started her third piece of strawberry short-cake, he leaned forward and brushed his fingertips against the corner of her mouth.

"Missed some whipped cream," he said, and then licked it off his fingertips. Belle's eyes went wide, and he heard her intake of breath. He almost kissed her then. Instead, he leaned back in his chair to look at her.

"So why did you do it, Belle?" he asked quietly. "Why did you deliberately have surgery at twenty-one, to prevent pregnancy? Knowing you as I do, it doesn't make sense."

For a moment he thought she might not answer. Then she set down her spoon.

"My dad died when I was a baby," she said haltingly. "My mother remarried a few years later, and had my broth-ers…"

"I know."

Belle looked surprised. "You know?" She glanced down as his hand enfolded her own, then said with a tinge of bitterness, "Of course you know. Your private investiga-tor told you, right?" She gave a humorless laugh. "So you know my mother died when I was twelve and my stepfather six years later. I couldn't let my brothers be sent to foster care. So I gave up my dream of college and stayed home to raise them."

Santiago tried to think of a time he'd made a sacrifice that big for anyone. He couldn't.

"It wasn't easy," she continued in a low voice. "They were angry teenagers. Sometimes I wasn't sure I could make it. Then I met Justin." She blinked fast. "He was so strong and sure. He said he loved me. Even when I told him I was old-fashioned and wished to wait until marriage to have sex, he still wanted me..."

Santiago gave an incredulous laugh. "No sex until marriage?"

"I know." She smiled wistfully. "Crazy, right? But he'd just gotten divorced. His wife'd had an awful miscarriage that broke them up. Justin was ten years older than me, but he said that didn't matter. He was even willing to help me raise my brothers, who desperately needed a male role model."

"Did they?" he said evenly, remembering all the times his own mother had married so-called "male role models" who hadn't been worth much and hadn't lasted more than a year.

"It seemed like the perfect solution for everyone to be happy. There was just one catch." Her voice was small. "Justin couldn't go through losing a baby again. So he only agreed to marry me if I...he and I...made sure to never have a baby of our own. Ever." She looked down at her lap. "So a few weeks before our wedding, I did it. It seemed like the only way to make everyone happy."

"What about you? Did it make you happy?"

A strangled laugh escaped her lips, and she looked away. "Not exactly."

The final light of the setting sun streaked across her pale, troubled face. He said grimly, "What happened?"

"He left me. Right before our wedding." She gave him a small smile. "He'd had a hard time waiting for sex and ran into his ex-wife at a bar. One thing led to another, and she became pregnant. After that, he wanted to give their relationship another try. He told me he'd never stopped loving her."

He gave a low, heartfelt curse in Spanish.

"It's all right," she said quietly. "They're happy now. They're married, living in El Paso. Last I heard, they have a big rambling house and five children."

Santiago fell silent, his jaw tight.

"I know what you're thinking." She looked up, her eyes suddenly shining with unshed tears. "Go ahead. Tell me how stupid I was, to sacrifice my own dreams for the sake of love."

Rising moonlight frosted the dark lake, and he heard the plaintive call of unseen birds. He looked at her beauty, at the way her dark eyelashes trembled against her cheeks.

Rising to his feet, he took her hand. "Dance with me."

"No, I…"

"Why?" He gave her a wicked smile. "Are you afraid?"

"Of course not. I'm just not a good dancer, I…"

But he didn't listen to her excuses. Gently, he pulled her from the chair, into his arms. He felt her body tremble against his. The fairy lights twinkled above the terrace, as they looked out at the moon-swept lake. They were alone.

"I'll lead," he murmured, and he twirled her slowly around the flagstone terrace. He watched her sway, light as air. Saw the beauty of her. The kindness. The way she'd sacrificed for her younger brothers. The way she'd sacrificed for the man she'd once thought she would marry.

Damn, he thought. What a mother she will make.

What a *wife*.

He whirled her close, then caught her tight in his arms. Her eyes widened, and she sucked in her breath as she saw his intention.

Slowly, never taking his eyes from hers, he lowered his mouth to hers.

She didn't fight him, but closed her eyes, letting him hold her close. He closed his eyes and kissed her, really kissed her.

Lightning shattered through his body, through his soul, in the embrace. He felt her tremble, pressing her body against his.

Then she ripped away, her eyes tortured.

"Why are you doing this?" she choked out.

"Doing what?"

"*Romancing* me," she said bitterly, "like the night you seduced me. I'm not going to fall for it again, so you can break my heart!" She pressed her palm against his chest, pushing him away. "Just tell me what you want from me."

The stars above them sparkled in the wide, velvety black sky as he looked down at her. It was too soon. He had barely started to seduce her as he wished. But she wanted him to speak plainly, so he would. He had that much respect for her.

"Very well," he said quietly. Reaching into his tuxedo jacket pocket, he lowered himself to one knee, holding up the huge diamond ring. It glittered brighter and bigger than the full moon shining across the endless Texas sky. "I want you to marry me, Belle."

She gaped at him, looking from the ring to his face and back again.

"I know I've treated you badly," he said. "But I'll never make that mistake again. I'll never lie to you, Belle. We'll be more than lovers. We'll be partners. Parents. I know you want love, and I regret I cannot give you that. But I offer you something better."

"Better than love?" she whispered. He nodded.

"My loyalty. You never betrayed me. I will never betray you. I've made very few promises in life, but I'm making one to you now. If you marry me, I'll make sure you're never alone again. Our marriage will be for life."

"For life?" She looked stricken. She said hoarsely, "I might consider a temporary marriage…to give our baby a name…"

"No." His expression hardened. "A real marriage, Belle. A real home. Isn't that what you want? Isn't that what our baby deserves from us?"

She looked away and whispered, "I don't know."

Rising to his feet, he pulled her close and growled, "I think you do."

Her dark gaze seared his. "I want to marry someone I can love and respect. And you're not that man, Santiago, you know you're not."

The words caused a stab in his solar plexus. He hadn't known he could still be hurt by rejection. He'd thought he'd buried his heart long ago. To be hurt now, when he was trying his best to please her, when he was trying his best to be honest, stung him to the core.

He took a deep breath. "Love—perhaps not. But we both love our daughter. And if you give me a chance," he said in a low voice, "I will earn your respect. I swear it."

She looked at the fairy lights and the flowers on the stone table, at the diamond ring still in his hand.

"I'm not your toy," she said in a small voice. "Just because we slept together once and conceived this child, you can't just have me whenever you want amusement. You don't have any permanent claim over me."

"You're wrong." He lifted his gaze to hers. "I do have a permanent claim. Just as you've had a claim over me, from the moment you came to my bed."

"What are you talking about?"

"You," he whispered, cupping her cheek. "And how you've bewitched me."

Her eyes were big as she looked up at him. "You can find someone else—"

"*No.*"

"Yes you can! You've been with dozens of women since that night. Supermodels, actresses, socialites…" Her voice cut off as their eyes met. She choked out, "Haven't you?"

Never looking away, he shook his head, his jaw tight. "There's been no one. Because I don't want any other woman. I haven't, since our night together. I've only hungered for you." He narrowed his eyes as he looked down at her. His voice was a growl. "You will belong to me, Belle. You have no choice. I already belong to you."

I already belong to you.

It wasn't romantic. At all. He said it, Belle thought, as if he felt trapped. Oppressed, even. His dark eyes glittered.

"Are you telling me," she breathed, "you've been celibate all these months?"

"Yes." His voice was a low growl.

"But—but why?"

His eyes were dark. "You've ensorcelled me."

Ensorcelled. Such a strange, old-fashioned word. Such a gleam in his dark eyes and his powerful body towering over her with all his strength. She suddenly felt like she'd gone back hundreds of years, to a simpler time.

Belle shivered, struggling not to feel so aware of his body close to hers. His eyes were dark beneath the softly swaying lights. She saw the arrogant curve of his dangerously seductive mouth.

He was right, she realized. She did belong to him. From the moment he'd kissed her that cold January night.

No. She couldn't pretend it had been just that. It had been more.

She'd been able to be honest with him that night in a way she hadn't been since her mother died. She never had to pretend with Santiago. She didn't have to act cheerful and happy all the time. She could actually be herself.

She did want him. His warmth. His strength. She wanted the man who'd seduced her that cold winter's night, not just with his body, but with his words.

The only thing that kept her from falling into his arms now was remembering how she'd felt waking up alone that gray January morning, and all the mornings after, when he ignored message after frantic message.

"But I can't trust you," she said in a small voice. "Not anymore. If I give myself to you, how do I know I won't be left broken-hearted and alone?"

"Your heart will be safe. I'll never ask for it." Reaching out, he stroked her shoulder. His soft touch over the fabric of her red dress felt like fire. "And you'll never be alone again." He lifted her hand to his mouth. She felt the warmth of his breath as he kissed her palm, then the back of her hand. "Never," he whispered.

She couldn't hide her shiver beneath his seductive caress. Looking up at his darkly handsome face beneath the moonlight, at his powerful body towering over hers in the tuxedo, she wondered wildly if he could hear the pounding of her heart. "I can't…"

"Are you sure?" he whispered. Brushing back her hair, he kissed her forehead. Her cheeks. She trembled in his arms, hovering on the edge of surrender.

"Please don't do this." Pressing her palms against the lapels of his tuxedo jacket, she lifted her tearful gaze to his. "You don't know what you're asking me."

"So tell me."

Her hands tightened.

"To give up all hope of being loved," she choked out. "Now and forever."

"That kind of love is an illusion." He drew back. "I know. My mother was a maid working in my father's palace when she got pregnant with me. He was already married, and his duchess was heavily pregnant. He must not have found his wife sexually appealing, because one afternoon he pushed my mother into a closet and kissed her." His lips twisted. "She was barely nineteen, and so wrapped up in fairy-tale dreams she convinced herself the duke loved her. That only lasted until she got pregnant, too, and he threw her out of the palace. She was suddenly poor, a single mother, and dreams don't pay the bills. She thought only love could save her. So she married. Five times."

Santiago had never told her anything about his childhood before. Not one word. She sucked in her breath. "Five marriages?"

"And each husband worse than the last. Each time, her heart was broken. She didn't want to raise me alone," he said lightly. "She couldn't relax at night. Couldn't sleep. So she took sleeping pills. One night she took too many and died."

"How old were you?" she said, aghast.

"Fourteen. I called an ambulance when I found her. The authorities dragged me from the house and I was sent to an orphanage."

"Why didn't you go to your father?"

He snorted. "My father already had a son and heir. He did not care to recognize the bastard result of his affair with a maid. When I tried to see him at his palace in Madrid, he set the dogs on me."

"How could he?" Belle breathed.

Santiago turned away, blankly staring toward the pearlescent moonlight trailing across the lake. He finally looked at her.

"The man did me a favor," he said flatly. "And I'm doing you one now by telling you this. The fairy-tale dream doesn't exist. Only when you give it up will you have any possibility of happiness."

Belle could understand why he might think that, after everything he'd gone through. And yet… She bit her lip. "You never tried to speak to your father again? Or your half brother?"

"They had their chance." His eyes were hard. "I might have Zoya blood, but they mean nothing to me now."

Santiago looked down at her. "So now do you understand? I never intended this to happen. I never meant to marry, or have a child. What do I know of being a husband, or a father?" His eyes narrowed. "But I will not allow my child to have the lonely existence I had. She will not be rejected, raised in poverty by a delusional mother and a succession of uncaring stepfathers. She will have my name." He looked at her evenly. "You will marry me."

Belle licked her lips as she tried desperately, "But there are other ways besides marriage…"

Reaching out, he cupped her cheek.

"You will agree to marry me, Belle, or I will keep you here until the baby is born, and take the child from you. Do you understand?"

His tone was so gentle, it took her a moment to understand the meaning. Then her eyes went wide as she drew away sharply.

"You wouldn't."

"You are mistaken if you believe I am as soft-hearted as you. I am not."

She shivered, not doubting it. "So you're threatening me?"

"I am telling you how it will be. I won't let you put your own foolish dreams above the needs of our baby. Either you leave here with this ring on your finger, or you don't leave at all."

"You can't want to be married… To be loyal and faithful to one woman for the rest of your life? You don't even love me!"

"I will keep my vows," he said impatiently. "I expect you to keep them as well."

She blinked fast. "It's easy for you to give up all dreams of love. You've never loved anyone."

Her harsh words echoed in the silent evening. He stared at her for a long moment, his jaw clenching. When he finally spoke, his voice held no expression.

"So you agree?"

"Fine," she choked out.

"You accept my proposal?"

"You've left me no choice."

"As you've left me none." He slid the enormous platinum-set diamond over her finger. "This ring symbolizes how we are bound. For life."

The precious metal felt cold and heavy, both on her hand and on her heart. "Now what, a shotgun wedding at the nearest justice of the peace?"

He snorted, then sobered. "We will be married in New York."

Back to New York, the city that had chewed her up and spat her out, with a man who would never love her, and who for all his fine words, was practically blackmailing her into marriage? "This gets better and better."

"Our wedding will be a society event. As my wife, you will take your rightful place in New York society."

Belle looked at him incredulously. "Have you lost your mind? Me? A leader in New York society?"

"You will be."

Belle lifted her chin. "I told you. You don't own me."

Santiago looked down at her, his black eyes glittering. "You're wrong," he said softly. Taking her hand in his own, he looked down at the sharp shine of the ring in the moonlight. "From this moment on, I do."

She felt his hand enfolding hers, his palm rough and warm against her skin, and a skitter of electricity went up her spine. Her lips parted.

He pulled her into his arms, cupping her face in his hands. Deliberately, slowly, he lowered his mouth to hers.

The smooth caress of his hot satin lips seared her, making her weak. Ruthlessly, he deepened the kiss, tilting back her head, tangling his hands in her hair. Need raced through her, quickening her heartbeat, making her lose her breath.

Pressing her against the thick white column of the pergola, amid the bloom of pink flowers beneath the fairy lights, he slowly kissed down her throat. Her head fell back, her dark hair tumbling down, as her eyes closed against the sweet pleasure of sensation.

He ran his hands down her arms, over the soft red knit fabric of her low-cut dress. She felt his touch like a whisper over her full breasts, over her belly, over her hips. He lowered his head to kiss her naked collarbone, then the bare cleavage between her breasts.

"I want you," he whispered. Leaning forward, he whispered against the sensitive flesh of her earlobe, making her shiver, "Come to my bed tonight."

Belle opened her eyes. Frosted by moonlight and the silvery lake behind him, Santiago's face was in shadow as he towered over her like a dark angel. That had been the Spanish playboy's nickname in New York, she remembered. Ángel. Now she understood why.

And she could no longer resist. She could only surrender.

Santiago looked at her, then scooped her wordlessly into his arms. He carried her into the sprawling ranch house, down the silent hallway, into the enormous master bedroom, dark with shadows except for the shaft of moonlight pooling through the large windows.

He set her down almost reverently, and she stood in front of him, unsteady on her feet. Kneeling in front of her, he pulled off her shoes, one by one. Rising, he stood in front of her and kissed her again, deeply. When the kiss ended, as she tried to catch her breath, he circled her, his fingertips lingering against her body, and slowly unzipped her dress in the back. Gently, he drew the dress down her body, slipping it off her full breasts, down her arms. He tugged it slowly over her belly, to her hips, until the dress finally fell like a soft whisper to the floor.

She stood nearly naked in front of him, wearing only a silk bra and panties. Still fully dressed in his tuxedo, Santiago looked down at her in the moonlight.

"So beautiful," he whispered, reaching out to touch her shoulder. His hand traced down to cup a full breast over the sensuous silk bra. She nearly gasped as she felt the warmth of his hand pressing the smooth fabric against her heavy breast and aching nipple, which hardened beneath his touch.

He drew closer. His palms explored the full curve of her belly, down to her hips, stroking the naked skin along the edge of her silk panties. Reaching around her, he put his hands over her backside, taking her firmly in his grasp, pulling her hard against his body.

When he lowered his mouth to hers, his kiss was hungry, as he reached beneath the flimsy silk to cup her naked breasts. His thumb stroked her aching nipple. As she gasped with pleasure, he unclasped the sliver of silk and dropped it entirely to the floor.

He cupped both her breasts with his hands, as if marveling at their weight, then lowered his mouth to gently suckle her.

The sensation was so intense she jolted beneath his hot mouth, gripping his shoulders. Pleasure was rising so hard and fast inside her, she wondered if she could climax like this, with only his lips against her breast, his tongue swirling around her nipple, sucking her deeply into his hot, wet mouth.

She gasped, her fingernails digging into his shoulders. She realized with shock that he was still wearing his jacket. Reaching down, she undid his tuxedo tie, then roughly yanked his jacket down from his shoulders.

Rising, he looked down at her intently. Gaze locked with hers, he undid the buttons of his shirt and trousers then dropped them to the floor, along with his silk boxers. He stood naked, his body hard and jutting toward her. She looked down at him in amazement. Reaching out, she took his hard shaft fully in her hands—it took both her hands—and relished the soft, velvety feel of him, so thick and hard as steel.

Now he was the one to gasp.

With a low growl, he pulled her toward the king-sized bed bathed in moonlight, and drew her on top of him. She was shy and uncertain at first, until he pulled her head down into a kiss. Her dark hair tumbled down like a veil, blocking the moonlight, leaving their faces in darkness.

She felt his hands on her hips, moving her until her legs spread wide over his. She felt the hardness of him, insistent between her thighs, demanding entry. That single movement, feeling him pressing against the wet, aching center of her desire, was enough to make her hold her breath. Involuntarily, she swayed against him. With an intake of breath, he tightened his hands on her hips, lifting her off his body, positioning her. Then, with agonizing slowness, he lowered her again, filling her, inch by delicious inch.

She gasped from the pleasure as he slid inside her. Just when she thought her body couldn't take any more of him, he somehow went even deeper, all the way to the hilt, all the way to the heart.

He was hard and thick inside her as his large hands

gripped her backside, spreading her wide. She gasped, tossing back her head.

Then slowly, instinctively, she began to move her body against his, feeling the deliciously exquisite tension rise and build inside her as she slid against his flat, muscular belly. She felt his rough fingertips gripping into her hips as she began to ride him, harder, faster. Her breasts bounced against the swell of her belly as she rode him, soft and slow, then hard and deep. She rode him until her whole body started to tremble and shake.

As she cried out, she heard his low roar join hers, rising to a shout as he filled her so deep she exploded with joyful ecstasy. Her cry became a scream she didn't even try to contain, and he screamed with her, his body jerking and pulsing as he spilled himself inside her.

Exhausted, she collapsed beside him, and he held her. He cuddled her close, gently kissing her sweaty temple. But as she closed her eyes, she heard his dark whisper, so soft she wondered if she'd imagined it, like a whisper of her heart's deepest fear.

"You're mine now."

CHAPTER FIVE

THE LIGHTS OF New York City were dazzling and bright, but in the deep canyon between skyscrapers, Belle could no longer see the sky.

Sitting beside Santiago in the chauffeured black Escalade, with bodyguards following in another SUV, she'd felt numb as they traveled from the airport in New Jersey through Midtown, passing within blocks of the Broadway and Off-Broadway theaters that had rejected her so thoroughly.

As the saying went, if you could make it in New York, you could make it anywhere. But Belle hadn't made it here. She'd thought if she could be an actress, if she could earn a living by pretending to be someone else every day, she could be happy. Instead, the city had laughed in her face.

And Santiago expected her, a small-town girl who'd never gone to college, to know how to be a socialite in this wealthy, ruthless city?

All she'd ever done was work as a waitress and raise her brothers. If Santiago had needed her to remember six different dinner orders with special instructions and sauce on the side, and serve it all at once balanced on her arms, no problem. If he'd wanted her to rustle up a double platter of brownies for ten hungry teenage basketball players in no time flat, Belle could have handled it.

But knowing how to blend into high society? Knowing how to swan around being chic while making small talk to the highly educated and fashionable glitterati he mingled with?

It was all Belle could do not to hyperventilate.

She glanced mutinously at Santiago sitting beside her in the SUV. "I'm not going to do it."

He didn't even bother to look up from his phone. They'd been having this same argument since before they'd left his Texas ranch that afternoon. "You will."

"I'd only embarrass you. I don't know how to talk to rich people!"

This time, Santiago did look up. His dark eyes flashed with amusement. "You talk to them like people."

She sat back sulkily against the soft black calfskin leather of the luxury SUV. "You know what I mean."

"They're not people?"

"Not *normal* people. They all have advanced degrees from places like Oxford and Princeton. They're billionaire entrepreneurs and ambassadors and famous artists. They all grew up in castles with a full staff of servants..."

"You really are a romantic, aren't you?"

"The point is, we have nothing in common."

"You do." His dark eyes gleamed. "Me."

She stared at him, stricken. Then she turned away, looking out silently at the dark, sparkling city.

Last night, Santiago had brought her to the heights of ecstasy in bed. But he'd also proven how thoroughly he commanded her body, even when her heart tried to resist.

He'd given her deep pleasure, made her feel things— *do* things—she'd never imagined. But that morning, she'd once again woken up alone. Only now, she had a big diamond ring on her left hand.

She'd surrendered to his marriage demand, both for their child's sake and because he'd left her no choice. She'd given up any hope of love. She looked at her engagement ring, glinting beneath the city lights. So hard. So cold.

Like the man who'd given it to her.

Alone in the ranch's master bedroom that morning, she'd gotten dressed in an old stretchy T-shirt from high school, the faded words *Bluebell Bears* emblazoned over the picture of a bear that stretched over her big belly, and a pair of loose khaki shorts and flip-flops. She'd found him sitting at the breakfast table drinking coffee, wearing a sleek black button-up shirt and black pants, more sophisticated than she'd ever be. She'd trembled in the doorway, still feeling last night's kisses, wondering how he would greet her now they were engaged to be married for the rest of their lives.

"Good morning," he'd said, barely looking at her. "I trust you slept well. We will be returning to New York today."

That had been it. No warmth. No friendliness. No acknowledgement of the night they'd spent in each other's arms. No matter how exhilarating, amazing, explosive the lovemaking, it was empty, with no love to fuel the fire.

And now he'd dragged her back to the fairy-tale city that had broken her heart.

Belle whispered in the back of the SUV, "I can't possibly be your hostess in New York society."

"What are you afraid of?"

"They'll laugh in my face. Society people are even meaner than casting directors. I saw what they did to Letty, ripping her apart just because her father went to jail..."

"That was different."

"They're meaner than rattlesnakes." Belle looked down, feeling a lump in her throat as she stared down at the gorgeous, obscenely huge diamond engagement ring. "And they'll all think the same as you did. That I'm a gold digger who tricked you into marrying me, by deliberately getting knocked up."

"No one will think that," he said firmly, and his arrogant expression made her roll her eyes. Santiago really thought he could control everything, even the thoughts of strangers. She shook her head.

"You're just not the kind of man who marries a girl like me. And this ring…"

"What about it?" he said shortly. He sounded on edge. She wondered if she'd offended him.

"It's beautiful, but it looks weird on my hand. I've spent my life working. This ring should belong to a princess who's never had to lift a finger." She looked down at her casual shorts and high school T-shirt over her baby bump. "Your trophy wife should be an heiress or supermodel or movie star or something. Not a short, dumpy waitress."

"Don't talk about yourself like that." His jaw tightened, and his dark eyes turned hard in a way she didn't understand. "And movie stars are highly overrated."

Belle frowned, looking up at his handsome face. "Did you ever date one?"

He blinked, then abruptly turned away, looking at the bright city lights sliding past their chauffeured SUV.

"Romantic love is a dream of lust and lies," he said in a low voice. "It all turns to ash in the end." He turned to her. "Be grateful it's not part of our relationship."

Belle started to protest, then remembered how she'd felt when Justin dumped her right before their wedding. How she'd felt when she'd found out he was not only getting back with his ex-wife, but they were also expecting the baby she could no longer conceive. Love hadn't felt so great back then.

"It's not always like that," she tried.

His cruel, sensual lips twisted. "Give me an example of a romance working out."

"Um…" She tried to think, then said triumphantly, "Letty and Darius."

"That just proves my point. They didn't marry for love.

They got lucky. Or else they decided to make the best of things."

She bit her lip and said in a small voice, "Maybe we can do that, too."

He rewarded her with a smile. "My executive assistant has already planned a meeting with the most exclusive wedding planner in the city."

"You will meet with this planner?"

"No, you will. You're the bride. I have a company to run."

"I didn't realize you were so old-fashioned, with the gender roles."

He flashed a grin. "I know my place. The wedding day always belongs to the bride."

The dread in Belle's stomach only intensified. "I don't need a big wedding. We could just go to City Hall…"

"Like Letty and Darius?"

That shut her up. Though Letty and Darius were happy now, their wedding had been awful, no matter how Belle had tried to put a positive spin on it. "Fine," she said in a small voice. "Have it your way."

Reaching out, he touched her shoulder. "At least we know what we're getting into. Our marriage will last. No delusions of hearts and flowers. You won't expect me to fulfill your every girlish fantasy."

Pulling away, she tossed her head. "You couldn't, even if you tried."

Santiago gave her a sideways glance, his eyes suddenly dark as he murmured, "I could fulfill a few." As she shivered at the huskiness of his voice, the SUV stopped.

"We're here, sir."

"Thank you, Ivan. Come." He turned to Belle. "The staff is waiting to meet you."

"By staff, do you mean that butler I met?" she said nervously.

"Yes, but Jones isn't the only one. We have three live-in staff members. Four others live out."

"Just for you?" she said in dismay. He smiled.

"For us."

The door was opened by their driver, Ivan. As he and Kip, a bodyguard who had tattoos on his neck and a mean stare, brought in their luggage, Santiago helped Belle out of the SUV. Looking up at his brownstone mansion, she gulped.

When she'd first come here a few days ago to tell Santiago she was pregnant, she never could have imagined she'd return as his fiancée and mistress of the house!

Inside the front door, seven uniformed members of staff stood waiting in the enormous foyer beneath the skylight. At the head of the line was the butler who'd been so cold to her when she'd last visited the house. Looking at her, the man narrowed his eyes in a scowl.

Nervously, she tried to draw back, but Santiago held her hand securely.

"Good evening to you all," he said gravely. "Thank you for waiting for our arrival." He glanced at Belle. "I'm pleased to introduce you to my future bride, Miss Belle Langtry."

"Hello, miss."

"Welcome."

"Lovely to meet you, miss."

As each staff member introduced themselves to Belle in turn, she felt embarrassed. She felt like a fraud. Like she belonged in the staff line herself. What did she know about being the lady of the manor? Her friend Letty had been born to it, but Belle didn't have a clue, and she was sure it showed. She ducked her head bashfully.

"As my wife," Santiago continued, "Belle will be in charge of the house, so please teach her everything she needs to know." He glanced at the butler. "I'm relying on you, Jones."

"Of course, sir," the butler intoned, but the sideways glance he threw Belle was far from friendly. *I'm sure we'll be friends in no time*, she told herself, but she felt more ill at ease than ever.

"That's all for now. You may go," Santiago said. After the staff departed, he looked down at her and said softly, "I'll show you around your new home."

He drew her down the hallway of the mansion. The ceilings were high, with molded plaster and chandeliers. Their footsteps echoed on the hardwood and marble floors, walking past walls with oak paneling and stone fireplaces. "How old is this house?"

"Not very. It was built in 1899."

"That's older than my whole hometown," she replied in awe. "And three employees actually live here? Doesn't that feel weird, having your butler around when you're slacking on the sofa in sweatpants, eating chips and watching football on TV?"

He gave a brief smile. "The staff have their own quarters in the evenings. On the fifth floor."

"The *fifth*? How many floors are there?"

"Seven, if you include the basement."

"This isn't a house, it's a skyscraper!"

His smile spread to a grin. "Come on."

Belle's eyes got bigger as he showed her the rest of the house, from the wine cellar and home theater in the basement, to the ballroom—"but it's small, for a ballroom"—on the main floor, through five guest bedrooms and nine bathrooms.

"Why so many bathrooms?" she said curiously. "Is it so when one gets dirty, you don't need to bother cleaning it, but can just move on to the next one?"

He gave her a crooked half grin. "That's not necessary.

The staff takes good care of us. Let me show you my second favorite place in this house."

He led her onto the elevator, causing Belle to exclaim in wonder, "You have your own elevator?", and pressed the button for the roof. As she walked out into the warm, humid July night, she gasped.

A rooftop pool was illuminated bright blue, with lounge chairs and cabanas surrounded by flowers and plants. But the real star was the view. As they stood on the rooftop, fifty-floor skyscrapers surrounded them, shining brightly.

Going to the edge of the railing, Belle saw, far below, the noise and traffic of the street. There was only one dark spot, directly to the left: Central Park.

"Wow," she breathed, then looked at Santiago. "If this is only your second favorite part of the house, what's your first?"

His eyes were dark, his voice low. "I'll show you."

He led her back to the elevator, and pressed the button for the third floor, which she realized she hadn't seen at all yet. The elevator door opened on a small foyer. Beyond that was a single door.

"What's this?" she asked.

His hooded eyes looked at her. "Open the door."

Hesitantly, she obeyed. Behind her, he turned on the light.

She saw an enormous spartan bedroom, bigger than even the one in Texas. It had an enormous bed and a wall of windows covered with translucent curtains. There was a sitting area with a reading chair, a vanity table, a wet bar and a small library of books. Peeking into two side doors, she saw a large wood-paneled walk-in closet filled with dark suits, and an en suite bathroom in chrome and marble. The bathroom was so expensively minimalist that even the towels were tucked away.

Though this bedroom suite was huge and elegant, she

didn't see what could possibly make it more spectacular than the rooftop pool. Frowning, she turned back in puzzlement. "Your bedroom?"

He nodded.

"What do you love so much about it?"

Coming forward, he put his hands on her shoulders, his eyes alight. "That you'll be in it."

Belle shivered, remembering the heat and passion they'd shared at the Texas ranch. She wasn't hypocritical enough to pretend that the thought disgusted her. She bit her lip. "What would the staff think?"

He looked amused. "That I'd share my room with my pregnant fiancée? You think this will shock them?" He gave a low laugh. "Ah, *querida*, you are such an innocent. The servants think what I pay them to think."

She snorted; then paused. "Is that what you'll expect of me, too? That I'll just do what you tell me to do and think what you want me to think?"

His dark eyebrows lowered. "No." He pulled her into his arms, and ran his hand softly along her cheek. "You are not my servant, Belle. My expectations are different for you. I expect you to be yourself. And say what you actually think."

She looked at him skeptically. "You do?"

"Of course." His lips curved upward. "So I can convince you around to my way of thinking. The correct way."

She rolled her eyes. "Right."

"I have no interest in a silent doormat as a wife. I would rather have sparks between us, and yes, hatred at times, than be married to a ghost. I expect you to tell me when you are angry, rather than hide from me. You will be my wife and soon, the mother of my children…"

"Children?"

"Of course." He tilted his head. "You know how important siblings are. I was an only child. My life might have been very different if I'd had a sibling. Imagine how your younger brothers' lives might have turned out if they'd not had you to take care of them."

The thought gave her a chill. Her brothers would have been separated, sent to foster care. Or an orphanage, even, like Santiago. She bit her lip. "Of course it's important, but…"

"But?"

"This is all just so new to me. I feel like my life is already becoming unrecognizable. Planning a society wedding? Have more children? I don't know anything about running a mansion, or managing a staff."

"You will learn."

"I don't know about designer clothes, obviously—" she looked down at her stretchy *Bluebell Bears* T-shirt and shorts "—or elegant manners or…"

"I've arranged an appointment for you tomorrow at eleven with a personal stylist. Ivan will take you. Kip will go with you."

"Why would I need a bodyguard?"

"Consider him an accessory. You certainly won't be the only one with a bodyguard. Your stylist is…" He named a celebrity stylist so famous that even Belle had heard of her. "She'll provide you with clothes and everything else."

"Bodyguard. Stylist." She gave an incredulous, half-hysterical laugh. "I'm not some celebrity!"

"You are now, because of that ring on your finger." He gave her a slow, seductive smile. "As for the rest of what you'll need to learn, I'll teach as we go. It will get easier."

"How?" She was almost near tears. "How is this ever going to work?"

Reaching out, Santiago ran his hands down her arms, making her shiver with sudden awareness and desire as they stood in the shadowy bedroom.

"I'll show you," he whispered, drawing her to the enormous bed. "Starting with this."

And he kissed her.

Golden sunlight poured in through the high windows when Belle woke up the next morning. For a moment, she just stretched languorously in bed. She still felt him all over her body. Remembering last night curled her toes.

Then her smile faded as she realized she was waking up in New York just as she had in Texas: alone. His side of the bed was empty.

Last night, he'd made love to her so passionately he'd made all her fears disappear. She'd been lost in the sensuality of his body against hers. She'd felt need so hot and intense it burned everything else away.

But in the morning, reality felt as cold as his side of the bed.

Belle looked at the clock. It was ten in the morning. She sat up, eyes wide. She couldn't remember the last time she'd slept so late. Even in the earliest stages of pregnancy, when she'd been exhausted, she'd worked the early shift, forcing herself to get up at five on dark, cold winter mornings. She couldn't remember the last time she'd slept till ten. It felt sinful.

Rising from the bed, still naked as she'd slept, she stretched her arms and toes, and felt the baby kick inside her. She rubbed her belly, murmuring happily, "Good morning, baby."

Going to the en suite bathroom, she took a long, warm shower. Her meager belongings from her suitcases had already been unpacked. She wondered if it had been the butler or the maid who'd unpacked her clothes last night, when Santiago was giving her the house tour. She hoped it was the young maid. She felt uncomfortable at the thought of the supercilious butler looking down his nose at her simple clothing, all purchased from discount stores and washed many times.

"The servants think what I pay them to think," Santiago had told her grandly yesterday.

But Belle's own experience said otherwise. As a waitress, she'd been paid to serve breakfast and refill coffee; her opinion had always been her own. Her tart temper had gotten her in trouble more than once. Belle always believed in being polite, but that was different than letting a bully walk all over you.

"I have no interest in a silent doormat as a wife," he'd told her.

It was obviously true in bed. It was also true that in some ways, he made her feel stronger, braver and like she could really be herself, without pretending. But if Santiago thought Belle could ever be some kind of high society trophy wife, he'd soon realize his mistake. She was just afraid she'd humiliate all of them in the process.

After brushing out her wet hair, she pulled on a clean T-shirt and pair of shorts. They were getting too tight around her belly. Maybe a new wardrobe wasn't the worst idea, she thought. Brushing her teeth, she glanced at herself in the mirror. And heaven knew a stylist couldn't hurt. It would have to be a brave stylist, though, to want to take her on.

Ignoring the elevator—it seemed so pretentious—she went down the gleaming back stairs. She was just grateful Santiago had given her a house tour, or she'd have gotten totally lost. Approaching the kitchen, she heard a woman laugh.

"He can't be serious. We're really expected to follow her orders? That nobody? It's humiliating."

Sucking in her breath, Belle stopped outside the kitchen door, listening.

"Humiliating or not, we'll have to take her orders. At

least for now." The butler's voice was scornful. "However ridiculous they might be. Who knows what she might want?"

A different woman said, "A stripper pole?"

"Silver bowls full of pork rinds," the other suggested.

"But Mr. Velazquez has chosen her as his bride," the butler intoned, "so we must pretend to obey her for as long as the marriage lasts. But do not worry. Once the brat is born, she'll soon be kicked to the curb. Mr. Velazquez is seeing his lawyer today, hopefully drawing up an iron-clad prenup…"

Belle must have made some noise, because the butler's voice suddenly cut off. A second later, to her horror, his head peered around the door. Her own cheeks were aflame at being caught eavesdropping.

But Jones didn't look ashamed. If anything, his expression was smug, even as he said politely, "Ah, good morning, Miss Langtry. Would you care for some breakfast?"

Belle had no idea how to react. He knew she'd overheard, but wasn't remotely sorry. The butler was in charge here, not her, no matter what Santiago had said. Suddenly not the least bit hungry, she blurted out the first thing she thought of—the morning special she'd served at the diner. "Um…scrambled eggs and toast would be lovely… Maybe a little orange juice…"

"Of course, madam."

But as she walked forward with hunched shoulders, he blocked her from the kitchen, and gestured smoothly down the hall. "We will serve you in the dining room, Miss Langtry. There are newspapers and juice and coffee already set out. Please make yourself comfortable."

Comfortable was the last thing she felt as she ate alone at the end of a long table that would have seated twenty. Huge vases of fresh flowers made her nose itch, and she

didn't find the *Financial Times* enough company to block
out the memory of the staff's cruel words.

"Who knows what she might want?"

"A stripper's pole?"

"Silver bowls full of pork rinds?"

*"She'll soon be kicked to the curb... Mr. Velazquez is
seeing his lawyer today."*

Santiago hadn't told her what his plans were today. He
hadn't even said goodbye. He'd just made love to her hot
and hard in the night, then disappeared before dawn. Like
always.

Was he really with his lawyer right now, devising some
kind of ironclad prenuptial agreement?

Of course he was, she thought bitterly. He wouldn't trust
her, ever. That was what their marriage would be, in spite
of all his fine words about friendship and partnership. It
would be a business arrangement, based on a contract,
where even the people running her own home despised her.

This mansion wasn't home, she thought with despair,
looking up at the soaring chandeliers, the high ceilings of
the dining room. She didn't belong here. She rubbed her
belly. Neither did her baby.

She missed her brothers. She missed Letty, who was in
Greece with her family. She missed her old friends back
in Bluebell. Most of all, she missed having control over
her life.

Why would any woman want to get pregnant by a billionaire, if it meant you'd always feel like an outsider?
Would even her own child, raised in this environment,
someday despise her?

Jones served her breakfast on a silver tray, then departed with a sweeping bow. But Belle saw his smirk. She
managed to eat a few bites, but it all tasted like ash in her
mouth. She was relieved when Kip, the muscular, tattooed
bodyguard, appeared in the doorway.

"Ready to go, Miss Langtry? Ivan has already pulled around the car."

Belle had dreaded the thought of the appointment with that famous personal stylist, but at that moment hell itself sounded preferable to remaining in this enormous, empty house, filled with employees who scorned her. She got up from the breakfast table so quickly that Kip's eyes widened to see a pregnant woman move so fast.

But later that afternoon, when Belle finally returned to the house, she felt worse, not better. She'd been poked and prodded, manicured and, most of all, criticized. Her awful hair! Her awful clothes! Her ragged cuticles! The famous stylist had cried out in shock and agony, right in front of Belle, and sent her assistants scurrying. They seemed to think Belle was a rock, incapable of thinking or feeling, just the brute clay from which they, the long-suffering artists, would sculpt and construct their art.

Ten different assistants had worked on her at the stylist's private salon, which the stylist herself, the famous owner of the establishment, called her *atelier*.

Belle had never cared much about her appearance. She'd always had more important things to think about, like raising her little brothers and putting food on the table. So she'd tried to remain patient and silent as they picked out a wardrobe and hairstyle appropriate to her station as a rich man's wife.

Seven hours later, as Kip finally carried out her new wardrobe to the waiting car, the famous stylist had showed Belle a mirror. "What do you think?"

She'd sucked in her breath. Her dark hair was now perfectly straight, gleaming down her shoulders. Her face felt raw from the facials, shellacked with expensive lotions and makeup, including lipstick and mascara. Her pregnant shape was draped in a severely chic black shift dress, black capelet, her hips thrust forward by uncomfortably high heels.

Startled by the stranger in the mirror, Belle replied timidly, "I don't recognize myself."

To which the famously pretentious personal stylist responded with a laugh, "Then my job is done."

Now, Belle trudged into the brownstone mansion feeling ridiculous in the jaunty black capelet.

Tomorrow she was supposed to meet with the wedding planner. She could only imagine how that would go. Santiago had already mentioned an engagement party he meant to hold in two weeks, "after you've gotten a chance to get comfortable." Comfortable?

She felt sick with worry.

Belle saw the maid and the cook as she walked wearily into the house. The two women elbowed each other as they saw her new chic appearance.

"You look nice, ma'am," the maid said meekly. Belle wondered if she was mocking her.

"Thank you," she said flatly, and went up to the third floor bedroom suite to take a nap. The same maid knocked on the door a few hours later.

"Mr. Velazquez is home, miss. He's requesting that you join him downstairs for dinner."

Groggily, Belle smoothed down her dress and hair from her nap, then went down to the dining room.

Santiago's dark eyes widened when he saw her. Rising from the table, he came forward to kiss her.

"You look very elegant," he said, helping her into her chair. Sitting beside her, he smiled. "Who is queen of society now?"

He didn't seem to notice her lack of enthusiasm or her absence of appetite for dinner. But there was one thing he noticed fast enough. When he took her upstairs to bed and kissed her, she didn't respond. He frowned. "What is it?"

"It's this makeup," she improvised. "It feels like a Halloween mask over my face."

He stared at her, then gave her a slow-rising grin. "I can solve that."

He pulled her into the shower, turned on the water, and scrubbed the day off her until she felt almost like herself again. It was only then, when her skin was pink and warm with steam, as she stood in front of him with her baby bump and pregnancy-swollen breasts, that she felt like she could breathe again, and started returning his kisses.

"That's better," he whispered appreciatively and kissed her in the shower until her knees were weak. Turning off the water, he gently toweled her off and pulled her onto the bed, their bodies still hot and wet. Lying down, he lifted her over him and put his hand gently on her cheek.

"You're in charge," he whispered, and she was. It was ecstasy. It was glory. Their souls seemed to spark together into fire, as well as their bodies. When they were together in bed, she could forget all her fears. She felt nothing but pleasure. She was his. He was hers.

But when Belle woke up in the morning, she was alone.

CHAPTER SIX

TWO WEEKS LATER, Santiago came home from his forty-floor skyscraper in Midtown with a scowl on his face.

His company, Velazquez International, had spent two weeks in negotiations, trying and failing to nail down the acquisition of a Canadian hotel chain. He'd offered them an excellent price, but they continued to hold out—not for more money, but for his promise that he'd keep all their employees and stores intact. Santiago scowled, narrowing his eyes. What fool would promise such a thing? But now, because of their stubbornness, he was going to be late for his own engagement party. And no deal had been struck.

That was what was making him tense, he told himself. The business deal. Running late.

It had nothing to do with the thought of giving Belle the prenuptial agreement tucked into his briefcase.

Rushing up the stone steps of his brownstone, he ground his teeth. The wedding was planned for early September, just a month away, just a few weeks before her due date. Of course the agreement had to be signed. He was a billionaire. Belle had nothing. Without a prenuptial agreement, he'd be risking half his fortune from the moment he said "I do."

But his scowl deepened as he entered his Upper East Side mansion, lavish with flowers and additional hired serving staff, awaiting the first guest for their engagement party, when he would introduce his future bride to New

York society. He took the elevator to the third floor, then stopped when he saw Belle.

She was looking into a full-length mirror as she put on diamond earrings, wearing a sleek black dress, her dark hair pulled back into a tight chignon. Her face was perfectly made up, and the diamond earrings he'd given her yesterday sparkled as brightly as the ten-carat engagement ring on her finger. But as she turned to him, he saw that beneath the dramatic black sweep of her lashes and red ruby lips, her creamy caramel skin was pale.

"What's wrong?" he demanded.

She gave him a trembling smile. "I was starting to worry you might make me host this party alone."

"Of course not." Dropping his briefcase, he kissed her, stroking her soft cheek. He searched her gaze. "You look beautiful."

"I'm glad. So maybe the pain is worth it."

"Pain?" he said, surprised.

She held out her foot, shod in a sexy black stiletto heel. "And you should see my underwear," she said wryly.

"I'd like to."

She returned his grin, then sighed. "At least the baby is comfortable. All the clothes are loose around my waist." She glanced down at the briefcase. "So when are you going to spring it on me?"

His hand stilled. "What?"

"The prenuptial agreement."

He blinked. How had she known?

Of course she knew, he chided himself. Belle was intuitive and smart. "You know it's necessary."

"Yes. I know."

She didn't argue. Didn't complain. She just looked at him, her dark eyes like big pools in her wan, pale face. And he felt like a cad. That irritated him even more. Turning away, he changed his clothes, pulling on his tuxedo.

"Santiago, am I a trophy wife?" she asked suddenly.

"What are you talking about?"

"I met some other brides while waiting for my appointment with the wedding planner yesterday. They told me all about the life of a trophy wife. They made it sound like being an indentured servant." She looked at the closet. "I already have the uniform. Shift dresses in black and beige."

He felt irritated as he sat down on the bed to put on his Italian leather shoes. "I didn't tell you to only wear black and beige."

"No, but the stylist did. And she insisted I must always wear stilettos, to be taller. They're like torture devices…" She peered down at her feet, then looked up with a sigh. "I'll sorry. I'm doing my best. I'm just afraid I'll fail you," she said in a small voice. "That I can't be what you need, or ever fit into your world—"

"Fit in?" He looked up from tying his shoes. "I wasn't born in this world either, Belle. Growing up in Madrid, I had nothing. And I've learned the hard way there's only one way to fit into a world that doesn't want you. By force. You have to make it impossible for them to ignore you."

She stared at him for a moment, and he wished he hadn't brought up his own childhood. He was relieved when she shook her head. "Force? I can't even force our wedding planner to consider any of my ideas. Our wedding is going to be awful."

"Awful?"

Belle rolled her eyes. "She called it 'postmodern'. I'm to hold a cactus instead of a bouquet, and instead of a white wedding cake, we'll be serving our guests gold-dusted foam."

"Really."

"When I told her I didn't want to hold a cactus in my bare hands and just wanted a wildflower bouquet and a regular wedding cake, the woman laughed and patted me on the head. She *patted me on the head*," she repeated for emphasis.

Santiago gave a low laugh. "*Querida*, her weddings might be unconventional, but she is the best, and I told her I want you to have the most spectacular wedding of the season…"

"*Spectacular* means wasting millions of dollars on stupid stuff we don't want, to impress people we don't even like?"

"You said you want to fit in. A big wedding is a show of power."

"She won't even let me invite my brothers. She said it was because she didn't think a plumber and a fireman would be comfortable at such a formal event, but I think she was just afraid they wouldn't fit in with her décor!"

Not letting Belle invite her little brothers? He was willing to accept cactus and gold foam, but excluding beloved family members was unacceptable. Santiago frowned as he finished putting on his tie. "I'll talk to her." Rising to his feet, he held out his arm. "Shall we go downstairs?"

He felt her hands shake a little as they wrapped around the arm of his jacket, heard the sudden catch of her breath. "So many guests are coming tonight…"

"It will be fine," he said, but he understood why Belle was nervous. Their 'impromptu engagement party' had ballooned out of proportion. On August weekends, the city usually was so deserted he wouldn't have been half-surprised to see tumbleweeds going down Fifth Avenue. But to his surprise, everyone they'd invited had instantly accepted. Not only that, but more had asked to come, even coming in from Connecticut and the Hamptons.

Everyone, it seemed, was curious to see the pregnant Texas waitress who'd tamed the famous playboy Santiago Velazquez.

"Gossip has spread about me," Belle said glumly.

"Ignore it."

"The butler's right, I'm nobody."

"So was I, when I came to America at eighteen," Santiago pointed out.

"That just adds to your glory," she said grumpily. "Now you're a self-made billionaire. I bet you've never failed at anything."

That wasn't true. Just five years ago, Santiago had failed in spectacular fashion.

But he wasn't going to tell Belle about Nadia. Not now. Not ever.

Pushing the button for the elevator, he turned to her with a sudden frown. "What did you mean, the butler was right? Did he say something to you?"

Averting her eyes, she nodded. "I overheard the butler and cook and maid talking a couple weeks ago. They weren't happy about having me as their mistress. Mr. Jones told them I was a nobody, but they should pretend to obey me until the *brat* was born, when you'd get rid of me."

"What?"

"He knew I heard them talking, but wasn't even sorry." Lifting her gaze, she tried to smile. "It's no big deal. I'll get used to it."

But Santiago's jaw was tight with fury. That his own employees would dare to scorn his future wife, his unborn child, in his own house! His dark brows lowered like a thundercloud.

Once the elevator opened on the ground floor, he took Belle by the arm and led her down the hall, past all the extra hired staff who were setting out appetizers and flowers for the party.

In the kitchen, he found the butler busy with preparations for the meal, along with the two other live-in members of his staff—Mrs. Green, the cook, and Anna, the maid. The front doorbell rang, and the butler started to leave the kitchen.

"Jones, stay," Santiago ordered harshly, then turned to one of the temporary waiters walking past with a tray. "Tell Kip he's in charge of answering the door."

"Kip?"

"The one with a tattoo on his neck."

"Right."

Santiago turned back to face his employees.

"What is it, Mr. Velazquez?" Anna said anxiously.

"I should be answering the door for your party guests, Mr. Velazquez," Jones intoned.

Santiago looked at the three of them coldly.

"You are all fired."

They stared at him in shock, their mouths agape.

"Pack up your things," Santiago continued grimly. "I want you out of here in ten minutes."

"But—my food for the party—" Mrs. Green stammered.

"What did we do?" Anna gasped.

"You told him to fire us." The butler looked at Belle with venom in his eyes. "You just had to tattle, didn't you?"

"I never meant for this to happen…" Belle looked at Santiago. She put an urgent hand on his shoulder. "Please. You don't need to—"

But he moved his shoulder away. His fury was past listening as he stared at the three employees who'd dared to be rude to Belle. "This party is no longer your concern, and you now only have nine minutes left."

The butler drew himself up contemptuously. "I'll go. It would destroy my professional reputation to work for your wife, anyway. She doesn't belong here!"

"You think your reputation would be destroyed?" Santiago said coldly. "See what happens if you ever speak rudely about Belle again to anyone."

"Santiago," Belle said, tugging on his sleeve desperately. "I don't want anyone to lose their jobs. I just thought…"

"I should have known you'd rat us out, after you heard us talking that first day," Jones snarled.

The plump cook whirled to Belle with a gasp. "You heard us?"

But Belle was staring at the butler, and so was Santiago. So was the maid.

Jones's accent had slipped.

Suddenly Santiago knew why the butler had hated Belle on sight. She wasn't the only one who felt out of place.

"You're not even British," Santiago said accusingly.

"Nope." Jones yanked off the apron that had been over his suit and tie. "Born in New Jersey. I'm done with this butler stuff. No amount of money is worth this." He looked at Belle. "You might be stuck here till he dumps you. But I'm not. Forget this. I'm going to go start a band."

Throwing away his apron, he left.

Santiago looked at the two women. "Any last words?"

The young maid, Anna, turned to Belle, her cheeks red. "I'm sorry, Miss Langtry. I sneered at you about pork rinds because, well, I like them myself. But I eat them in secret. I didn't want Mr. Jones to know… "

The cook stepped forward, abashed. "And I taunted you about the stripper pole, because, well—" the plump middle-aged woman's cheeks reddened "—I was a stripper myself for a few months when I was young. It's not something I'm proud of, but my baby's father had abandoned us. I was desperate…" Turning to Santiago, she pulled off her cap. "That bit of employment wasn't listed on my résumé. I understand if you don't want me cooking for you no more. Especially after what I said. I'll go."

"Please don't fire me," Anna begged. "I need this job.

I'm working my way through law school and the hours are hard to find. The wages, too."

"It's not your choice." Santiago looked at Belle. "It's my fiancée's."

Belle glanced at the two women. The younger of them was looking at her with pleading eyes, as the older stared woodenly at the floor with slumped shoulders.

"Please stay." Her voice trembled slightly. "If you're not too embarrassed to work for me…"

"Oh, no!" Anna exclaimed fervently. "How could I be embarrassed of you? I'm only ashamed of myself."

"Me, too," the cook said softly. Looking up, her soft blue eyes filled with tears. "Thank you."

Belle gave them a wobbly smile. "I know what it feels like to be pregnant and alone. No one would judge you badly for doing whatever it took to take care of your baby." Glancing at Santiago out of the corner of her eye, she added, "In fact, you both get a raise."

"What?" the women said joyfully.

"Of thirty percent!"

"What?" Santiago said, not so joyfully.

"A raise," Belle repeated firmly, "as our household will be doing without a butler. Their extra responsibilities deserve it."

She made a good point. Santiago scowled at her. And he had to admit to himself that having a butler, especially a sniffy one like Jones, hadn't added much to the comfort of his home life.

"Fine," he said grudgingly, then turned to the others. "Don't give my bride reason to regret her generosity. There will be no second chance."

"Yes, sir!"

"Back to your duties."

"Right away!"

Mrs. Green scurried back to the enormous ovens, her plump face alarmed. "Oh, no—my salmon puffs!"

Taking Belle aside in the hallway, he growled, "Thirty percent?"

She lifted her chin. "They will be worth it."

"Right. And here I thought the most expensive thing would be getting you a new wardrobe."

"What about this?" She smiled, lifting up the huge diamond ring on her left hand. "I can't even imagine how much it cost."

Try free, he thought. He cleared his throat, then brightened. "And your earrings." Those, at least, had been specifically purchased for Belle.

She touched one of the diamonds dangling from her ears. "You could have bought me fake ones, you know. No one would have been able to tell the difference, least of all me. Big waste of money."

"You really are terrible at being a gold digger."

"I know," she agreed. She looked down at her ring. "It's beautiful, but it makes me feel guilty. This ring could have probably bought a car."

When he'd bought it five years before, the amount he'd spent could actually have bought a house. But of course he'd bought it for a different woman, so Belle had nothing to feel guilty about. He was tempted to tell her, but kept his mouth shut. Somehow he thought this was one situation when no woman on earth, even an ardent environmentalist, would think highly of recycling.

The doorbell rang again, and he saw the seven-foot-tall Kip head for the front door. Flinging it open, Kip glared at an ambassador, who looked startled, and his skinny, bejeweled wife, who looked terrified.

"Oh, dear," Belle sighed, following his gaze.

"I'm not sure Kip has the right skill set to be butler," Santiago said, hiding a smile.

"Let's go take over for him."

He frowned at her. "Answer the door ourselves?"

"What, don't you know how?" Giving him an impish smile, she took his hand. "Come on, Santiago. Let's give 'em a big Texas welcome."

Her hand was warm in his own, and as he looked down at the curve of her breasts revealed above the neckline of her gown, a flash of heat went through his body. "I thought you were afraid of society people."

"I am." She added with a rueful laugh, "But my mama always said there's only one way to get through something that scares you, and that's by doing it."

Looking at the resolve in Belle's beautiful face, at the gleam in her dark eyes and her half-parted ruby-red lips, Santiago was tempted to give her a counteroffer: that they throw all the guests out, lock the door, and make love right here, on the table between the flowers and the cream puffs.

Instead, as the doorbell rang again, Belle pulled him toward the door.

"I just fired Jones," Santiago told Kip. "Make sure he doesn't make off with the silver."

"Yes, sir," Kip said, looking relieved, and he fled.

Santiago stood beside Belle as they answered the door, welcoming all their illustrious, powerful guests. The people were all strangers to Belle, and yet she gave each of them a warm smile, as if she were truly glad to see them. Some of the guests seemed pleased, others slightly startled.

Santiago was enchanted.

Over the next few hours, as he watched Belle mingle at the party, he felt a mixture of pride and desire. He couldn't take his eyes off her. She was breathtaking.

In that dress and those high heels, with her makeup and hair so glossy and sophisticated, she might have fit in perfectly, except for one thing.

She stood out.

Belle was the most beautiful woman there.

Only he knew the fear and insecurity she'd hidden inside. That somehow made him even prouder of her. Tonight he admired her courage and grace even more than he admired her beauty.

The house had been filled with bright-colored flowers, and the hors d'oeuvres, overseen by Mrs. Green, were exquisite. But not half as exquisite as Belle, feverishly bright-eyed and lovely. The party was a huge success.

Because of Belle, he thought. She was the star.

Later that evening, he watched her across the crowded ballroom, now smiling at three of the board members of the Canadian hotel chain. He'd invited them to the party in an offhand way, but he hadn't really expected them to come. He watched as Belle smiled and said something that made all three men laugh uproariously.

Belle was as good at this as Nadia, he thought in astonishment. Maybe even better.

He'd met Nadia his first night at the orphanage in Madrid, when he was fourteen. She was blonde, beautiful, a year older, with hard violet eyes and a raspy laugh. He'd been immediately infatuated. When he told her he was breaking out to go live with his father, the Duke of Sangovia, she'd been awed. "Take me with you," she'd begged, and he'd agreed.

Nadia had watched from the bushes as the palace guards tried phoning his father, then at the duke's answer, turned on Santiago scornfully, setting the dogs on him. He'd run away from the snarling jaws and snapping teeth, staggering past the safety of the gate, to fall at her feet.

"No luck, huh?" Nadia had said, looking down at him coolly. She'd looked past the wrought-iron walls, ten feet tall, over the palm trees, toward the rooftops of the palace, barely visible from the gate. "Someday, I'll live in a place like this."

"I won't." Wiping blood from his face, Santiago had looked back at it with hatred, then slowly risen to his feet, ignoring the blood on his knees, the rips in his pants. "My house will be a million times better than this." He'd looked at the beautiful blonde girl. "And you'll be my wife."

"Marry you?" She'd looked at him coolly. "I'm going to be a movie star. There's no reason I'd marry you or anyone. Not unless you could give me something I can't get for myself." Her lovely face was thoughtful as she looked back toward the palace. "If you could make me a duchess…"

That was one thing Santiago could never do. He wasn't the legitimate heir. He was just a bastard by-blow, whose father couldn't be bothered to give him a home, a name, or even a single minute of his time. A sliver of pain went through him, overwhelmed by a wave of rage.

He would be better than his father. Better than his half brother. Better than all of them.

Lifting his chin, he'd said boldly, "Someday, I'll be a billionaire. Then I'll ask you. And you'll say yes."

Nadia had given a low, patronizing laugh. "A billionaire?" she'd said, putting out her cigarette. "Sure. Ask me then."

He'd officially made his first billion by the time he was thirty. But too late. The day his company went public, he flew his private jet to Barcelona, where Nadia was filming her latest movie. He'd fallen to one knee and held out the ring, just as he'd imagined for half his life. And then he'd waited.

One never knew where one stood with Nadia. She knew how to charm with a glance, how to cut out someone's heart with a smile. Sitting on her film set, looking beautiful as a queen, she'd fluttered her eyelashes mournfully.

"Oh, dear. I'm sorry. You're too late. I just agreed to marry your brother." She'd held out her left hand, showing off an exquisite antique ring. "I'm going to live in the

Palacio de las Palmas and be a duchess someday. I can only do that if I marry the Duque de Sangovia's legitimate heir. And that's not you. Sorry."

Strange to think that Nadia was living with his father and brother, Santiago thought, while he himself had never met either of them. Nadia had been married to his brother for five years now, and as she waited to be duchess she comforted herself with the title of *marquesa*, along with the other title given her by the European tabloids—"the Most Beautiful Woman in the World."

"Hell of a girl you've got there."

Coming out of his reverie, Santiago abruptly focused on the man speaking to him. It was Rob McVoy, the CEO of the Canadian family firm. "Thank you."

"Any man who could make a woman like Belle love him must be trustworthy. So I changed my mind. We'll take the chance." He gave a brusque nod. "We agree to the deal."

Santiago blinked in shock. "You do?"

The man clapped him on the shoulder. "Our lawyers will be in touch."

Santiago stared after him in amazement. After weeks of stalled negotiations, accusations of double-dealing and an almost total lack of trust, the Canadians were suddenly willing to sell him their family company, just after spending twenty minutes talking to Belle?

He was still in shock hours later, when the appetizers and champagne were almost gone, the flowers starting to wilt and the last guests straggling out. Belle had already gone upstairs. As a pregnant woman, no one thought less of her for being tired, and they'd all said goodbye to her with fond, indulgent smiles. Santiago was amazed. How had she become so popular with so many, so fast?

Not with everyone, of course. Some of the trophy wives and girlfriends, some of the more shallow hedge fund billionaires, had indeed looked askance, and whispered behind their hands, smirking.

Everyone else had loved her.

Going to the third floor, Santiago found her in their bedroom, sitting on their bed, her shoes kicked off. His gaze swept over the curves of her breasts as she leaned over to rub her bare feet, wincing. "These shoes. Murder!"

Dropping his tuxedo jacket and tie to the floor, he sat beside her on the enormous bed. Pulling her feet into his lap, he started massaging them.

"That feels fantastic," she murmured. Her eyes closed in pleasure as she leaned back against the pillows.

"Did you enjoy the party?" It took several moments for her to answer.

"Um. It was great."

He stopped rubbing her feet. "How was it really?"

With a sigh, she opened her eyes.

"Fine?" she tried, and it was even less believable. He snorted.

"You really are the worst actress I've ever seen," he observed. He started rubbing the arches of her feet, and she exhaled in pleasure.

"All right, it wasn't easy. Those shoes are like instruments of death. And people kept talking about things I didn't understand—effective altruism as related to overnight borrowing rates, for example…"

"Those aren't at all related."

She glared at him in irritation. "That's exactly my point. I don't know, and don't care." She yawned. "Then others started discussing the gallery show of an artist I never heard of. When I confessed as much, they were horrified and said you owned one of his paintings. Then they made me go take a look at it."

"Which painting?"

"The—um… Mira?"

"Joan Miró?"

"Yeah. They said you'd gotten it at a steal for ten million dollars. I barely restrained myself from yelping, 'That squiggle? I've seen better art done by preschoolers!'" Shaking her head, she added defensively, "And I have."

"Very diplomatic to restrain yourself from saying so."

"Took a lot of willpower, I'll tell you."

He smiled. "You were amazing tonight. Every time I glanced over at you, whomever you were talking to looked enthralled."

She blushed shyly. "Really? You're just being kind."

"Excuse me, have we met?"

She smiled. "Well, I tried my best. Any time I felt nervous, I forced myself to smile and say something nice, like my mama taught me. You know, 'Beautiful dress!' 'What a lovely necklace!'"

"What about the men? Did you compliment their neckties?"

She fluttered her dark eyelashes coyly. "I brought up football, or if that didn't work, horses. You apparently know a lot of polo players. As a last resort, politics."

"Do you follow politics?" he said, surprised.

"Not at all. But generally if you just start the ball rolling, the other person's happy to take it and run. At that point, all you have to do is make sympathetic noises." She rubbed the back of her neck and yawned again. "I'm exhausted. This must be what it's like to act in a play all night. The role of trophy wife."

"You closed a multi-million-dollar deal, Belle."

She frowned. "What?"

"The McVoys…"

She brightened. "Oh, the guys from Calgary? They were hilarious. They were talking about this action movie they saw last night, with that Spanish movie star, you know, the famous one…" She rolled her eyes. "I think they have a crush on her. She's married to some kind of prince already, but I told the guys it never hurts to dream." She gave a sudden grin. "Movie stars get married and divorced dozens of times, don't they? And you never know. She might decide what she really wants next is a middle-aged Canadian with hockey skills."

Santiago's body felt like ice. He cleared his throat. "I've been negotiating with the McVoys for weeks, trying to buy their company." His voice was still a little hoarse. He forced his lips into a smile. "They just agreed to the deal only because of you."

"Me?" she said, astonished.

"They said any man you love couldn't be all bad."

"Oh." Her cheeks went red as she said quickly, "I never told them I loved you."

"I guess they just assumed, since we're getting married and all," he said dryly. "Turn around." Reaching out, he started massaging the back of her neck, her shoulders, brushing back the dark tendrils of her hair. As she leaned against his hands, he breathed in the scent of her, like vanilla and orange blossoms.

She leaned back, looking at him over her shoulder. "Can I ask you something?"

"You'll ask it, whether I say yes or no."

"You're right." She flashed him a sudden grin, then grew serious. "What turned you against the idea of love?"

His hands stilled on her shoulders.

"I told you about my parents."

"That wasn't all, was it? There was something else. Someone else." She took a deep breath, and raised her eyes pleadingly to his. "You know about my sad romantic history, but I know nothing about yours…."

"You're right," he said slowly. "There was a woman."

Belle sat up straight. He saw that he had her full attention. He wasn't sure why he was telling her this. He'd never spoken about it to anyone.

"When I was a teenager, I met a girl in the orphanage. She was blonde, beautiful, with violet eyes…" He tensed, remembering how he'd felt about her as a boy. "She was older than me. Street-smart. Brave. We both had such big dreams about the future. We were both going to conquer the world." He gave a humorless smile. "At fourteen, I asked her to marry me. She told me to ask her again after I proved myself. So I did."

"How?"

"I earned a billion-dollar fortune. For her."

Her eyes went wide. "What?"

Santiago turned away, his jaw tight. "It took me sixteen years, but when my company went public five years ago, I went to Spain with a huge diamond ring."

His eyes fell unwillingly to Belle's left hand, but fortunately she didn't notice. Sitting across from him on the bed, she was staring at him with wide eyes.

"What happened?" she breathed.

His lips twisted at the edges. "I came too late. She wanted more than I could give her. She'd just gotten engaged to my brother."

Her expression changed to horror. "Your *brother*?"

He gave a crooked half grin. "She told me that she'd been attracted to Otilio in part because he reminded her of me. An upgraded version of me." His voice held no emotion. He'd had a lot of practice at showing none. Feeling none. "I couldn't even begrudge her choice. Marrying into the official Zoya family meant she would not be merely rich, but famous and powerful across Europe, and someday, after my father is dead, a duchess."

"Of all men on earth—your brother!"

"Their marriage was a huge social event in Madrid, I heard later."

"What a horrible woman!" she cried indignantly. Her lovely heart-shaped face was stricken as she faced him across the shadowy bed. "No wonder you think so little of love. And marriage, too. What did you do, after she told you she was marrying your brother?"

He shrugged. "I came back to New York. I worked harder. My fortune is bigger than theirs now. The Zoya family owns an *estancia* in Argentina, so I bought a bigger ranch in Texas. They have an art collection. Now mine is better. I don't need them now. They're nothing to me."

"They're your family," she said forlornly.

"They chose not to be."

Reaching out, Belle put her arms around him, hugging him close to her on the bed, offering comfort. For a moment, he accepted the warmth of her smaller body cradled against his. He exhaled deeply. He hadn't even realized his jaw had been tense, until now, as the tension melted away. Drawing back, he looked down at her, and gently tucked a dark tendril of hair back into her loose chignon.

She'd offered him comfort tonight, and loyalty, and her charm had even helped him close a business deal. She'd given it all without asking for anything in return.

He wanted to show his appreciation. Give her a present. But she wouldn't care about jewelry or clothes or art. *Especially* not art, he thought with amusement. So what?

Then he knew.

"I'll cancel the wedding planner, Belle. We can have any kind of wedding you want."

Her eyes lit up. It was worth it for that alone. She breathed, "Really?"

"I know you'll want your brothers to attend. I'll send my private jet to collect them. We don't have to hold the ceremony at the cathedral. I don't care about the details." He looked at her. "As long as we are husband and wife before our child comes into this world."

She tilted her head thoughtfully. "What about having the wedding here?"

"Here?"

She nodded eagerly. "I can have a flower bouquet, instead of holding a cactus. A real cake, instead of foam." She was beaming. "We can have good food that people might actually want to eat!"

"Ah, Belle." With a low laugh, he drew her closer on the bed, cupping her face. "Forget what I said about fitting in. You will never fit in." She looked hurt. Still smiling, he reached out and gently lifted her chin. "Because you were born to stand out, *querida*. You were the most beautiful woman at our engagement party. No one could even compare. I couldn't take my eyes off you."

Her cheeks flushed with shy pleasure. "Really?"

"Just one thing is wrong. That dress." He ran his hand along the black fabric. "It's driving me crazy."

Belle checked the back zipper self-consciously. "What's wrong with it?"

Sitting next to her on the bed, he pulled her into his arms.

"That you're still wearing it," he whispered, and lowered his mouth to hers.

CHAPTER SEVEN

For Santiago, sex had always been simple. Easy. A quick release. A brief pleasure, swiftly forgotten.

Sex with Belle was different than he'd ever experienced before. It was fire. A conflagration. A drug he could not get enough of.

But as with any drug, he was soon hit by unwanted, bewildering side effects.

Having Belle in his Upper East Side mansion, in his bed every night, he was shocked by the way their night-time pleasures started to bleed into his days. He could not refuse her anything.

First, he'd agreed to change their wedding, even though the celebration the famous wedding planner had proposed would have been the social event of the year. The wedding Belle wanted, small and private, without pomp or press coverage, would do nothing for the prestige of his name.

But he let Belle have her way. And it didn't stop there.

He found himself thinking about her during the day-light hours, when his focus was supposed to be on running his company. The Canadian deal had gone through, but other deals began to fall apart. He was distracted, and it was affecting his business. He found himself impatient, even bored, at meetings—even when he himself was the one who'd called them.

He'd spent almost twenty years focused on building Velazquez International to be a huge multinational conglomerate, owning a host of brands of everything from food and soft drinks to running shoes and five-star resorts. He'd spent the last five years at an almost obsessive expansion, buying up small companies with an eye to a future where he owned the world.

But now, as he signed documents to purchase his latest company, a valuable nutritional supplement firm based in Copenhagen, instead of triumph he felt only irritation.

He didn't give a damn about vitamins or protein powders. He wanted to be home with Belle. In her arms. In her bed.

And it was getting worse. At night, when he was in her arms, lost in her deep, expressive brown eyes, kissing her sensual mouth, he'd started to feel something he'd sworn he never would again. Something more than desire.

He found himself caring about her opinion.

He found himself...caring.

In daylight, the thought chilled Santiago to the bone. He couldn't let himself be vulnerable. He'd be marrying her in a matter of weeks, and soon afterward, they'd be raising a child together.

Marriage he could justify, as a mere piece of paper to secure his child's name.

But actually caring about Belle...

Needing her happiness...

Needing *her*...

That was something else.

He could never risk the devastation of loving someone again. He couldn't be that stupid. He couldn't.

But as the weeks passed and their wedding date approached, Santiago grew increasingly tense. Every day he was with Belle, every night, he felt intimacy building between them. The wedding he'd once insisted upon now started to feel like a ticking time bomb. Waiting to explode. To destroy.

It made him want to run.

I made a promise, he told himself desperately. *To Belle. To our child. I'm not going anywhere.*

But as their wedding grew closer, his fears intensified. No matter how much he tried to shove down his feelings. No matter how he tried to deny them.

I have to marry her. For my child's sake. It's just a piece of paper. Not my soul!

But the closer their wedding date became, the more edgy he felt.

Belle woke before dawn on her wedding day, and when she opened her eyes in the gray September light, she looked across the bed. A smile burst across her face brighter than the sun.

It was an omen. Today was their wedding day. And it was the first time she hadn't woken alone.

Santiago was sleeping in bed beside her.

With a rush of gratitude, Belle smiled to herself happily, listening to his deep breathing beside her in the shadows of their bedroom.

After all her fears and plans, she would marry him tonight. And just in time, since at three weeks from her due date, her belly had gotten so huge that she barely fit into her simple, pretty wedding dress. Tonight, in a candlelight ceremony on their rooftop garden, she would officially become Mrs. Santiago Velazquez.

The past month in New York had been filled with unexpected joys, like fixing up this house. It hadn't been a makeover, but a make-*under*. Seven stories, elevator, rooftop garden, wine cellar and all, it had become a real home as she believed a home should be: comfy and cozy. She'd softened the cold, stark modern design, replacing the angular furniture with plump sofas that you could cuddle in.

The master closet, sadly, was now full of fashionable,

scratchy black dresses and stiletto heels, but on the plus side, if she still hated going out into society, at least she loved coming home.

This house had somehow become her home.

After their rocky start, she'd become friends with the live-in staff—Dinah Green, the cook, and Anna Phelps, the maid. Belle often helped them with their tasks, just for the company, and because she liked taking care of her own home. She'd helped Anna study for tests for law school. Dinah had taught her some delicious new recipes, and Belle had already volunteered to cook on every holiday so the older woman could have the time off to visit her grown-up son in Philadelphia.

Together, the three women had worked together to plan everything for the wedding tonight.

It would be a simple affair, a short ceremony attended by family and friends, followed by a late dinner. A judge friend of Santiago's was going to officiate. They already had the marriage license. Afterward, there would be a sit-down dinner of roast beef and grilled asparagus on the rooftop desk, then dancing to music provided by a jazz trio, cake and champagne toasts, and all done by midnight.

Planning the event hadn't been too hard. Belle wasn't that picky, and besides, she'd discovered that living on the Upper East Side, with a driver and unlimited money, was an entirely different New York experience from when she'd shared a walk-up apartment and struggled to make the bills in Brooklyn.

Here, she had a concierge obstetrician who made house calls. Here, she had time. Here, she had space. Her heart fluttered when Santiago came home each night, and they ate dinner together at the long table. He was very busy with his company and often worked long days. But on weekends he would take her out to little cafés—which she enjoyed—and trendy restaurants—which she didn't.

He'd taken her to see a certain famous musical sold out on Broadway, with front-row tickets that the whole world knew were impossible to get. Sitting next to him in the audience that night, Belle realized that she wasn't wishing she could trade places with the actress on stage. She liked where she was, at Santiago's side, with his hand resting protectively on her baby bump. She'd looked at him in the darkened theater. Feeling her look, he'd squeezed her hand.

Then, a minute later, he'd abruptly dropped it.

It was strange. One minute she felt so close to him, as their eyes met in mutual understanding, or a shared joke. But the next minute, he would suddenly seem distant, or literally leave the room. She didn't know which was worse.

Maybe he was having annoyances at work. Maybe he was nervous about their baby's upcoming due date, in just three weeks. She could hardly wait to meet their baby and hold her in their arms.

She intended to have their baby sleep in a bassinet next to their bed at first, but she'd already decorated the nursery to be ready. It was a sweet room, with pale pink walls, a crystal chandelier, a pretty white crib, changing table and rocking chair. And a huge stuffed white polar bear in the corner.

That stuffed bear, twelve feet tall, had been brought home yesterday by Santiago, carried into the nursery with the assistance of Kip.

Belle had laughed. "And you say you have no idea how to be a father. Didn't they have a bigger one?"

"I'm glad they didn't. I would have had to bring it in with a crane through the window. It barely fit in the elevator."

"You're a genius," she'd proclaimed, kissing him happily. "And to think all I've done today for the baby is look through the baby name book."

"Find anything?"

"Well, maybe," she said shyly. He seemed in such a good mood, she'd ventured, "What would you think about naming her Emma Valeria, after both our mothers?"

Santiago's expression immediately turned cold.

"Name her after your mother, if you like. Keep mine out of it."

And he'd abruptly left the nursery.

She shivered. He was always going from hot to cold. It was bewildering. You never knew what might set him off. Even during their happiest moments, he could suddenly become remote. He could be passionate, demanding, infuriating; he could be generous and occasionally, even kind. But aside from the night after their engagement party, when he'd told her about that horrible woman who'd broken his heart, Santiago had never again let her close. Never let her in.

Thinking about it now, Belle shook her head firmly. There was no point in worrying. Today was her wedding day. She should just relish her joy that Santiago had actually woken up beside her.

Careful not to wake him, she rose quietly from the bed. Going to the bedroom's tall windows, she brushed aside the translucent curtains and looked down at the New York street, which was already starting to stir into life with taxi cabs and pedestrians, in a pale haze of pink and gray.

Tonight after dusk, she and Santiago would be bound together in lifetime vows, surrounded by family and friends. Letty and Darius had come back from Greece with their fat, adorable baby, specifically to attend. Letty would even be coming to the house a few hours early, to help Belle do her hair and makeup for the ceremony. And that wasn't all.

Two days ago, Santiago had sent his private jets to collect Belle's younger brothers: Ray from Atlanta, where he now owned his own plumbing business, and Joe from Denver, where he was training to be a fireman.

Belle had cried when her brothers arrived. It was the first time she'd seen them in two years. For a long time, the three siblings just hugged each other. Her brothers were excited to be uncles. They'd exclaimed both at the size of her belly and the luxurious brownstone mansion.

"You're in a new world now, Belle," Ray had said, pulling off his John Deere cap to survey the foyer in awe. Even their guest rooms had amazed them. Joe confided he was afraid to use the towels, until she'd tartly told him that this was her house and she wouldn't accept any more foolishness. Joe looked at her.

"You're happy, aren't you, Belle?" He shook his head. "I mean, I know this guy's got private jets and mansions and all that. But does he love you? Do you love him?"

And looking at her baby brother's hopeful, pleading face, Belle had done the only thing an older sister could do. She'd lied.

"Of course Santiago loves me." Then she'd realized something horrible. Something that wasn't a lie. She'd whispered, "And I love him."

Two days before her wedding, she'd been forced to face the truth. She was in love with Santiago.

When she'd first accepted his proposal—when he'd blackmailed her into it—Belle had told herself she shouldn't take it personally if Santiago didn't love her. He was just a hard-edged, ruthless tycoon who couldn't love anyone. Love wasn't in his character. She'd told herself she could live with it.

She was wrong.

"I earned a billion-dollar fortune. For her."

She could still hear the raw huskiness of Santiago's voice when he'd told her the story of the woman he'd once loved with all his heart. The night of their engagement party, all her rationalizations had fallen off a cliff.

Santiago did know how to love. Her stomach churned

now as she stared out the window at the waking city. He'd once loved a woman so much he'd spent literally years trying to win her, just like in the fairy tales Belle used to read her brothers when they were little. A peasant boy proves his worth by killing a dragon or vanquishing an army or sailing the seven seas to win the hand of the fair princess.

Only Santiago hadn't won his true love. Instead, the princess had just been one more privilege he was denied because he'd been born the bastard son of a maid. And everything he'd done to prove he didn't care about his father's rejection—from buying the historic ranch in Texas, to building a world-class art collection, to amassing a bigger fortune than him—only proved the opposite.

It doesn't matter, she told herself desperately. It all happened long ago. The woman had married his elder brother and they all lived in Spain, on the other side of the world.

But here in New York, the fairy tale was different. Belle was the peasant, and Santiago the handsome, distant king. She'd have given anything to win him. Slay any dragon, conquer any army. But how?

She might bear his child, but would she ever claim his heart?

Belle looked back at Santiago, still sprawled across their bed. The cool light of dawn was starting to add a soft pink glow through the windows. Her eyes traced the contours and outlines of his muscular, powerful body, with the white sheet twisted around his legs. She longed for him to be hers, really hers.

And in a way, he was. She would be his wife. His partner. His lover.

But never his love.

Going to the en-suite bathroom, she took a long, hot shower, trying to get the anxiety out of her body, and the growing fear of marrying a man she loved, but who would never love her back.

A man who, for all she knew, was still in love with that woman from long ago.

Maybe our baby will bring us together, she tried to tell herself, but she knew this was a delusion. Santiago would be a caring father, and he'd love their daughter. That didn't mean he'd feel anything more than respect for Belle as a partner. Anything more than desire for her in the night.

He would never let her in his heart. He would never slay dragons for her, sacrifice his life for her, as he had for that beautiful Spanish woman long ago.

Getting out of the shower, she wrapped herself in a white fluffy robe. Wiping the steam off the glass, Belle looked at herself in the bathroom mirror. Today was supposed to be the happiest day of her life, but her eyes were suddenly sad.

She looked down at the enormous diamond ring sparkling on her left hand. As ridiculously impractical as it was, as heavy and cold, it was beautiful and special. He'd picked it out just for her. Didn't that mean something, at least?

When she came out into their bedroom, Santiago was gone. He'd told her he would be at the office until shortly before their candlelight ceremony was due to begin, at seven, but she'd somehow hoped he would change his mind and be with her, today of all days. She was desperate for reassurance about their upcoming marriage. She was suddenly terrified she was about to make the biggest mistake of her life, and that she wouldn't be the only one to suffer for it.

Right or wrong, she told herself, the choice has already been made. *I'm marrying him today*.

But the day passed with agonizing slowness, with too much time for her to worry. She saw her brothers at breakfast, right before the two young men set out to see the Statue of Liberty and Empire State Building. She got one last checkup from her obstetrician, then finished last-minute wedding details.

In the late afternoon, it was finally time. She went to her closet and stroked the empire-waist wedding gown of cream-colored lace, tailored to fit her eight-months-plus pregnant belly. She'd found it at a vintage shop in Chinatown, and loved it.

She took a deep breath.

Smoothing rose-scented lotion over her skin, she put on her wedding lingerie, an expensive confection of white satin bralette, panties and white stockings with garter belt. Any moment now, Letty would be here to help with her hair and makeup. Belle would have to somehow pretend to be a blissfully happy bride, hiding how scared she really was that she was doing the wrong thing, permanently giving her life and heart to a man who would never love her back.

I'm marrying him for our daughter, Belle told herself desperately. But would her daughter grow up thinking it was normal for married parents not to love each other? That it was expected and right, to live without love?

Belle felt like she was hyperventilating as she went to the huge closet and took the beautiful wedding dress from the hanger. She heard a hard knock at the door.

Expecting Letty, she called, "Just a sec!"

But the door was flung open. Belle turned with a yelp of protest, trying to hide her half-naked body with the wedding dress. Then she gasped.

"Santiago! What are you doing here? Don't you know it's bad luck to see the bride in her wedding dr—?" Her voice cut off when she saw his face. "What's wrong?"

"My brother..."

"Your brother? Is he here?"

He gave a strangled laugh. "He's dead."

"What?"

His expression was pale and strange. "He died two days ago."

"I'm sorry," Belle whispered. Her wedding dress dropped unheeded to the floor as she went to him. Without thinking, she wrapped her arms around him, offering comfort, not caring that she was wearing only the bra and panties and that it was bad luck. "What happened?"

"Otilio had a heart attack and crashed his car. It's just lucky no one else was hurt."

"I'm so sorry," she repeated, her eyes filling with tears. "Even though you never met, and your relationship was complicated, he was still your brother and…"

"The funeral is tomorrow morning in Madrid."

Belle sucked in her breath. "You'll miss it. You…"

Then he met her eyes, and she suddenly knew.

"You're not going to miss it," she said slowly. "You're going to Madrid."

Santiago gave a single short nod. "I'm leaving immediately."

"But our wedding…" she whispered.

"I've already had my executive assistant start making calls. I'm sorry, Belle. Our wedding must be temporarily put off."

Belle had just been arguing that they were family, but now she said in a small voice, "But you don't even know them."

"My father needs me."

"He called you?"

His jaw tightened. "No. It was my brother's widow who called. She asked me to come, for my father's sake."

"Your brother's…" It took several seconds for this to sink in, and then Belle staggered back a step.

His brother's widow.

His *widow.*

The only woman Santiago had ever loved was free now.

Single.

What must the woman be like, since Santiago had spent years trying to win her love? Beautiful, chic, witty, powerful, sexy, glamorous? All of the above?

How could Belle compare with that?

She couldn't.

She felt sick inside.

"Belle?"

"Um." She tried to gather her thoughts. "It must have been…strange to talk to her again, after all these years."

"It was," he said in a low voice. "She said my father wants to see me. He has no one else now. His wife died years ago. Otilio and Nadia never had any children. I'm the last Zoya."

Belle's lips parted. "Are you saying…?"

"After thirty-five years, the Duque de Sangovia is willing to recognize me as his son."

And with that, Belle suddenly knew that her whole life, and her baby's too, had just changed, because a man she'd never met had had a heart attack in Spain.

"I'm sorry I have to postpone the wedding," he added, but something about his voice made her wonder how sorry he really was. Even as she had the thought, she reproached herself for it. How could she selfishly think about her own hurt, when Santiago's brother had just died, and his father was reaching out to him for the first time?

She put her hand on his arm urgently. "I'll come with you. To Madrid."

He shook his head. "It's across the Atlantic. You're getting too close to your due date to travel."

"I'll manage. I mean—" she gave an awkward laugh "—isn't that why you have a private jet? I just had a checkup this morning and I'm not anywhere close to labor. I'll be fine for a few days."

He looked at her, his jaw tight. "You would be willing

to go to so much trouble, to attend the funeral of a man you've never met? At your state of pregnancy? After I canceled our wedding like this?"

"Of course I would," she said over the lump in her throat. "I'm going to be your wife."

He set his jaw.

"Come, then."

She didn't get the sense that he was overjoyed.

"Unless you don't want me..."

"That's not it. I just don't want you to be uncomfortable."

"I'll be fine. I can't let you face it alone."

"That's very thoughtful." His eyes were unreadable as he looked down at her. "But then, I'd expect no less of you. Such a loving heart."

His words should have cheered her, and yet somehow, they didn't feel like a compliment. They felt like an accusation.

He looked her over in the white silk wedding lingerie, as if not even seeing her. "Change your clothes. Pack as quickly as possible. We leave in ten minutes."

She stared after him, her heart sick with fear.

When she'd woken up that morning, she'd been so scared of marrying Santiago and spending the rest of her life loving him, when he didn't love her back.

But now she realized there could be something even worse than that. Watching as Santiago fell back in love with the beautiful, aristocratic woman who'd once claimed his heart.

CHAPTER EIGHT

MADRID. ROYAL CITY of dreams.

The city was the third largest in Europe, built on a grand scale, from the classical grandeur of the Plaza Mayor to the world-class art of the Prado Museum and designer shops on the wide, graceful Gran Vía.

Santiago hadn't been back to this city since he'd fled at eighteen to make his fortune. Now he was back, no longer a desperate, penniless teenager, but a powerful tycoon, a self-made billionaire.

At fourteen, he'd begged his father to see him. Now the Duque de Sangovia was doing the begging, not him.

Actually, it had been Nadia who'd begged on his father's behalf. It had been strange, unpleasant, to hear her voice on the phone, like resurrecting a long-dead ghost. He'd felt nothing, not even hatred.

Perhaps he should thank her, he thought. She was the one who'd spurred him to become the man he was today. Powerful. Rich.

Heartless.

He stared out the car window as the Duque de Sangovia's chauffeur drove the limousine through the city's clogged morning traffic, carrying Santiago and Belle and their two bodyguards from the private airport. Madrid had once been a medieval dusty village, until King Phillip had moved the royal court here during the Spanish Golden Age. And even back then, the Zoya family had served their king, fighting his battles to build an empire of their own.

Each generation had become more powerful, with a better title to pass on to their heirs. His elder half brother Otilio had been born with the title of *marqués*, raised to be the next duke. But now his brother was dead.

Brother. Such a meaningful word for what had been, in their case, such a nonexistent relationship. Second only to *father.*

Today, at Otilio's funeral, he would finally meet his father in person. All Santiago knew of him came from the news and from his mother's scant stories, when he was very young. And he would see Nadia, the woman he'd once loved, whom he'd thought a kindred spirit. They'd both achieved the dreams they'd had at the orphanage, some twenty years before. He was a billionaire. She was a world-famous actress.

But not a duchess, he thought. That dream, at least, had been lost to her, from the moment her husband died.

He looked out at the weak morning light of Madrid. The September weather was chilly, the sky drizzling rain. He couldn't imagine a more perfect setting for a funeral.

Belle was sitting beside him in the back of the vintage Rolls-Royce limousine, wearing an elegant black shift dress with a long black jacket. It should have been chic, but was somehow ill-fitting and uncomfortable-looking on Belle's pregnant, curvaceous body. She wouldn't meet his eyes.

She'd barely spoken two words to him on the overnight flight across the Atlantic, leaving him alone with his own dark thoughts. She hadn't reproached him about canceling their wedding. Not a single word.

Not one woman in a million would have been so understanding, he thought. But of course Belle was always so kind. So loving.

Emotions were bubbling up inside him, hot as lava. He'd pushed his feelings down for most of his life. He wasn't sure how much longer he could keep it up.

He hadn't gone to his mother's funeral, twenty years before, because there hadn't been one. She'd had no money, the husbands she'd divorced were long gone, and in her frustration and bitterness, she'd alienated most of her friends. Her son was the only one left, and she'd done her best to make him hate her as well, knowing he couldn't leave.

As a young boy, he'd noticed other boys getting hugs and kisses from their mothers, and wondered why Mamá never treated him with such devotion. "Because you're bad all the time," she told him angrily. "You make your stepfathers angry when you don't put away your toys. You make them leave." It had hurt him when he was young. But by the time he was fourteen, he'd realized the real reason she never loved him. She blamed him for all the fairy tales gone wrong. Starting with his father, the duke.

Living in the orphanage, at least he'd known where he stood. He was on his own.

He'd loved New York from the beginning. The city was heartless and cold? Well, so was he. They were perfect for each other.

"Oh, my word," Belle breathed next to him. "Is that the crowd for your brother's funeral?"

Santiago blinked as he saw huge crowds of well-wishers and gawkers standing on the sidewalk outside the cathedral, held back by police. The driver pulled up to the curb, then opened their door.

Santiago got out of the backseat, turning back to assist Belle, who glanced nervously at the crowds, then looked up at him with dark stricken eyes.

Reaching for her hand, he helped her from the limo toward the gothic stone cathedral. The driver held an umbrella over their heads as the rain continued to drizzle from the gray clouds, falling against the vivid yellows and reds of the trees in September.

"It's like all Madrid is here," she whispered. "How famous was he?"

"They're not here for him," he ground out.

Belle frowned. "What do you mean?"

"There's something you should know about his wife…"

But before he could finish, the oversized door of the cathedral opened, and they entered. The nave of the cathedral was crowded with people who'd come to pay their last respects to Otilio, Marqués de Flavilla, the only legitimate son and heir of the powerful Duque de Sangovia, and the husband of the Most Beautiful Woman in the World.

"He died so unexpectedly," he heard someone say sadly as they passed. "Of a heart attack, and at only thirty-six. Such a tragedy to die so young."

"His poor wife…"

"Oh, her. I heard they've been separated for years. She's probably already thinking this will make spectacular PR for her next movie."

Setting his jaw, Santiago walked heavily up the center aisle of the cathedral in his black suit, holding Belle's hand tightly. The crowds parted for them like magic, people whispering around them, their eyes popping out of their heads.

"The duke's secret son…"

"His bastard son…"

"A self-made billionaire from America…"

Everywhere, he saw admiring eyes, curious eyes. All of them, these aristocrats and royals and politicians from around the world, seemed to admire him as he'd once only dreamed of being admired.

Ironic. All it had taken was the death of his brother, and suddenly Santiago had become a Zoya.

His jaw was taut as he came down the aisle, Belle directly behind him. Then he froze.

At the altar, surrounded by flowers, he saw a closed casket covered with a blanket embroidered with the family's coat of arms. The brother he'd never met, the chosen one, the rightful heir. Surrounding the coffin were flowers, tall silver candlesticks and officiants, ponderous in their robes.

Santiago's attention fell on two people in the front row. An old man in a wheelchair. His father. He looked old, compared to the pictures he'd seen. His face looked querulous, and his skin so pale it was almost translucent.

Beside him, patting him on the shoulder, a woman stood in a sleek, short black dress and chic little black hat with netting. Nadia.

At thirty-six, she was tall and thin and blonde, delicate and fragile, like an angel, severely elegant in her dark mascara and red slash of lipstick. He felt the shock of her beauty like the metallic tang of a remembered poison that had once been tasted and nearly been fatal.

Looking up, Nadia's violet eyes pierced him. She lowered her head to whisper to the man in the wheelchair, and the Duque de Sangovia's rheumy eyes abruptly looked up to see Santiago, his thirty-five-year-old bastard son, for the very first time.

For a second, Santiago held his breath. Then he exhaled. What did he care what the man thought of him now?

Behind him, Belle gave a soft, breathy curse that made him turn and stare. She'd never used a curse word in front of him before. Her eyes were wide with horror.

"That's your ex?" she said in a strangled voice. "Nadia *Cruz*?"

"So?" he said shortly.

"So—she's famous! I've seen her movies! She's one of the biggest movie stars in the world!"

"I know," he said impatiently, and strode forward to the end of the aisle, Belle trailing behind him.

"Santiago! Thank the heavens you are here at last," Nadia greeted him in Spanish, anxiously holding out her hands. "Quickly, quickly, it's about to start. We saved you a place…" She drew back with an irritated look as she saw Belle behind him, still clinging to his hand. "Who is this?"

"My fiancée," he responded in the same language. "Belle Langtry."

Belle's hand tightened. She didn't understand Spanish, but she understood her own name.

Nadia gave a smile that didn't reach her eyes and switched to say in clear English, "We only saved one place in the front row. For family only. She'll have to go behind."

"She stays with me," Santiago said automatically, but he was distracted as his father wheeled himself forward.

The Duque de Sangovia was even older than he'd expected. He seemed to have shrunken since last photographed, in the days since his heir had died. He said imperiously to Santiago, "You will sit between Nadia and me." He didn't look at Belle. "Your companion must find another place."

Bereaved or not, Santiago wasn't going to let the old man boss him around. "No, she stays."

But he felt Belle's hand pull away.

"It's fine. I'll get a spot in the back," she said quickly, and disappeared into the crowd. As the choir started to sing, everyone took their seats and Santiago found himself sitting between his father, whose attention he'd once craved so desperately, and the woman he'd once loved so recklessly.

Twisting his head, Santiago saw Belle in her dark black dress and coat sitting three rows behind them. Her lovely face was pale, her dark eyes luminous and sad. Was she so affected by the death of a man she'd never known? But when she met his eyes, she gave him an encouraging smile.

Always so thoughtful. Such a loving heart.

Luring him to trust her. To love her. Luring him to his own destruction.

Santiago turned away, a storm raging inside him.

The priest began the ceremony and he sat numbly, hardly able to feel anything. He barely heard the words as one officiant after another praised his brother, who apparently had been a paragon, beloved by all.

His heart was pounding as he stared at the closed casket, covered with the embroidered Zoya coat of arms and surrounded by flowers, barely hearing the eulogies.

He'd never imagined he would someday be seated beside his father, the duke, in a place of honor, for all the world to see. The old man actually looked at him once or twice during the ceremony, his wizened expression a little bewildered, tears in his eyes.

After the ceremony, they were whisked into the waiting limousine, which had been altered for his father's wheelchair. They were to be taken to the funeral reception at the Zoya *palacio*, a mile away from the cathedral. But as he was led to the limousine behind his father and Nadia, Santiago paused, looking around with a frown.

"Where is Belle?"

"Family only," Nadia told him firmly. He ignored her.

Striding back into the cathedral, he found Belle. "Come with me."

"Where?" She looked uncertain, ill at ease.

"The palace." This time, he wasn't going to let her slip away. Holding her hand tightly, he pulled her into the back of the stretch limousine, where Nadia and his father were already seated.

Belle sat beside him in silence, looking awkward and

uncomfortable and very pregnant, as they faced Nadia and his father, seated opposite. He saw Nadia and the duke both look at the swell of Belle's pregnancy, then look away, as if her condition were a personal affront.

Deafening silence filled the limousine as the driver took them from the cathedral to the Calle de la Princesa. In the middle of Madrid, surrounded by high-rise buildings, was the duke's city residence, the Palacio de las Palmas, with acres of lush greenery behind tall wrought-iron walls and a guarded gate. The same gate from which Santiago had been bloodily barred as an orphaned fourteen-year-old.

They drove past the wide open gate and past the luxurious gardens with the exotic palms for which the neo-classical palace was named. The limo stopped. Santiago's eyes were wide as he saw the nineteenth-century palace for the first time.

But as Santiago started to get out, the duke reached out a shaking claw to his shoulder.

"I thank God you've come to me, boy," he rasped in Spanish. "You are all I have left." He looked at him intently with his hooded gaze. "Truth be told, *mi hijo*, you are the only one who can save this family now."

It had been a very long day, Belle thought wearily. One thing after another. Her interrupted wedding. A private flight across the Atlantic. An elaborate funeral. A palace in Madrid. And oh, yeah, discovering that Santiago's ex was *Nadia Cruz*.

Now this.

Belle felt exhausted and overwhelmed as she looked up at the five-hundred-year-old castle. After the funeral reception had ended in Madrid, they'd traveled ninety minutes to the village of Sangovia, nestled in a valley beneath the castle on the crag, heart of Zoya history and power.

She nearly stumbled over the cobblestones, still slippery with rain in the darkness. Santiago grabbed her arm, steadying her.

He frowned, looking at her. "Are you all right?"

Belle tried to smile encouragingly. "I'm fine."

But she wasn't fine. Not at all. She hadn't been fine since Santiago had canceled their wedding yesterday.

She'd slept fitfully on the private jet over the Atlantic, tossing and turning. Then at the funeral she'd discovered it was even worse than she'd feared.

Santiago's ex, the widowed marquesa, was a famous movie star—famous, beautiful, powerful…everything that she, Belle, was not. And his father, the elderly Duque de Sangovia, had yet to acknowledge Belle's existence, even when he'd been sitting inches away, facing her in the limousine.

After the funeral, at the reception in the Palacio de las Palmas in the center of Madrid, she'd watched as Santiago stood beside his father and Nadia to gravely thank each of the illustrious, powerful guests—prime ministers, presidents, royalty—for coming to honor the late marqués.

Belle stood back, near the tables of food, feeling awkward and alone. The reception lasted for hours, until her belly felt heavy and tight and her feet throbbed with pain. She did not belong here, surrounded by all these wealthy, powerful people, in the gilded palace.

How could she compete with this—any of it?

She'd been intimidated by Santiago's mansion in Manhattan, but the Palacio de las Palmas, with its classical architecture and Greek columns, was an actual palace. There were layers of wealth on every wall, paintings and frescoes on the ceiling and sweeping staircases that led to more gilded rooms with yet more paintings of more illustrious Zoya ancestors.

When the reception finally ended, Belle had breathed a sigh of relief, hoping against hope that Santiago would shake hands with his father and Nadia—or better yet, just wave to the woman from a distance—and he and Belle could get back on a plane for New York.

Instead, Santiago had informed her that he would be remaining in Spain, staying at the castle of Sangovia with his father and Nadia.

"Just until Otilio's will is dealt with."

"Do we have to?"

"You don't. You can go back to New York tonight."

She'd looked up sharply. "No!"

"You are three weeks from your due date," he replied coolly. "You should be home."

He seemed as if he could hardly wait to get rid of her. Once, it would have been a dream come true for her to be sent away. But now, she could hardly bear the thought of it. She'd glared at him. "I'm staying with you."

He ground his teeth. "Belle—"

"We just got to Spain." Her voice trembled, but she lifted her chin. "I'm not going to turn around and fly back to New York. I'm exhausted. I'm staying."

He'd stared at her for a long moment.

"Fine. Stay. Just for a day or two. Then you're going back."

And he hadn't spoken to her again, the whole ninety minutes it took to drive with the duke and the movie star and their bodyguards to the medieval village of Sangovia, tucked in a green valley, beneath the looming castle at the top of the crag.

The castle had looked beautiful from a distance, but as Belle walked through the enormous door, she thought it felt impersonal and cold inside, far worse than the palace in Madrid. The castle of Sangovia wasn't gilded or gleaming like the neoclassical Palacio de las Palmas. The windows were small and far between, and the walls were cold stone. This castle came from an earlier, more brutal time of battles and blood.

The duke said something in Spanish to Santiago, and he replied with a nod. His father disappeared down the cold hallway, past a suit of armor, into a room she couldn't see.

Nadia then said something lightly in the same language, before she too disappeared. For a brief moment, Belle and Santiago were alone in the dark stone hallway. She was suddenly tempted to throw herself in his arms, to ask why he'd been so distant, to try to feel close to him again.

Then they heard a cough, and turning, they saw a uniformed maid. She said in English, "I'm here to take you to your rooms."

"Of course," Santiago said smoothly. "Thank you."

The maid led them through the castle, and up the stairs. A less homey or cozy domicile could scarcely be imagined. It was cold, drafty and damp. The stiff chairs they passed in the hallway all looked hundreds of years old and Belle feared might break if she actually tried to sit on one. Why would anyone choose to live here? she wondered.

The maid led Santiago and Belle to the east wing of the second floor. "All the family's bedrooms are down here," she said shyly, and pushed open a door.

The bedroom was formal and old-fashioned, filled with antiques, including a curtained four-poster bed. Belle glanced out the window at the view of the valley in the twilight.

"What do you think?" Santiago asked in an expressionless voice.

"It's very nice," Belle said politely.

"Thank you," the maid said. She turned to Belle. "I will take you to your room now, *señorita*."

Santiago suddenly scowled. "What are you talking about? My fiancée is staying with me."

"I am sorry, *señor*," the maid replied uncomfortably,

"but His Excellency does not approve of unmarried persons sharing sleeping quarters."

"Oh, really?" Santiago ground out. "Is that why he always used to seduce his maids in closets?"

The woman looked scared. *"Señor—?"*

"Forget it." He gritted his teeth. "You can just tell His Excellency—"

"No, Santiago. It's fine. Really." Belle put her hand on his arm anxiously. "This is his home. He just lost his son. I can sleep in a separate room for a night or two." She gave him a wan smile. "I'm tired. I just want to go to bed."

He started to argue, then scowled at the maid. "Fine. Take us to her room, then."

Rather than looking relieved, the maid looked even more nervous. "His Excellency asked that you come back down immediately to the salon, *señor*. I can take Miss Langtry the rest of the way upstairs."

"Upstairs? How far is it?"

"Um…"

"It doesn't matter," Belle interjected. "Your father needs you. Go to him."

He turned to Belle. "Are you sure?"

"I'm sure."

"I'll check on you later." His expression seemed distant. "And kiss you good night."

Maybe then, she thought hopefully, when they were alone, they could actually talk and try to work out whatever was making him so distant. "All right."

He kissed her gently on the forehead, his lips cool. "Until then."

"This way, *señorita*."

Belle followed the maid down the hall. They went up a sweeping staircase, then a tightly winding flight of steps, then another. Belle's legs started to ache, and once or twice she leaned against the stone wall to catch her breath. The maid seemed to have no trouble whatsoever.

"How many people are on staff here?" Belle asked, to fill the silence as the maid waited.

"Thirty, *señorita*."

"Thirty people work here? To take care of how many?"

"Two."

Reaching a tower, they went up another tightly twisting flight of stairs, this one of rickety wood. Ducking her head, the maid pushed open a door at the back. She sounded embarrassed as she said, "Here is the room assigned to you, *señorita*."

Belle realized they'd put her in the attic, as if she were a mad relative, four floors above Santiago's room in the family wing.

"There's the bathroom," the woman added reluctantly.

Belle peeked past the door to a tiny bathroom, smaller than a closet, with a toilet, bare sink and shower so small she was afraid her belly wouldn't fit. A bare light bulb hung from the ceiling.

The family's opinion of her, and intention for her future, couldn't have been more clear.

"I'm sorry, *señorita*."

Belle forced herself to turn with a bright smile. "No, it's fine."

"You are too kind." The maid added under her breath, "If the marquesa had been assigned to such a room, we would have heard her screaming for miles."

Which was why, Belle reflected, beautiful women like Nadia Cruz ended up with everything they wanted, while girls like Belle ended up in rooms in the attic.

Soon after the maid left, Belle's overnight bag arrived, held by a huffing and puffing porter who glared at her, as if it were her fault he'd been forced to climb so many tightly twisting stone steps. "I'm sorry," she apologized, feeling guilty even though it hadn't been her idea.

Getting on her pajamas, she brushed her teeth and climbed into the tiny single bed, with the sagging mattress and squeaky metal frame, to wait for Santiago.

She looked out through the curtainless small round window. Sweeping moonlight showed all of the tiny village of Sangovia in the valley below the castle. With a shiver, she pulled up the thin blankets around her baby bump, and stared out into the starlit night.

Cuddling her belly, she leaned back against the lumpy pillow, yawning as she tried to stay awake until Santiago came to kiss her good night as he'd promised. She waited. And waited.

But he never came.

CHAPTER NINE

SANTIAGO STARED ACROSS the chilly salon, over a glass of even chillier Scotch, and looked down into his father's eyes, the chilliest of all.

"What are you saying?" His voice sounded strained, even to his own ears.

The old man's reply was a harsh rasp from the bowels of his wheelchair. "You will stay in Spain. As my heir."

Santiago paced a step in the oversized salon, which was filled with Renaissance art and leather-bound books that he'd wager no one had touched in years, except perhaps by the maids dusting them. The two men were alone.

When he'd come downstairs to see his father, the man had wheeled over to the liquor cabinet, poured him a drink, and then spoken his demand without preamble.

Once he would have killed to hear his father say those words. But now...

Santiago took a gulp of Scotch, then said coldly, "You've ignored me for my whole life. Why would I want to be your heir?"

"It is your birthright."

"It wasn't my birthright for the last thirty-five years."

"Everything changed with the death of my son." Suddenly, the old man sounded weary. He ran a hand over his wispy head. "I am dying, Santiago. You are all that is left of the Zoyas now. If you do not take over this family, there will never be another Duque de Sangovia."

Santiago's jaw tightened. "Why should I care? You abandoned my mother. You abandoned me before I was born. What is the dukedom to me? I have my own company. My own empire. My life is not in Spain."

"It could be."

"I came to Otilio's funeral to show my respect, nothing more. And because I was curious to meet the man who never wanted to recognize me as his son."

The elderly Duke said slyly, "And to see Nadia?"

That brought Santiago up short.

The man continued, "She has been a good daughter-in-law to me. She is beautiful, elegant, powerful, famous. The perfect consort." He paused. "Except for her inability to conceive the Zoya heir, but as for that, perhaps it is not too late."

Santiago's eyes narrowed. "What do you mean?"

"I know you and Nadia have a history. Perhaps this is fate. She could still bear the Zoya heir. To you."

Santiago stared down at him, unable to believe what he was hearing. "Have you lost your mind, old man? You've met my fiancée. Belle is upstairs right now. Our baby is due in weeks—"

"You must give that woman up," the Duque de Sangovia said harshly. "She will never be accepted, this country girl, not in Madrid nor in the elite circles of international aristocracy where you belong. It would be cruel to force her into a place where she would always be awkward, rejected, based on her unfortunate background."

"Oh, so you're just looking out for her—is that it?" Santiago said acidly. "You forget I was raised a bastard, without money or formal education—"

"You are different. You are my son, with Zoya blood. You have single-handedly built a business empire that must inspire respect."

In spite of himself, Santiago felt a strange zing of pride

at hearing his father speak those words. Then he caught himself. "So you expect me to abandon her," he ground out, "as you did my mother?"

"*Sí*, and for the same reasons," the duke said calmly. "I could not divorce my wife, the duchess, to run off with a maid. I would have lost all the fortune that came with her, and damaged my family honor and my name."

"Seducing an eighteen-year-old maid and then abandoning your own son is what you call honorable?"

"Sometimes difficult choices must be made. This girl, this Belle, has nothing. She is nothing. Toy with her if you must, even have a child with her, but do not marry her. If you wish to be my heir, you must marry as befits the future Duke of Sangovia."

"I will marry as I choose, and you and Sangovia and Nadia can all go to hell."

"Do not marry this American girl." The old man's rheumy eyes turned hard. "Do you really think she could ever be happy here, in this world? It would be cruel to her. And the child. Let her go."

Santiago opened his mouth to argue. Then he snapped it shut, thinking of the sad, haunted look in Belle's eyes ever since they'd arrived in Madrid.

"Excuse me, Your Excellency." A male nurse appeared at the door. "It is time for your medicine."

The duke nodded grimly. He started to push his wheelchair out of the room, but as he passed Santiago, the duke gripped his arm with a shaking hand.

"You have the power to choose, *mi hijo*. Let the girl go. Accept your birthright as my son. Become my heir, and the future duke, to continue a legacy that has endured for hundreds of years. The dukedom, combined with your vast business empire, plus a marriage to Nadia, would make you one of the most powerful men in the entire world." His beady eyes burned brightly in the shadowy salon. "Think about it."

Santiago was left alone in the salon, with nothing but the glass of Scotch and his own bleak thoughts for company.

His father was offering him everything he'd ever dreamed of as a boy.

A vindication of his worth.

Everything he'd hungered for as a young man.

But that wasn't the only reason he was suddenly tempted. He clawed back his hair.

For the last few months, he'd found himself growing closer to Belle in a way that he'd enjoyed at first, but now terrified him. As their marriage approached, he'd become increasingly on edge. In bed with her, he'd experienced physical joy beyond anything he'd ever imagined. But he'd started to have feelings for her, beyond partnership or even friendship. Against his will, Belle had become too important to him. Her beauty. Her kindness. Her wit. The deep luminosity of her brown eyes.

He found himself drawn to her. *Needing* her.

Like today. Even after he'd made the decision to send her back to New York so he wouldn't worry about her going into labor so far from home, all she'd had to do was raise her poignant gaze to his and ask to stay, and he'd immediately given in. Because he couldn't bear to see her unhappy, not even for a moment.

He didn't like it.

Santiago didn't want to need anyone. He didn't want to be dependent on their happiness for his own peace of mind. Because if you depended on someone—if you cared for them—it left you weak and vulnerable, to be crushed at will by their inevitable betrayal. He'd learned that from childhood. From Nadia.

I know you and Nadia have a history. Perhaps this is fate. She could still bear the Zoya heir. To you.

The thought repelled him. Nadia, for all her angelic beauty, had the soul of a snake. A mercenary, gold-digging snake. The thought of touching her disgusted him.

But at least Nadia would never again tempt him into risking his heart. Not like Belle.

If he was honest with himself, when he'd gotten the call about his brother's death, and realized it gave him the perfect excuse to cancel the wedding—the same wedding he himself had insisted on, demanded, blackmailed Belle into—part of him had been relieved.

Something inside him was afraid of marrying her now. He, who'd never been afraid of anything, was afraid of what would happen if he spoke those vows to Belle, the one woman on earth who held power over him.

Wearily, Santiago left the salon and went up the sweeping stairs toward the second floor. He stopped in front of his own door, suddenly remembering how he'd promised Belle he'd come up and kiss her good night.

He pictured her beautiful face. Her wide, haunting brown eyes, fringed with black lashes. Her full ruby-red lips. Her softness. Her sweetness.

She'd hated him when they'd first met, with good cause. Santiago had pushed people away for most of his life. It wasn't just a game to him; it was necessary for survival. But he'd known from the night he first seduced Belle that she, idealistic and romantic and good-hearted as she was, could be dangerous to his peace of mind. So he'd pushed her away.

That had all changed when he'd found out she was pregnant. He'd forced her into an engagement in Texas. She'd hated him for that.

But Belle didn't hate him anymore. Something had changed in her during their time living in New York. She'd been his hostess. She'd redecorated his home. She'd even traveled with him to Spain when, by rights, she should have slapped his face for canceling their wedding to attend the funeral of a virtual stranger half a world away.

Santiago wanted her. So much. Even picturing Belle now, stretched out on a bed somewhere upstairs, he yearned to see her, hold her, touch her. He'd meant to ask the housekeeper for directions to her bedroom, which he assumed to be even larger and more comfortable than his own, as any pregnant woman deserved. But now...

Hesitating at his own bedroom door, he looked down the dark hallway toward the stairs. His body yearned for the electricity and comfort of her touch. He longed to feel her sweet, hot, lush body naked against his own.

But the cost to his soul was suddenly too high.

Setting his jaw, he turned back to his own bedroom, going inside, closing the door firmly behind him.

He would sleep alone.

Belle woke up alone in the shabby little attic room of the castle, and sat up in a rush. He'd never come up to kiss her last night.

Trying to ignore the hurt, she stretched her muscles, aching from the lumpy mattress. She took a quick, awkward shower in the tiny beat-up bathroom with peeling linoleum, then freshened up, putting on a new dress that, with her full pregnancy, made her look as lumpy as that bed.

Going downstairs, she went to Santiago's bedroom, only to discover it was empty. So were the other bedrooms in the wing. She wandered downstairs, feeling lost, until she found an English-speaking maid who directed her to the breakfast room.

"You should hurry, miss. I'm afraid you're late," she said anxiously.

Late? How could she be late? No one had told Belle anything about breakfast being at any certain time.

She found the formal breakfast room, with its long elegant table, with food spread out on a side table and big arrangements of flowers that made her want to sneeze. When she arrived, Santiago set down his newspaper, his breakfast plate already empty. His dark eyes were cool as, rising from the table, he came forward.

"I missed you last night," she said, staring up at him.

"Sorry. I was busy." He barely looked at her, and kissed her on the cheek as if she were a stranger.

"Did you enjoy sleeping in, Miss Langtry?" cooed Nadia, also rising from the table, looking sexy and chic in a perfectly cut black skirt suit, her light blond hair pulled back into a chignon, a jeweled brooch on her lapel.

"Sleeping in?" Belle stammered.

"We expected you an hour ago."

The duke muttered something darkly in Spanish, but didn't bother to look in Belle's direction, as his servant pushed his wheelchair from the room.

Belle bit her lip as she looked between Santiago and Nadia. "You expected me at a certain time?"

"Breakfast begins strictly at eight," Nadia said sweetly. "As the housekeeper mentioned in your wake-up call this morning."

"I didn't get any—"

"Don't worry." The blonde swept her arm in a generous gesture. "You are a guest, so of course you are free to ignore the rules of our household, no matter how much trouble it might cause everyone. The food has grown cold, so I've instructed the servants to prepare you a fresh breakfast, in addition to their other duties."

"I didn't mean…" Belle stopped when Santiago kissed her forehead. He was dressed in a dark suit. "Are you going somewhere?"

"The lawyer's office," he said. "And to Madrid, to discuss the possibility of donating art to the museum and creating a wing in my brother's name."

"Otilio was an art lover," Nadia purred. Her stiletto heels clicked against the marble floor as she looked up at Santiago with a smile. "Shall we go?"

Oh, *hell* to the no. Belle looked between them. "I'll come with you."

"That's not necessary," Santiago said.

"But I want to."

"It will be very boring for you."

"Please," she implored, holding out her hand.

With visible reluctance, he took it. "As you wish."

She exhaled.

"It's really unnecessary, Miss Langtry," Nadia said. She looked seriously annoyed.

Belle was glad. The other woman might be in charge in this castle, arranging to exile her to the attic room and sabotaging her in front of Santiago and the household, but Belle wouldn't give up Santiago without a fight.

But, it seemed, neither would Nadia. Later that morning, as the duke and Santiago were in the adjoining office, speaking to the lawyers, the two women sat together in the posh waiting room.

Bright sunlight was pouring through the windows, and cushy chairs lined the walls. The sound of secretaries typing on keyboards came from the next room. Sitting across from Nadia, Belle felt nervous and awkward and tried to hide it by reading a magazine. In Spanish. Upside down.

"How charming," Nadia said suddenly.

Sheepishly, Belle turned around her magazine. But the other woman wasn't looking at her reading material. Reaching out, she touched the diamond on Belle's finger.

"Oh, the ring?" Belle smiled. "Yes, I love it. His proposal was very romantic, too." Maybe it was stretching the truth to call the way he'd blackmailed her into marriage in Texas romantic, but she hated the smirk on the movie star's face.

"Was it?" Nadia smiled back. "I mean, I know it's very *au courant* to recycle these days, but this is taking it a bit far, don't you think?"

"What do you mean?" Belle said stiffly. She guessed from the context that *au courant* meant trendy, though for all she knew it could have been a type of jam.

"Oh, didn't you know?" The blonde's smile widened. "That's the same ring Santiago once used to propose to me."

Belle's heart fell to the wooden parquet floor.

"No," she stammered. "You're mistaken. He picked it out just for me."

"Oh, didn't he tell you? That naughty creature." Nadia's smile turned wicked. "He tried to give it to me five years ago. Regrettably, he'd waited too long and I'd already been spoken for. But I know my diamonds."

Belle wrapped her hand around the ring, feeling completely betrayed. But she couldn't show it, couldn't let the other woman see how her barb had found its target. She tried to shrug. "Even if it's the same ring, we have a totally different situation. I never betrayed him."

"No, you just got pregnant."

Belle's eyes narrowed. "While you made him chase you all those years, then married his brother."

Nadia looked at her with a taunting smile on her red lips. "I'm not married to him anymore. Now I am free."

Belle stiffened, trying to hide her growing fear. "You think you can take him from me."

Nadia tilted her head, considering. "You're not so stupid after all."

Belle's cheeks flushed. "You don't deserve to be Santiago's wife."

"I'm more deserving than you."

"I love him."

"That I can easily believe." The movie star's famous violet eyes cut through her. "But does he love you?"

The burn on Belle's cheeks intensified.

Because that was the heart of it. Santiago didn't love her. He never had. He never would.

That was the truth she'd been fighting to deny, to hide, even from herself. Even though he'd once told her to her face that he would never love her, she'd dreamed he might change.

She mumbled, "He proposed to me…"

"He proposed to me first. With that exact ring." Nadia gave her a hard smile. "Curious, don't you think, that he kept it all these years?"

Belle tried to fight the emotions swirling inside her beneath the other woman's hard gaze. "He was the one who demanded marriage when he found out I was pregnant…"

"And he obviously felt strongly about it, since he couldn't even be bothered to get you your own ring." Nadia leaned forward in her chair, smiling pleasantly. "The ring was mine. As his love was mine. And both will be again."

Belle couldn't breathe. Her heart was pounding frantically. "You're wrong…he won't…"

"No?" Grabbing her arm, Nadia said, "I am Santiago's equal as you never were. We are meant to be together."

Each word hurt more than the last. "You gave him up," Belle choked out, struggling to pull her arm away.

"I had to be ruthless to get what I wanted. Santiago of all people will understand this, and respect it." Her red lips lifted in a smile. "He's loved me since we were teenagers. He's ached for me. Hungered for me. We belong together. My choice to marry his brother only made Santiago want me more." She looked Belle over contemptuously. "Do you really think he would ever choose you, now I'm free?"

No, she didn't. That was what hurt the most.

"There are two ways to do this," Nadia said sweetly. "Either give Santiago up gracefully. Or watch helplessly as I take him from you."

"You can't…"

"If you love him like you say you do, at least leave him thinking of you with some respect."

Pain ripped through Belle. She felt her baby kick inside her as if her daughter was angry, too. She put her hands over her belly. "He's the father of my child."

"After we are wed, I will give him another baby. He will forget yours." Nadia smiled. "Santiago is an honorable man. He will always provide for you and your child, as a matter of duty. You will never have to work again. Consider yourself lucky. Leave Spain. Go seek the love that Santiago will never give you."

Belle swallowed, her heart pounding.

As the door to the lawyer's office opened and the men came out, Nadia whispered, "End it quickly, and it will be better for everyone. Especially you."

With a final friendly pat to Belle's shoulder, Nadia rose to her feet with a beaming smile to greet the duke and Santiago, who was pushing his father's wheelchair.

"Are you boys finally done? Because we are due at the museum." She added teasingly, with her violet-blue eyes flashing between the duke and Santiago, "You men always like to talk and talk…"

Numbly, Belle pushed herself up from the chair. No one was paying attention to her. The three others were talking in Spanish as they walked ahead of her out of the lawyer's office.

In the limo, she sat silently beside Santiago as they traveled through the sun-drenched streets of Madrid. He gave her a curious glance.

But this time, she was the one avoiding his gaze.

"He's loved me since we were teenagers. He's ached for me. Hungered for me. We belong together."

Belle swallowed over the ache in her throat as she watched the passing city through the car window. She'd only met Santiago a year ago. He'd never loved her. And what did they even have in common, when she barely knew the name of her great-grandparents, compared with Santiago, who had an aristocratic bloodline that went back to the Middle Ages?

"After we are wed I will give him another baby. He will forget yours."

Belle knew Santiago's determination to uphold his honor and give their unborn daughter a better childhood than he himself had had. He would not abandon his promise to marry Belle.

She shivered as they traveled in luxury, in a limousine through the streets of Madrid.

The real question was, could she actually let him keep his word, and marry her, trapping them both forever in a cold marriage without love?

CHAPTER TEN

SANTIAGO GLANCED AT the duke as they drove through Madrid. His father had actually thanked him for helping deal with some legal business at the lawyer's office, some contracts that Otilio hadn't signed properly.

His father. It was strange thinking of the old man that way. For the first time, he had a real, flesh-and-blood father.

The old man wasn't affectionate, or even kind. He was arrogant and controlling, and seemed to think that he could boss Santiago around, using his inheritance as bait. Just look at his ridiculous demand that Santiago betray his promise to wed Belle...

He glanced at her now, sitting quietly beside him in the backseat, biting her lip as she stared out at the city streets. She'd been strangely quiet since they'd left the lawyer's office. It wasn't like her to be so quiet. Usually she couldn't wait to tell him exactly what she was thinking, particularly when it insulted him.

No, Santiago suddenly realized. That wasn't true anymore. She didn't insult him anymore, not like she used to. Now, she treated him with encouragement. With...love?

The limo bounced over a bump in the road, and his shoe hit the stiletto across from him. He looked up at Nadia, who was sitting across from him, beside his father. She lifted her dark lashes and smiled.

His father obviously wasn't the only one who believed he could get power over Santiago.

It made him incredulous. How could Nadia not realize he had nothing but contempt for her?

Both she and his father were trying to buy him. They offered him a dukedom like a prize, and thought they could use words like honor and fate, and welcome him into the castle, and Santiago would be grateful. They thought he'd never grown up from the childhood dream he'd had as a lonely, fatherless boy. They thought that all they had to do was offer and Santiago, a self-made independent billionaire, would instantly become an obedient son to the father who'd abandoned him, a grateful husband to the woman who'd betrayed him.

But Santiago Velazquez was no man's pawn—or woman's. His jaw tightened as he looked from Nadia to Belle, who was still staring out the window as if her life depended on it. He was just grateful that she had no idea what his father had proposed. He didn't want her hurt. Especially since...

As his gaze traced over her full rosy lips and the plump curves of her body, something twisted in his heart.

Belle was a woman like no other. Her loyalty and courage and honesty didn't just inspire respect, but reverence. She drew him in. He wanted to let her love him.

He wanted to love her back.

His heart was suddenly pounding.

No.

He couldn't be that stupid.

No one could be as honest, or loyal, or good as he thought Belle was. However she might seem. If he let her inside his heart, he would regret it.

When they reached the famous art museum in the heart of Madrid, he got out quickly, opening his passenger door before the driver could. Belle, too, stepped out quickly, as if she were afraid he might offer his hand to help her out.

At least they were in agreement on one thing right now, he thought grimly. Avoiding each other.

They were parked on the quiet side of the museum, far from the long queues of tourists. He pushed his father's wheelchair toward the side door, which led to the museum's administrative offices. Nadia walked beside the duke, chattering to him charmingly in Spanish. Belle walked silently behind, with the bodyguards and his father's nurse, as if she preferred to be with the staff, rather than with the aristocrats.

She probably did, Santiago thought.

Castilian-accented Spanish whirled around him as they were escorted into the lobby and whisked into the director's office, where they were offered champagne or coffee. Through it all, Belle held herself back from the others, looking miserable and wan and as if her feet hurt.

Becoming a duchess in Spain, traveling with the jet-set, would require more rules that Belle wouldn't like, Santiago thought. He would have to live by new rules as well, but at least he spoke Spanish. At least he was of Spanish blood. Belle wasn't.

Plus, she'd have to temper her honest, enthusiastic, joyful nature to be cool and calm, to know how to smile pleasantly while speaking cutting words, to maneuver the hard merciless edges of the highest of European high society— a world of not just mere money, but hundreds of years of history and breeding, of jostling for position.

Santiago knew he could win in that world, if he chose, because of both his heritage and his personal ruthlessness. He'd spent twenty years fighting in business, tearing other men's companies apart. He knew how to battle. He wasn't afraid of war. He had a thick skin and sharp weapons.

Belle was different. She wasn't a gold digger; she wasn't

a social climber. She'd barely seemed to tolerate New York City. He suspected she'd be happier just tending flowers in their garden, baking for their children, volunteering at their school and caring for her neighbors. She would be happy to be with a man who appreciated her every day when he hugged his family in a warm, loving home. A man who would fix things around the house. Who'd sit on the floor with their young daughter and patiently have a tea party with her dolls.

Belle didn't want to marry a powerful billionaire, or a sexy playboy, or a famous duke. What she really wanted— what she *needed*—was a good man who would love her.

His father's hoarse words came back to haunt him.

"Do you really think she could ever be happy here, in this world? It would be cruel to her. And the child. Let her go."

Belle climbed wearily up the last flight of stairs to her bedroom in the top tower of the castle, then fell exhausted into her small bed.

After the day she'd had, watching Santiago and Nadia and the Duque de Sangovia be fêted and honored in Spanish while she was shunted and ignored, she felt weary to the bone. To the heart.

They'd finally arrived back at the castle, and the others had gone for a drink in the salon. She'd come upstairs for a nap. She barely felt the late afternoon sunlight from the tiny round window warm her skin, and she fell asleep.

When she woke, the room was shadowy and gray, and she saw Santiago's handsome face above her, his jaw tight, his eyes hard.

"This is your bedroom? This—closet?"

She was startled, still half lost in the sensual, heart-breaking dream she'd been having about him. "What are you doing up here? What's wrong?"

"I came to get you for dinner. Nadia never sends any-one to tell you, does she?"

"No," she said frankly. "She wants you for herself."

His startled eyes met hers. "You know?"

"Of course I know. But she can't have you." Belle put her hand on his sculpted cheek, rough with a five-o'clock shadow. Something suddenly gave her courage. Maybe it was this moment of intimacy, of honesty. Maybe it was because, just a moment ago, she'd been dreaming of him making love to her. But looking him straight in the eye, she whispered, "Because I love you, Santiago…"

For a moment, she trembled with terror that she'd ad-mitted it. She couldn't meet his eyes, so leaning up, she kissed him, full on the mouth. It was the first time she'd ever initiated a kiss, and she embraced him with all her pent-up hunger and desperate love.

And in the tiny single bed, tucked by the attic win-dow, a miracle happened—Santiago gripped her shoulders tightly and kissed her back even more desperately than she'd kissed him. He held her as if he were drowning, and Belle was his only chance of saving himself. Exhilaration flooded through her body. She pulled away.

"I love you," she repeated joyfully, searching his dark gaze. "Could you ever love me?"

But when he looked down at her, his handsome face was suddenly cold.

"I never asked for your love, Belle. I never wanted it."

She sucked in her breath, annihilated by pain. How could he kiss her so desperately one moment, then push her away so coldly the next?

Then suddenly it all made sense.

The coldness. The distance. It had all started weeks ago.

He wasn't a fool. He must have realized she was fall-ing in love with him, probably before she even realized it herself. So he'd started pulling away, acting cold. He must have started regretting his decision to propose. When he'd first heard the news of his brother's death—that was why he'd seemed almost relieved to have the excuse to cancel their wedding.

He didn't want her love.

Her shoulders fell. "You told me from the beginning that you'd never love me." Her voice was low. "But I fell for you anyway. For the man you are and the man you could be. I couldn't stop myself from loving you…"

Santiago gripped her shoulders. "Stop saying that." Taking her hand, he pulled her from the bed. "We'll discuss this later. We should go down to dinner. They're waiting for us."

He didn't look at her as they went down the twisting wooden staircase, and all the stairs after that, to the great hall.

Belle's throat ached with unshed tears as they reached the enormous room, two stories high, with paintings that looked hundreds of years old. At the center of the room was a long table that could have easily fit thirty people, but tonight had only two at the end: the elderly duke, who as usual didn't acknowledge Belle's existence, and Nadia, who as usual looked wickedly sexy and beautiful.

Behind her on the wall was an old portrait of a beautiful woman in a black mantilla and elaborate gown, with expressive eyes and a hard smile. Just like Nadia's.

Who was the obviously correct consort for Santiago now? Belle, with her average looks and former job as a waitress, a regular girl from small-town Texas? Or Nadia, an international movie star, the most beautiful woman in the world, who knew how to smile sweetly as she cut you to the heart—the woman Santiago had once loved so much that he'd literally earned a billion dollars to try to win her?

The duke muttered something in Spanish beneath his breath.

Looking up, Nadia said to Belle, "Late again? Honestly, you don't look like the kind of girl who's always late to meals."

Belle growled under her breath, but to her surprise, Santiago answered for her. "Thanks to you."

Nadia tilted her head innocently. "I don't know what you mean."

"You know perfectly well. Sticking Belle up in the tower. You've been doing your best to sabotage her. Stop it," he said sharply, then his voice turned gentle as he said to Belle, "Sit here. Beside me."

A moment later, Belle was eating dinner without much appetite, and drinking water as the others drank red wine and spoke in Spanish. She'd just told her future husband she loved him, and nothing had happened. Wasn't courage supposed to be rewarded in life?

But she didn't think it would be.

She ate numbly, then rose to her feet to escape the dreary, formal table. Santiago stopped her with a glance and four quiet words.

"We need to talk."

And looking at him, Belle was suddenly afraid.

He led her outside, to the Moorish garden behind the castle courtyard. She could see the lights of the castle above and the village below. A few lampposts dotted through the palm trees and fountains of the dark-shadowed garden. Moonlight silvered the dark valley.

Folding his arms, Santiago stood over her, handsome as a fierce medieval king. "Take back your words."

"I can't." She felt like she was going to faint. It was one thing for her to think of leaving him, but something different if he told her to go. Much more final.

His forehead furrowed as he came closer. He was

dressed in a sleek suit, his dark hair cut short. She missed the rougher man she remembered in New York. The one who could laugh, whose hair was a little more wild, especially when he raked it impatiently with his hands. "You don't even like it here."

"Because I don't belong here," she said quietly. "But neither do you."

For a long moment, he looked at her. She saw the clench of his jaw in the moonlight. When he spoke, his voice was hard.

"I'm sending you back to New York."

"You're staying?"

"Yes."

"And you're glad." She choked out a laugh, wiping tears that burned her. "Right. I get it. Let's face it, I was always your second-choice bride. You never really wanted to marry me. You just wanted to do the right thing for our baby."

"I still do," he said quietly. "But as I told you from the beginning, love was never supposed to be part of it."

Her honesty had ruined any chance they had, she realized. When she'd told him she loved him—that had been the thing that had made him finally decide to end this.

"I'm sorry," he said quietly.

She tried to smile, but couldn't. Her cheeks wouldn't lift. She turned away.

Suddenly, she just wanted this to be over as soon as possible. She pulled off her diamond ring, tugging it hard to get it off her pregnancy-swollen finger. Afraid to touch him—afraid if she did, she would cling to him, sob, slide down his body to the ground and grip his leg as she begged him never to let her go—she held it out. "Here."

He stared at the ring without moving to take it. Why was he trying to make her suffer? Why wouldn't he just take it? She slid it into his jacket pocket. She again tried to smile, and again failed. "The ring was never really mine, anyway. You bought it for her."

Santiago stared at her. "She told you?"

"At the lawyer's office." With a choked laugh, Belle looked up at the castle towers overhead. "You know, every time I hear the tap-tap-tap of her stiletto heels, I've started to feel like a swimmer seeing a shark fin in the water." Lifting her gaze to his, she took a deep breath and forced herself to say simply, "But she's like you. You've known her half your life. I can see why you love her."

"Love her?" He sounded shocked. "Don't be ridiculous. She's my brother's widow. He's not even cold in his grave."

Why was he trying to deny what was so plain, even to her? "And now she's free. The only woman you ever loved. The woman you spent years trying to deserve, like a knight on a charger, determined to slay dragons for her. Just like in a fairy tale." She looked up. "And now you'll be duke and duchess. You'll live in a castle in Spain." She looked up at the moonlit castle in wonder, then down at herself as she stood in the garden, heavily pregnant and with ill-fitting, wrinkled clothes, and whispered, "I'm no man's prize."

Reaching out, he cupped her cheek. "It's better for you, Belle," he said quietly. "I can't give you the love you deserve. Now, you'll have a chance at real happiness."

She felt frozen, heartsick. "And our baby?"

"We will do as you suggested in Texas, and share custody. Neither you nor our daughter will ever want for anything. You will always have more money than you can spend. I will buy you a house in New York. Any house you desire."

A lump rose in her throat. "There's only one house I want," she whispered. "*Our* house. The one I decorated, with our baby's first nursery. With Anna and Dinah. Our house, Santiago."

He looked down at her. "I'm sorry."

She looked down at her bare left hand. Once she left him, she thought, all his childhood dreams could come true. He would be a true Zoya. He'd have his father. His position as heir. The woman he'd once loved.

Life was short. Love was all that mattered.

She had to accept it. To set him free, and herself free as well.

Weak with grief, Belle looked up at him. And with a deep breath, she forced herself to say the words that betrayed her very soul. "I'll leave you, then. Tomorrow."

"Tonight would be better. I'll call my pilot and order the plane ready."

Santiago's voice was so matter-of-fact, so cold. As if he didn't care at all. While her own heart was in agony. She wanted to cry. Her voice trembled. "You're in such a rush to get rid of me?"

His jaw set. "Once the decision is made, it's best to get it over with. You deserve better than me. A good man who can actually love you back."

"You could be that man," she whispered. She struggled to smile, to find a trace of her old spirit, even as her eyes were wet with tears. "I know you could."

Emotion flashed across his handsome face, but before she could identify it, it was gone. He looked away.

"I am doing the best I can," he said in a low voice. "By letting you go."

It was a civilized ending to their engagement. They could both go forward as partners raising their baby, telling friends that the breakup had been "mutual" and their engagement had ended "amicably."

But Belle couldn't end it like that.

She couldn't just leave quietly, with dignity. Her heart

rebelled. She couldn't hold back her real feelings. Not anymore.

"I know I can't compete with Nadia," she choked out, "not in a million years. I'm not beautiful like her. I can't offer you the dukedom you've craved all your life. There's only one thing I can give you better than anyone else. My love. Love that will last for the rest of my life." She looked up at him through her tears. "Choose me, Santiago," she whispered. "Love me."

For a moment, blood rushed in her ears. She felt like she was going to faint in the moonlit garden. The image of the looming castle swirled above her. She swayed on her feet, holding her breath.

Then she saw his answer, by the grim tightening of his jaw.

"That's why I'm ending this, Belle," he said in a low, rough voice. "I care for you too much to let you stay and waste your life—your light—on me."

The brief hope in her heart died. Her shoulders sagged. "All right," she said, feeling like she'd aged fifty years. "I'll go pack."

But as she started to turn, he grabbed her wrist. "Unless…"

"Unless?" she breathed.

"You tell me you don't love me after all. Tell me you were lying. We could still be married, like we planned. If you don't ask for more than I can give."

He was willing to still marry her?

For a moment, desperate hope pounded through her.

Then she went still.

Seven years ago, when Justin had first proposed to her, she'd known even then, deep down, that he didn't love her. When he'd demanded Belle have the medical procedure to permanently prevent pregnancy—a monstrous demand, when she'd been only a twenty-one-year-old virgin—barely more than a kid herself—Belle had deluded herself into thinking she had to accept any sacrifice as the price of her love for him.

No longer. She looked up at Santiago in the moonlit garden.

"No," she said quietly.

He looked incredulous. "No?"

Belle lifted her chin. "I might not be a movie star, I might not have a title or fortune, but I've realized I'm worth something too. Just as I am." She took a deep breath. "I want to be loved. And I will be, someday." She gave him a wistful smile. "I just wish it could have been by you."

"Belle..."

Her belly suddenly became taut. Her lower back was hurting. She was still weeks from her due date so she knew it couldn't be labor. It was her body reacting, she thought, to her heart breaking.

"I will always love you, Santiago," she whispered. Tears spilled down her cheeks as she reached up to cradle his rough chin with her hand one last time. "And think that we could have been happy together. Really happy."

Standing on her tiptoes, she kissed one cheek, then the other, then finally his lips. She kissed him truly, tenderly, with all her love, to try to keep this last memory of him locked forever in her heart.

Then, with desperate grief, she pulled away at last.

"Goodbye," she choked, and fled into the castle, blinded by tears. She went up to her room in the tower and packed quickly. It was easy, since she left all of the expensive, uncomfortable new clothes behind. When she came downstairs, she saw a limo in the courtyard waiting for her.

"I'll take your bag, miss," the driver said.

Belle climbed in to the limo, looking back at the castle one last time. She had a glimpse of Santiago in the library window, alone in the cold castle, the future Duke of Sangovia, the future husband of a *marquesa*, a self-made billionaire, sleek and handsome with cold, dead eyes staring after her.

Then, like a dream, he was gone.

CHAPTER ELEVEN

SANTIAGO STOOD AT the library window, watching Belle's limo disappear into the dark night. He felt sick at heart. It was the hardest thing he'd ever done, letting her go.

"Finally. She's gone."

Nadia's voice was a purr behind him. Furious, Santiago turned to face her with a glare. She smiled at him, with a hand on her tilted hip, in front of the dark wood paneling and wall of old leather-bound books. She looked like a spoiled Persian cat, he thought irritably. He bared his teeth into a smile.

"You did your part to get rid of her, didn't you? Sticking her in the tower, undercutting her with the staff, telling her the engagement ring had once been yours?"

"She didn't belong here," she said lazily. "Better for her to just go."

Yes, Santiago thought dully. It would be better. That was the only reason he'd let Belle go. He couldn't bear to be loved by her, and she refused to marry him without it.

Belle, of all women on earth, deserved to be happy. She deserved to be loved.

The truth was, he had no idea what she'd seen to love in him. He'd taken her from her Texas hometown against her will, and yet she hadn't just gone back with him to New York: she'd done her best to fit into his life and play the role of society wife. He remembered how scared she'd been, but she'd done it anyway. Because he'd asked her to.

She'd redecorated his Upper East Side mansion, turning it from a cold showplace to a warm, cozy home. She'd reorganized his staff, removing the arrogant butler, making the household happier.

Belle had been unbelievably understanding when he'd canceled their wedding hours before the ceremony. She'd even insisted on coming to Spain with him.

"I can't let you face it alone," she'd told him.

But now he was alone, in this cold place.

"It was unpleasant, having her always hovering around us. Such a pushy girl," Nadia said, then gave him a bright smile. "Your father sent me to find you. He wants to discuss how soon you might take over the family's business interests." She gave a hard laugh. "You'll do better than Otilio did, that's for sure."

Santiago turned to her abruptly. "Did you love my brother?"

She blinked. "*Love* him?"

"Did you?"

Nadia laughed mirthlessly. "Otilio spent most of his time getting drunk and chasing one-night stands. You heard he died from a heart attack?"

"Yes…"

She shook her head. "He was drunk, and crashed his car into the window of a children's charity shop. It was night and the shop was empty, or else he might have taken out a bunch of mothers and their babies, too. That would have been awful…for our family's reputation." She sighed. "But he wanted a beautiful, famous wife, and I wanted a title. We were partners, promoting the brand of our marriage." She shrugged. "We tried not to spend too much time together."

Partners, Santiago thought dully. Just like he'd suggested to Belle. As if it would be remotely appealing to anyone with a beating heart to accept marriage as a business arrangement, as a brand, as a cheap imitation for what was supposed to be the main relationship of one's life.

He could hardly blame her for refusing.

I love you, Belle had whispered in the shadowy light of that threadbare little attic room. *Could you ever love me?*

And he, who was afraid of nothing, had been afraid.

Santiago told himself that he was glad Belle was gone, so he didn't have to see her big eyes tugging at his heart, pulling him to...what?

"The duke wants you to be on a conference call regarding the Cebela merger."

"Right." He hadn't been listening. He followed Nadia out of the library toward his father's study, feeling numb. He liked feeling numb. It was easy. It was safe.

But late that night, he tossed and turned, imagining Belle on his private jet, flying alone across the dark ocean. What if the plane crashed? And she was so close to her due date. What if she went into labor on the plane? Why hadn't he sent a doctor with her?

Because he'd been so eager to get her away from him.

Not eager. Desperate.

"I love you. Could you ever love me?"

When Santiago finally rose at dawn, he felt bleary-eyed, more exhausted than he'd been the night before. It was the middle of the night in New York, but he didn't care. He phoned the pilot. The man politely let him know that they'd arrived safely in New York, and Miss Langtry had been picked up at the airport by his usual driver and the bodyguard.

"Is there a problem?" the pilot asked.

"No problem," Santiago said abruptly and hung up.

He pushed down his emotions, determined to stay numb. He went downstairs in the castle and ate breakfast, reading newspapers, just as Nadia and his father did. Three people silently reading newspapers at a long table in an elegant room filled with flowers, the only sound the rustle of paper and the metallic clank of silverware against china.

Santiago went numbly through the motions of the day, speaking to his father's lawyers, skipping lunch for a long conference call with a Tokyo firm in the process of being sold to Santiago's New York-based conglomerate.

He didn't contact Belle. He tried not to think about her. He was careful not to feel, or let himself think about anything deeper than business. He felt utterly alone. Correction: he didn't feel anything at all.

Exactly as he'd wanted.

At dinner that night in the great hall, both his father and his sister-in-law were lavish in their abuse of the woman who'd left them the previous night.

"Nothing but a gold digger," Nadia said with a smirk. "As soon as I told her you'd always support the baby she left, didn't she?"

Santiago stared at his crystal goblet with the red wine. Red, like blood, which he no longer could feel beating through his heart.

"You did the right thing, *mi hijo*," the old man cackled, then started talking about a potential business acquisition. "But these money-grubbing peasants refuse to sell. Do they not know their place? They refused my generous offer!" He drank more wine. "So we'll just take the company. Have our lawyers send a letter, say we already own the technology. Check the status of the patents. We can ruin him then take his company for almost nothing."

"Clever," Nadia said approvingly.

Santiago didn't say anything. He just stared down at his plate, at the elegant china edged with twenty-four-carat gold. At the solid silver knife beside it. He took a drink of the cool water, closing his eyes.

All he could think of was Belle, who'd tried to save him

from the cold reality of his world. From the cold reality of who he'd become, as dead as the steak on this plate.

Belle had tried to be his sunshine, his warmth, his light. She'd loved him. And for that, he'd sent her away forever. Both her and his unborn daughter.

"You are very quiet, *mi hijo*."

"I'm not very hungry. Excuse me," Santiago muttered and left the dinner table with a noisy scrape of his hard wooden chair. In the darkened hallway, he leaned back against the oak-paneled wall and took a deep breath, trying to contain the acid-like feeling in his chest. In his heart.

Tomorrow, his father intended to hold a press conference to announce that Santiago would be taking the Zoya name as rightfully his, along with the Zoya companies, eventually folding his own companies into the conglomerate. The duke also would start the process of getting Santiago recognized as the heir to his dukedom.

He was going to be the rightful heir, as he'd dreamed of all his life. He was about to have everything he'd ever wanted. Everything he'd ever dreamed of.

And he'd never felt so miserable.

If he closed his eyes in the hallway, he could almost imagine he could smell the light scent of Belle's fragrance, tangerine and soap and sunshine.

Suddenly, he had to know she was doing all right. It was early afternoon in New York. Reaching for his phone, he dialed the number of the kitchen in his Upper East Side mansion.

Mrs. Green answered. "Velazquez residence."

"Hello, Mrs. Green," Santiago said tightly. "I was just wondering if my wife—" Then he remembered Belle was not his wife, not even his fiancée, and never would be again. He cleared his throat. "Please don't disturb Belle. I just wanted to make sure she is doing well after her trip home."

There was a long pause. Her voice sounded half surprised, half sad. "Mr. Velazquez, I thought you knew."

"Knew what?"

"Miss Langtry is at the hospital... She's in labor."

He gripped the phone. "But it's too soon—"

"The doctors are concerned. Didn't she call you?"

No, of course Belle hadn't. Why would she now, when he'd made it so clear he wanted nothing to do with her? Or their baby girl?

"Thank you, Mrs. Green," he said quietly and hung up. He felt sick, dizzy.

"Something wrong?"

Nadia found him in the hallway. He didn't like having her so close, blocking the sunshine and soap with her heavy smell of exotic flowers and musk.

She frowned, looking at the phone still clasped tightly in his hand. "Bad news?"

"Belle's in the hospital."

"She was hurt?"

"She's gone into labor early."

Nadia shrugged. "Maybe things will go badly. Otherwise you're on the hook for the next eighteen years. If you're lucky, they'll both conveniently die and... Stop, you're hurting me!" she suddenly cried.

Looking down, Santiago saw he'd grabbed her by the shoulder in fury, and his fingers were digging into her skin. He abruptly let her go. The skin on his hand still crawled from touching her.

"You are a snake."

Rubbing her shoulder, she said, "We both are. That's why we're perfect for each other."

He ground his teeth. "My brother is barely in his grave."

"It was always you I wanted, Santiago."

"You had a funny way of showing it."

Nadia shrugged, smiling, still certain of her charm.

"I had to be practical, darling. I didn't know then that you would turn out to be worth so much." She tilted her head, fluttering her long eyelashes. "And what can I say? I wanted to be a duchess."

His lip curled. "You disgust me."

Nadia frowned in confusion. "Then why did you send that girl away? Wait. Oh, no." Her lips spread in a shark-like smile. "You *love* her," she taunted. "Sweet, true, *tender* love."

His voice was tight. "I don't."

"You do. And that baby as well. You wanted to kill me just now, for speaking as I did. You love them both."

Santiago stared down blindly at Nadia in the castle hallway.

Love Belle?

Love her?

He'd let her go because it was better for her. That was all. Because she deserved to be happy. And because his family needed him here in Spain.

But he suddenly realized that wasn't the *whole* reason.

For months now, he'd been fighting his feelings for Belle. Because since he was a boy, every time he'd loved someone, they'd stabbed him in the back. He'd vowed to never play the sucker again.

But with Belle, he'd been tempted more than he could resist. He'd come to care about her too much. He'd started feeling that her happiness was more important than his own.

He hadn't sent Belle away so he could be with his family, but because he was fleeing from them.

Belle was his real family. Belle and the baby.

And that fact terrified him.

Santiago's knees trembled beneath him. He felt a wave rip through his soul, cracking it open.

He'd let her go because he was afraid. Afraid of being

vulnerable. Afraid of getting hurt. Afraid of what would happen, who he would become, if he let her love him.

If he loved her back.

"So it's really true." Nadia looked stunned. Her violet eyes narrowed with rage. "You'd choose that little nobody over me?"

Santiago thought of Belle's many joys, her tart honesty, her silliness, her kindness. He thought of her luminous eyes and trembling pink lips as she'd whispered, *"There's only one thing I can give you better than anyone else. My love."*

For the first time, he saw the truth.

When he was a boy, he'd dreamed of being loved by his father, who was rich and powerful and able to command people from a palace. He'd thought if he could just get the duke to call him son, he'd be happy.

As a young man, he'd dreamed of being loved by Nadia, with all her cold beauty and utter lack of pity. He'd thought he'd be happy if he could just win her. Like a trophy.

But today, at thirty-five, he suddenly realized happiness had nothing to do with that kind of so-called love. Wealth and power, physical beauty, what did they have to do with love? Those things didn't last.

Real love did.

Love was having the loyalty and devotion of a kind-hearted, honest woman. A woman who could make you laugh. Who always had your back. Who would protect and adore you through good times and bad. Who cared for your child. A woman who was the heart of your home. The heart of your heart.

There was only one way to be happy: to give everything he had, just as she had done.

He had to be willing to die for her. And even more important: live for her.

Choose me. Love me.

This was what love meant. What family meant. It didn't mean requiring someone to jump through hoops. It didn't mean a lifetime of ignoring someone until you found a use for them, as his father had done. It didn't mean abandoning them when you had a better offer, as Nadia had.

Love meant acceptance. Protection. It meant a lifetime of loyalty through good times and bad.

Love that will last for the rest of my life.

It meant forever.

Santiago sucked in his breath. Belle was his true family. She was his love.

And right now, Belle was in New York. In labor with their baby. Utterly alone.

Turning sharply, he checked for his wallet. He had his passport. He said, "I have to go."

"But—where are you going?" Nadia sounded utterly bewildered. "What about your father's press conference tomorrow?"

"Tell him to forget it."

"You're leaving us?"

Santiago looked at Nadia one last time. "I'm sorry. I don't really care about you, or the old man, either. Be honest. Neither of you really care about me. You ignored me until you had a use for me."

"But you're supposed to be the heir," she wailed. "You're supposed to make me a duchess!"

He snorted, shaking his head. "Tell my father that if he wants an heir, I recommend he marry you himself."

Leaving her behind, Santiago left the castle of Sangovia for good.

He was done with his old childish dreams. There was only one dream he wanted now. One dream that was real, and for that, he would risk everything he had. Heart and soul.

* * *

"Just a little longer…" her friend Letty pleaded.

Belle panted for breath, choked with tears of pain as the contraction finally ended. Stretched out in bed in the private room in the hospital, her legs beneath a blanket, she'd wanted to be brave, so she'd told the doctors she didn't need an epidural. It was a choice she was now sorely regretting.

The labor had already lasted for hours and hours, and it still wasn't time to push. Her daughter, after demanding to be born early, was suddenly taking her time.

"You're doing fine," Letty said, letting go of her hand with a wince, to reach for a cup of ice chips.

Belle took the cup gratefully and sucked on an ice chip, thirsty and exhausted in this brief respite between contractions. She knew that soon, the pain would start again, and hurt so much throughout her body that if she'd had anything left in her stomach, she would have thrown up.

"Thanks for being here with me," she whispered. "I just hope I didn't break your hand."

"It's fine," her friend said, stretching her hand gingerly. Her eyes narrowed. "It's nothing compared to how my hand will hurt after the next time I see Santiago's face. After what he did to you… The bastard! The total bastard!"

"Don't talk about him that way," Belle said weakly as she started to feel the beginnings of the next contraction. "He tried his…best. He couldn't…love me. So he let me go…"

They both turned their heads as they heard some kind of commotion in the hospital hallway, outside the door. It was loud enough to be heard over the medical equipment monitoring her heartbeat and the baby's with beeps and lights.

"What on earth…?" With a frown, the nurse who'd been hovering by Belle's bed went out to check, closing the door behind her.

But the noise only increased. Clutching her belly, Belle panted, "Go see what's happening."

"I'm not leaving you," Letty said stoutly.

"Any…distraction…is better…"

With a reluctant nod, Letty went out into the hall.

And then the yelling really started. For a moment, Belle lost track of her labor pains in her sudden fear that World War III had just started in the hospital hallway.

The shouting abruptly stopped. The door exploded open to reveal the last person she'd expected to see. Standing in the doorway was Santiago, tall and broad-shouldered, his dark eyes bright.

Was she dreaming? Had she died?

As the pain started to crest, she stretched out her hand to him with a choked gasp, and in two seconds, he crossed to her side, putting his hand in hers. With him there, though the pain was worse than ever, suddenly she felt stronger and braver, and knew she could endure. With his hand in hers, she knew she could squeeze as hard as she wanted, and it wouldn't hurt him. She didn't have to hold back. So she didn't. Clutching his hand tight, she screamed through the pain.

When the contraction finally was over, he had tears in his eyes. She was shocked.

"Did I hurt your hand?" she said anxiously.

"My hand?" he looked down at it in bewilderment, then shook his head. "It's fine."

"Then why—"

"Forgive me," he choked out.

Then to her astonished eyes, Santiago fell to his knees beside the hospital bed, next to the blanket that covered her legs. He looked up, his dark eyes searing her soul.

"I was a coward," he whispered. "Afraid to admit what was in my heart. I thought I could send you away and stay safe and numb the rest of my life. I can't." He set his jaw. "I won't."

"What are you saying?" she croaked out.

"You are everything I was ever afraid to want. Everything good. Everything I thought I didn't deserve. I need you, Belle." He took a deep breath. "I love you."

She gaped down at him. "I thought you could only love Nadia…"

"Nadia?" He snorted. "She was a trophy. Like art on my wall or a million-acre ranch. You are no man's trophy, Belle."

Her heart fell. She bit her lip. "No. I'm not."

"You're no trophy," he said in a low, intense voice, "because you're far more. You are my woman. My equal partner. My better half. My love. And if you'll have me," he said humbly, "my wife."

She sucked in her breath. "Your—"

Then the new contraction hit, and she reached desperately for his hand. Rising to his feet, he took it immediately, holding it close, against his heart. The pain built sharply, leaving her gasping for breath.

For what seemed like hours, he held her hand unflinchingly, speaking to her in Spanish and English, calming her with his deep voice, giving her his strength, helping her through the pain. As the contraction finally subsided, the nurse checked her beneath the blanket, then gave a quick nod. "I'm going to get the doctor."

Belle and Santiago were alone. She took a deep breath.

"Thank you," she whispered. "For being here. For our baby."

His expression turned sad. "Just for the baby?" he said slowly. "It's too late, isn't it? I've hurt you too badly to ever hope for forgiveness…"

She said in a trembling voice, "Do you really love me?"

Sudden, shocked hope lit his dark eyes.

"With everything I have. Everything I am. I love you." Leaning over the hospital bed, he kissed her sweaty forehead tenderly. "Love me," he whispered. "Forgive me. Marry me."

Belle wondered if she was dreaming. Then she decided she didn't care. "Yes."

He drew back, looking down at her with joy. "You'll marry me?"

Wordlessly, she nodded. Rushing to fling open the door, he called two people inside: a man dressed in a plain black suit and Letty, following behind, holding a bag from the hospital gift shop.

"This is John Alvarez, the hospital pastor," Santiago told her. "He's going to marry us."

Her jaw dropped. "Right now?"

"What, are you busy?" he teased.

She snorted, then grew serious. "But…what about the big wedding you wanted?"

"We already have a license. I don't want to live another moment without you as my wife." He cupped her cheek. "I love you, Belle."

A slow-rising smile lifted her lips.

"I love you too," she whispered, tears falling down her face unheeded. Pulling on his hand, she brought him closer to the hospital bed and kissed him, laughing her happiness. Then she groaned, as she felt the next contraction begin to rise. "But we'd better do this fast."

And so it was that, plain gold bands from the hospital gift shop were slipped within minutes on both their hands, and they were declared man and wife. And just in time.

"Anyone that's not family, get out!" the nurse said, shooing the pastor and Letty into the hallway. In that moment, the doctor hurried into the room.

"All right, Belle," the doctor said, smiling. "Are you ready to push?"

Forty-five minutes later, their daughter, named Emma Jamie Velazquez after the baby's grandmother and grand-father, was brought into this world. A short while later, as Belle watched her husband—her *husband!*—hold their daughter, who was a fat eight pounds ten ounces, tenderly in his arms, she was overwhelmed with happiness.

"Someone wants to meet you," Santiago said, smiling, and gently placed their newborn daughter in Belle's arms.

As she looked down at their precious baby, the miracle she'd once thought she could never have, tears fell from Belle's eyes that she didn't even try to hide. She whispered, "She's so beautiful."

"Like her mother," Santiago said. Leaning down, he kissed her forehead with infinite tenderness, then kissed their sleeping baby's. He looked down at Belle—his *wife*—in the hospital bed. "I love you, Mrs. Velazquez."

She caught her breath at hearing her name for the first time.

Letty peeked around the door into the room to make sure it was safe, then entered, beaming at the baby before she turned to Santiago. "Um, you forgive me for slapping you earlier, right? I feel kind of bad about it now."

"I had it coming," Santiago said, adjusting his jaw a little ruefully. "Thanks for helping with the rings."

Letty grinned. "No problem. It was easy. It was either gold bands or the candy ones. Hey, you two lovebirds, there was one part of the wedding the pastor had to cut when we got kicked out." Letty looked between them. "You may now kiss the bride."

Santiago looked down at Belle with a gleam in his black eyes. "The perfect end to a perfect day."

Belle smiled through her tears.

Once, she'd thought that all her chances for love and happiness had passed her by. She'd thought that her choice to take care of her brothers instead of herself, to sacrifice her own dreams for others, meant that she'd ended her own chance for a bright future.

Now she realized that life wasn't like that.

Every day could be a new start. Every day could be a fresh miracle. And today, the first day of their marriage, the first day of her daughter's life, she knew it wasn't the end of anything. As her husband lowered his head to kiss her in a private vow that would last the rest of their lives, she knew it was all just beginning.

Santiago got married in a quick hospital ceremony just minutes before his baby was born, and his two best friends never let him forget it.

"And you said you'd never get married in some tacky quick wedding," said Darius Kyrillos, who'd married at City Hall.

"You said you'd never get married at all," said his friend Kassius Black, who'd wed at an over-the-top grand ceremony in New Orleans.

Santiago grinned. "A man can change his mind, can't he?"

He was on his third helping of Texas-style barbecue, and the three men were sitting across a huge sofa in a corner of the ballroom of his Upper East Side mansion. Officially, it was a party to celebrate the christening of six-week-old Emma. Unofficially, it was also a wedding reception. The house was crowded, decidedly a family affair filled with friends and relatives, including Belle's two brothers who'd come up to New York for the event, and neighbors, employees and their families. For dinner, they'd had champagne, beer, barbecue, corn on the cob and homemade ice cream. It was November, the time of Thanksgiving. But Belle had definite ideas about how she wanted this party to be.

"Fun like home," she'd said with a grin.

So there was a bluegrass band playing, to the mild shock

of the foreign dignitaries that had been invited. But they seemed to like it, and even strangers had become friends, with people dancing and kids running around. And did he actually see someone's golden retriever running madly across the house…?

The only family not in attendance was his father, the Duke of Sangovia, who had recently, and rather shockingly, wed his former daughter-in-law, the famous movie star. Another marriage "partnership." Santiago shuddered thinking of it. And those were the people he might have spent his life with, like a prison sentence, if Belle hadn't saved him. If she hadn't taught him to be brave enough to risk his heart and soul.

If she hadn't taught him what love actually meant.

Now, as the three husbands sat together, drinking frosty mugs of beer and watching the crowd, Santiago looked down at his daughter, who'd fallen asleep in his arms. After six weeks, he was starting to feel like a pro as a dad.

Kassius and Darius, who'd also brought their wives and children to the party, looked down at the fat baby in Santiago's arms.

"Babies are adorable," Kassius said.

"Especially when they're sleeping," Darius said.

"That's what I meant," he said.

"To sleeping babies—" Santiago raised his beer mug "—and beautiful wives." They all clinked glasses. Softly, so as not to wake the baby.

Across the crowd, Santiago saw Belle, and as always, he lost his breath.

She was beautiful—the center of this house as she was the center of his world. Her long dark hair tumbled over her shoulders, over her curvaceous body in the soft red dress. As she felt his glance, their eyes locked across the crowd. Electricity raced through his body.

Santiago had spent his whole childhood dreaming of

having a place in the world. A home. A family. It had come true, just not in the way he'd expected.

He hadn't been born into this family. He'd created it. He and Belle together. From the moment they'd fallen into bed and accidentally conceived a child.

Had it been an accident? he suddenly wondered. Or was it possible he'd always known, from the moment he first met Belle, that she would be the one to break the spell?

Because that was what she'd done. It was funny. Belle had once compared him to a knight, saying he'd slain dragons for Nadia like something out of a fairy tale. But he hadn't. All he'd done was make a lot of money. He'd never risked anything. He'd never saved anyone.

Not like Belle.

She was the true knight. She was the one who'd slain the dragon. She was the one who'd saved his soul. He would always be grateful for that miracle.

Tomorrow, they would leave on a two-month honeymoon—bringing baby Emma, of course—on a trip around the world. Belle had planned this reception, so he'd insisted on organizing the honeymoon. "What are your top five dream travel destinations?"

"Paris," she'd said instantly, then "London." She'd bitten her lip. "The Christmas markets in Germany. The neon lights of Tokyo. Or maybe—" she'd tilted her head "—a beach vacation in Australia? The Great Barrier Reef?" With a sigh, she'd shaken her head. "I'm glad I'm not the one who has to decide!"

But as it turned out neither did he. Because they were going to see everything. Emma would be a very well-traveled baby before she even had her first bite of baby food.

Their family would see the world together, all of them for the first time. It would all be new to Santiago, too. Because this time, he'd be leading with his heart.

In the ballroom, Belle came up to the sofa, smiling. "You boys having fun?"

"Yes," they all said cheerily, and in Kassius's and Darius's case a little tipsily. Belle grinned at Santiago.

"Want to help cut the cake?"

"Absolutely." He rose to his feet, their sleeping baby still tucked securely against his chest. With his free hand, he suddenly pulled his wife close and kissed her. Not a little kiss, either. He kissed her long and hard, until they started getting catcalls and whistles and cheers from the guests, and he felt her tremble in his arms.

She drew back, her eyes big. "What was that for?"

"It's the start of a whole life loving you," he whispered, cupping her cheek. "I wanted to do it right."

Belle leaned her head against his shoulder, and for a moment, the three of them stood nestled together. Then they heard someone yell, "Come quick! The kids are coming at the cake with spoons, and there's a dog close behind!"

Laughing, Santiago and Belle, with their sleeping baby, went to cut the cake. And as they were toasted and cheered by their family and friends, he looked down tenderly at his wife, who smiled back at him, her eyes shining with love. And Santiago knew, for the first time in his life, that he was finally home.

* * * * *

MILLS & BOON®

MODERN™

POWER, PASSION AND IRRESISTIBLE TEMPTATION

A sneak peek at next month's titles...

In stores from 10th August 2017:

- **The Tycoon's Outrageous Proposal** – Miranda Lee
  and **At the Ruthless Billionaire's Command**
  – Carole Mortimer
- **Claiming His One-Night Baby** – Michelle Smart *and*
  Cipriani's Innocent Captive – Cathy Williams

In stores from 24th August 2017:

- **Engaged for Her Enemy's Heir** – Kate Hewitt *and*
  His Drakon Runaway Bride – Tara Pammi
- **The Throne He Must Take** – Chantelle Shaw *and*
  The Italian's Virgin Acquisition – Michelle Conder

Just can't wait?
Buy our books online before they hit the shops!
www.millsandboon.co.uk

Also available as eBooks.

0817/19

MILLS & BOON®

EXCLUSIVE EXTRACT

Natasha Pellegrini and Matteo Manaserro's reunion
catches them both in a potent mix of emotion, and they
surrender to their explosive passion. Natasha was a virgin
until Matteo's touch branded her as his and when Matteo
discovers Natasha is pregnant, he's intent on claiming his
baby. Except he hasn't bargained on their insatiable
chemistry binding them together so completely!

Read on for a sneak preview of Michelle Smart's book
CLAIMING HIS ONE-NIGHT BABY
The second part of her Bound to a Billionaire trilogy

'For better or worse we're going to be tied together by our
child for the rest of our lives and the only way we're going
to get through it is by always being honest with each other.
We will argue and disagree but you must always speak the
truth to me.'

Natasha fought to keep her feet grounded and her limbs
from turning into fondue but it was a fight she was losing,
Matteo's breath warm on her face, his thumb gently moving
on her skin but scorching it, the heat from his body almost
penetrating her clothes, heat crawling through her, pooling
in her most intimate place.

His scent was right there too, filling every part of her, and
she wanted to bury her nose into his neck and inhale him.

She'd kissed him without any thought, a desperate
compulsion to touch him and comfort him flooding her, and
then the fury had struck from nowhere, all her private thoughts
about the direction he'd taken his career in converging to
realise he'd thrown it all away in the pursuit of riches.

And now she wanted to kiss him again.

As if he could sense the need inside her, he brought his mouth close to hers but not quite touching, the promise of a kiss.

'And now I will ask you something and I want complete honesty,' he whispered, the movement of his words making his lips dance against hers like a breath.

The fluttering of panic sifted into the compulsive desire. She hated lies too. She never wanted to tell another, especially not to him. But she had to keep her wits about her because there were things she just could not tell because no matter what he said about lies always being worse, sometimes it was the truth that could destroy a life.

But, God, how could she think properly when her head was turning into candyfloss at his mere touch?

His other hand trailed down her back and clasped her bottom to pull her flush to him. Her abdomen clenched to feel his erection pressing hard against her lower stomach. His lips moved lightly over hers, still tantalising her with the promise of his kiss. 'Do you want me to let you go?'

Her hands that she'd clenched into fists at her sides to stop from touching him back unfurled themselves and inched to his hips.

The hand stroking her cheek moved round her head and speared her hair. 'Tell me.' His lips found her exposed neck and nipped gently at it. 'Do you want me to stop?'

'Matteo...' Finally, she found her voice.

'Yes, *bella*?'

'Don't stop.'

Don't miss
CLAIMING HIS ONE-NIGHT BABY
By Michelle Smart

Available September 2017
www.millsandboon.co.uk

Copyright ©2017 Michelle Smart

Join Britain's BIGGEST Romance Book Club

- **EXCLUSIVE offers every month**
- **FREE delivery direct to your door**
- **NEVER MISS a title**
- **EARN Bonus Book points**

Call Customer Services
0844 844 1358*

or visit
nillsandboon.co.uk/subscriptions

* This call will cost you 7 pence per minute plus your phone company's price per minute access charge.

MILLS & BOON®

Why shop at millsandboon.co.uk?

Each year, thousands of romance readers find their perfect read at millsandboon.co.uk. That's because we're passionate about bringing you the very best romantic fiction. Here are some of the advantages of shopping at www.millsandboon.co.uk:

* **Get new books first**—you'll be able to buy your favourite books one month before they hit the shops

* **Get exclusive discounts**—you'll also be able to buy our specially created monthly collections, with up to 50% off the RRP

* **Find your favourite authors**—latest news, interviews and new releases for all your favourite authors and series on our website, plus ideas for what to try next

* **Join in**—once you've bought your favourite books, don't forget to register with us to rate, review and join in the discussions

Visit **www.millsandboon.co.uk**
for all this and more today!